The Peace Tree Mystery

Stephen L. Brayton, Editor

A collaborative novel written
by members of
The Marion County Writers Workshop

ISBN: 979-8-218-02436-9 (Paperback)

Any references to historical events, real people, or real places are used fictitiously. Some of the places depicted are fictitious embellishments of actual places but beyond that, names, characters, and places are products of the author's imagination.

Printed by Ingram Spark, Inc., in the United States of America.

First printing edition 2022.

Marion County Review
1699 Highway 14
Knoxville, IA 50138

www.Nearwoodwinery.com/Peacetreemystery

Contributors

The Marion County Writers Workshop

Stephen L. Brayton, Editor in Chief

Michael Van Natta
Mary Walker
Elin Babcock
Teresa Tallman
Bob Tallman
Ashley Lovell
Larry Brown
Robert Hutzell
Carol. M. Reed
Lee Collins
Kathryn Daugherty
Cassandra Albee
Charlotte Shivvers
Helen Boertje
Jacqueline Sharp
Joann Schissel, Cover Art
J. Scott Evans, back cover photograph

THE PEACE TREE MYSTERY
ORIGIN STORY

In the fall of 2013, now some 9 years ago, the members of the Marion County Writers Workshop, in a moment of frivolity, hatched an idea of writing a collaborative novel. As has always been the case, we had among our group members of the local historical organization, who suggested we write about the Peace Tree, a local landmark of historic note.

Ideas flowed like scattered buckshot and over the next few weeks, what started as a snowball, destined to melt within minutes, got rolling down the hill, took on heft and momentum. Enthusiasm for the project grew, and, as will happen in writers groups, everyone had ideas about plot, locations, characters, tone, timelines, on and on. So, in the guise of the "Weekly Writer's Challenge," we all worked out scenes on the page. Somehow, this disparate work coalesced into the semblances of a loosely cohesive novel.

Plot lines firmed up, characters appeared before us, and true to its inception, a tone of frivolity and humor dominated. In short, all of us decided, for this book anyway, that we wouldn't shoot for a Pulitzer Prize in fiction, but rather find a way to entertain, to educate, and to celebrate the land in which we all lived.

As my memory serves me, about eighteen months later, while also working on our other individual projects, we had the majority of the book written. What remained was for us to simply piece it together, write some linking scenes, some missing scenes and throw out stuff that simply didn't work.

This is where my memory gets fuzzy. The "Writer's Challenges" moved on to other prompts and each of us pursued our own writing and publishing goals. Members dropped out or moved on to other groups. New members came in with their own writing agendas. Enthusiasm waned, momentum declined, work product suffered. Soon, I began to think of the project as simply another step along each of our individual writer's lives, like so many first drafts that never come in front of our alter-egos, the editor.

Stephen Brayton made an attempt to gather me in to do just that, two or three years later. While sitting at a picnic table on a glorious autumn day in the Marion County Park as part of our traditional "Camp Write," we made an attempt to 1) find all the individual pieces, now lost in buried files on our devices; 2) determine if the original writers wanted to contribute - if they could even be located; and 3) develop a method to finally get the work to completion. It seemed a waste to not.

I'll confess here and now that I was not as enthusiastic as Steve. I had my own stuff to work on, didn't I?

Somewhere along the way, the actual Peace Tree, the long-dead Sycamore which had for decades been a landmark and nautical reference point, sticking up above the surface of Lake Red Rock as it did, disappeared. How to account for that? Was it simply rot? Vandalism? It was a mystery.

Five years later, during the pandemic, Steve found himself with some time on his hands. One day, he announced he was working on the project. By himself.

At about the same time, I had begun hatching ideas of starting up an annual publication to highlight especially good short writing and had enlisted some enthusiasm from our membership. The two efforts seemed to gather strength from each other and the next thing we knew, we were moving forward with both. Me, with what we called tentatively, The Marion County Review, and Steve, with spearheading the renewed effort to get The Peace Tree Mystery into final form.

We held weekly meetings, assignments were made, people got busy. Six months later, we knew we were going to publish the novel. If you're reading this, then we have succeeded. Excuse the cliche, but it does feel a lot like watching the Phoenix rise from the ashes.

Michael Van Natta

Chapter 1
Thursday, Present Day

Jacob Wildcrow tossed about on his blanket. Alone in his teepee, the old man's eyelids danced in dream-sleep. In his vision, he saw the scene from the eyes of the red-tailed hawk making lazy circles in the sky over the land that would become Iowa. Through the hawk's eyes he saw a gathering of people—his people—on the south bank of a river to be named Des Moines.

* * *

1790.

The bird allowed the updrafts to determine the direction of its journey, save for slight adjustments to keep the flight path localized within a half mile diameter. Despite the veiled sun, the vague shadow of the hawk wavered over the winding river, crawled up the rough escarpment of the rust-colored bluffs, and floated among the blades of the late fall grass.

Often, and not unnoticed, the hawk flew over the group of Indians who encircled a gigantic Sycamore. Twenty in number were seated, a half dozen tribes represented. Ancestors had honored the giant Sycamore with the name Peace Tree. On certain occasions—celebrations, times of dispute, holy days—any given number of men from scores of miles distant, congregated to discuss those matters of importance. Tribes, even those who warred with each other, knew the Peace Tree's environs allowed no bloodshed, but was a place to honor the dead and bless the newborn. For those in conflict, the locale offered a safe haven to seek resolution.

This day and this meeting differed from those in other years, lasting longer, with a more somber tone than previous gatherings. This time, those present commemorated no sacred observances, had no acknowledgment of a tribe's new chief, not even to discuss warring factions unable to agree to terms. Rather, each man reflected upon his past... and his future.

A man who had witnessed sixty summers, respected and experienced by time, sat in the leadership position. Skin darkened by his ancestors and the sun, his dark eyes missed nothing, not the concerned expression upon each of the other faces nor the revered avian friend above.

He wore the vestments befitting his rank of Chief of the Sac tribe. Breeches and a stole of deer hide. A scarlet cloth draped over one shoulder. Upon his head of black hair rested a band from which sprouted a plume of finely tailored feathers the same color as the hawk's tail. Behind his left shoulder, inserted into the earth, was his arrowhead tipped staff, fashioned with the feathers of various birds. Other tribes respected his character, wisdom, and mien. They admired, even envied, his ability to calm troubled waters within his tribe. Decisions handed down were firm, fair, and brooked only silent protest.

Images of tomorrow and years to come disturbed his mind. For this reason, he had called the gathering. One by one, the others' eyes were caught by his stare.

"I have foreseen many changes," Chief Saunuk intoned in his bass voice. His words held power, but with a dire note. "In our land and in our very way of life." He gestured at the hawk and the Sycamore. "The hatchling grows into a mighty hunter and passes on his skills. The seedling becomes a symbol of earth's glory and, in time, releases of itself to continue unto another generation. We have grown strong, learning the values from our fathers and mothers. Those customs and traditions will pass to our children."

The Chief sighed and gave a resigned nod. "As the hawk will become bones to return to the earth and one day this tree will be but a stump, so shall we pass on. I have foreseen our heritage waning. Our numbers will fade to precious few who will seek to continue our traditions. Some will succeed, many will fail."

The Chief raised a hand toward where the sun rose each morning. "Over the horizon men from other lands travel toward us. Already, we have met their scouts and traded with their explorers. Fourteen summers ago, they warred with their mother country. Their victory meant more freedom for them to expand their numbers, to occupy our land. I have foreseen no end to our people being exploited, subverted, and decimated."

He indicated the river and the ground around them. "My visions show how this sacred valley will become a mighty lake, the waters extending from bluff to bluff and a day's journey in length."

He paused to allow the others to contemplate his words. "We must preserve our heritage until one of our descendants who, even in his elder years, will continue to remember and resurrect our traditions. He shall pass along our knowledge to another individual who will have chosen to forget, to one who will have spurned our life.

"Come, my brothers, let us collect items for a bundle to be given to one of our finest braves. He will undertake a journey of remembrance and honor. He shall not rest until he has secured the bundle in a place of our choosing. There it will stay until such a time as it can be unearthed, and its knowledge can be reborn and understood."

Overhead, the hawk screeched once as if in agreement. It descended to perch upon an upper branch of the Peace Tree as if to oversee the subsequent discussion and plans.

***

The screech of the hawk in his dream was repeated by a screech outside his teepee. Jacob Wildcrow blinked and returned to consciousness. The images from his vision remained clear in his mind, the words still resonating in his ears.

He sighed and looked around the inside of his teepee, his blankets spread upon the hard November ground. Dressed in deerskin with his feathered headdress beside him, he came to a decision in a matter of seconds.

Before he could act, the sound of car tires crunching over gravel reached his ears. Jacob rose and pulled back the flap at the teepee's slit entrance. Above him, a red-tailed hawk sat perched on the branch of the nearest maple. Wildcrow stepped out and watched the car with its distinctive markings stop fifteen yards away. The door opened and a large man stepped out. He wore a brown uniform, a Sam Browne belt across his shoulder, and a holster on his right hip. His big-boned frame projected as much of an aura of authority as did the badge on his left breast. Black eyes stared, and Wildcrow felt the weight of their exasperation upon him. Marion County Sheriff Brett Lockridge.

Chapter 2

With every car she passed, Grace Snow glanced at the speedometer of her Ford Escape, then checked her rearview mirror.

"Good," she muttered. "No flashing lights. I don't need another ticket, and I don't need to be slowed down right now. I want this over with!"

Chow sat in the passenger's seat watching her. The woman knew the sixty-pound Siberian Husky paid attention whenever Grace put on 'that face.' Grace's jaw clenched. A vein stood out on her forehead. Her eyes stared ahead. Deep in thought, Grace drove the miles on Interstate 35. In times of stress, whether mild or intense, and only when she was out of earshot of others, she talked aloud to herself. "Change in plans. Looks like I'm skipping the Big Animal conference and going to Knoxville instead. Not what I wanted!"

Only an hour before, she sat not a block from her home in Ames, Iowa, eyeing the arrival of her favorite breakfast treat at Hickory Park Restaurant, a black licorice malt. About ready to savor the first scoop, she heard the cell phone in her purse warble. She thought it would be an emergency at her small-animal veterinary practice or maybe something about her research project at Iowa State University. But the number displayed wasn't local.

"Hello," she answered.

"Is this Grace Snow?"

"Yes."

"This is Sheriff Brett Lockridge down here in Marion County. Do you know a Jacob Wildcrow?"

"Uh, what is this about?"

"Mr. Wildcrow gave me your name and number. Could you verify that you are related to him?"

"I'm his granddaughter. What happened?"

"Well, he's made an illegal camp on land overlooking Lake Red Rock. We've had complaints. This isn't the first time. He's been wandering around, putting up a teepee here and there, doing some kind of dance, yelling some sort of chant...."

"Okay, Sheriff, but what is it you want me to do about it?"

"Well, ma'am, it's like this. He's been kind of a... character around these parts for a long time."

"Yes, I understand," Grace said."

"Normally, he just sets up his teepee where it doesn't belong and goes through some of his rituals. May cause a minor disturbance, but there's no real harm."

"What's the problem now?"

"Like I said, there ain't been real harm done and he doesn't damage any property, but, well, the number of these complaints are adding up."

"What is it you think I can do?" Grace asked.

"I was hoping you could come talk to him, maybe persuade him into moving on or at least to stop his antics. He's been around the area for a long time. I know he and his wife had that little store over in Harvey, selling trinkets and artifacts, but, well, that's been many years ago. I just don't want to see anything happen to him. I'm concerned someone will get mad enough and challenge him. Or some teenagers will get wind of his activities and taunt him, and we'll have an incident. He wasn't all that cooperative when I talked to him just a few minutes ago but like I said, he gave me your name and number and said he would talk to you. I can wait around if you think you can come down right away."

She heard an inhalation over the phone and knew an ultimatum was coming.

"Look, I don't want to, but if you can't get him to move out, I'll have to call in some deputies, and we may end up arresting him."

"Sheriff, can I just talk to him on the phone?" Grace asked.

"I tried that. He said he would only speak with you in person." He rambled on. "I don't know, something about a hawk and a map, and you, and some words I didn't understand. Well, I'd appreciate it if you could come."

Grace looked at her malt and sighed. Maybe she could take it with her. "Okay, Sheriff. I can be there in about an hour and a half."

Sheriff Lockridge gave Grace directions to Wildcrow's camp, off the road to Pleasantville and just north of Ruckman Cemetery. He had agreed to meet her at the cemetery gate and direct her from there.

"Meeting me at the cemetery gate." Grace glanced at the speedometer. At this rate, she'd beat the hour and half she told the sheriff by at least twenty minutes. She stared ahead and passing a line of semis, her thoughts traveled back to recent weekend visits. Grandfather had been agitated, repeating phrases, usually in the Sac language, and obsessing about an old map. The same one the sheriff mentioned? She had hoped this was just a passing phase. Now, she was beginning to think his behavior had been a sign of something more serious.

Chow watched traffic during the high-speed silence. Grace turned and looked straight at Chow. "Indian stuff, Chow. It's Indian stuff. I know it is!"

Chow straightened his head and widened his eyes.

"He and his Native American Indian stuff are going to drive me crazy."

Chow adjusted himself in the seat, still looking at her.

Grace's hands squeezed the steering wheel. She recalled the family history. Her jaw tightened, and her eyes stared ahead. She put on 'that face' again.

Grandfather's ancestry was from the Sac tribe. Grandmother came from Meskwaki stock. She remembered the store in the small town of Harvey, about fifteen minutes east of Knoxville. Grandfather was good at procuring authentic Native Americans items. Grace had faint mental images of herself, very small, going with Grandfather on buying trips. Grandmother did the selling. After Grandmother became seriously ill, Grandfather treated her with old-time traditions, ignoring modern medicine, in spite of Grace's father insisting he to take her to the hospital.

She turned toward Chow. "He wouldn't take her to the hospital!"

She recalled when Grandmother passed away, Grace's father became so angry that he disowned his own father and moved to Ames with six-year-old Grace, and he never talked to Grandfather again. Ever since, Grace's father avoided anything to do with Native American culture.

Grace had no voice in the matter. No choice but to grow up with that same attitude. She hadn't seen Grandfather until after she finished her university degree. She considered the old man to be different, even weird, though he'd always been good to her. Over time they renewed their relationship, and she came to love the old guy again. She feared, however, that he would pull her into what she considered 'Indian stuff.' With the recent conversations she'd had with him and the uptick in complaints Sheriff Lockridge mentioned, he might be doing just that. The sheriff said Grandfather had been 'dancing and chanting.' That sounded like what Father had always warned her about.

Grace took the exit into Carlisle on Highway 5, the final leg of the trip. Iowa fields stretched to each horizon. Most of the harvest had been completed, but random acres of Iowa corn and beans still awaited the combines. Around a long curve outside of Hartford, Grace slowed to a crawl behind a string of traffic. Six cars ahead, a big, green John Deere combine chugged along, moving from one field to another.

Grace gritted her teeth as the line of cars formed a reluctant parade. She thought of the Clinic arrangements she'd made leaving Ames. Mrs. Parker's shih tzu needed an operation to remove a tumor. Grace called in her assistant, a young man capable of handling the operation, but she was miffed she wouldn't be around to oversee the procedure. Not knowing how long she'd be away, she also asked her receptionist to reschedule other appointments and to only bring in the part-time help for Friday's patients. Nothing major... except two regulars, a Rottweiler and a Maine Coon cat. Both were owned by the same man, who, along with his pets, had an irascible nature. All three would need a firm and stolid resolve, but Grace felt her staff could handle matters.

Two long miles later, the combine crept into a field on the right and traffic picked up speed. A couple miles from Pleasantville, she slowed again behind an even longer line. Peering ahead once more, Grace saw another huge piece of farm machinery. The blood red color could have meant International Harvester or Massey Ferguson.

"More time on the road," she grumbled out loud. "How can I get Grandfather to move, Chow?" Then she remembered Grandfather loved the Hometown Meat Market. Maybe, with a decent meal, he'd listen to reason.

She adjusted her visor against the bright November sun. The fall weather hadn't been chilly. In fact, the dog days of summer had made a re-appearance in the last two weeks, keeping temps in the upper sixties and even low seventies.

In another three miles, she saw the sign pointing toward Pleasantville. She drove through most of the small town, meandering around the curves of a county highway called by locals the Stringtown Road. Fifteen minutes later, she turned on the gravel lane that led to the cemetery. Buzzards in the trees swarmed skyward when she passed underneath. Nearing the cemetery, at the end of the dead-end, close to the south shore of Lake Red Rock, she saw the sheriff's car. He'd waited for her, as he said he would. Beside him, stood the aged but regal bearing of her grandfather.

"I wonder if the fact that he's come out to meet us is a good sign?" she murmured.

Chapter 3

An hour later Grace held her grandfather's left arm as he pulled open the door to the Hometown Meat Market where Grace would finish her interrupted breakfast with an early lunch. She stood in the doorway for a moment waiting for her eyes to adjust. The store was narrow and deep with a long aisle fronting a display counter offering several cuts of meat, cheeses, and vegetables. A handwritten chalk menu hung on the wall behind the counter. It listed a variety of sandwiches, side dishes, and drinks. The dining area contained only four tables with chairs, but there were three high tables where one could stand and eat. Wildcrow chose his favorite table, facing the door. Grace went to order their meals then waited at the counter.

Two men in their twenties stood at the far end, discussing what kind of sandwiches they wanted. One was tall, gangly, with a horse face. The other stood much shorter, overweight, with a face that had never quite lost its 'fat baby cheeks' features. Grace noticed, however, even though they had different physiques, they shared a family resemblance in the oily black hair, squinty eyes, and similar jaw lines. Their general appearance—dirty jeans and old flannel shirts—turned her off. She curled her toes in her shoes and turned away from them.

Grace watched her grandfather with one eye as she paid for the food and took the plates back to the table. She set his tenderloin sandwich down then slid onto the bench seat across from him with her own chicken wrap. He glared at her, ignoring the food in front of him.

"What's wrong, Grandfather? Did you change you're mind on what you wanted?"

He looked down at his plate then back to her. "Meat okay." He placed his hands on each side of his plate and leaned forward. "I don't understand why you took me away from my home. Why we here?"

Grandfather knew how to speak proper English, however, sometimes he fell into stereotypical pronunciations, leaving out words.

"That land where you set up your teepee is not your home," Grace said. "It belongs to someone else. The sheriff was going to put you in jail if we hadn't left."

"All this land our land." Wildcrow waved a hand to indicate, Grace thought, the entire state, maybe the country. "From long ago. It's ours."

Grace sighed and picked up her fork. "That used to be true, but we don't live in the past, Grandfather. The land isn't ours today."

Wildcrow nodded. "The Spirit of the Land is ours. Will always be that way. I will show you." His voice rose in volume, attracting attention.

"You don't prove anything just by putting a teepee wherever you want. It was outside a cemetery for heaven's sake," Grace said. "You can't just say it's your land. You need proof. Something in writing. The White Man's way, Grandfather." Grace looked around the Meat Market. An Asian-appearing man sitting at the corner table gave her a smile which she didn't return. When he dropped his gaze, she turned in her seat to the two guys still at the counter. They covered their mouths with their hands and talked to each other in whispers. They kept glancing her way. She felt her face getting warm.

She lowered her voice. "Grandfather, you have to be careful about wild talk. People are listening."

Wildcrow bent down and pulled a rolled object from his bag beside his chair. "Here." He unrolled the object, and Grace recognized it as a piece of animal skin. Scraped free of hair, one side had a variety of markings. "I had a vision. It said I would find the way back to our heritage. This will help us."

"What is that, Grandfather? Where did you get it?"

"This has been handed down through many generations in our family. Until my vision I didn't know what it meant. The Spirits told me. It is a map that will lead us to the truth. We will find the treasured bundle, then everyone will know."

"Bundle? What are you talking about?"

Grace saw the two men stand straighter when Wildcrow laid the map on the table. The taller guy paid for their purchase, wiped his mouth with his sleeve, and motioned to his partner to leave.

When the two men passed their table, the tall one pointed his cell phone at the skin map. What? Grace thought. He's taking a picture?

"Roll that up, Grandfather. There are people here who don't need to know about it."

Wildcrow slapped his hand on the table and his face turned red. "White men need to know." His angry voice carried throughout the restaurant.

The manager, wearing a white apron hustled around the end of the counter and came over beside Wildcrow, his hands on his hips. "You folks about finished?" The meaning was clear.

Wildcrow stood, the map in his hand. "You'll regret this. We will find the bundle and then you will know."

"I'm sure I will." The manager pointed toward the door. "I think it's time to leave."

"Grandfather, we have to go." Grace apologized to the manager and guided Wildcrow by his elbow to the door. When they got to her car, she glanced over her shoulder but didn't see anyone following them. The two men who had been so curious about Wildcrow's map disappeared around the corner on the Square. With one last look in her rearview mirror, she started her car and headed back to the place where Grandfather's tent had been erected near the cemetery. With reluctance, the sheriff had agreed Wildcrow could spend one more night but had to vacate the area come morning as there was a burial scheduled.

When he wasn't occupying that land, her grandfather lived in an old Airstream trailer at Elk Rock Park. He offered it to Grace and Chow to spend the night. She accepted but was determined that come morning, she would help pack up his possessions and move him to Ames.

Chapter 4

Wu Jin-dien Hardware, locally known as Woo Hardware, was just about a block from the Hometown Meat Market. It had been a fixture in the tow for years but was now owned by a foreign company. Hank Oliver had managed the business for years and continued to do so after the transition. Folks called him Hardware Hank. He was a friendly guy but a man who tended toward brusqueness in minor matters. He fit the picture of a hardware store man with his square face, beefy build, and western-style shirt. A sprinkling of dust from his rooting around in back corners always seemed to coat his sandy brown hair.

Other than managing the store, he drove an ambulance when needed, directed the volunteer fire department, and served on the City Council. For years, whenever there was an emergency, Hank would close the shop and hang a sign on the front door indicating that he had gone to do his duty. Most customers were used to the fact that Hank might be gone, but some complained that letting Hank close the store even to chase fires was a bad way to do business. The owners, usually content to let Hank run things, had by the spring of that year, received one too many of those complaints. They insisted that he hire someone to keep the store open during regular hours. Though he felt he had handled business quite well on his own, he relented and had taken on a man named Kyle Brewer as a new clerk. At first, the decision seemed to work out because in recent months, Hank kept getting called out more often, usually for fires.

Kyle had stuck around after the annual sprint car championships back in August. Not much time had passed before Hank began to wonder about his choice of this former pit crew helper. Kyle had been deferential and productive at first, with an attitude matching his boyish, friendly face. Maybe a bit too chatty some days, Hank thought, but the customers liked to listen to his stories about growing up on a ranch out west. While that was fine, Hank felt Kyle tried to get a little too personal with the customers, asking about their habits and homes. Hank considered some of the inquiries nosy and unnecessary but figured it was part of Kyle's personality. The man could turn on the charm when needed. A little too slick looking, though. Black hair, square jaw, nose broken at least once sometime in his past. Not unattractive and Hank had noticed some of the women eyeing the guy's 'bad boy' hardness.

Near eleven that Thursday morning, Hank sat at his desk looking through his list of new merchandise ordered earlier that week. He moved his finger down the order sheet and realized there was an item missing. Damn it, Kyle! He grabbed the paper and went out front. "Kyle, where in the Sam-Hill are the shovels that I asked you to order?" Kyle was silent.

"Well?"

"Sorry, boss."

"I put you in charge of that for a reason." Hank walked behind the counter. "I have a City Council meeting at noon, and you'll need to man the store while I'm gone." He scratched his jaw. "Look, I don't like to come down on you, but you need to be more diligent in your duties. We have only five shovels left. I'll write down some other items we need. Also, I'll make a list of some basic office supplies. Close the store for about half an hour during lunch and go over to Papers, Pens & Stuff. Mandy will know what we need."

"Yes, sir," Kyle replied.

"I know you haven't been here very long but if you want to continue, you'll have to be more careful."

He considered saying more, but decided he'd berated Kyle enough. What really bothered Hank, though, was that some of the inventory had gone missing in recent weeks. Smaller items, flashlights and batteries, screwdrivers and hammers, were unaccounted for when he compared items sold with what remained on the shelves and display boards. Balancing the bank deposits took more time because the figures didn't always add up correctly. A little bit here and there, sure, maybe simple calculating errors, but Hank often wondered if Kyle was pocketing items and cash.

"You should know you're still in a probationary period," Hank told his clerk. "If there weren't so many fires breaking out recently, I wouldn't even need you."

"Boss," Kyle said, changing the subject – something Kyle was quite good at – "Can you believe the fire that burned the hotel out on the highway? Who do you think did it?"

"No one knows," Hank said. "Not even sure if it was accidental or arson. The department and the police are still investigating."

Hank turned to go back to his office but stopped when two customers entered. He sneered when two men ambled up the center aisle. Bubba and Cole Smith. There were plenty of lowlife losers in town, but Hank thought these were two of the worst. He'd heard stories about their drug dealing, beer drinking, and causing general mayhem on the weekends. Hell, he'd even considered them culprits to some of the fires around the county. Who knew, maybe they'd been screwing around at the hotel at the time of its blaze. The least they could do was dress a bit better than thrift store jeans and faded, flannel shirts.

When they stopped at the front counter, Hank thought they looked like they belonged in a circus sideshow, Bubba, shorter and flabbier than his string bean brother. Both Hank and Kyle took a step back. The Smiths reeked of marijuana.

"We need shovels," Bubba said without even a greeting.

Not caring about courtesy—the two ingrates certainly hadn't—Hank grabbed the Febreze bottle from under the register and sprayed the air. After ten full seconds, he stopped and pointed. "They're right over there behind you. Aisle three."

Bubba and Cole walked away. Hank sprayed the space where they'd stood. He tried not to breathe until the pot odor had dissipated.

Kyle waved his hands in the air. "Oh my god, they stink, man."

Hank nodded, grabbed a notepad, plucked a pen from a Mason jar near the register, and started writing a list of items for Kyle to order and another list for supplies he needed from Mandy's office supply store around the corner. Kyle returned to general cleaning duties. The store wasn't too large, and the Smiths' voices carried.

"Holy cow," Bubba said. "Look at all the different kinds of shovels. What kind do we need?"

"Duh, you dumb head," Cole said. "A regular one! What a stupid question."

"There's a long flat one, there's one with a round pointed blade, and there's a smaller one."

Cole grabbed the round pointed blade and asked, "This one should get us the treasure."

"Did you get a good picture of the map when he had it rolled out at the table?" Bubba prodded. "Are you sure it was focused?"

"Sure, I did, you idiot." Cole held up the shovel. "If we can follow the old Indian's treasure map, this'll work."

"It might be buried really deep."

Cole smacked Bubba across the head. "Then we'll get two, and you can help."

"You know I don't like shoveling stuff," Bubba said.

"'Less it's food in your mouth," Cole said. "Stupid. Get outta my way before I stomp you."

Hank and Kyle looked at each other with raised eyebrows. Kyle walked over to the boys.

"Treasure?" Kyle asked. "What's up, guys?"

"That old Indian Wildcrow was bragging about a map and treasure," Bubba said. "We're gonna find it before he does."

"Shut up, stupid. Do you want the whole town to know our business?" Cole slammed his brother in the chest and grabbed the shovels. "He's just kidding. We want to plant some flowers out by our trailer."

The boys paid for the shovels and left, pushing and shoving each other as they departed.

"Treasure? Sounds like Cole and Bubba have been smoking way too much of their own product," Hank remarked and headed back to his office.

Before Hank entered his office, he noticed Kyle still staring after the two brothers. His expression was a mixture of curiosity and contemplation, as if his thoughts ran toward plans for following up on the Smiths' conversation.

While Hank gathered notes for the council meeting, he muttered, "I'll have to keep an eye on Kyle."

Chapter 5

The Knoxville City Hall hadn't weathered well over the years. It had the look of a rundown senior center and, coincidentally, a senior citizens group did hold regular meetings in the basement. That Thursday, cars lined the streets and spilled over into the library and nearby church parking lots. Most of the owners were attending a special city council meeting.

Justin 'Digger' Clay pulled up to the library and parked. He rolled a Gran Habano Corojo #V between his fingers, took in a final drag, and smothered the last ember in the ashtray. The musty, spicy aroma of the quality cigar was always a welcome and calming smell.

He stepped out, and the contrasting crisp fall air filled his lungs. At least it wasn't as dusty as it was where he lived outside of town. There he could smell the crops, but waves of dust from the gravel roads rolled in like tidal waves to blanket him in a fog. He coughed just with the thought. Digger, a history teacher at the local high school, had a three-day break from classes for teacher development and had agreed to meet his girlfriend, Kathryn, to take her to lunch after the council meeting.

He turned to his prized 1978 Gremlin, olive green with black stripes. He'd picked it up for a steal while he was finishing undergraduate courses, and the combination of his self-taught knowledge of cars and the local mechanics had kept it running well. It was a statement and a reflection of himself—sturdy, reliable, and cool with a touch of retro style…if sometimes covered in dust. He'd thought about running it through the car wash on the way into town, but he felt it a waste of time and money since the drive home would just get it dusty again.

As a squirrel darted across the road and some red-breasted robins bounced across the grass by the sidewalk, Digger heard the familiar alarm sound of his phone playing, *Even If It Breaks Your Heart.*

"Crap!" He hurried toward City Hall, across the parking lot and the street, but pulled up short at the east end of the building. The main entrance lay on the west side.

"I hope she's not going to be mad at me for being late," he mumbled.

He pushed through the front door to a landing with flights of ascending stairs to the main floor or a descending flight to the lower level. He charged up, glad for all the leg exercise he had gotten this summer working out in the yard and setting fence line.

Only one woman occupied the hall to the meeting room. Cheryl Lockridge, the sheriff's wife, leaned against the wall with her phone to her ear. Seconds later, doors opened, and people flowed out. He'd missed the whole meeting. Caught behind a Claas combine on the way to a late harvest, Digger had been unaccountably delayed.

The local treasurer, a balding man with glasses, held the attention of three other men to his left. Other council members spoke with groups of the general public. Digger let out a sigh of relief when he didn't spy Kathryn. She hadn't sounded happy on the phone about going to this meeting.

"Digger, boy!"

Digger turned, recognizing Hank's deep bellowing voice that always filled whatever room he was in. The barrel-chested man offered a wide smile.

"Hank. Good to see you," Digger said.

Hank unhooked his thumbs from his suspenders. He had on a tan button up western shirt and jeans. "Same to you." He clapped Digger on the back which threatened to send him forward on his face. "How you been?"

Digger shrugged. "Same ole."

"Son, you're too young to look that down. You and VanSteele still getting along?"

Digger nodded. He and Kathryn VanSteele had been together for four years now. They hadn't moved in together, but often had discussed the idea. The main concern on her part was that she didn't like his farmhouse but would consider the idea if he completed the remodeling. This meant he had spent the greater portion of the past four years at her apartment on the couch. She had a double bed which had been big enough at the beginning of the night. He remembered the nights they had when they first started dating. Wild, hot, and steamy nights.

Not anymore. Over the years, her sleep had become disturbed, restless. She couldn't explain the change. In the last six months, whenever she started thrashing and snorting in her sleep, he found the couch felt better than an abrupt shove out on the floor or the feel of putting his hand in some sleep drool on a pillow. He couldn't stand that drooling. That and other personality quirks of hers had cooled his emotions toward her. The idea of living together didn't have the amount of importance it once held.

Hank cut into Diggers drifting thoughts. "Well, you've heard the latest, I take it?"

"No, what's happening?" Digger knew he was about to be privy to the latest gossip.

"Kyle and I heard the town fools, those Smith brothers, talking about a map that Jacob Wildcrow has. He and a young woman were at the Meat Market earlier. Not sure who she is, but she called him her grandfather. Anyway, other people also heard it and word has spread about a buried treasure. You know how people can latch onto a rumor."

Digger didn't know Wildcrow had any relatives, at least none in the area. A treasure map? Cole and Bubba were known around town for the petty crimes they committed. Selling marijuana, traffic violations, causing general mischief. So far, they'd been relatively harmless. Everyone had learned to take what claims they made with a grain of salt. He knew the boys well, having thrown them both out of his history class multiple times for being disruptive back in the day. Poor boys. No one knew why they weren't in jail. Digger just assumed that instead of being too smart to get caught, they were just too dumb.

He had made friends with Jacob Wildcrow years ago. The elderly guy still possessed a lot of spunk and vitality and had turned Digger's archaeologist hobby more toward Native American artifacts. Yes, he would have preferred Jurassic Park dinosaur finds, but here in the Midwest, those were few and far between. Recently, he had been looking into the area's Indian mounds.

"I guess the boys think it's a big deal," Hank said. "I personally think they've been smoking a little too much pot. But still, I hear Mr. Wildcrow's been quite the nuisance lately, setting up his teepee all over the county. Sheriff Lockridge has had to roust him out several times."

Digger nodded, only half listening. It was strange. Treasure.... Just the mention of that one little word sent Digger's mind spinning into intrigue and adventure. What if Wildcrow had knowledge of a treasure? Digger, a novice hunter of artifacts, imagined discovering 'the big one' like Nicholas Cage had in the movie *National Treasure*.

Hank's tone dropped to a sullen note. "Oh, well. Did you hear what the council meeting was all about? Seems like things in this town are a lot worse than we thought."

Digger nodded and at the same time wondered if the treasure had something to do with the mounds he'd spotted over by the river. Wildcrow talked about them often. Then again, he talked about a lot of things during Digger's visits out at Elk Rock campground where Wildcrow was a part-time caretaker. They'd discuss any arrowheads or potsherds Digger found. Many times, he just listened while Wildcrow told stories of Native American history.

Hank's booming voice, which seemed to come from deep within his belly, grew louder, interrupting Digger's daydream. "You know, when that big box store came in and the square lost some businesses, the city borrowed money to try to keep stores from closing and provide incentives for local ownership," Hank continued. "Looks like it backfired, 'cause the town's going to default on this loan soon. A guy by the name of LeMay from Zygote Development told us about this same thing happening in a town down south. A lot of the town pretty much got re-possessed and turned into a new multiplex China Town."

Digger frowned. He hadn't imagined Knoxville's problems to be so bad, but he had seen the city hurting for a while since the big store came in. There were a few empty retail spaces on the square, two being a former appliance and furniture store. Many others struggled and survived by community loyalty and sheer will. Wildcrow had made a lot of comments about the 'white man stores.' He never said it in a racist way, always like a joke, yet Digger heard some of the underlying tones.

Digger recalled Wildcrow's little trailer at Elk Rock where he stayed during the summer. Sunflower seed shells littered the floor around Wildcrow's easy chair. Books stacked on homemade shelves, many historical tomes about Iowa and Oklahoma. What were some of those titles?

Wildcrow had been subdued all this last summer, always seeming to be lost in thought. He hadn't been rude, but their conversations felt stilted, distant.

Now, if Cole and Bubba were to be believed, the old Indian had a map. A treasure map? Once again, the idea sent a heart-revving thrill through him.

A high-pitched voice shattered Digger's thoughts. "We're bringing in a casino, Justin!"

Digger jerked and turned to face Kathryn VanSteele. Her business clothes always surprised him. Only five feet five inches tall and very compact, she displayed never ending full curves. Dishwater blonde hair fell in ringlets to the bottom of her earlobes. Bright chocolate drop eyes sparkled with excitement. The gray business suit she wore only intensified those curves, holding hostage large breasts, clutching her waist sensually, and clinging to her hips. He wished her skirt was a touch longer though, because her knobby knees poked out. He had never noticed that fact in the first couple years they were dating, but now it drove him wild, and not in a good way.

He drew a long breath, took her hands, and placed a brief kiss on her lips. "Good to see you. What did you say about a casino?"

She smiled. "We're getting a casino, baby. Isn't that wonderful?"

"What?" She had talked about a big project several times in the past, wanting to bring a casino to the area. He had always tried to sound supportive and encouraged her, because he thought no one would be crazy enough to approve it.

Her smile widened as she nodded. "My plan went through to bring in a casino which will protect the city from defaulting. James LeMay, from the Zygote Casino Development Group, convinced the council that tons of money and dozens of jobs would come to Knoxville and solve all our problems."

"That's... great." Digger tried to sound pleased but wasn't. Iowa had enough casinos. While the city may have approved it, he wondered if the state gaming commission would. The closest casino,

Prairie Meadows, was only a forty-five-minute drive. One placed in Knoxville would mean mass development of land and most likely ruin natural wildlife areas. "Where is it going to be built?"

"That open hunting land out by the cliffs at Lake Red Rock."

"What cliffs?"

"The ones by that tree they use as a kayaking marker." She snapped her fingers together. "What's it called again?"

"The... Peace Tree." He didn't want to say it, because he didn't want it to be real. Developing the private land by the Peace Tree would destroy a perfectly good piece of wildlife habitat and ruin a crucial part of Native American history. The land was hilly, so the whole area would have to be bulldozed and leveled. He'd tried to discourage her whenever she brought up the topic. Damn, he thought. He should have been more persuasive.

"Yes!" She smiled and raised her hand triumphantly. "And I'm overseeing the entire project."

"That's... good," he forced out. "Kathryn, you might need to think a bit more about this idea. That land isn't stable enough to support large buildings."

A casino would destroy everything. First the wildlife would leave, and how long would it take before they sold off Elk Rock and other sites around the lake, too, in order to build hotels and other businesses? Just like what had happened at the Meskwaki Casino near Tama. They might even name it Peace Tree Casino as they devastated everything the Peace Tree stood for. He pictured the casino, hotels, shopping malls, restaurants, and internally shivered.

"Yes. I'm so excited," said Kathryn. She was too wound up to hear a word Digger said. "I can't wait to tell you more, but I'm starved." She smacked her hand on her stomach.

"Where do you want to eat?" he asked.

"Oh, anywhere."

He narrowed his eyes as a vague idea came to him. "How about Cone Corner? They're serving sandwiches now."

"Delicious."

He raised a brow. "And afterward, we can take a peek at the land you're looking at. Give you a better idea of what would happen with what you're planning."

She clapped her hands together. "That would be perfect. Oh, Justin, I love how smart you are." Her voice rose to a high pitch, the kind that always made him feel like a small soft fluffy puppy. At any moment she would break out into baby talk and tickle him under his chin, another thing he had liked when they first were dating but now couldn't stand. Maybe it was just him. He'd been told couples go through rough spots and... dry spells.

Digger smiled at her as he sorted out a very sketchy plan. Maybe if he took her to the Peace Tree area, she might realize a casino would be a bad idea.

Chapter 6

After a quick bite and sundaes at Cone Corner, Digger drove out to Red Rock. On the way, he and Kathryn argued—she would have described it as discussing—about the wisdom of developing the Peace Tree land. A couple years older than Digger, she'd made her mark almost from the first day she moved to Knoxville. She started as a real estate agent, but soon after, established herself as a real estate *developer*, having an innate sense of how best to utilize new land and already existing businesses. This project, though, in his opinion, went too far.

"Your ideas are too extreme for the available land," Digger offered. "There's too steep a slope to have a good footing for any very big complexes. If we had a rainy summer, which is very possible, the land would flood and undermine the foundation."

"I'm sure that the engineers can make accommodations for any of the natural features," Kathryn said.

As a history teacher and amateur archaeologist, Digger was familiar with the historic significance of the land. It was one reason he was trying to convince Kathryn not to desecrate the place with all the folderol she was talking about.

"I'll show you what a bad idea it is to build there," he said.

"I'm willing to look it over, but I think this will really work," she replied. "Let's not waste time. I have a lot of planning to do and calls to make."

She was caught up in the excitement and novelty of a casino, without acknowledging the realities of the matter. He pondered again about what he was doing with this woman as his girlfriend. Having decided to stay in Marion County, he had wanted to settle into family life in the area. Kathryn VanSteele seemed energetic, successful in her work, and involved in a number of activities that fit with Digger's own interests.

The two of them had worked, played, and loved well together. In bed, they had a playful manner. Often, they engaged in a game to see who could excite the other the most with sexy talk and innuendos.

Early on, Digger expected he and Kathryn would someday tie the knot. Lately, however, the idea of marrying Kathryn had lost its appeal. Rather, his thoughts kept returning to previous girlfriends, which were not many in number, and a crush he'd had briefly one post-grad summer at Iowa State.

Digger turned onto the gravel road that led to Ruckman Cemetery. The area under consideration for development lay off to the west, but there was an access point just beyond the cemetery that gave a good view of the land. Through the cemetery gate, he drove the perimeter road to the trail that led to the access point. Digger was about to reiterate his argument against the casino when he spotted the familiar teepee he'd often seen at his friend's Airstream trailer. It had been erected in a clearing at the head of the trail. This late in November, the lack of foliage allowed a broad view of the lake. About thirty yards from the teepee, the land dipped sharply down a bluff to the rocky shoreline. He couldn't see it, but Digger knew the recent drought had lowered the water level by several feet.

Two figures stood near the teepee. One he recognized at once, dressed in traditional Native American breeches and leather tunic. The other…well, the slender young woman looked vaguely familiar.

"There's Jacob Wildcrow," Digger said. "I was talking to Hank just before you came out of the meeting. He told me the Smith brothers had started some excitement about a map and possible treasure, and that Wildcrow was at the center of it all. Now here he is."

Kathryn perked up and jumped from the car, straightening her skirt and patting her hair. By the time Digger could extricate himself from the Gremlin, Kathryn had gone right up to the two to introduce herself.

"Kathryn VanSteele." Digger heard her say, extending her hand. "You must be Jacob Wildcrow. I've been hearing stories about you."

Wildcrow's face took on a quizzical look. He stared at her outstretched hand. The young woman beside Wildcrow took a step forward "I'm his granddaughter, Grace Snow. Can I ask why you are here, Miss VanSteele?"

Kathryn turned her attention to the woman. Digger thought she sensed that Grace's alliance might be useful. From then on, Wildcrow was ignored. "I see. As I said, I'm Kathryn VanSteele. I'm a realtor and always on the lookout for economic development." She gave them her best saleswoman smile. "This is my boyfriend, Justin Clay."

"Call me Digger," he said. "How have you been, Wildcrow?" No one outside his high school teaching world ever called Digger anything else, and Kathryn's continuing to call him Justin was another annoyance these days. That, and her self-aggrandizement.

"We're looking at the land as a prospective site for development." Kathryn waved her arms to indicate the space around them. "Look around you. This is the future home of the largest casino in Iowa. Well, not here at the cemetery, of course, but around the next bluff."

Wildcrow just gazed at her. Then, he shook his head, turned, stepped several feet away, and began to dance and sing in his native language, spitting and whooping. Digger guessed there might have been a few profane words mixed in there. Digger had attended pow-wows in Tama, and those dancing men weren't half so animated as old Wildcrow was in response to Kathryn's words.

Kathryn stepped back and clutched Digger's arm. Wide-eyed, she stared at Wildcrow. Digger felt the tension in her body, as if she were ready to bolt at the first sign of an attack. He knew Wildcrow wouldn't assault Kathryn but readied himself to defend her if necessary. After the man calmed, Grace placed a hand on his arm. She spoke almost in a whisper, the way one would soothe an angry dog. Wildcrow froze in his frenzied movements, then relaxed. He dropped his head to his chest and stood still.

Uh-oh, Kathryn, now you've done it, Digger thought. One more reason that building here is a bad idea. He watched Grace with Wildcrow and a moment later, he realized where he had seen her before. She was one of the girls he'd been thinking about on the drive out to the lake, the one he'd seen walking across the Iowa State campus by the Campanile six years before.

****

The day had been bright and warm. He'd taken himself out on the commons, enjoying the sunshine, sitting on the grass, nose into his textbook *The Anasazi and Pre-American Culture*, a summer post-grad class at ISU. He all but ignored pairs and groups of students who strolled by, laughing and joking, and those out walking dogs. The sound of hard-soled shoes *tap-tapping* on the sidewalk in what he perceived as a no-nonsense rhythm caught his attention. He looked up to see a stately brunette beauty, nose in the air, heading toward the library. Her darker skin tone looked natural, not from a tanning salon. Latino? Maybe, but her facial features didn't have the soft roundness of women from south of the border. Rather, they reminded him of books he'd read about other Native American tribes other than the Anasazi. At that moment, all he knew was that she was gorgeous.

Digger jumped up, deciding to make a trip to the library—or wherever else she was going. He brushed off his jeans and took long strides to catch up with her.

He might have been a mosquito or a passing breeze for all the attention she paid him.

"Excuse me miss," he said when he came alongside her.

The woman glanced at him but didn't slow her stride. "May I help you?"

"Well, I wondered if you knew the campus myth about this area, the Campanile?"

She ignored him. Undaunted, he continued. "Yeah, I sure wish it was midnight so I could steal a kiss and your heart."

He was only using the line because of the decade's old story told that a midnight kiss by the Campanile was a magical way to assure a lasting relationship. In retrospect, it was pretty nerdy of him to use the cheesy line. She curled her lips in disgust at his brazenness and walked on. He then asked for her number, but she just turned away from the library and headed across the quad toward the animal buildings. He followed but slowed when an undergrad female came toward her and greeted her as Dr. Snow. Digger paused but made a mental note to look her up in the faculty directory. It took quite a search, but once found, he called her office and started to explain that he was the fellow who had talked to her by the Campanile.

"Annoyed me, you mean," she said. "Sorry, I'm not interested." Digger heard the phone click.

Digger checked the office number in the directory and walked over to see if his third try would yield charm. Was she really a Native American, as he'd deduced? Her facial features weren't from a European background, but he couldn't figure out her ancestry. Standing outside her office—he had called once again to be sure she was still there—he built a fantasy in his mind of the midnight kiss.

When the woman did come out, she took one look at him, whirled, and stalked back inside. In a short while campus security, in the form of a uniformed bruiser who looked like he outweighed Digger by a hundred pounds or so, suggested that he move along and stop loitering.

The summer term ended, and Digger returned to teach at Knoxville High School. He met Kathryn at the Swamp Fox the next year. They dated off and on, until eventually they were going steady.

The enigmatic Doctor Snow drifted into to his memory bank.

***

Now, here she was again. What a coincidence. Wildcrow's granddaughter? Maybe not a coincidence. Maybe Fate had stepped in at a time when he had some relationship concerns. Watching Kathryn try to proclaim the wonders of a casino, Digger felt the urge to protect Grace rather than his girlfriend. Wildcrow, standing near the tree line, had unrolled what looked like a thick parchment. Digger joined him. He still overheard the conversation between Kathryn and Grace.

"Do you know the harm you are doing to even consider a casino here?" Grace asked.

Digger cut in before Kathryn could gain steam. "This is fascinating."

"What is?" Kathryn stepped to his side.

"This map! I've seen something like this elsewhere, I'm sure." He held up the map Wildcrow had unrolled.

"What are you talking about?" Grace asked. "Are you saying you think this is real?"

"I'm not an expert by any means, but it seems old enough to be authentic."

She sighed. Digger wondered if she doubted the map's veracity. They were nuisances, but could Cole and Bubba have been right?

"You actually can't think this is a real treasure map," Grace said.

"Well, it's a map to something. Maybe treasure. Hard to tell. There are plenty of reports that old and valuable artifacts were buried around these parts by the natives. Even a rumor that someone once buried gold, precious stones, other valuable items in one of the mounds, but it has never been confirmed."

Grace shook her head. "Surely those are just myths."

"Some are." Digger gave her a pointed look. "Others... may not be."

He glanced at Kathryn who didn't look at all pleased with the talk of maps and treasure. They could mean possible government intrusion and delayed plans for her pet project.

From the look on her face, though, he feared she'd plow through any obstacles, including him.

Chapter 7

After the council meeting, Hank Oliver decided to pick up some stamps at the post office before he returned to the hardware store. He pushed open the door to the post office and saw Sheriff Lockridge coming out, unzipping his jacket as he entered the heat. "Nice morning isn't it, Sheriff?"

"Sure is, Hank. You headed to lunch? We could get a bite together."

"No, I need to get back to the hardware store so Kyle can get his lunch. I'll pick up a burger and take it back with me. I've been at the city council meeting over the lunch hour. That was a trip and a half. Did you hear about the casino and the 'Indian treasure?'"

"Indian treasure, I know about. I had to call Wildcrow's granddaughter down here from Ames to avoid an incident. She'll get the old man to move his teepee."

"Bubba and Cole were spouting off in the store this morning that they are going to find the treasure for themselves," Hank said. "I've never seen such idiots as those two."

"What were you talking about when you mentioned a casino?" the sheriff asked. "There have been rumors, sure, but they rise and fall as fast as the water level at the dam. There have, come to think of it, been some rich-looking strangers driving around town in Mercedes, Cadillacs, even a nice-looking Crown Victoria. The mayor mentioned the buzz about a local casino, but it seems like so much pie-in-the-sky. About as likely as Wildcrow finding a real treasure around here."

"We're one step closer after this noon's council meeting." Hank said. "A guy from St. Louis made a presentation, laying out the chances of the city defaulting on some bonds. You know your cousin Kathryn has been pushing the casino idea. Well, the meeting ended with an approval for a commission to explore the whole concept."

"Hmm. Well, that's city business, I guess," Lockridge said. "Still, as county sheriff, I think they ought to have let me know about it."

"I'm sure you'll get a notice in the official minutes. I thought your wife filled you in on such stuff."

Lockridge laughed. "Yeah, she does whenever we have a few minutes together."

"What's the latest on the rash of fires we've been having? Any more evidence of who's setting them?"

The sheriff scratched his neck. "Well, you're the fire inspector around here. You tell me. To my eyes, they look like accidents or maybe kids playing around. The majority of the buildings damaged were old."

"I'm getting tired of going out on these calls," Hank said. "Wish something could be done."

"Don't worry," Lockridge said. "We'll catch whoever's setting them one day. I'm more worried about those sinkholes. Had another call yesterday northwest of the lake about one in a farm field. Luckily, the combine stopped before it fell in."

"What is that, Sheriff, about the third or fourth incident?"

"Yeah, always up on the north side of Red Rock. Hate to have them start appearing in the middle of town."

"No explanation?"

"Nope. We've had some so-called experts come in, but they haven't determined anything yet. Freak of nature is what they say."

In a few moments, they wrapped up their conversation. "Take care, Sheriff," Hank said.

After finishing at the post office and buying a cheeseburger and fries at Taso's, Hank returned to Woo Hardware. A parade of cars drove by on Marion Street. None of them was any of the luxury cars Lockridge had mentioned, but one was a very dilapidated van with rust around the rear fenders. For all the honor of having the title of Mayor, Larry Stubbs remained true to himself, a good ole boy with rural roots. He didn't mind driving the old beater van. In fact, he was kind of proud of it.

Originally from Ozark, Missouri, he had moved to town when his father took a job after the 3M plant completed its facility in 1973. He had an acne scarred face under a trimmed white beard. Matching white hair had receded to curl around each ear.

Hank threw up his hand in a wave and hollered. "Hey, Mayor, how's it going?"

"Mornin' Hank. Caught any arsonists, lately?" the mayor yelled.

"Very funny, Mayor. Wasn't that a trip at the city council meeting? Casinos? Default on our loans? I guess I contributed to the confusion when I mentioned Bubba and Cole's latest wild goose chase. Next, we'll be hearing that big time gangsters are hiding out in Knoxville." Hank laughed and shook his head.

The mayor laughed, too. "Well, that last one might be true. I didn't bring it up at the meeting, but have you heard the rumor the FBI might have sent an agent to the area as part of a manhunt to find a wanted felon from Chicago? Heard the guy was into the drug trade and is wanted for several murders."

"You're kidding, right?"

"I've had no official notice about it, but you know how talk is once someone gets a notion," Stubbs said. He took on a more serious tone. "Normally, the feds get in touch with the local police, but as I understand, there's been someone in town all mysterious like, asking questions at some of the restaurants. People say he drives one of those unmarked Crown Victorias. You know how gossip is: 'Gotta be the FBI.'"

"Check with your wife," Hank suggested.

"I'd better check in with my wife," Stubbs said as if he hadn't heard Hank. "She's good at sorting rumors from truth. Hey, good to see you Hank."

Mayor Stubbs drove off and Hank entered the hardware store to relieve Kyle.

***

Hank's mention of his wife during their conversation sparked a romantic notion in Sheriff Lockridge. Before returning to the office, he stopped in at Candi's Flowers and inquired about one of those Christmas cacti. Fern, one of the employees said she had one left. "Would you like it delivered?"

"That'd be fine," Lockridge said, then added, "Uh, why don't put in about half a dozen carnations with that?"

Fern gave him a sly grin. "Come on, sheriff, you can do better than that. Carnations are for high school boys. Now, I'll make you a good deal on a dozen roses."

Lockridge considered. Fern did have a reputation for buying flowers that lasted longer than usual, but a dozen? He hadn't bought that many roses in... well, he couldn't recall.

Fern leaned over the counter and said in a mischievous low voice, "If you don't want all hot sexy red, I'll add some whites and pinks."

Lockridge felt his face grow warm. "Fern...."

Fern laughed at his embarrassment. "What do you say, Sheriff? I'll knock three bucks off the price."

Lockridge pulled his wallet from his pants pocket. "Fine, but don't be talking about this."

"Aw, you know me, Sheriff."

"Yeah, I do know, and that's what I meant. Just keep this to yourself, all right?"

He left the store and ambled south along the sidewalk, feeling more light-hearted. Maybe the flowers and the cactus would help make up for last week's interruption. Another fire had taken out an abandoned farmhouse north of town and threatened to burn the neighboring cornfield that hadn't been harvested. Lockridge had wanted to splurge at a fancy restaurant in Des Moines, make it a romantic night with his wife. The fire had canceled those plans. Maybe they could try again. Maybe, start the weekend early tonight....

Lost in thoughts of enjoying the pleasures of being in love with his wife, near the bank, he recognized Hank's new salesclerk. What was his name? After a moment's thought, he remembered. Kyle was gazing intently at the Swamp Fox, his jaw clenched.

"Excuse me," Lockridge said from twenty feet away, but Kyle didn't acknowledge him. His focus was aimed at someone standing across the down the block near one of the patio tables outside the Swamp Fox bar. The man, average looking, about forty or so, stood out because of his attire: a black suit coat over a black turtleneck shirt and black slacks. The clothes looked completely out of place here in the middle of rural Iowa. Average height and build, sandy blond hair. Lockridge was sure he had never seen the man before and wondered who he was and what business he had in town.

Kyle, still staring toward the bar and the stranger, made an abrupt turn. Lockridge watched him walk down Marion to First

Street, taking the long way to what Lockridge assumed would be the Casa Grande for lunch.

Lockridge wondered what it was all about.

Chapter 8

Ten miles north of the city of Knoxville, two Cadillacs and a Mercedes sat at the gate below the Cordova observation tower overlooking Lake Red Rock. James LeMay, of the Zygote Casino Development Company, had combined a business trip with a family vacation to see the sticks and stalks of Iowa. Most of their time, however, had been spent seeing the sites in Des Moines—the Blank Park Zoo, the Science Center, and a comedy act at the new club downtown—but they had gotten a good taste of the country. LeMay, tired of his hometown's barbecue, wanted the local fare. Thick hand-breaded tenderloins and Maid-Rite loose meat sandwiches. Cholesterol-laden diner breakfasts and Dutch letters from the bakeries in Pella. His two brothers and their wives had joined him for a small vacation, and he talked his daughter into letting his grandson come along during a school break. While his wife had looked forward to the experience, he wasn't so sure his grandson would be. However, to his surprise everyone was excited about the wild outdoors, previously viewed only from thirty thousand feet in travels from one coast to the other. They enjoyed the walking trails and even laughed about the odors of dead skunk and hog farms.

LeMay had come at the invitation of Kathryn VanSteele to discuss the possibility of financing a casino on the shores of the lake. After getting himself assigned to the project by the boss, he figured he could add a bit extra to the expense account to cover a family vacation at no added cost to him.

After everyone exited the rented Mercedes GLK, he clicked the key fob and heard the chirp of the lock. Standing on the gravel parking lot, he laughed to himself.

"What's so funny," asked his brother, Bob.

LeMay shrugged. "Locking the door out here. I doubt some dimwit hayseed from Iowa will come out here just to steal a Mercedes."

He knew in St. Louis, an unlocked Mercedes could disappear as soon as the owner entered an office building and sometimes before.

His grandson, Reggie, tugged on his arm. "Granddad, can I keep the key in my fanny pack while we're climbing? I'll be real careful with it."

LeMay looked at the towering edifice before him, remembering what he'd read in the travel pamphlet. One hundred and six feet tall, the Cordova tower was the tallest observation tower in the Midwest.

He looked back at his grandson. "Well, Reginald, keys are for grownups. But I'll tell you what I'll do. If you want, you can put the quarters in the turnstile so we can get in the gate. Here, I brought a bunch of them. I'm appointing you as the official gatekeeper for everyone."

Money clinked into the steel box as the members of the extended LeMay family passed through the gate. The boy smiled with pride as he inserted the quarters one by one and when everyone had entered, he dropped the last quarter and pushed through the metal pipes that provided entrance to the monstrous structure.

"Look, Granddad, I have two quarters left."

"That's correct, Reginald. Because your Uncle Bob and Uncle Mike and their wives decided to enter two at a time instead of one at a time like the sign says." They kind of mauled each other as they quick-stepped through. Worse yet, they hadn't done so with their own wives, but each other's.

"You mean they cheated, Granddad?"

"Ah… Listen, Reginald, why don't you just keep those extra quarters in your fanny pack, if you promise to be very careful with them. We might need them for something else later.

***

Cole and Bubba Smith sat at the worn-out kitchen counter in their sagging mobile home. Cole looked through one of the cracked windows, past the dirt lawn strewn with rusting car parts and discarded beer cans, and down the weed-choked drive leading to the main road.

"Come on, Bubba. I wanna go looking!"

Bubba took a bite out of his sandwich and spoke while chewing. "Shut up, Cole. In case you haven't noticed, I'm having my lunch here, sitting in my favorite chair, and I'm savoring."

Cole scratched his head. "Whatta you mean, you're savoring? Looks to me like you're slobbering, and you could just as well be slobbering at the park while we're looking! So, let's go Bubba, you big slob."

Speaking though his food, Bubba chose the opportunity to educate his brother. "Savoring, Brother Cole, not slobbering. Savoring is what rich folks do when they're pigging-out real slow. And they say things to each other like 'ain't these sardines delightful' or 'why, I believe these are the best chicken parts I've ever had.' They call that highbrow conversation while they're savoring. You, Cole, ain't capable of any high class conversating, so I'm just savoring without conversation."

Cole shook his head in disgust. "Bubba, you're still a big slob. The only way you'll have a reason to do high class anything is if we cash in on that treasure. We got to get to looking and scout things out, if we're going to find it. What if someone else gets to it first? I think the lookout tower is the best place to start. Gives us a chance to see the area. Let's get out of this old trailer and go. Time's a-wasting."

Bubba leaned back, lifted his feet onto the worn, green-and-white Formica countertop, and tore off another enormous hunk of bread and meat before responding. "I wanna finish my lunch first. Ah... a double-decker baloney sandwich from the Meat Market. This ain't your usual snouts and ears and wet sawdust baloney. It's that real good Pella baloney, made out of genuine cow meat and such. And, I figured if I was eating high class baloney I might as well go all the way top-class, so I splurged on a bottle of that fancy-schmancy mustard."

He looked at the odd-shaped remnant of his sandwich and licked some spillover mustard from the fingers of his other hand.

"Although now that I'm eating it, I have to admit, I don't see what's the big deal with this fancy mustard. Next time I go grocery shopping, I'm gonna steal another squeezer of that yellow mustard. It tastes better, and you don't have to mess with it to get it out of the jar. Just shake it around a little, turn it up-side-down, and give it a good squeeze. Which is what I'm gonna do to you if you don't leave me alone 'til I finish my lunch."

"Bubba, you may be able to shake me around, but don't you forget, I'm the brains of this outfit. I'm telling you, if you eat all of that gigantic sandwich, you're gonna flounder, and we ain't gonna enjoy climbing that park-tower or doing our looking."

"Cole, you may think you're the brains of this outfit, but I'm gonna have to correct your language."

Cole hated when his brother tried to act all uppity. As kids, Bubba always tried to correct him when he thought Cole had made a mistake, whether in how to speak or how to prepare a meal. Lately, he'd been messing about with their supply of pot and meth.

Bubba chomped off another chunk and chewed with deliberation. Cole knew he was trying to goad him into losing his temper demanding to know what he'd said wrong.

Bubba gulped down half his can of Pabst, belched once, then said, "The word ain't 'flounder,' big brother, it's 'founder.' Like when Daddy's cows used to break into the wrong pasture. He didn't say they were gonna 'flounder.' He said they were gonna 'founder.'"

Cole waited, rolling his eyes. Bubba took forever getting to the point.

"Think of it this way, we're Iowans. Have we ever seen a cow 'founder?' The answer is 'Yes we have.' And I'll point out to you that we've done a lot of fishing, and we have never once caught a 'flounder.' And you know why? Cause there ain't no flounders in Iowa! Oh, we got catfish, bluegills, carp, bass, and the like, but we ain't got no stinking 'flounders.' So, the word to use in Iowa is 'founder' not 'flounder.'"

Bubba packed the final remains of the baloney sandwich into his mouth and took on a satisfied air as he stared at Cole.

Cole sighed and tried to be patient. He could never figure out why he always got roped into arguments with his dippy brother. They were talking about the difference of a single letter, for stinking's sake. "Bubba, there's a difference. It ain't depending on where you live. Being the brains of the two of us, I paid attention in school. I remember the English teacher told us that 'flounder' means struggling; 'founder' means failing. She used the example that I was gonna 'flounder' in school, but you were gonna 'founder.' Everyone laughed, except you, 'cause you weren't paying no attention. You were googly-eyeing Becky Robertson across the room again, who, by the way, was laughing too, 'cause she was paying attention to the teacher, not to you."

Bubba made an exaggerated swallow of his last bite of sandwich. "Cole, with all your yip-yapping, I'm finished savoring my sandwich. I'm ready to go."

"You sure you're full enough, Bubba?"

Bubba patted and then rubbed his swollen stomach. "Oh, yeah. I'm really full. That was one mighty big sandwich."

Cole seized the opportunity. "Bubba, you think you can climb all those stairs when we get there? There's a ton of them you know. World's longest continuous set of fiberglass stairs. I read that on the sign at the bottom."

"Well, Cole, I am pretty full, and I may have a little trouble getting up all those stairs... they're mighty high... but, for the treasure, I guarantee you that I'll make it to the top, even if I have to crawl."

Cole rolled his eyes. "So, you're going to make it, even if you have to crawl. Now that's the dedication I'm looking for."

"Yep, even if I have to struggle all-out, I guarantee I'm gonna make it."

"So, Bubba, you're gonna flounder up those stairs. 'Cause flounder means to struggle. Founder, of course, means to fail, and you're telling me that you're not gonna fail. So, you're gonna flounder, right here, in Iowa."

"Shut up Cole. Let's just get in the truck."

***

Each member of the LeMay family had ascended as far as his or her endurance lasted, viewed the landscape, and gathered again at the bottom. Blouses—previously unwrinkled—were now untucked. Shirt collars unbuttoned, ties askew. Expensive suit coats had been removed.

They started toward the exit gate when Reggie called out, "Look, Granddad, what's that? Something's coming toward us.

"What? Oh, crap!" Twenty feet to the north, a swarm of bees had migrated into the tower's enclosure, pausing fifty feet away at the exit turnstile, then continuing south, the LeMay party in their path.

"Quick, push on through hat turn-style we came in through, and let's get out of here," LeMay said.

"Granddad, I'm pushing, but it won't budge. I'm scared. Momma says I'm 'lergic. If they sting me, I might die!" Reggie flailed away as the first of the bees buzzed nearby.

"Don't swat at them, Reginald. Don't make them mad. We brought your EpiPen, but it's in the glove box. Push harder, Reginald. Here, let me try."

"See, it won't move, Granddad. Ouch, ouch, ouch! One just stung me. Granddad! Granddad! Am I going to die?" The little boy jumped up and down.

Just then, a rusty, battered, red and white Ford truck careened around the blacktop heading straight toward the entrance gate.

"Stand back, Reginald!" LeMay yelled. "Stand back everyone! That truck's coming right toward us."

The truck smashed into the fence, tore a hole in the wire, and came to a rocking stop. Two men all but fell out of the truck. Immediately, the bees swarmed. The men screamed, waving and slapping at the bees. LeMay sidestepped the new victims and rushed toward the Mercedes to retrieve the EpiPen.

"Hit 'em, Bubba. Hit every last one of 'em."

"I'm hitting them, Cole, but there's gazillions of them!"

"They're all over me, Bubba. Stinking bees."

Most of the swarm had attacked the two men, giving the rest of the LeMay family room to reach the safety of the Mercedes. LeMay himself retrieved the EpiPen from the glove compartment and punctured his grandson's jeans and thigh.

In another minute, the swarm had moved off. LeMay, the only one of his family still outside the car, tried to regain his composure, still out of breath.

"You boys all right?" he called. "I don't know how you did it, but you managed to attract the bees away from us. One of them stung my grandson and if I hadn't been able to get the EpiPen, well... I'm just glad no one was seriously hurt. Here... here... let me give you a reward." He pulled out his wallet and waved a hundred-dollar bill toward the brothers. "Here's a hundred dollars."

"Well, Cole, what do you think about that?" exclaimed the heavier of the two men. "He's giving us a hun'erd dollars. It's our lucky day!"

The other man looked at the money, then at LeMay. "Bubba, I'll tell you what I think. I think we just saved this guy's grandkid, so they can all drive outta here in those fancy SUV's they came in, and he thinks his grandkid's life is worth only one hundred dollars."

LeMay looked toward the car, then back at the men. "Okay, you two boys were really brave. I'll make it five hundred dollars. That sound fair?" He withdrew four more bills from his wallet.

Cole looked at the bills, then at his brother. He reached and grabbed the cash. "Yeah. I think that's about right."

"Thank you, men." LeMay said. "But I'm curious. What are you going to do with all that money?"

"Yeah, Cole, what shall we do with it?"

Cole looked at the cash in his fist and then at the red and white Ford. "Well, I'll tell you all. The first thing is get the steering on that old truck fixed. I knew it was bad, but as we rounded the curve here, it completely gave out. Otherwise, I could have avoided smashing into that fence in the first place."

Chapter 9

The first exhausting day had ended. Instead of heading back to Ames, it appeared that Grace and her big husky, Chow, would be dealing with these latest delusions of Grandfather's wandering mind for a while longer. In the morning, she'd help him dismantle his teepee and return to Elk Rock Park. She thought for a few minutes about a plan to persuade him to return to Ames with her.

"We're here for the duration, Chow," Grace muttered. "We might as well make the best of a bad bargain. I know getting Grandfather away from all this Indian business won't be easy. Until I can convince him that his idea is pointless—wishful thinking, I suspect—I guess we'll hang around."

Even though this Digger person claimed that there might be some substance to Grandfather's ideas, Grace wanted to put all this behind her. While the sheriff had agreed to allow Grandfather one last night in the teepee, Grace wondered if that would only prolong the obsession with the map. She'd accepted his offer of his Airstream at Elk Rock. But then Grandfather got her to agree to at least hear him out about the quest that preoccupied him.

She felt restless in the trailer, used to her spacious apartment in Ames, but relieved it had enough room that she and Chow didn't feel too confined and a nearby dog park provided a way to exercise for them both.

Grandfather had allowed his trailer to become cluttered, just as he had allowed the store to become a mess after Grandmother died. Books, papers, artifacts, knick-knacks, figurines, and arrow heads cluttered tables, counters and shelves. Tufts of feathers that crumpled to dust at the merest touch stuck out between statuettes. A dirty cracked leather shift, maybe worn long ago by Grandmother, hung on a hook on the bathroom door. While the bathroom itself and the kitchen were relatively clean, dust coated every other surface. Chow had sneezed several times after entering and snorted in discomfort. He circled, stepped on a portion of loosened carpeting near the couch, eventually finding a place to rest. Sunflower shells littered most of the floors.

She had changed the linen on the bed and now flicked off the light to try to sleep. Not only did the situation with Grandfather bother her but for a reason she couldn't understand, Justin Clay kept intruding into her thoughts. She hadn't recognized him at first when they met at the cemetery, but after a minute or two she remembered. He was the twerp who had tried to pick her up with those corny lines that one day on the Campanile. The one who kept bothering her until she called campus security.

How did he come to be in Knoxville and know Grandfather?

After the last time she'd seen him, she'd soon forgotten him. She hadn't cared. His nerve at coming onto her so persistently turned her off.

Yet, she recalled, a small part of her had felt a momentary attraction. She considered that it was normal, the desire to be desired. Okay, not full-blown desire, but.... Maybe if he had waited a week or two and apologized, tried again with a more casual approach....

Five years didn't seem a long time but maybe long enough? People change. Had he recognized her? She didn't think so. If he did, at least he didn't come on to her this time. Of course, he had arrived with another woman, that Kathryn VanSteele. Hadn't *she* been a treat with her smarmy attitude gushing about a casino? His girlfriend? If so, what did that say about Digger? Was that his nickname? He hadn't looked too pleased with Kathryn's obvious false demeanor, greeting Grandfather like he might be an exhibit for the new gaming establishment. The more Grace recalled the scene, the more she realized how much Digger had ignored Kathryn but showed a genuine interest in Grandfather and his map. No, he hadn't supported the casino idea.

Five years... Justin hadn't been some muscle-bound jock during their brief encounters at the university. Lean, but fit, apparently, he had maintained that physique, maybe filled out in the arms and legs a bit. And that mop of light red hair. Her face grew warm as that small part of her momentary attraction flared again.

Maybe...grew brighter... for an instant?

Unable to sleep, she beat the pillows into submission, tossed back the covers, and decided on another shower to relax. Afterward, eyelids heavy, she stumbled back to bed, observing that Chow slept without a care. She listened to a soft rain on the window. Concentrating on the white noise effect, she drifted off.

***

Chow's deep barks startled her awake. The gentle rain had become a driving torrent, a barrage of machine gun bullets on the trailer roof. Lightning flashed nearby and a horrendous clap of thunder followed. Chow barked again.

"Hush, dog," Grace whispered. "It's just a storm." She beckoned Chow to join her in the over-soft bed. They tumbled together into the sag in the middle. Chow only whimpered, eyes wide.

Fully awake, Grace looked around as another lightning flash lit up the interior of the trailer through the drapes. "Don't worry, Chow, I think the storm is moving on. I wonder how close it is to Grandfather's teepee. I hope he's doing okay."

Grace stretched out on her right side with her back to the dog. Its low snuffle comforted her as the lightning became less brilliant and the space between flash and thunderclap grew longer. She recalled a time when she was only five years old, and a storm had frightened her. Her grandmother told a story that relieved her fears.

"Thunder was the grandfather of our people and the Moon our grandmother. Long ago, when our people forgot Grandfather Thunder, they remembered and honored our grandmother Moon. Grandfather Thunder became bitter and angry because he felt neglected. He shot lightning arrows down at the Earth, killing people, burning houses, and shattering trees. Our people became most fearful at the sight of dark clouds. Then Nanapush, the trickster spirit, took pity on our people. He told us, 'You have hurt Grandfather Thunder's feelings because you do not honor and respect him. Grandfathers need to be remembered and honored too, for they also, like grandmothers, have shared in the gift of life and in helping their grandchildren into the future.'"

Grace rolled over and sat up. Grandfather Thunder. She'd not thought of those stories in many years. Grandfather Thunder was in charge of the rains that watered the earth and made things grow. He demanded our respect.

She thought of her own grandfather. Didn't he deserve the same respect? "I'll make an effort to listen to him when I see him tomorrow," she mumbled to Chow.

The rain maintained a steady rhythm and lulled her back to sleep.

Flash!

Suddenly, the room lit up, bright as the sun. Before the flash could fade—*Crash*—a cannon-like boom shook the entire trailer, rattling the windows.

Grace jerked from sound sleep to sitting up-right, bed covers flung into the air. "Chow, what's that?"

Chow's growls and gruff barks drowned her out.

Another flash—this one not as jolting—a peel of thunder and Grace recognized the sound of rain pelting the metal roof like an avalanche of BB's.

"Chow, shut up! It's just the storm."

Chow growled once but remained in a protective stance at her feet.

She laid a hand on his head. "It was lightning, Chow," she explained in a soothing voice. Reaching for the lamp on the old, wooden table next to the bed, she turned the switch. Nothing. She turned it again. Still nothing. Once more. Nothing.

In the intermittent lighting of the thunderstorm, she stood, got her bearings, and took three steps to the wall switch. Nothing. She flicked it off and on several times. Still nothing.

"Electricity's out," she said, as if the husky could understand. He cocked his head and looked at her. The calm tone in her voice put him more at ease.

Flash! Crash!

"Wow, another close one, Chow."

The husky whimpered and barked three times.

"Hush, Chow." Chow padded to her side, at the ready if needed.

The pounding on the roof abated. Grace recalled that pop-up thunderstorms had been forecast in the ten o'clock news. She worried again about Grandfather. How could he sleep in that teepee? The cone-shaped structure might have been waterproof but what about the ground on which Grandfather slept? Looking out the window, Grace saw only darkness.

Lightning flashed. In the second of brightness, something moved between two of the huge oak trees not far from the trailer. Another flare of lightning danced among the clouds. Another flitting movement near the trees. Not a dog or a deer, but.... Fear overwhelmed her. A person.

"Someone's out there," she told Chow.

A third blaze of lightning showed the figure... no, *two* people. They moved to hide behind another tree.

"Cell phone!" She had connected her cell phone to its charger and left it on the table below the window. She stepped back into the bedroom and felt for the phone, while her eyes stayed on the window.

The doorknob rattled, and the door vibrated as someone tried to pull it open.

"Oh, my God," she whispered. Chow growled low and stood between her and the door. Grace looked around for something heavy, something long, something she could defend herself with.

Wham! Something smashed against the door.

"Chow!"

The husky bristled, emitting a deep, throaty *woof.* Grace didn't attempt to quiet him this time. She located the cell phone on the edge of the table, snatched it up, and activated the screen.

Then she saw the five vertical bars indicating a level of connection to the phone lines. They were all dark. No service.

Another slam at the door. The Airstream's construction held, but it wouldn't last. Chow now alternated between growls and barks. A mental image of a hatchet flashed into Grace's mind. A hatchet tearing through the door. It came again. Whack after whack. Chow was big and powerful. He would defend them, but what chance would he stand against a weapon?

She looked around for another escape. Through a window? Did she have time?

Another big bang on the door. Grace screamed.

Over the rumbling thunder, she heard a resounding screech. An inhuman, air horn-like squawk, loud and grating. It blared again followed by an all too human scream. Yells and commotion. A scuffle? Something thudded against the trailer. Chow barked again.

Then silence. No more sounds came from the front door. Neither Grace nor Chow moved.

Lightning re-ignited the sky. Through the window, Grace saw two men running back into the woods. One slipped, fell, scrambled to his feet, and dashed off. Each man covered his head with his arms, thrusting fists up in an awkward punching pantomime.

Another squawk and during the intermittent flashes of lightning, she saw a stop-motion image of what looked like broad wings flitting around the men. First on one side, then the other. Above, then behind them. The men slapped and punched but were always two moves behind. Both men and their tormentor disappeared into the trees.

Grace's face streaked with tears, her breath ragged. Chow leaned against her for comfort. She sat on the bed and hugged the dog, willing her tremors to subside. She didn't understand what had just happened. Who were those men? What did they want.?

And what attacked them? Drove them away?

She looked Chow in the eyes. "I don't know what that was, but it just saved our lives." Her voice dropped to almost a whisper. "It looked like some sort of bird, like a furious, half-crazed eagle, or a hawk."

Chapter 10

A covering of deer hide over a thick layer of straw protected Jacob Wildcrow from the rain that seeped under his teepee. Warmed by his blankets, he slept, but not without dreams. Another vision played out, again at the Peace Tree, again through the eyes of the red-tailed hawk perched upon one of the sycamore's branches. He knew mere days had passed since the gathering of the various tribal representatives.

***

The same group of men formed a half circle around the fire. At the head of a circle, stood Chief Saunuk and a taller, younger man, Running Eagle.

After witnessing twenty annual seasons pass, Running Eagle stood six feet tall, with the handsome features of his father, a skilled hunter, and bearing a buffalo shaped birthmark on his neck. A similar mark adorned the neck of his mother. Because of this distinction from the Spirit gods, both mother and son had been given positions of honor. No one knew what higher purpose the gods had planned but that day at the Peace Tree, all was revealed.

With skin three shades shy of the nearby red bluff, lean and muscular appendages, Running Eagle stood in profile to the eastern horizon. Women, silent in their movements, tied ceremonial beads to his shoulder length brown hair with rawhide babiche. Chief Saunuk, with two fingers, painted red patterns on Running Eagle's bare chest, neck, and arms. Afterward, he presented Running Eagle with the wrapped and bound bundle to be hidden away to await an unknown descendant.

"Let nothing deter you." Chief Saunuk drew a single line of paint along the other's jawline. "Be not mindful of storms, the creatures of the land, or personal injury."

"Only death," Running Eagle said. "And even the great black spirit shall understand struggle before success."

Saunuk met the stare of the young man. "When you return, our people will have scattered. Some may remain with the hope of continuing our traditions. I fear, though, the pale skins will soon outnumber the buffalo and our future will be washed away as the flood waters wash away the earth. Though our numbers may dwindle like melting snowflakes, part of us will always remain. Like the ancient ones who built burial and ceremonial mounds throughout the land, we have created this bundle by which future generations may remember us."

"I shall protect this to my last breath," Running Eagle vowed.

Chief Saunuk then presented a beaded necklace and placed it around the young brave's neck. "Our story began many moons ago, but one season, a chief decided his people needed an item to pass down to descendants so they could remember their history. He fashioned a necklace with one bead. As each chief succeeded him, another bead was added. Some chiefs proved themselves deserving of the position, others not. However, in his own way, each has kept sacred our people's traditions."

Saunuk's face softened. He grasped the other's shoulders with both hands. "You have expressed interest in my granddaughter."

Running Eagle stood straighter, muscles tense. "Only if I am deemed worthy."

Saunuk stared deep into the other's eyes. A slight smile formed. "I believe you are," he said. "Complete this journey, return, and we shall see if she is of the same mind." He leaned forward, and his voice dropped to a whisper. "I may be chief, but a mate provides guidance and wisdom beyond even my capabilities. Mine has been exceptional in these regards. I foresee a day when you shall sit in my place with your mate beside you to give more than children and comfort in your later seasons."

He released the brave's shoulders. "Let us sit. I shall explain how you will leave markers along your path for those who follow in a season yet to arrive. You shall keep watch for the hunter hawk, as his shadow will guide you."

The old chief's expression hardened and a look of... regret? Hope? Resignation?... gleamed in his black eyes. With a grip on Running Eagle's shoulder, he nodded once.

Thus, began Running Eagle's quest.

***

A streak of lightning and a kettle drum roll of thunder penetrated Wildcrow's dream. The gathering he'd seen in his visions disappeared to be replaced by one lone man. Wildcrow recognized himself sitting cross-legged under the Peace Tree. For an unknown reason, the sycamore wasn't where it was located now, nearly covered with brown lake water. He and the tree were on high ground—and he had a sense of floating above that ground—the dark branches reaching tall and strong toward a cerulean Iowa sky. Wildcrow hummed the chants his grandfather had taught him, and he felt almost one with the tree, the sighing wind, and yet feeling the damp earth beneath. With eyes half opened, he caught sight of something drifting still higher in the air over him. The hawk, spiraling down in ever smaller concentric circles until it hovered like a hummingbird in front of him. It was so close he could feel the soft rush of air from its wings, bringing him an even deeper sense of connection with the world around him and the assurance that he, too, would fulfill his quest.

Chapter 11

Digger shifted position in one of the wrought iron chairs that surrounded the small tables outside the Swamp Fox, satisfied with how the building shielded him from the crisp late night westerly breeze. Under the faint glow of a light fixture mounted to the outside brick, he steadied the business end of his ten-dollar Cu-Avana cigar, palmed his Blaze lighter, and flicked to life a low-roaring, dark blue and red flame. He thought about the dickering exchange over the lighter he had with Roma, the Jamaican who owned Sam's Haberdashery in Oskaloosa. As he puffed in the fragrant smoke and watched the cigar's cherry end grow brighter, he couldn't help but smile. The mini blowtorch cost him a pretty penny. It was worth every bit of that penny—but at half the retail price.

Ominous clouds had moved in during the last half hour. Lightning chased itself across the sky. Portentous thunder rumbled in the distance, but the storm remained to the north and west.

His thoughts drifted to his short talk with Wildcrow's granddaughter, Grace, at the cemetery earlier that afternoon. He doubted that she remembered they had met before. He pictured the glint in her eyes as she spoke about her dog, calling the husky 'best friend.' It was that same glint he'd seen, that same compassion he'd felt, those many years before, qualities which had attracted him to her. Digger didn't believe in love at first sight, well... not before that day, anyway. But there had been that certain something, right?

He closed his eyes and drew in deeply, feeling the warm smoke swirl in his mouth, tasting that peculiar tint of sweet pumpernickel so characteristic of a Cu-Avana. How lovely, he thought. "How lovely, indeed," he said aloud.

Grace was lovely, too. Digger wished she'd have at least gone out on one date with him. On reflection, he had to admit he'd come on a bit strong. Two strangers, and instead of a proper greeting, he threw out an immature line about kissing in the moonlight. The past didn't matter, though. She had reentered his life. Despite the paper grading he knew he had to complete before the fall break, despite the problems brewing at City Hall, and despite the waning feelings he had for Kathryn, he found his thoughts returning to Grace throughout the afternoon and evening, not wanting to take the long drive back to his house. She was damn hard to get out of his mind, and he felt loath to try.

What of Kathryn?

He blew the warm smoke into the air, watched it blow away east over Second Street.

Warm cigar smoke, a cool breeze, but the word regarding his feelings toward Kathryn was 'tepid.' He wondered if he'd be able to finally get up the nerve to break it off with her. It was the right thing to do. He hadn't felt the thrill of the relationship in the last few weeks. No, more like months. Still, he'd vacillated. A bird in the hand and all that? Still, it wasn't right to keep stringing her along.

Digger thought about being alone. Alone like he'd been most of his life. Even growing up, his father slaving long hours and mandatory overtime at 3M, his mother long dead by the time he reached first grade. A string of babysitters, a nanny, daycares, and preschools. A lot of people, but always alone. Not for the first time, Digger wished he'd grown up with a brother or sister.

Kathryn, at least, could be counted on as someone to take out, have dinner at The Peppertree in Oskaloosa or Kaldera's in Pella, someone who led the way on shopping forays at Jordan Creek Mall in Des Moines. He had to admit she was nice to cuddle up with while watching a movie on cold winter evenings. Not to mention her wild abandon between the sheets.

He'd been with her for four years. They should have been talking marriage, buying a house together, but no. They'd just kept dating and sleeping together.

Maybe the relationship, in its monotony, had stagnated. With nothing new to spur him on, he'd become complacent. The emotions and passion, for him, had faded.

No sooner did he think these thoughts than he saw Grace's body appear in his mind's eye. He tapped his cigar with his index finger, letting the growing ash fly free. He imagined what her tiny waist would feel like in his hands, what her arms around him might conjure within him. Just his imagination made him feel needful, left him at once satisfied and yet longing.

"Excuse me, sir, last call."

He flinched when the waitress spoke. She approached his table holding a round plastic serving tray with two empty glasses. She had a pretty smile, but her tired eyes wanted the night to end.

"Ah, sure. A beer would be good. No, let's make it a glass of wine."

"What kind?" she asked.

"I don't know. Anything red from Nearwood Winery? I like to buy local if I can."

"We have Storybook," she suggested.

"Excellent." He approved of the choice. The name of the wine fit the current situation. The beginning, he hoped, of a new story for him.

He watched the girl skip away and up the stairs into the brick building. Red wine was a good choice, he thought. Nothing like red wine and cigars. Grace, he thought, it would sure be nice if she were here.

She and Wildcrow each held something to pique his interest. Grace excited him, and the idea of a map and treasure hunt intrigued him. What type of treasure? If related to Wildcrow's ancestry, it wouldn't be precious jewels or gold coins. However, it might be something that would better assist in the town's misfortunes than a blasted casino. He sat back, puffed on the cigar, and marveled at how his life had changed in so short a time. How figurative windows had opened up onto a lush and vibrant world where as little as two weeks before he had only bare unpainted walls and stale air to breathe.

He crossed his legs and contemplated an overview of the past. He'd always been practical to a fault but had to be just to survive his growing up. Since becoming a teacher at the high school, most people thought of him as a stereotypical professorial type. At times—usually when exploring the Indian mounds or other historical sites—he thought of himself as this type of man, too. But Grace....Grace's showing up in his life made him feel different, feel... what?

He inhaled another draft of Pumpernickel, and a frisson of adventure sizzled through him. Errol Flynn, swashbuckling actor of silent films, swinging from the rigging of tall ships, rescuing the distressed damsels and sailing away with... the treasure.

The surge of fresh energy of an adventure and the elation of a possible new romance both surprised and amused Digger. The storm had moved closer to town but at the moment, all it displayed was a sound and light show. He looked at the wine the waitress had placed on his table and thought he should have ordered the beer. That way, he could chug it like those pirates did with their ale in those movies. Oh well, he could fantasize another night. It was nice to relax with a glass of wine. However, as he tipped up the glass and the rich red smoothness entered his mouth, he heard the voice of Errol Flynn in his own ears. No man of Flynn's character would ever be caught dead with the likes of a washed-up has-been realtor like Kathryn.

"It's over," he said to the night and puffed again on the cigar.

Chapter 12
Friday

"Hello, Mrs. Lane, thank you for getting back to me so soon." Grace listened to the voice on her cell phone. "Your retirement center does have an opening for my grandfather? Great. I can't come by this afternoon. I'm out of town for a day or two." Grace dug in her purse to find her credit card. "I realize my grandfather and I will need to come in for an interview, but if I give you my credit card number will that hold a space until we can arrive to fill out the paperwork? Would that be all right? Thank you." She gave the required information from the card to the woman from the retirement home, replaced her card, and said good-bye.

After the two men had been driven off by a mysterious hawk-like creature, and after she felt it was safe again, Grace packed her suitcase and Chow into the Ford and sped away from the trailer. The whole experience had seemed surreal. She would find a motel room. While Knoxville was a straight shot down Highway 14, she thought Bos Landen near Pella would be safer, maybe more secure. Thank goodness the Holiday Inn allowed pets for an extra fee. In her room, she settled in and with a bit of effort and Chow's bulky warmth beside her, she managed to sleep.

In the morning she remembered she'd forgotten to phone the police the previous night when she reached an area of better reception. Should she phone now? The men wouldn't return, would they? IN any event, she and Chow were safe now.

She ate breakfast in the hotel's restaurant and snuck some bacon strips and a couple sausage patties back to the room for Chow. The dog snarfed them up in three seconds. The meager offering wouldn't be enough, but maybe it would satisfy him until she managed to buy some actual dog food. In her haste to drive to Bos Landon, she'd left his food at the trailer.

She had waited until eight o'clock before calling the Good Faith home in Ames. The facility owned several cats she'd treated. The cats had the run of the place, wandering from room to room offering the residents affection and companionship or else resting in the recreation room waiting for people to come to them. In time, she'd become friends with many of the staff and was able to better see how the facility operated. Calling that center to see if they had any vacancies, was the logical choice.

Now comes the difficult part, Grace thought. She knew Grandfather would be reluctant to move to the senior living home in Ames, but it was in his best interests. It wouldn't be an easy sell, but the craziness of the previous day had convinced her the sooner she managed to get him out of Knoxville, the better. Grace grabbed her jacket and keys, loaded Chow into her car, and headed to Elk Rock to Grandfather's trailer. She'd retrieve Chow's food, and she wanted to do some cleaning up before she helped him with his teepee.

On the drive across the dam, she once again talked to Chow as if the dog understood her words. "Chow, look at the beautiful pelicans. There must be hundreds of them."

In groups of about twenty, the birds swooped below the dam near the water, then back up to be replaced by the next group. Above, the main flock glided in a holding pattern, circling. The lake was a precious spot during their migration.

The drive across the Red Rock dam always took her breath away. The lake's and the dam's primary function was flood control, but recreation came a close second. Already that morning, a few vessels were skimming the water. Mostly bass fishers and other flat bottom jon-boats, but she saw a catamaran and two sailboats. Fishing season was winding up, but the weather stayed warm enough for people to enjoy the lake.

She wondered if many drivers were annoyed at the fact the speed limit while crossing the dam dropped down to forty-five. Had the Corps of Engineers deemed the lower limit for safety, or had they been clever to allow the people to enjoy the scenery? To her left, she saw where the Des Moines River flowed from the spillway and the campsites at Howell Station. Both vistas could make a person long to stop and visit for an hour, a day, or longer.

"Oh, shoot," she said and took her foot off the accelerator.

She was going in the wrong direction to get to Grandfather's trailer. Elk Rock lay on the south side of the lake, but she needed to reverse her course from the previous night, taking the north shore perimeter road. Continuing across the dam meant a longer drive through Knoxville or winding through back roads to get around the lake's contours. Muttering, she turned onto a descending road that led to another camping and fishing area at the base of the dam, waited for northbound traffic to pass, then reversed onto the highway.

At least she'd enjoy the view from the dam once again.

Chapter 13

Friday morning started clear and cool. Jacob Wildcrow woke before the sun peeked above the horizon. After quiet meditation and with a disheartened resignation, he dismantled and bundled up his teepee along with the folded blankets. While he waited for his granddaughter to arrive, anticipation replaced resignation. From the previous night's vision, he knew his assignment. His mission. His... destiny.

Just when the sun began its vain effort to warm the bluffs around the lake, he heard a vehicle approach. Instead of Grace's Escape, a Ford Explorer kicked up dust along the cemetery road. The SUV stopped twenty feet from Wildcrow, and a frowning Sheriff Lockridge stepped out.

"Thought your granddaughter was going to be here this morning to help."

"Maybe still at my trailer," Wildcrow said.

Lockridge sighed and shook his head in exasperation. He unlocked and opened the rear of the Explorer and helped Wildcrow load up his teepee and other belongings. They didn't share much conversation on the drive to Elk Rock. A few mutterings about the night's storm but the only significant talk came when Lockridge commented, "You know, with your antics yesterday at the Hometown Meat Market, you have some people agitated over a supposed treasure map you may or may not have."

Wildcrow displayed no reaction but internally, he was concerned. Many people knew he owned a trailer at Elk Rock. If people visited, wanting more information or a look at the map, they could ruin his plans for the day. There were too many troublemakers already; he didn't need more. He regretted his spouting off the previous day at lunch, but it had come at a time when he himself was riled up.

Grace's Escape wasn't at Wildcrow's trailer when Lockridge braked and shut off the engine. They hadn't passed her on the way. Wildcrow figured she and the dog must have gone into town for an early breakfast and would meet him at the cemetery afterward. When she didn't find him out there, she'd come back to the trailer.

Lockridge wiped perspiration from his forehead. "Listen, Jacob. Why don't you just lay low for a while? Take it easy. Your granddaughter's here, you two enjoy the weekend together. And for heaven's sake, put that teepee in storage and stop causing a ruckus all over my county." He shook his head again and the gruffness left his voice. "Look, I'll help you get all this stuff packed away. Will that be all right?"

Wildcrow nodded once.

"Okay, then," Lockridge said. "How you got out there in the first place is beyond me."

Lockridge helped store the teepee in the shed. Before he drove away, he said, "Take care of yourself. I'll be back to check on you later."

Wildcrow studied the dents in the trailer's door, wondering what had happened. Inside he found the bed unfolded but not made up. Grace's suitcase was missing. Had she gone back to Ames? She had promised to help him that morning and then listen to him explain the map and what his ancestors had done centuries before. He had hoped to persuade her to join him on his journey.

During his morning meditation, he felt the promise of warm weather. It would aid his plan to start tracking the first of the markers on the map. Grace would be angry if she knew he was going out alone, but he didn't want to waste the day waiting for her. He hadn't promised her that he would stay put but since his run-in with the local police, she had made it clear to him that he was not to do much of anything without her being told of it. It was only a matter of scouting around a little, wasn't it? He knew these woods better than any of the local rangers.

Still, he needed to be careful. If news of his map had spread much further than Lockridge had indicated, he could have people with shovels digging up the park. He knew rumors grew with each retelling. How far afield would the greed extend? The markers had been placed over a large area around the lake, but if people started searching willy-nilly, they might delay his travels.

Wildcrow stepped toward the back of the trailer, remembering at the last second to avoid the small section of carpet that had unglued near the couch. In the bathroom, he washed his face and looked in the mirror. Bags had grown under dark eyes. Over the years, his cheeks had withdrawn, and his lips tightened. The skin had browned to a fine leather, but age spots, instead of deteriorating his countenance, had reinforced the regality within. Time and nature had weathered his body, but not his mind, his spirit, or his determination.

After Wildcrow's wife died, he had been despondent. Despondency turned to outright depression. He found he had no ambition to continue their business in Harvey selling artifacts. When a job opened up to oversee Elk Rock, he took it because the travel trailer that came with the job promised better living conditions than lodging in the back of the run-down store with the drafts and the leaky roof. The change of scenery seemed to break the hold that grief had on him. He locked up the shop in Harvey and just never went back. Never, that is, until a television documentary on the public network about Wounded Knee reminded him of something he remembered as a boy.

Back to Harvey he went and after tearing through shelves and boxes not touched for years, he found it.

The map.

His memory, though he knew it to be somewhat questionable these days, was clear on distant events. He recalled his father and uncle discussing the map but refusing to embark on the quest the map seemed to require. Both were heavily involved in getting the nascent Meskwaki Casino off the ground and just too busy with politics.

Jacob Wildcrow was not busy, though. Not anymore. When the dreams and visions started, Jacob knew he was the one.

He now retrieved the map from his pack and laid it on the table that he folded down from the trailer wall. The map was supple despite its age, made from auburn colored deer hide with crimson and ocher markings. He had been puzzled by certain symbols on the upper right area that did not seem to correspond to any recognizable landmarks. He knew the map was at least three hundred years old and the landscape would have altered substantially since that time. Of course, when the area was flooded in the 1960's during the building of Lake Red Rock, many landmarks had changed. Seven small towns had been abandoned and were now covered by water.

He studied the first symbol closer. It had to be the north outcropping of the painted rocks bluff. The particular curve of the land was still very unusual and high enough that it had not been covered by the reservoir. With that realization, other markings seen in this light had new meaning. In fact, he'd be able to check out one location now. When he returned, maybe Grace would be here.

***

"You comin' or not, meathead?" Cole shouted at the reposed lump of his brother.

The lump did not stir, so Cole lifted a foot and gave Bubba's hip a quick shove. "Come on, brother, treasure's waitin' for us."

"Huh?"

The lump turned under the threadbare blanket, his face looking like the doughboy on that cake box they never figured out how to bake.

"Bubba, you allergic to bees now? Look at you. Your face is all swollen. I can't even see your eyes! You okay, brother?"

"Huh? Yeah. Just itchy and the like, but I sure slept well."

"Well, take a Benadryl, and let's get going," Cole said.

"Naw, that medicine knocks me out. This will go away in a bit." Bubba slipped to the side of the bed, rubbed his buried eyes, opened his mouth, tilted his head, and managed to just get his peepers open. "Where we going?"

"Treasure hunting, of course. What's wrong with you? Maybe the bees caused some sort of brain enema."

Bubba turned his head to his brother. "Brain edema, Cole. I think you mean brain edema. That's what grams died of."

"Whatever. In your case, brain enema probably fits anyway."

Cole walked to the home-made kitchen table and pointed to a plastic bag. "Grab a couple doughnuts, Bubba, while I study the map to check where we need to start digging."

While Bubba stuffed his swollen face with doughnuts, one after another, Cole looked at his cellphone photo of Wildcrow's map they'd taken at the Meat Market. It was his turn to rub his eyes. The image looked blurred.

He stood and went to a double set of Rubbermaid drawers, their newest furniture acquisition from the local thrift shop. He pulled a drawer out, rummaged through it and shoved it back in, grumbling as he did.

In the fourth drawer, he retrieved a pair of bent wire rim eyeglasses. He'd worn them in school to read small print, but otherwise he didn't use them. He adjusted the frames, fit them over his eyes, and looked at the cellphone again. He reached behind him smacked his brother on the back. "Bubba!"

"Wha?" his brother said amid a shower of flying chewed dough. "Don' scare me li' tha! Wha?"

"When you took the picture of Wildcrow's map, did you hold the camera still?"

"You too' the pisher, brother."

"That's not possible, Bubba."

"Why not?"

"Because, dimwit, if I took the picture, it would be crystal clear. So, it stands to reason that you took the picture and when you did, you moved the phone and blurred the picture. Look!" He thrust the ghostly image of the map on the table at the Meat Market in front of Bubba's face."

"Yeth, and no." Bubba slurred.

"What do you mean, 'Yes and no?'"

"I mean yeth, it's blurred and no, I din' take it. You took it."

Cole walked away, shaking his head, adjusting the zoom on the image. After a minute, he turned back to his brother. "You know what this means?"

Bubba swallowed and swallowed until he managed to clear his mouth. Finally, he smiled, barely discernible on his swollen face. "We gotta go take the picture again?"

"No, you idiot. Wildcrow has the map. We got to go get it. I think he's still out yonder at Elk Rock Park."

"Okay, don't forget your phone," Bubba said.

"My what?"

"Your phone. And this time, hold it still, so it doesn't blur."

"Listen, Bubba. Listen carefully so you understand this simple fact. I don't think old Wildcrow is gonna be too keen on us taking a picture of it. So, we're going to have to get him to give it to us."

"You think he will?"

Cole rolled his eyes. "It's the two of us against an old man. I know he will."

* * *

After a quick meal of dried fruit and venison jerky, Wildcrow grabbed a supply of sunflower seeds, bundled the map under his deerskin jacket, and went out into the cool November day. The wind was light with a wisp of high clouds. It was perfect hunting weather. He headed toward what he thought might be the best route toward the curious marking on the map. He strode through heavy timber avoiding crisp leaves and sticks, making a silent path to the lake. The woods had a sharp smell of decaying foliage, and he heard the gentle rustling of deer deeper in the thicket. As he reached the south shore of the lake, he pulled out his map and scanned the shoreline. Even from this distance, his old eyes picked out the beak shaped outcropping across the lake on the north shore that corresponded to the map marking. As he turned the map in various directions, he realized that the bluff enabled an orientation for the remaining symbols. He felt a rising sense of excitement and stuffed the map back under his deerskin jacket.

Wildcrow hurried back to his Airstream, not caring now about treading through the woods with his usual caution. His mind raced thinking about the implications of where the next set of markers might lead. A fast-moving band of clouds obscured the sun. The wind cut sharper, and he blew into his cupped gnarled hands to warm them. When he reached the clearing, he heard the sound of a pickup truck in the distance. He went into the trailer, placed the map back into an old Cheerios cereal box as a hiding place and set it in a tiny, veneered cupboard.

From the bookshelf he had created from a couple of glass blocks and painted boards, he pulled a couple of thick, worn books. One was titled *History of Marion County 1850-1929*. The other was a topographical print collection of the Red Rock Dam area. He opened the second of these and scanned the fragile pages until he found a particular page that showed a closer view of the lake and its surroundings. Remembering the symbols, he ran a finger along an imaginary line from the beak outcropping on one of the northern bluffs gradually northeast. It passed through another historical landmark. He felt satisfied he was on the correct path to the Bundle.

Wildcrow laid the book down on the floor and leaned back on his threadbare easy chair. He thought about the Bundle, his life quest. It was so close, but sometimes he was afraid that he would not live to fulfill his mission. That would be a catastrophe, unacceptable, an insult both to his life and to his heritage.

Wildcrow looked at the only picture of his granddaughter he owned, set in a tarnished silver frame propped on the counter. In the photo, she stood with a group of half a dozen other young women all smiling for the camera. Her staff at the veterinary clinic had posed for a Christmas card. Her hair was short and curved around the front of her face. It would be so lovely, he thought, fixed in the Indian fashion and straight flowing behind her back in a dark braid. That was the way Evie, Wildcrow's wife, had worn hers, and he had loved running his fingers through the black silky locks. Had Grace ever thought about growing her hair out like that? He doubted it. She doesn't even know who she is, he thought. Wildcrow shook his head. By rejecting her heritage, she could not acknowledge the very core of her being. The old man had seen what had happened to other Native Americans who shunned their past. On a deep level they were aimless, uprooted, and unhappy. He didn't want that to happen to his granddaughter.

Maybe when she was still a child, he could have persuaded her to remember the old ways, but as a grown, independent woman, she made her own choices. He hoped one of those choices would involve his friend, Digger.

Wildcrow had known Digger for many years, ever since he came to Knoxville to teach history. He often visited Wildcrow's trailer or walked with him along the lake trails. They discussed arrowheads Digger had found or talked about the Indian tribes who used to inhabit Iowa. Digger had a firm footing in the present but respected the past.

What Wildcrow could not understand was Digger's attraction to Kathryn VanSteele. Sure, she was a beautiful woman but a Nukpana, a cold witch, on the inside. No love for anything or anyone except amassing what money and prestige she could in this little corner of the world.

Scuffling footsteps outside attracted Wildcrow's attention. He went to the dusty window, peered out into the gray day, but saw no one. Possibly a deer or ground squirrel on the loose gravel, Wildcrow thought. He threw some newspapers off the couch and stretched out. He'd just closed his eyes when a loud tapping on the metal frame of the camper door startled him. He rose again, stiff jointed, and frowned when, through the window, he saw Knoxville's most unwanted, Bubba and Cole Smith, out front. Why are those two damn fools coming around here, when I'm just getting settled for a nice nap? Wildcrow opened the trailer door and the two brothers rushed in, pushing him back against the far wall. They smelled of sweat and stale beer. Cole backhanded Wildcrow across his face.

"What are you doing?" Wildcrow staggered to the couch. "Leave me alone."

Bubba stepped to loom over him. "We want that treasure map, old man. We tried to get it last night but were chased away by some crazy bird. Now, be a nice old geezer and give it to us, and we'll leave without any problems."

"I don't know what you're talking about." Wildcrow rubbed his face. "I don't have any treasure map."

"We hear differently, Redman," said Cole. "We heard you at the Meat Market while you were yapping it up about your treasure hunt. We're going to find it first." Cole raised his hand to strike. "You don't deserve any loot. You ain't even from around here. You're a foreigner. Bubba and I now, we was born and raised here, native sons you know. We came here for that map and we're gonna leave with it, understand?"

Wildcrow nodded slowly but said nothing. Bubba and Cole stood before him, breathing fast, eyes darting around the room looking for anything that resembled a map.

"Take a look back there in the bedroom, Bubba."

Bubba loped through a short hall to the tiny room, and Wildcrow heard him pull off the sheets and overturn boxes. Cole, grinning now, sat down on the couch next to where Wildcrow was slumped. "It would make clean up a lot easier if you just gave it to us, you know."

Wildcrow eyed Cole but remained silent. There was a hunting knife around the trailer, but he didn't exactly know where it was located. Damn memory. Bubba, finished with trashing the bed and bathroom area, lumbered into the kitchenette. As he started pulling cans of beans down from the cabinet, Wildcrow felt an ache in his heart. If they found the map, he didn't think they were smart enough to interpret the symbols. They might even destroy it just for spite.

Bubba gave a short whoop when he emptied the Cheerios box onto the floor. "Were you gonna have cowhide for breakfast with your cereal, Mr. Pow-wow?"

Cole slapped Wildcrow on the shoulder, stood, and joined his brother. "Nice going, Bubba. This has got to be it," he said. "It looks really old, too. I'll bet it's even older than you, geezer."

Just then Wildcrow remembered. Quick as a cat, he reached underneath the couch and pulled out a sheathed knife. Pulling it free, he flashed it upward. The Smiths, both wide-eyed, stepped back with cries of protest.

"You give me the map." Wildcrow stepped forward, then felt his foot catch on the bubble of carpet. Unable to regain his balance, he fell forward. The brothers separated to avoid the flailing knife; backs pressed against the sides of the trailer. Wildcrow tried to raise an arm to shield his face, but his forehead cracked against the edge of the table. He collapsed to the ground.

Through his waning senses, he heard Bubba wail "Is he dead?"

Cole said, "You saw him, Bubba, he tried to kill me!"

"Yeah, but did we kill him? He's bleeding."

Wildcrow felt a hand on his neck. "He's still breathing," Cole said. "Let's get outta here."

"You think we should tell someone?" Bubba's voice wavered in fear. "Maybe we should make an ominous phone call."

"You mean anonymous," Cole said.

"No, I meant what I said. When we tell them about this, our voices are going to be, you know, dramatic. Ominous."

"We ain't callin' nobody," Cole griped. "If we do, they'll think we did this. No, we gotta go. He'll be all right."

"Yeah, we got what we came for," said Bubba.

Wildcrow heard them leave without closing the door. It banged against the trailer with each gust of wind. He tried to raise up to hands and knees but the woozy, swirling mental maelstrom overwhelmed him. He dropped to the floor, unconscious.

Chapter 14

Brandyn Antonaccio drove his rented Crown Victoria to the Knoxville town square and admired the majestic Romanesque style Marion County Courthouse. Its clock tower rose high above the three-storied limestone building. Iowa courthouses were a delight to study, if what one mostly viewed was city bricks and skyscrapers. This current assignment gave him a nice break from metropolitan bustle and noise, even if the final aim proved to be a very somber one.

He parked in front of the Swamp Fox. Best not to go to the courthouse yet, since he was still gathering information. He'd traced his quarry to this small Midwestern town, but who knew if the man hadn't already moved on? No use raising alarm if it wasn't necessary. The previous day he did some initial surveillance, talked to a few shop owners, but hadn't asked any questions to raise suspicions. While he knew the man he was after was dangerous, he didn't want to cause a panic. He'd adopted a style different from his coworkers. He didn't rush in and lock down an area. Instead, he took his time, familiarized himself with his surroundings, and learned about the residents. Through conversations, rather than intense interrogations, he discovered useful facts, and sometimes leads. Yes, his manner ran into difficulties in those big cities, but he gained more positive results than negative because even the largest were nothing but a bunch of small neighborhoods, some even as large as Knoxville.

He'd learned the local bars often offered up the most information. Bartenders and a few friendly patrons were wonderful sources to tap. He stepped into the building after climbing the six curved concrete steps. Right or left, up or down. Right, the stairs went upward to what looked like an apartment overlooking the street. To his left, the stairs descended, and he heard voices drifting up to him. On the wall were pictures of soldiers from World War II, Korea, Vietnam, and some that looked like those of recent battles in the Middle East and Afghanistan. Young men whose optimistic faces were so innocent, they should not have been subjected to the horrors of combat.

Memories of his own time in the service threatened to rise up and distract him. He forced them back into his mental cellar and locked the door. No need to relive what he'd never forget. After eight years of orders, guns, and killing, he wanted to bring the fight home, to right the wrongs in his own country. His first stop after Iraq was Quantico, Virginia, to enroll in the FBI Academy. Instructors soon found they had a unique specimen with skills and abilities different from the other agents-in-training. In time, he escalated from bank robberies and drug sting operations to more serious cases. Kidnappings and serial killers. The Bureau shifted cases to him that stymied other agents. He had an outstanding closure record, mostly by doing his own thing, much of the time working solo, with the guarantee of the government behind him.

Burnout came to every agent sooner or later, in one form or another. Too many years of chasing rapists, gangsters, and the most heinous pieces of human debris had driven many agents to suicide, either quick and easy with a bullet or slow and drawn out with alcohol. Ten years had been the limit for Antonaccio. With no family, save for distant cousins, no wife or children, he had retired to a split log home in North Carolina, with two dogs. Besides, he couldn't imagine any woman sticking around with someone who'd witnessed the horrors he'd endured.

To be honest he was only semi-retired. Every now and then the Bureau came a'calling, either his former supervisor or one of his lackeys. A 'special case' they said. A really *bad* guy, they said. Could you help us with this one, they asked, usually with an apologetic attitude. We know you said you were done, but....

He'd refused some cases but accepted others that piqued his interest if there were unusual aspects of the crimes. Something inside him had to feel challenged by the killer.

So, what was he doing in small-town Iowa? No major crimes here other than a few meth labs, some assaults when some guy knocked around his wife, or vandalism from stupid teenagers. Every now and then some child or young woman disappeared. Residents and the media kept the story hot for a couple weeks. Either the victim was found alive and reasonably well or the corpse was discovered in a ditch or bean field. Sometimes a perp was arrested but other times remained unknown. Too often, the case grew cold when no further leads were found, and the media moved onto more interesting stories. The victim stayed missing, with only the family suffering.

This time, Antonaccio wasn't after a killer who moved from state to state leaving bodies nailed to walls or a rapist with a fetish for ice picks. His quarry was a Chicago gangster. It might have seemed a normal everyday assignment, but this one rankled. This one hit a little too close to home. Or rather, work.

Peter White was an up-and-coming mobster out of the Windy City. Usurping his former boss, he seized control of his faction. Within a month he had instituted new rules, killed off internal rivals, and set goals for expansion and wealth. Unfortunately for him, his goals were a bit too lofty, and they conflicted with a couple of the other better-established organizations. He soon found himself literally under the gun and on the run. Most of his crew had been wiped out along with all but a small portion of the territory the gang claimed. The latest word had him hiding out, forming plans to reorganize, build up funds, personnel, and materiel to take his revenge.

The point at which the case became personal for Antonaccio came when White, hunted by the Bureau, escaped capture, but in doing so had fatally injured one of the agents. Crystal Harris had been Antonaccio's partner on many investigations back before he had moved onto special crimes. After Harris had been killed, Antonaccio requested inclusion into the hunt for White. To be more accurate, he had blackmailed his way in, saying he'd refuse any more cases if he wasn't allowed to go after White. His supervisor understood he'd go after White on his own if he wasn't made official.

Now, after four months of investigation, interrogation, and using his ability to read patterns, Antonaccio had traced White to Knoxville, Iowa. Through research and other contacts, he'd learned about the community and some of its more colorful residents. The sprint car track, the annual holiday festivities, and farmer's market. Red Rock Lake. The 3M plant. The former Veterans Administration Hospital. All these made the little town unique. One of the FBI investigators who grew up in Iowa told him about a sacred Indian tree in the area. The previous day he'd heard rumors about a treasure map. If Peter White were in the area, the chance to steal a quick fortune—if it existed—might entice him to stay.

At the bar's entrance, he had his first look at the Swamp Fox. His mind immediately noted patterns about what didn't fit or seemed to stand out against orderliness. The first anomaly was that the bar opened up early. While it didn't serve a full breakfast, Antonaccio smelled the tang of hot ham mixed with cheese and egg. He spied a microwave on the far side of the counter.

A single hanging lamp floated above each of ten round-top tables. Four wooden chairs were pulled up to each table. One chair at one of the tables was two inches shorter than the rest. Antonaccio momentarily focused on that chair until he realized the legs didn't have the rubber end caps the other chairs had. It looked as if someone had sawed each leg, maybe after one cracked or broke.

A television was mounted on each side wall. One broadcast The Price Is Right, while the other aired a morning talk show. Antonaccio deduced it was from the Des Moines Fox affiliate because the capital city skyline was displayed in the background, overlaid by a listing of weekend activities.

Two men sat at the table nearest the door. They wore identical dust-streaked blue work pants and shirts and identical drawn out, tired expressions. Neither looked up at Antonaccio when he stepped into the room. He couldn't imagine anyone drinking so early in the morning, but they must have worked a late shift. For them, it was the end of the day. Heads bowed over their half-filled mugs of beer, they looked as if they could be either praying or asleep.

The main bar stretched most of the length of the far wall. Antonaccio's mental ruler measured it at twelve and a half feet. A man who could have played football in college or wrestled in a heavier weight class stood behind the bar slicing lemons into wedges. He was bald, with a small gold hoop adorning one ear lobe, and the edge of a tattoo showing above the collar of his shirt, the color of a UPS truck. He acknowledged Antonaccio with a half nod, "Hi, what can I help you with?"

That morning Antonaccio chose black clothing, but normally every day he chose black. Most of his wardrobe in his home closet consisted of trousers, jacket, a turtleneck shirt, and Tony Lama boots, all in the same coal color. He knew his clothing choice set him apart from the general population, but sometimes that fact worked in his favor. People didn't know what to make of him and for some ironic reason, they weren't suspicious, just caught off guard. Instead of clamming up, they had an urge to talk.

Antonaccio adopted a friendly but not overly large smile and approached the bar. In his pocket, he kept a folded selection of bills. Without withdrawing the money to find the correct denomination—he knew how many of each there were and in what order—he took out a twenty and laid it on the bar. "Manhattan," he ordered. "Make it a double."

He didn't expect to drink it all, but, again, an unusual and large order sometimes encouraged bartenders to be more talkative.

"Haven't had an order for that in a while," the bartender said. "Especially in the morning." Finished with the last lemon, he placed the wedges in a glass jar, ran the knife under a stream of water from the sink, dried it with a towel, and set it on the counter. "Nope, don't get a call for that too often. Buchanan, Woodford or...."

"Crown," Antonaccio said.

"Good choice," the bartender said and reached for the squat blue and yellow labeled bottle. While he mixed the drink, he added, "New in town?"

"Been here a couple days."

The bartender nodded, placed the Manhattan in front of Antonaccio, and leaned closer over the bar. Not intimidating, just conspiratorially friendly. He raised his eyebrows in a silent question before he said, "Word is, there's an FBI agent around town. It has the sheriff all in a lather, 'cause he don't know who he is."

Antonaccio sipped his drink. "Want to see my identification?"

"Why? You ain't old enough to be drinking?"

Antonaccio smiled.

The bartender smiled. "Just kidding. I don't care what you are. By the way, most people call me Spike."

"Because of the railroad spike tattoo?"

"Nah, they called me that in the Army. See, after the initial head shave at basic training, for some reason my hair didn't grow back like it used to, all curly and such. Instead, it came out sticking straight out, you know, like spikes. So, the guys gave me that nickname."

"You used to have curly hair?"

"Yeah, kind of strange, big guy like me, right?" Spike lowered his voice. "I tell you, the chicks really went for it. I may have looked like a male Orphan Annie, but the girls loved it."

"Who knows women…"

"Right. Anyway, I didn't like the way it grew back out, so I just kept it shaved. Somehow, the nickname stuck around and followed me back to Knoxville."

"Grew up here?" Antonaccio asked.

"Born and bred."

Antonaccio paused, sipped his drink. Spike had measured out the ingredients in the right proportions. The perfect combination of whiskey, vermouth, and bitters made the cocktail sweet to the taste and easy to swallow. With a graceful hand movement and a short head turn directed at the two men at the far table, he laid another twenty on the counter. "Think our conversation could be kept on the QT?"

Spike uttered a single *ha* of a laugh. "The Handy boys? Don't worry about them."

"Don't you mean the Hardy boys?"

"Naw," Spike drawled. "Jeff and Tom Handy out south of town on Highway 5. Neighboring houses. Both work at Pella Windows. They're in here most every morning after their shift. They'll sit there until one of their wives calls to bring their butts home. They don't hear anything, they're half asleep as it is."

"How about you? I don't want to attract too much attention right off."

"With that outfit?" Spike said and laughed again. "Just kidding. I think you're too late, anyway. As I said, word's already spread."

Antonaccio edged the bill closer to Spike. "Well, any *more* attention."

Spiked shrugged and Antonaccio appreciated the fact the man didn't automatically snatch up the money.

"Anything of interest going on in town?" the agent asked.

"Not much happening," Spike said. "Living Windows celebration is coming up in a few weeks. Things get lively then. Once the sprint car races are over, it's a bit dead around here."

"Ah, the Knoxville Nationals."

"Right. Except for Tulip Time in Pella, it's the biggest event around the area."

"You go to the races?"

"I'd like to," Spike said. "I mean, it's sacrilege to stay home, but with thousands of people coming around, I stay pretty busy. All my part-time help want the days off, so I'm stuck here. That's all right. There's a local channel that broadcasts the races, so I have it on the televisions."

"Do you see a lot of new folks around once the races are over?" Antonaccio asked.

"Oh, sure. A lot of people take their vacations, stick around to do some fishing, go up to Des Moines."

"How often do you see people staying around longer than a couple weeks? New people moving to the area."

Spike shrugged. He wiped down the small cutting board he'd been using for the lemons and took a handful of limes from beneath the counter. Knife in hand he started slicing wedges. "Every now and then. Usually nearer September, you know, when the new school year begins. Course, we get a few drifters coming and going. Knoxville's not that large of a town, but if people stick around long enough, word gets passed."

"Anyone in particular stand out?"

Spike smiled. "Looking for someone, eh?"

Antonaccio shrugged, noting that Spike cut each lime into eight sections.

"Well, let me think," Spike said. "Guy named Kyle Brewer took a job at Woo Hardware after the races. Young gal... what's her name? Gia. Yeah, Gia Marie, moved here in October with her two-year old son. She works at the library. Oh, and the Handy boys got talkative one morning about a new guy over at the windows plant. They don't like him because he's always bragging about how he used to play for Ohio State. That kind of talk don't go well around here. You're either a Hawkeye or a Cyclone. If you wanna root for another team, then you keep it to yourself. Anyway, there are probably some other folks hired newly somewhere."

"Popular place."

"Well, we're close enough to Des Moines without having the big city headaches. A couple major industries what with the window plant and Hormel. Heck, we even got ourselves a winery. Nearwood Winery is a couple miles south of town, and they produce great stuff. I can't keep enough of their Raceway Red when Nationals come around."

"Appropriately named," Antonaccio said. "Who are the movers and shakers around town? Any local troublemakers?"

Spike finished with the limes, cleaned the knife and cutting board. "I'm not one to gossip, you understand, but there's a guy named Joe Dirkson. Makes a round of the bars. Gets into a scuffle now and then when he tries to pick up some gal who's already taken, or if he gets too friendly with the waitresses. Most of the time he's busted for disturbing the peace. He'll stand out on his front porch at one in the morning yelling about how he hates the world and his job. However, no one really knows what he does."

"Anyone else?"

"I guess two that come to mind are Bubba and Cole Smith. Couple brothers who live a few miles south of town. They're not major criminals, more nuisances than anything. Not real bright, but they manage to get into trouble pretty easily. Into pot, maybe a bit of meth, yet the law can't seem to get 'em except for a couple speeding tickets or, like Joe, a couple of fights every now and then."

"How about on the other side? The people who get things moving?"

"Well, there's the mayor, of course. Decent guy. Doesn't get too radical on anything. Stays middle of the road."

Antonaccio sipped his drink.

"Old guy named Lindville Wagner. He's an interesting character. His family saw the end of the coal mining around the area and invested what savings they could in oil and other commodities which made them a pretty good fortune. Lindville continued the practice and gave back to the community. A lot of donations to building funds, helping the school with new band uniforms and equipment for the sports teams. That kind of thing. Stays in the background a lot, doesn't invite too much publicity."

Antonaccio remained silent. Sometimes silence helped people to reveal more.

"Oh, then there's Kathryn VanSteele. Now, there's a woman for you. Go getter, wants everything done now, can't wait to bring something new to town. If you were around yesterday, the big talk was the casino they want to build out near Red Rock."

"I did hear about that."

"Yeah, folks themselves might be doing okay, but the town itself... well, I don't know all the details, but there are some financial problems. A lot of people think a casino is what we need. Kathryn's been leading the pack on the issue for a long time."

"Was that the discussion people were having around the Municipal Center earlier this morning?"

Spike shook his head in mild disgust. "I caught some of that on my way into the bar. It's an example of the fuss that the Smith brothers can stir up. They started a rumor that there's a Native American treasure buried somewhere around the lake. I don't know why anyone would take them seriously, but some people, you know, once they get a notion in their head, well, common sense takes a hike."

"Treasure? As in gold? I doubt if the Native Americans buried much gold anywhere in these parts," Antonaccio said, "Maybe money but not from Indians. Jesse James robbed banks around here back in his day. There's even some speculation that he hid one of his sacks of loot in Marion County."

"Could be. I haven't heard any talk about that."

"Tell me more about the treasure," Antonaccio said.

"Jacob Wildcrow. He's another local character. Never lost his Indian heritage to join the modern world. I'm not criticizing him, he's just one of those people you smile about when you see him. He and his wife used to run a trading post in Harvey years ago selling artifacts and knick-knacks. Well, the shop closed after his wife died and he's been caretaking at Elk Rock. This fall he's been... well, not causing major trouble, just being a pest. Setting up his teepee on private land, doing some dancing and chanting late at night. Sheriff Lockridge has had to roust him out a number of times. Yesterday, Wildcrow was ranting in the local meat market about a map. Guess his granddaughter came down to try to help. Anyway, the Smith boys thought he was talking about a treasure map and word spread.

"Now, this granddaughter. I haven't seen her, but people say she's pretty attractive and that she came down from Ames with a

Siberian Husky. I don't know, maybe she can calm down the old guy."

Antonaccio asked a few other questions but didn't gain any more useful information. "Thanks for the drink. I might see you around in the next few days. Have a good one."

As Antonaccio left the bar, he thought about the Smith brothers, Jacob Wildcrow, the granddaughter with a Siberian Husky, and a possible treasure. Peter White, the gangster looking to score some easy money, definitely would be interested in treasure. He'd have to do some quick research into all the players. He might get to Peter by following those involved in a treasure hunt rather than looking for new tenants at apartments or rental houses.

Chapter 15

"Chow, Grandfather has company," Grace said, as she drove up the path to the Airstream. "Oh, no. That's the car I saw up at the Peace Tree overlook the other night. I hope it's not that VanSteele woman riling Grandfather again. I don't know Chow, would a woman like that drive a green Gremlin?"

Then Grace noticed the Iowa State University sticker plastered across the rear window. She placed fingers on her temples and massaged small circles. "Oh, no. Looks like that Justin, the one who tried to pick me up. I knew I remembered him."

The memory of their meeting returned. She had finished her surgery class for the day and had paused to stare up at the Campanile. This guy came over with a line about kissing under its shadow at midnight. Grace had brushed him off, but he tracked her down and waited for her outside her office. After she called security, he didn't bother her any longer.

"Now here he is again," Grace muttered to Chow. "The other night at the Peace Tree land he and Grandfather seemed well acquainted. I hope he hasn't been encouraging Grandfather in this outrageous quest."

A low growl and a bark from Chow pulled her from her thoughts as Justin came running out of the trailer. Was that blood on his hand? She braked hard, opened the car door, and rushed forward. "Oh, my God, what happened? Are you all right?" Chow followed, and she ordered him to lie down.

"Wildcrow's hurt. I'll call an ambulance," Justin yelled.

"What are you talking about? Grandfather! Did you hurt Grandfather?" She raced to the trailer, not waiting for answers from Justin who was taking his own cell phone from the car.

Grandfather lay on the floor. A small pool of blood surrounded his head which apparently came from a two-inch laceration just above his right eyebrow. She leaned over to listen for his breath and checked his heartbeat. Both were weak and ragged.

Justin entered. "Grace, the ambulance is on the way. Don't worry. A head wound usually looks worse than it really is."

Grace whirled on him. "What happened here? Did you do this?"

"Of course not! Your grandfather and I have been friends for a long time. I came to discuss the map with him. He didn't answer when I knocked, but the door was ajar. I found him here, on the floor"

At the mention of the map Grandfather stirred. His lips cracked open. A low moan issued followed by mumbled words. "The map...."

"Grandfather, are you all right?"

"The... map," Wildcrow wheezed. "They... took... map."

"Grandfather, quit worrying about that damn map. Talk to me. Who did this?" Grace turned on Justin again. "Did you steal it for yourself?"

Grandfather barely lifted his hand to wave for Grace's attention. "Not him. Two men."

"Wildcrow, did you get a look at them? Can you identify them?" Justin asked.

"The brothers. I smelled them, putrid smell. Like dead skunks." Grandfather slipped back into unconsciousness.

Through tears and sobs, Grace did what she could to stabilize his neck, keeping a close tab on his pulse. There were no other obvious wounds or injuries. "Where's the damn ambulance?"

Minutes later, she heard the distinctive wail.

"I'll get them," Justin said. Moments later, she heard him say, "Hey, Jerry, he's in there. Head wound."

Jerry and another EMT entered the trailer, and Grace moved aside.

"He was talking just a minute ago," Grace said. "I've put pressure on the wound, but it looks like he has lost quite a bit of blood."

"We'll thoroughly examine him," said one of the EMT's with the name tag of Russ Collins.

Digger and Grace stood back while the two talked to each other and radioed in various vital signs.

"All right, we have the gurney outside," the first EMT announced. "We'll take him to the hospital. Digger, why don't you and Grace step outside."

The two EMTs stabilized Grandfather, transferred him to the gurney, and into the back of the ambulance.

"I'm coming along," Grace said.

"No, sorry, ma'am, there isn't room." Jerry looked over at Justin. "Digger, could you take her?"

Digger looked at Grace and gestured to the Gremlin. "This thing looks like it's ready for the auto graveyard but it's reliable. And I know the way to the hospital. I'd be glad to take you with me."

"All right," she murmured through clenched teeth. She still did not know if she trusted this man, but her grandfather seemed to be friends with him, and she wanted to get to the hospital as quickly as possible.

"Good. Get your dog and we'll follow the ambulance to town."

Chapter 16

Grace sat quietly during the ride, stroking Chow's neck. The dog took up most of the back seat, its head stuck between the front seats. She tried to push aside every negative thought and replace them with positive beliefs: Grandfather is strong and healthy, except for his mind. He's not really all that old. He's been through worse, I'm sure.

Just before they arrived at the hospital, Grace prayed. She promised God that if Grandfather lived, she'd listen to him about his map and even read that Indian heritage book he'd pushed on her years ago.

When Justin found a parking spot, he asked, "Can the dog stay in the car?"

"Leave the window down a little, and he'll curl up and go to sleep in the backseat."

They hurried to the emergency entrance. The two EMTs wheeled Grandfather inside and through a set of double doors deeper into the hospital. Justin stood near while Grace registered with the receptionist. Afterward, Justin sat on a cushioned chair in the waiting area while Grace paced. She looked at the doors, at the clock mounted on the wall, then at the doors. Minutes passed like hours. She remembered her drive down the previous day being stuck behind the two combines. Worry had gnawed at her then. This time it was worse. Anxiety threatened to overwhelm her.

A half-hour later, a short man with Asian features and a name tag that read Doctor Browning entered the waiting area. Grace pounced on him to barrage him with questions, but he held up a hand. "Mr. Wildcrow is going to be fine. The head wound isn't as bad as it appeared. He's awake and talking, though some of it doesn't make any sense. He's babbling about a map and a treasure. I want to do a CT scan just to be sure there's nothing else going on."

"But he's awake," Grace said. "Can I talk to him?"

"Let's get the scan over with, then we'll all sit down and discuss things. It will take about an hour and with his agitation, it'll probably take longer. I'll need to sedate him for the scan."

"Just for a few minutes," Grace insisted.

"I think it's best if we let the nurse handle it. He needs to be calm for the scan to be effective. As I said, let's talk afterward. He'll need to stay overnight, just so we can keep watch. "

Grace didn't know how to react. She wanted to make sure Grandfather was all right, but.... Confusion and fear for the worst clouded her thoughts.

"May I suggest you get some coffee?" Browning said. "I'll come get you when I have the results."

"Thank you, Doctor Browning," Justin said. "Coffee sounds like a plan. Come on, Grace. I'll buy you a cup." He pointed to the sign indicating the direction of the cafeteria.

Once seated in the cafeteria, coffee mugs in front of them, Grace relaxed a bit. At least her breathing was not as erratic.

"If he's awake and talking, I'm sure your grandfather is going to be fine," Justin said.

Grace half-smiled. "I'm glad. It's just that I made a promise, and now I have to read something I've been able to avoid for years."

He cocked his head in question. "I don't understand."

"In the car I made a promise to God that if Grandfather lived, I'd read a Native American book he has been nagging me about."

Justin leaned back in the chair. "I'm glad you made that promise. I think your ancestry is important to know. Wildcrow would be pleased to know that you want to learn more about your people."

"My people?" Grace stared at Justin and shook her head. "My people are not only Grandfather and Grandmother Wildcrow, and my father, Mahkah, but my Dutch-American mother and her ancestors who came to Iowa in the 1840s with Dominie Scholte."

"From the Netherlands," Digger said.

"You know about him?"

"I'm a history teacher. He broke away from the organized church and led a bunch of followers to America. He's credited with the founding of the town of Pella."

Grace nodded. "Yes, well, my mother named me Gray Swan in honor of my father's heritage, but my Dutch relatives, who had never approved of her marriage to my father, changed it to Grace. We lived with them in Pella a short while after my mother died when I was only five. Father and I then lived with the Wildcrows for close to a year, until he packed me up one day and took me to Colorado. Father wouldn't explain what made him move."

Grace tensed. "He wouldn't even tell me until years later that his mother—my grandmother—had died, and it was because Grandfather wouldn't seek out the white man's medicine which might have cured her. Father rejected his heritage because of Grandfather's stubbornness. After that, my father repeatedly told me the Native Americans were not my people. I was raised in a white neighborhood. I made myself as white as I could be, and we shunned anything related to 'Indians.' In retrospect, it was a terrible move. The kids found out my background and teased me unmercifully. They called me a squaw and a papoose, or worse, a half-breed."

"Kids can be cruel," Justin said. "I'm sorry."

Grace paused as thoughts drifted back to the day her father stormed away from Grandfather. Even after all these years, she recalled Father's final words. She had a vague recollection that her father had thrown something at Wildcrow.

"Your traditions end here," he'd said, harsh and biting.

What had father thrown? Grace saw a blurry image of glittering beads on a string. While some memories remained stark and clear, some had been driven from her by her father's vitriol and resentment that lasted for years.

She returned to the present and waved away Justin's sympathy. "It was only after I attended ISU and wanted to contact Grandfather that Father told me how the Indian ways killed my grandmother. Now, here I am mixed up in this thing about a stupid map and talk of treasure. He's been talking about this for months. I had hoped it would pass. Once Grandfather is well, I'm taking him back to Ames. I've made a deposit on a room at the Good Faith Home and I pray he'll put this whole map and treasure garbage behind him."

"I know nothing of your childhood, so I have no right to judge," Justin said. "I do know your grandfather, though, and I think you could very easily break his heart. He's stubborn, I'll grant you, but if you push him, you might crush his spirit. I hope you'll think about all of that before you go forward with your plan for a retirement home."

Grace glared at him. "It's none of your business."

"Maybe not, but I respect your grandfather and that makes me care. Just give it some thought before you make a decision."

"You're right that you know nothing of my childhood." Grace looked away, a tear rolling down her cheek.

Justin reached out and touched Grace's face. "You showed them all by succeeding in school, Doctor Snow."

He smiled, but Grace did not. "How did you know I'm a doctor?"

Justin shrugged. "I should say 'Grace Snow, DVM.' I did a little checking on the Internet last night."

A cell phone rang, and Justin pulled it from his pocket. He frowned at the phone and Grace saw he swiped the option to reject the call. He set the phone on the table, sipped his coffee, then asked, "You mentioned you were young when you moved from the area. How well do you remember Wildcrow and your grandmother?"

Grace stared over Justin's right shoulder and was silent for a long while. "I remember pieces. Certain memories come to mind. The time when Father brought me to stay with Grandmother. It was shortly after my mother's death. Every night when it was time for me to settle down to sleep, Grandmother told me the old tales from her childhood. I loved the stories but hated the yelling between my father and my grandfather every evening. Grandmother was ill even then, but I didn't know it.

"Then one day, Father grabbed me up and took me to Colorado where he found work and put me into school. I was nearly seven, but my only schooling, except for kindergarten, had been at Grandmother's knee. I started as a first grader. Once I caught on to what school was all about, I did very well. I spent only half a year in first grade, half a year in second grade, and over the years, by putting my effort into showing them what I could do, I graduated at the top of my high school class and went to Iowa State on a full scholarship."

"You have done a good job of it, Grace. Did you ever think that maybe your heritage might be an important part of who you are?"

Grace wanted to reject that notion, as she had—sometimes forcibly—all her life. Something in his eyes, though, a *pleading*, like how Chow sometimes looked at her when he wanted something, softened her. Justin took Grace's hand, and she didn't pull away. Her breath caught in her throat. Even though he'd come on strong when they were at university, he had treated her with respect since they met at Ruckman Cemetery, helped her with Grandfather. Drove her to the hospital and sat and talked with her over coffee. He didn't have any responsibility toward her or Grandfather, even if they were friends. She saw him as he was now, not as he had been years ago. People can change, she thought, couldn't they?

With Grandfather injured, her anxiety spiking, and the concerns over the vet practice always present, at the touch of his hand, her list of concerns faded for the moment. How would she have reacted if he'd soft-pedaled his approach back then? Part of her wanted to remain stand-offish, but he was trying to help. Also, she had promised to read the book and listen to Grandfather's words.

"Grace, I've talked with your grandfather many times. He believes all the land around here belongs to the Indians. There may be something to that idea. Controversy will always exist, because history shows the settlers and the government didn't treat the Indians all that well at times. The settlement of the treaties that your people signed was taken back by trickery. The Sauk and the Meskwaki Indians ceded the land in the treaty of 1843, but the money to pay for it went chiefly to the traders who had extended credit to them with exorbitant interest. It isn't even clear that the individuals who received the treaty money had the right to collect it. I don't think the issue will ever be resolved, but we have to realize that these were small groups of immoral men who caused problems."

"The government wasn't small," Grace countered.

Justin held up a hand and nodded. "True. I'm not defending their actions. These were two nations in conflict over possession of the land and unfortunately, the original owners, the Native Americans, were unsuccessful against a more technologically superior and more numerous foes. By the time the westward charge got here to Iowa, the White Man had settled, conquered, civilized the tribes in the Eastern lands. Then, driven by Manifest Destiny, there was little to stop them from going coast to coast."

Digger took a breath, looked at Grace. "Sorry for the lecture. Still, there are a lot of examples of cooperation and prosperity between the two peoples. It's at least one of the reasons why cities and towns, sports teams, and songs have connections with Native Americans. Don't get me wrong, the Europeans were closed-minded and xenophobic—and maybe some still are—but times were different than they are now."

He didn't say what Kathyrn might have said, that now the Native Americans are taking it all back, raking in the dough with their casinos.

"What I'm saying is, some people haven't forgotten, and your grandfather wants to make sure more people know and understand. Erecting his teepee on private land may not be the best way to accomplish it, but his heart and mind are in the right place. I believe he thinks if he can... bring you back into the fold, as it were, he'll have passed on his legacy. If more people can learn and understand from the past, maybe fewer will be tricked when it comes to today's issues."

Grace considered Justin's words. This wasn't what she expected from the young man who had been such a nuisance. "Every people has trouble with tricksters," Grandmother had often told Grace. Justin was confirming Grandmother's words.

Her thoughts were interrupted by a tap on the shoulder. She looked around at Sheriff Lockridge. "Miss Snow, sorry to bother you. How's your grandfather doing?"

"I'm told he'll be fine," Grace said. "Thank you, Sheriff."

Lockridge slid a chair over and sat. "Look, I need a statement from each of you. You know, time of arrival at Wildcrow's trailer, what you saw, what you did."

Grace and Digger recited the earlier events while Lockridge wrote notes. Digger had arrived a few minutes before Grace, thinking Wildcrow had already gotten home.

"I found him on the floor and the trailer ransacked," Justin said.

Grace told her story and repeated the part where Grandfather described who stole the map.

"Sounds like the Smiths have really gotten in deep this time," Lockridge said. "You said your grandfather was talking about a missing map, maybe stolen. Do you know anything about that?"

Grace shook her head, exasperated. "That stupid map. He showed it to me yesterday at lunch, but I didn't want to listen to him.

I don't know what he did with it. When Grandfather is better, he may be able to tell you more about what happened."

"How about you, Digger?" Lockridge asked. "Know anything about this map?"

"I know Wildcrow had mentioned a map a couple times when I've visited him in the last few months. I did see it yesterday out at the cemetery. I didn't understand the symbols or what Wildcrow was trying to tell me. I don't think it was about a treasure as all the rumors say."

"I heard that, too," Lockridge said. "More people are getting excited about it. I hope it stays just talk and doesn't get out of hand. Ma'am, weren't you supposed to help him pack up his stuff at the cemetery?"

"Yes," Grace said. "However, I didn't stay the night. The storm woke me up and then...."

"Something happened?"

"Well, I don't know. I'm not too sure what happened. Two people tried to break into the trailer last night."

Lockridge leaned forward. "Suppose you start at the beginning."

Grace described being awoken by the storm, discovering the power outage, seeing two men approach the trailer, hearing banging at the door, and seeing them run away. With reluctance, she even mentioned the strange bird that attacked the men when they fled.

"And you didn't call the police?" Lockridge asked.

"I didn't have a cell phone signal."

"What happened then?"

"I waited for about ten minutes, then packed up my suitcase and put Chow in the car. I stayed at the Holiday Inn at Bos Landen."

"Can you describe the men you saw?"

"No, it was too dark."

"Did they say anything? Make any threats?"

"No, I think they tried to chop through the door with an axe. I was afraid, Then, like I said, one of them screamed. When I looked out the window, they were running away flapping their arms. Some sort of bird, at least I think it was a bird, attacked them. It was dark, so I couldn't be sure. Then they disappeared into the woods."

Lockridge narrowed his gaze. "A bird?"

"I don't know what it was, Sheriff."

Lockridge shook his head. "This goll' darn map. What's it all about? Either of you have any idea why Wildcrow's so obsessed with it? Why would anyone think it so important to attack an old man and steal it?"

Grace and Justin shook their heads.

"Treasure," Lockridge said with a snort. He stood and retucked his uniform shirt into his brown pants. "Well, I'll have to think on this. See if I can track down the Smith brothers. Any tire tracks left would have been obliterated by your vehicles and the ambulance. I suppose I could conduct a search in the surrounding woods to see if the intruders from last night left anything behind. I doubt it, but I gotta cover all bases." He stood. "If either of you think of anything, let me know. I hope your grandfather recovers soon."

"Thank you, Sheriff."

After Lockridge left, Justin said, "It might be better for you if you didn't have to drag around your dog while you get things in order for your grandfather. How about you let me take Chow out to my farmhouse. It's only a few miles from town. I could set him up with food and water, so you don't have to worry about him being cooped up in a vehicle or your hotel room all day."

Grace faltered with Justin's offer, then dropped her head.

"Something wrong?"

Grace gave a half-hearted shrug. "Can he stay in the house? He's a big baby when it comes to staying outside."

Justin smiled. "Of course. I'll take care of him. Does he get along well with other dogs."

"Yes. Why?"

"I have a couple dogs at home. They also like to be in the house, but I have a doggie door at the back entrance. It might be a bit of a squeeze for Chow, but he should be able to handle it. The three of them should keep each other occupied until we return. I'll be back in a little bit. If you hear anything, give me a call."

He scribbled his number on a napkin, set his empty coffee cup on the counter, and left Grace to her own thoughts. She had a lot to consider, including Grandfather's health and the reappearance of Justin—Digger—into her life.

Chapter 17

Outside the hospital, Digger found a bench down the sidewalk from the emergency entrance. The previous night's storm had passed, with only a few clouds drifting across the morning sun. The air was still, but Digger's mind was on the move. He sat down, hoping the solidity of the bench would ground and focus him as he sought to organize his thoughts.

Grace Snow had re-appeared in his life and within a day, he volunteered to dog-sit. He genuinely cared about the animal's well-being, but he also considered the fact that the gesture meant he and Grace would be spending more time together. When Wildcrow recovered, maybe he could persuade her to stay around town longer. Or else maybe he could take a weekend to visit her in Ames.

Again, as he had the previous night at the Swamp Fox, he wondered if she had recognized him at the cemetery. She gave no indication so far but with everything happening, maybe that short-lived encounter hadn't registered. He remembered sitting on the campus grass near the ISU campanile, when his eyes first lasered onto her shapely exotic features. He leaped to his feet and fast-walked to get close to her, then offered his best banter of charm. Her rejection had been clear.

"Ah, well." He tried to dismiss the past by taking a Macanudo cigar out of his pocket. "Now this is one fine cigar," he said to no one.

Before he could fully contemplate the smoke, his mind traveled back to that time at ISU. After he'd been rousted by security for loitering at her office, he'd thought about creating opportunities for Grace and him to 'accidentally' bump into each other. Every time he saw her, he couldn't go through with his plan, afraid she'd get mad and report him. He didn't want to risk suspension or expulsion.

Soon, he forgot about her. Almost. Every now and then he'd think of her, or she'd show up in a dream, apologizing for her behavior, and agreeing to go out with him. He'd wake up feeling guilty because of how *he* had behaved at their first meeting.

Now, Grace had re-appeared in his life as a result of Wildcrow's map. And the map was missing—stolen!

Digger always contemplated possibilities best while puffing a good cigar. And he wanted to strategize how he could add a few more positive encounters before memories of past buffoonery came up. He pulled out his cutter and took a thin slice off the cap of the Macanudo Baron de Rothschild. Examining it for any slight imperfections, he wondered about the history behind this cigar being named Rothschild. Technically, tts length and thin size indicated a Lonsdale.

In college, he'd leaned toward history, as well as archaeology and geology, in his coursework for his teaching degree. Now, as a teacher in Knoxville, his students appreciated how he brought all three together in his classes. Digger wondered if there was a way to mix Grace, Wildcrow, and the map into a history lesson for some upcoming lessons. Could doing so put another check mark in the plus column for him in Grace's eyes?

He clicked a flame on his butane lighter and toasted the foot of the Macanudo. Then he held the smoldering tip a quarter inch above the visible flame and puffed while rolling the body of the cigar back-and-forth. Soon, the end glowed a soft ember-red.

Leaning back on the bench, he felt energized, enlivened by the reappearance of Grace. Maybe something would come of it?

As smoke drifted upward from his cigar, he blew several rings. Years of smoking cigars had instilled a number of rituals he inevitably followed without giving it much thought. This morning, he tried to focus his attention on the mild, complex flavor.

Visions of Grace jumped back into his head. Not much ever interrupted his enjoyment of a cigar, but Wildcrow's granddaughter was difficult to resist. The passage of so much time and his intermittent thoughts and dreams had only enhanced her intrigue. In the few hours he'd been with her yesterday and that morning, he could tell that there was a lady underneath the hard veneer she'd shown him at university, a softness. Yes, she cared about her grandfather, but—and this was a huge hope—he wondered if his presence also brought out a tender side.

Digger wanted to help Grace and Wildcrow. The map tantalized him, and he wondered where it might lead. If not treasure, then maybe a second chance at a relationship with Grace? And who knew? Both, if he was lucky.

Drawing on his cigar again, he thought about his image. He wasn't the immature student anymore. He considered how he might show a more sophisticated and discerning self to her. He had, after all was said and done, succeeded in achieving his goals, had become a respected community participant with a meaningful job. If she wondered about his interest in the map, knowing he was a teacher and a friend of Wildcrow's might be enough. While the idea of a treasure hunt intrigued him, it was not, he knew deep down, his primary interest.

He paused to enjoy another long puff on his cigar when his cell phone rang. Seeing the caller ID, he didn't answer it. He didn't want to interrupt his line of thought, but the caller had been Kathryn VanSteele.

The image of her jolted him forward and cigar ash dropped into his lap. "Complication," he muttered and brushed away the ash with the side of his hand. Although he had decided he was through with her, well... it was still complicated. Wildcrow, Grace, the map, the casino, treasure. His head spun, and not from the cigar smoke.

He vowed to take it slow, proceed with caution, like he would pursue a new archaeological dig. After all, Grace was here, now, because of Wildcrow, not because of him. He needed be careful. Still, he couldn't help but envision a wonderful outcome. Even if a relationship didn't work out with Grace, he knew he was done with Kathryn.

Satisfied with his plan, Digger picked himself up off the bench. Feeling hopeful, he started the walk to his car, thinking he should let Chow out for a few minutes before taking him home. Stepping into the aisle where his car was parked, he saw someone standing next to his Gremlin. The person reached through the partially open window.

"Hey!" Digger called.

The figure moved to the right and Digger could not see Chow at all, just the back of the person.

Digger yelled louder, "Hey! What's going on?"

He hurried toward his car. A man in his forties, about Digger's own size with sandy blond hair and dressed all in black, didn't seem to have heard him shout. Just as Digger reached him, he withdrew his arm from the car.

"Oh, hi there." The man flashed a toothy grin. "Sorry, I was admiring the dog. It's a Siberian Husky. I have one myself."

The man spoke in a low tenor voice with a trace of a southern accent. Digger didn't recognize him, so surmised that he wasn't a local.

"I just love these big dogs," the man added. "They all seem to love me, so I decided to give him a pat or two. He sure seemed to like it."

Digger could now see Chow, as the man stepped to the side and held out his palms as if to say, *see, nothing in my hands.*

Chow didn't look out of sorts: Tongue lolling. Nose stuck out as far as he could get it through the narrow gap. Snorting for more attention. Nothing appeared abnormal. Maybe this was nothing more than some dog-loving stranger stopping to pet Chow through the window. Still, Digger wondered why the man didn't respond when he first yelled. In fact, he'd moved as if to shield himself.

Digger was just about to ask about the odd behavior, but the man turned and began walking away, saying over his shoulder, "He's quite a dog!"

"Yeah...." Digger replied. "Uh...."

The stranger tossed back, "Sorry for worrying you. No problem." He disappeared into the next row of cars.

Digger contemplated running after him, demanding answers, but thought the man pleasant enough and he didn't seem to be causing any harm.

His phone rang again. Kathryn again. Once more, he ignored the call. He opened the car door and let the dog out to relieve itself. Afterward, Chow, slobbering and huffing, tried to push his way into the front seat. Digger had to shove him back.

"Knock it off, big guy. Get back there and settle down. I'm taking you home to meet some new playmates."

He looked over his shoulder at the animal. The dog huffed at him. Even though his own pets were male, he wondered if the big husky had been neutered, but figured Doctor Grace Snow would have been conscientious enough to take care of that issue. At the exit to the hospital lot, he waited for traffic behind a Crown Victoria. The reflection in the side mirror showed part of the driver's face. Digger thought it was the same man who'd been petting Chow. He wondered if he ought to call the police, report the matter, but decided against it. There hadn't been any crime and the dog hadn't been injured.

By the time he pulled onto Lincoln Street, his mind had wandered back to Wildcrow and the map. He thought of a couple books in his classroom he could reference. If he recalled correctly, they mentioned some of the Native American tribes who occupied the land before Iowa became a state. He didn't remember if any of the texts referred to a map being created, but it wouldn't hurt to look.

He glanced at Chow in the rear-view mirror. "Quick side trip before I take you home, big guy."

The dog, as if resigned to the situation, stretched over the length of the back seat.

Chapter 18

Grace watched her grandfather who'd fallen asleep after the CAT scan. His breathing was steady, but a bit raspy.

His hospital room was stark, with a counter, a couple drawers for clothes, and a small bathroom. Pleated curtains had been pulled around the bed.

Grace thought of the conversation with Justin in the cafeteria about Grandfather and her Indian heritage. She wasn't sure if Justin understood her troubled childhood. She'd told him about her father taking her away to Colorado when she was a young girl, the teasing she received at school, but did he truly understand her pain?

She missed the stories her grandmother had told her. It was dreadful to have only those stories when her father enrolled her in a new white man's school in Greeley. None of her studies included Native American history except for token chapters about Sitting Bull and Geronimo. Her father had rejected his heritage and persuaded her to do the same.

"Oh, Grandfather, why does my father hold such a grudge?" she whispered and wiped her eyes on a discolored and frayed handkerchief. "Why can't he forgive you? He should be here with you."

She'd called her father after Justin left and before the nurse said her grandfather was in the recovery room. After no one answered, she left a message for him to call as soon as possible. Grace wanted to stay and be with her grandfather when he woke but didn't know how long he'd be out. They'd given him a sedative before the scan. However, she was getting hungry. She decided to see if any of the food in the cafeteria interested her and come right back. Grace placed a soft kiss on Grandfather's forehead.

At that second, his body flinched. He expelled a hoarse cough, then started mumbling. His eyes opened wide. The mumbling became rhythmic, chant-like.

"What did you say?" Grace asked.

The chanting became louder.

"I don't understand what you're saying. Speak English, Grandfather."

Even though his eyes were open she suspected he wasn't awake. She took up a pen and notepad on the nearby counter and wrote down as many words as she could decipher. Her knowledge of the Sac language was not strong enough to keep up.

Grandfather's body relaxed and he appeared to be coming around. He moved his arm which pulled on the IV tube and plastic bag of fluid. The slight resistance must have startled him because he bellowed a cry of alarm, lashed out, and swatted at the stand.

Grace found a nurse in the hall. "Come quick. Something's wrong."

The nurse followed Grace into the room and checked on the IV. Grandfather jerked his arm away. "Go away! Leave me be." He shook his finger at the nurse. "I'm fine. I was just having trouble waking up."

"Sir, I need to check the IV, make sure you haven't pulled out the needle," the nurse insisted. "Just relax."

"I'm all right," he said, but allowed her to examine the IV.

"Everything seems to be in order," the nurse said.

In all the excitement, Grace hadn't noticed the nurse's Asian features before. Now she saw the woman was around fifty. Her face had developed some creases, but her almond shaped eyes glittered with life. However, the nurse didn't appear to have pure Asian ancestry. In another setting, her long face but round cheeks could have passed for Native American. Grace found it interesting that both a nurse and Wildcrow's doctor shared Asian backgrounds.

When the nurse spoke, she had a calm sing-song cadence. "Are you feeling any pain?"

Grandfather shook his head. "No."

"Are you feeling light-headed? Nauseated?"

Another head shake. "No."

"You will if you keep moving your head like that, you gagiibaadad rascal." the nurse chided.

Grandfather's eyes widened, saw the nurse's teasing smile, and huffed once. It reminded Grace of when Chow responded to her words.

"What did you say to him?" Grace asked.

The nurse winked. "While my mother is Chinese and taught me her language, my father is descended from the Ojibwe and I learned a lot his old language." She laid a hand on Grandfather's arm and narrowed her eyes. "You are, perhaps, related to this man?"

"My grandfather."

The nurse nodded. "Well, I may not have used the word he is familiar with, but I'm sure he recognizes it." She looked down at Grandfather. "You rest and don't make me come back here again. Understand?"

He huffed again and the nurse left.

"Grandfather?"

"Ach!" he bleated.

"What did she say?" When he didn't reply, she added, "Did she insult you?"

"Ach!" he repeated. "She tried to be smart, a showoff. She called me foolish."

Grace smiled, leaned down, and kissed his cheek. "I think sometimes you are. Why did you get so frantic when you woke? You almost knocked over the IV stand."

Grandfather sighed. "I'm fine. I guess when I woke, I didn't know where I was. That contraption caught me off guard."

"Do you remember what you were saying? I tried to write down what I think you said, but I'm not sure I have it correct." She showed him the paper.

He sighed again. "Oh, Grace. Later. I'm tired. Let me sleep. I'll explain later."

"Okay, I'll be back in a while. I'm going to the cafeteria."

He nodded and closed his eyes. At the door, she heard him say in a soft voice, "Gagiibaadad! Humph!"

Chapter 19

Digger pulled into the high school lot and parked in front of the glass double door entrance. Only two other cars were in the lot, and their presence reminded him of a curiosity. Whenever he'd pass a large business, closed for whatever reason, there always seemed to be one or two cars in the parking area. Who owned those cars? Office workers in to finish reports? If so, why park so far away? It was one of those imponderables that came up every now and then.

He unlocked the doors. Inside, the tile floor and the acoustics served to amplify any small sound. When school was in session, students and teachers laughing and talking, lockers and doors opening and closing, all fell into a general hubbub of noise. With the school empty, he noticed that his footfalls, even wearing tennis shoes, filled the hall. He experienced a weird, momentary feeling of guilt, like he had sneaked into the school to cause mischief. If he met anyone, he could explain he was after some research material, which was true. He wouldn't want to detail the reason for those books. How silly would it sound if he said he wanted to look up references to Native American map making, perhaps a map to a treasure?

After unlocking his classroom door, he paused and let his gaze wander the room. Thirty desks, never all filled during any given hour. His old, scarred, wooden desk up front against the right wall. Four drawer metal filing cabinet against the other. Obligatory chalkboard. Framed images of Presidents Washington and Jefferson. Digger's predecessor had taped a ten foot long, two-foot-high poster depicting a timeline of notable events in American history to the wall his desk sat against.

Digger had added some personal touches with some mementos from home, artifacts he'd discovered during his explorations. Every so often he brought in new objects which invariably, invited questions from the freshman students. Many times, they learned more with an open discussion or question and answer session than they did by reading endless pages of a textbook.

Digger enjoyed teaching. While he had created a curriculum for his classes, he often deviated from it when more interesting topics arose. He had a good relationship with most of the students, with an open-door policy, often making acquaintances with some of the parents. He even allowed the students to use his nickname and even some of his fellow teachers fell into the practice.

Sighing with a touch of pride at his accomplishments since returning to Knoxville after college, he found the two books he thought might be of value to him on his research into Wildcrow's map. Back outside, he had his hand on the car door handle when he saw Kathryn's Audi A3 turn into the school lot. Inwardly, he cringed, remembering how he had ignored her phone calls all morning.

"*Darling*, I was worried something had happened when you didn't answer your phone." She slammed shut her car door and advanced upon him. "Were you ever going to answer my calls?"

Typical Kathryn. She didn't say, "I'm glad you're all right." Or "Did you turn off your phone when grading papers?" Nope, she'd make a scene, affronted at her perceived lack of courtesy from him. Previous times he'd turned off his phone for any number of reasons only to discover later she'd left several messages, each progressively more dramatic. Explanations were usually given, and the mood would shift. Some romantic play usually eased away the heightened tension.

This time, the results would be different. He *had* been discourteous, not accepting her calls on purpose because... well, because he was tending to an injured friend. Then there was Grace. Also, there was this new casino dispute that he figured would likely be ongoing. He wondered how now, in the light of day, to best to approach his decision the previous night to just end their relationship.

She stood in front of him, hands on hips, face scrunched up even more than usual, her nose tightened, eyes squinty, piercing like blue knives, lips forming a wolfish curl. "Well?"

"Kathryn—"

"I thought you might have called me yesterday afternoon. Maybe go to dinner, discuss the casino some more. I waited in the office until five, then went home. Nothing all night."

Of course, she hadn't tried to call him, either.

"What were you doing all day? All night?" she asked.

"I—"

"Don't you realize how important this casino is to this town? To me?"

Oh, he understood how it would affect her community standing.

She shook her head, exasperated. "I don't know about you, Justin. These last few months, it feels like you've been pulling away from me. I mean you didn't even go with me to the sprint car races when I met with some of the city's developers. That was the perfect venue to get in good with them, and it would have been good if you were with me, but you weren't there."

He had explained to her that, unfortunately, he had to miss that event because of a teachers' conference. He wouldn't have been good company anyway. The races interested him more than schmoozing with big wigs. There was an up-and-coming new driver this year, and he had hoped to watch his performance.

"Now you're hanging around an old Indian who's nothing but a nuisance," Kathryn said.

"Wait a minute—"

"He's got a lot of people in this town riled up over some supposed treasure. Indian treasure. Give me a break. What could it be? A bunch of arrowheads, more pottery shards, maybe a piece of a tomahawk?"

"Kathryn—"

"Did you see that teepee he had? Heavens, what century does he think we're in?"

"Stop it—"

"I don't understand you, Justin. I thought you were behind me on this. The casino will bring in business and boost our economy."

"And devastate a bunch of land near a beautiful lake," Digger said.

"We're not talking about the whole lake, only a few hundred acres. Look what they did down at Lake Rathbun with the Honeycreek Resort."

"A lot of good farmland gone," Digger said.

"Justin, stop. Just stop. I'm not going to argue with you about this." She swiped hair from her face, shook her head, and took a long breath. The feral nature left her face. When she spoke again, she tried for a conciliatory tone, but Digger knew it was false.

"Justin, please. We've always managed to get over the rough spots. You've been wonderful when my job gets stressful."

Too bad the feeling wasn't reciprocal, he thought. Whenever he had issues, she dismissed them or changed the subject.

"I'm really getting into the thick of things and was hoping for some support. I don't know what's come over you lately. Maybe you need to take some time and think things over, figure out what you want. This casino could take us places we can't imagine." She adopted a sly askance look. "Think what we could do with the money. Vacations, New York getaways. Who knows?"

Digger had no desire to visit New York other than maybe the northern part of the state for some archaeological explorations.

"Why don't you go home, sweetie, and relax for the rest of the day? I know you have papers to grade, but you can do that over the weekend. Think over things and call me tonight, okay?"

Without waiting for his response, she turned and walked to her car. Just before she entered, she blew him a kiss. Seconds later, she drove past him with a little wave.

Digger watched her leave the school grounds. Think it over, she'd said. Well, he had done a lot of thinking the previous night at the Swamp Fox. Today's meeting, with her always interrupting him, left no time for him to get a word in edgewise. He knew they did need to talk. What just transpired certainly hadn't changed his mind.

Yes, he thought. I will take some time off...maybe forever.

Chapter 20

In a cushioned chair next to Grandfather's bed, Grace tried to divert her anxiety with a couple magazines she found in the room. Unfortunately, neither helped. Upon seeing the content, she knew they must have been selected and brought in by the staff because Wildcrow was who he was.

The first, *National Geographic*, chose to dedicate the entire issue to Native Americans. Each article on the more well-known tribes. Cherokee, Apache, Navajo. Many of the other tribes including her own ancestors from the Sac and Fox were briefly mentioned at the end of the piece. Vivid images of today's Indians accompanied restored photos of life in the 1800s and early 1900s.

The other magazine, *Taste of Home*, contained many recipes from the American Indian culture—pumpkins, squash, beans—with suggestions on 'modernizing for taste,' or substitution of ingredients if one had certain allergies or dietary requirements.

Grace thought the tone of some of the suggestions were disparaging. They completely missed the point. Nowhere did the instructions say the best way was to use natural ingredients, cook over an open flame, or bake in a stone oven. Most of the ingredients listed were processed and cooking came from gas or electric appliances. One even explained how to cook in a microwave.

She remembered her childhood visits to her grandparents' store in Harvey. Along with artifacts, the store sold baked goods Grandmother created. She used a stone hearth in the back of the property. Yes, she 'modernized for taste' at times, but the pastries and cornbread were more delicious than the too-sweet stuff at the local bakery.

Grandfather also hunted deer every season, processing the meat for pemmican, adding his special dried berry combination. Grace remembered her five-year old jaw working on the chewy meat, how she enjoyed the wild, gamey taste. The hides, he turned into clothing with decorative patterns and beadwork.

Part of her missed those childhood times. Yes, she'd endured the ridicule and sarcasm in school but ultimately found her way through and even to thrive in the white man's world. Yes, she'd been hardened against her heritage by her father, and yes, she was a modern woman. She enjoyed her independence, her self-made life, but had no inclinations to bring her heritage back into her day-to-day existence. She'd moved past all that.

She knew quite a few Native Americans, even people her age, who were very active in their tribal affairs, but this was not her. Since her school days with all the bullying and ostracizing, she only wished to blend in with the rest of America. She eschewed the idea that she was born of Sac Native American people.

However, that had never kept her from recalling the days on Grandfather's knee or at Grandmother's table. The memories of her youth remained strong, clear: the stories and lessons, preparing traditional meals, working with her hands.

"Oh, Grandfather," she sighed. "Why can't we go back to those times?"

As if in answer, Grandfather began to mumble as he had earlier, as if even unconscious, he tried to impart whatever important message that haunted him.

She stood and leaned over him. "What is it, Grandfather? Tell me."

The mumbling faded to nasally breaths before he quieted. A nurse entered, the same one from earlier.

"He was trying to say something," Grace said.

The nurse checked his pulse, blood pressure, and changed out the IV bag of fluid. "Everything is normal," she said. "Yes, I've heard him at times during my rounds. I don't catch many words, but I think he'd been dreaming. Sometimes, head traumas have certain side effects where the mind remains active even in deep sleep. It's nothing to worry about." She typed her findings into the rolling computer workstation that seemed to be a physical part of her. She checked her watch. "You should take care of yourself. It's nearing dinner time. We'll monitor him throughout the night."

"I'm waiting for a friend to come back."

After the nurse left, Grace's thoughts turned to Justin. A friend, she'd said. Was he? She'd seen him yesterday for a short time, then again that morning. Before that, she'd seen him when he hit on her, trying in vain to ask her out.

A friend. How strange, she thought, to call him that after knowing him a short time. How easily she felt comforted by his presence and his support. Maybe that had to do with the friendship he had with Grandfather. She felt something, some connection to him. She couldn't put words to it.

She heard the scrape of a footstep on tile. Justin stood in the doorway, shoulders hunched, eyes darting to hers, then down. How long had he been standing there? Had he looked at her all that time? She felt her face warm with a blush. Justin didn't seem to notice.

"How's he doing?" He took a couple steps into the room.

Grace brushed hair from her cheeks but realized she was really trying to wipe away the evidence of her blush at the thought of Justin looking at her. "Fine, except for the times when he's restless, when he wants to say something but can't get the words out."

Justin stood on the other side of the bed. "Yeah, he's been anxious these last few months. This map has been pretty important to him."

"I don't know what I'm going to do," Grace said. "I reserved a spot for him at one of the senior living facilities in Ames, but I'll have trouble persuading him to go."

"He's set in his ways." Grace flashed him a glare, but he added, "That's not a criticism. I've talked with him often and once his mind is set on something, he's determined to follow through. Look at how many times he's camped out in his teepee at the cemeteries and on private land."

"What's it all for?"

"I think it's as if he's preparing for something. He has that map, maybe he's been planning a trip. No, more like a journey."

"Do you think he's getting ready to die?" Grace asked. "I've read about how it was thought native peoples knew... it was their time." Her voice cracked at the end.

"No," Justin assured. "I don't think it's that. This has to do with the map." He smiled. "I'll tell you, though, this map has gotten more people than your grandfather excited."

"What do you mean?"

"After I stopped at the school to pick up a couple books, I drove Chow out to my place. By the way, that's why I took so long getting back. I introduced him to my dogs, had some play time, let him settle in. I think he should be okay. Oh, then I heard some grinding in my engine, so I stopped by Hube's Garage. Turned out I was low on oil. My oil light doesn't turn on. Need to get it fixed one day."

Grace brought the conversation back to Grandfather. "You mentioned other people excited about the map."

"Well, you know how rumors spread in a small town. They get more enhanced with each telling. Anyway, I've seen a lot of folks with shovels. Some driving out toward the burial mounds."

"Why?"

"Looking for that treasure Wildcrow was talking about. I know, it probably isn't actual treasure like a gold coin-filled chest or a pile of money someone squirreled away fifty years ago, but you know how some people's imaginations can get the better of them. I'm afraid Sheriff Lockridge and his deputies might have their hands full."

"I don't understand it," Grace said.

"It won't come to much," Justin said. "Bunch of holes in the ground. I'd hate to see damage done to the mounds." He shrugged. "Anyway, I thought, um...."

His words trailed off. He shoved his hands into his pants pockets and his gaze drifted to the floor.

"What?" Grace asked.

"I was wondering... well, I mean, it's getting on in the afternoon, and I thought maybe you'd like to get some supper."

"Oh," Grace said, her attention went back to Grandfather.

"I'm sure he'll be all right," Justin said. "The doctor will call if anything changes."

Doctor Browning entered the room as if on cue. "Well, how's the patient doing?" He checked his tablet. He then checked Grandfather's pulse and the dressing over the head injury. "Everything looks fine. I wanted a last visit before I went off shift. We'll make routine checks during the night."

"Do you think he'll be all right?" Grace asked.

"Hard to tell with head injuries. He was awake this afternoon. That's a good sign. He seems stable enough except for the episodes when you said he talks in his sleep. It means his mind is active. Something in there is fighting."

Justin broke in. "We were thinking about getting some dinner."

"Good idea," Browning said. "You can come back later until visiting hours are over."

After the doctor departed, Grace still stared at Grandfather. She didn't want to leave him, wanted to be present when he woke up. However, her stomach rumbled. Hunger intervened.

"So, what about dinner?" Justin asked. Had he heard her stomach?

She sighed. "Where were you thinking?"

Justin pursed his lips and looked in the direction Doctor Browning had gone. "Chinese?"

***

For two hours, they lingered at Deng's Garden over cashew shrimp, moo goo gai pan, and shared egg rolls. Grace's thoughts never drifted far from Grandfather, but once again, she felt comfortable with Justin. Instead of waxing about kissing in the moonlight or at midnight as he had five years before, he asked about her veterinary practice and how long she'd been in Knoxville as a child. He related the story of how he became a teacher and told a few stories about his archaeological research exploring many Indian mounds and other area sites.

While Justin had offered to keep Chow overnight, she said she'd feel more at ease with the big dog around, even if they were at the hotel. Justin drove her to his rural home a few miles north of Knoxville. On a gravel road, the ranch home had a kennel in the back yard for his two dogs. Part of the property had been set aside for a garden, but Justin said he hadn't taken time to cultivate it. The land around the acreage consisted of soybean fields owned by a neighbor.

"It's a little too big for one person," Justin said. "However, the previous owner wanted out and gave me a good deal."

Chow bounded to the fence when Grace and Justin rounded the corner of the house. The husky was followed by a short-haired dachshund and a German Shepherd mix smaller than a normal Shepherd.

"Barney and Roscoe," Justin introduced.

The kennel allowed the dogs to run for short sprints. Several chew toys and old beef bones lay scattered around the grass. Three-sided, wooden shelters provided protection against the weather.

"Usually, they stay in the house during the night." Justin crouched to pet the dachshund. "Lately though, for some reason Barney here prefers to spend a lot of nights outdoors, even during the winter. I've had to reinforce the fence to prevent coyotes from getting inside."

Chow barked three times, and Grace wondered if he'd had enough canine playtime. Justin held back his dogs while Grace retrieved Chow and led him to the Gremlin. Justin then drove back to the hospital where Grace stayed with Grandfather until visiting hours ended. The night shift nurse said nothing had changed. The patient rested easily. No, he hadn't heard him mumbling any Indian words.

"He's been very quiet," the nurse reported.

Upon leaving, Justin drove her back to the Airstream where her Escape had been since that morning. She thanked him for dinner and caring for Chow.

"Why don't you call me tomorrow morning?" He handed her a napkin on which he'd jotted his cell phone number. "I'll stop by the hotel, and we can grab some breakfast."

"I'll think about it," she said. "Thank you."

During the drive to the Holiday Inn Express, Justin stayed in her thoughts. "What do you think of him?" she asked Chow.

The dog snuffled and Grace assumed he approved.

"I suppose you'd like to visit your new friends again."

Chow licked her cheek.

She took her eyes off the road only long enough to look at Chow. His dark eyes gleamed in the car's dashboard lights. "Tell me the truth, Chow, do you like Justin?"

The husky woofed low and breathy. Grace returned to the task of driving. Storm clouds had moved in, threatening more rain.

"Yeah," she whispered. "I do, too."

Chapter 21

Around eight that night, Kyle Brewer, known in Chicago as Peter White, sat in the storage room of Woo Hardware waiting for the Smith brothers. Because of their ineptness at keeping information to themselves, the two dolts had caused a stir around Knoxville with their talk of treasure and an old Indian map.

Kyle drank from a can of Schlitz beer and shook his head in exasperation. When he'd come to town in August around the time of the sprint car races, he never expected to stay long. He'd been surprised at the influx of people and the main race days weren't scheduled until a week later. After the races, Kyle wondered if he should have joined the exodus of racers, campers, and other tourists, maybe hide out in Des Moines. Then, he saw how things quieted down and figured he could blend in, scrape together some cash, and build up a decent amount. He couldn't go to major cities like St. Louis or Houston because of the already established organizations. Even Des Moines had a couple factions.

Kyle figured he'd find a small town, secure a job, make and steal a bit of extra cash from the locals, then move to the next town before the cops paid too much attention. He had enough reserves to tide him over, but he needed more—a lot more—before he could return to Chicago. Unfortunately, he hadn't taken into account how long he might need to obtain the amount of money required. At the rate he was going, it might be years before he could return to the Windy City.

A possible treasure, though....

He'd met the Smiths not two days after he rented an apartment and hired on at Woo Hardware. They were arguing between themselves at the Hometown Meat Market over roast beef or turkey. Kyle had smelled the marijuana odor emanating off their clothes from twenty feet away. He soon discovered they not only smoked weed but sold it along with a bit of meth they cooked up at their property south of town.

Now, they'd come across a map....

Kyle remained cautious with the Smiths, hadn't become too friendly with them. They had a knack for screwing up and not accomplishing much. Maybe that's why they stayed out of jail: *because* of their failures. They were too dumb to be arrested.

The previous day, they met after Kyle's shift to discuss the map and the purported treasure. Kyle looked at the image Cole had taken with his cell phone when the brothers had overheard the Indian spouting off in the meat market. Not much could be distinguished because Cole's hand had twitched, and the image came out blurry. Kyle made out enough features to recognize they most likely showed the land around Lake Red Rock, although the water symbols might have indicated a river, not a lake.

When the store wasn't busy, he'd looked through a small book published by the local historical society that detailed the history of the dam and the lake, the flooded over towns that had been sacrificed when the Corps of Engineers built it in 1969. It was a way to pass idle time.

Today, the brothers had found Kyle during his lunch hour and wanted to show him the original map they'd stolen from Wildcrow. Kyle wanted to punch them out right there in the diner for being so dense. He told them to come by the store after dinner.

A banging on the front door interrupted Kyle's thoughts. He stood and walked from the storage out into the main room of the store. Security lights showed two figures outside. Kyle recognized the Smiths, still wearing the same dirty jeans and flannel shirts they had earlier in the day. He huffed in disgust, drained the last of the beer, and tossed the can in the nearest trash can.

"You idiots," he said in a low voice once he'd exited the store and locked the door. "I told you to come to the back entrance."

"I thought you said to come back to the entrance," Bubba said.

"I knew you had interpreted it wrong," Cole said.

"No, I didn't," Bubba said. "Kyle here spoke good English."

"So what?"

"Interpreted means you change foreign words into English. Kyle spoke English, so I couldn't have interpreted what he said wrong."

"Well, you still—"

"Both of you shut up," Kyle interrupted. He'd heard these two argue back and forth over word definitions on several occasions, and it irritated him enough he wanted to shove a dictionary down their throats. "Do you have your truck here?"

"Around back," Bubba said.

Kyle stared at them. "Then why didn't you knock on the back door?"

"Because you said—"

"All right, never mind. Let's just get out of here. We're too out in the open. How far is your place? I think it'd be safer there."

"A couple miles out of town," Cole said.

"I'll follow you." Kyle thought it weird he'd never seen where the brothers lived. Their meetings were always in shadowy alleys or parks at dusk. "Your talk of treasure managed to get a lot of other people talking. We had a new shipment of shovels come in this morning, and I sold every one."

"I hope we find it first," Bubba said. "You don't think someone else found it, do you?"

"We'd have heard something." Kyle looked up and down the sidewalk. "Come on, let's go."

The Smiths meant trouble and mischief, and anyone seen associating with them too much could be under suspicion. Kyle had already seen one stranger in town the previous day who raised his own caution flags. Someone all in black who reminded Kyle of a call he'd received shortly after he'd gone on the run. One of his guys he'd talked to from Chicago said there was a federal agent sniffing around, asking questions. Said he was a bit weird, didn't act like other cops or agents. One thing that his guy mentioned was the agent dressed in all black clothes. Kyle didn't know if that same agent had tracked him to Knoxville, if he'd been the one Kyle had seen heading toward the Swamp Fox that morning. He did think it wise to be cautious.

South on Highway 14, Kyle followed the Smiths' truck. At the first road past the airport, they turned west for almost a mile before going south again. Just over the English Creek, the truck cut a sharp left onto a rutted dirt and gravel lane Kyle would have missed on his own.

The track went through a field and then entered a treed area. Tree branches on either side made woody scrapes against his car.

The old Riviera wasn't built for off-road driving, and the shocks jounced and protested each pothole and bump.

Kyle estimated he'd gone almost a quarter a mile before he came out into a small clearing with a double-wide mobile home trailer and another building that might have been an old barn. The headlights showed the trailer's rust-eaten skirting, the sides glinting unpainted silver, and the roof and gutters sagging.

When everyone had climbed out of their vehicles, Kyle saw Cole held a flashlight, one of those extra-large lights with a handle.

"Come on, we'll give you the quarter tour since you ain't never been out here," Cole said.

"I thought it was a nickel tour," Bubba said.

Cole stopped and turned the light so it shone full-on Bubba's face. "They called it a nickel tour because that's what it used to cost to visit some place in those days. A nickel. But now, we got taxes and inflation, so you have to raise the price. So, now it's a quarter."

There were times Kyle would just as soon shoot these bozos and leave them for the raccoons, coyotes, and other nocturnal scavengers. This was one of those times. Still, he followed the brothers to the barn. The wood had rotted away in many places and the swinging door shivered on loose hinges. Cole's flashlight illuminated a counter and table with empty two-liter soda bottles, boxes of Sudafed, and other common household items. These included coffee filters, bottles of Heet gas additive, and Drano. Also on the counter, Kyle saw a bunch of snacks and cookies.

"It ain't a large operation, but we cook up enough meth to keep our customers happy," Cole said.

"We even have a couple that come over from Oskaloosa," Bubba added.

Kyle knew Oskaloosa lay about twenty-five miles east of Knoxville.

"Come on," Cole said. "We'll show you what we like to call the pot patch."

"*You* call it that," Bubba said. "I think it's a stupid name."

"You should like it, then," Cole retorted. "You're a stupid person."

"Not stupid enough to call it a pot patch."

About thirty yards into the trees on the eastern end of the property, they stepped out into open ground perhaps sixty feet square. The dormant marijuana plants weren't very high, but Kyle thought they'd bring in a decent harvest.

"Ain't nothing until next spring," Cole said. "We have another small patch below the barn all set up with heat lamps and fertilized soil."

Kyle saw a glint of metal in the distance which caught in Cole's waving beam. "Hold on. Point the light back over there."

Cole moved the light and Kyle saw the partial profile of what looked to be a rusted delivery-type truck. Weather and time had eradicated most of the paint on the side panel, but he could still make out faint lettering: STAN, THE ICE CREAM MAN.

It was an old ice cream truck. Kyle had heard about them. They drove through neighborhoods playing a goofy tune all the kids recognized. The driver handed out treats from a side or rear window.

"What is that doing here?" Kyle asked.

Bubba laughed low, maybe in an attempt at a stereotypical spooky movie laugh. "Tell him, Cole," he said in an equally creepy gravelly voice.

Cole gave a closed mouth laugh that reminded Kyle of a Vincent Price movie he'd seen. "We don't know."

"What do you mean?"

"Come have a look." Cole walked toward the truck. Kyle discovered it was part of an outer circle of other rusted vehicles from decades ago. They lined yet another clearing about seventy yards long and forty wide. The flashlight's beam didn't show details of the vehicles at the far end, but Kyle made out junkyard type sedans, pickups, even an old school bus. Another group of flatbed trucks, panel vans and a couple convertibles formed an inner circle. Kyle guessed around thirty-five vehicles formed an oval 'track.'

"We don't know," Cole repeated, and Bubba laughed again. "Every so often we come back here and there's another car or truck. Don't know where they come from."

"Don't you own this property?" Kyle asked. "Isn't this part of your land?"

"Yep," Cole said. "Actually, it was our Daddy's. We just inherited it."

"He died when we was still in school," Bubba said.

"Your mother?"

"She run off long time ago," Cole said.

"We had an aunt who took care of us until graduation," Bubba said.

"Then on our 18th birthday, she gave us what little cash she'd saved up, the deed to the property, and she run off, too," Cole said.

"Were there cars here when your dad was alive?" Kyle asked.

"No. They started showing up 'bout ten years ago. One at a time. Don't know how they get here."

"We looked for tire tracks, but didn't find any," Bubba said.

"We even checked the fence line between us and the winery on the other side. Didn't find no holes or even a gate."

"They got good wine over there," Bubba said. "I sneak over there once in a while and steal a couple bottles."

"Wait a minute," Kyle said. "Back up. You have no idea about these vehicles? Why someone brings them here or how they get here?"

"Nope." Cole gave his Vincent Price laugh again. "Bubba thinks this place is haunted."

"It is," Bubba said. "Me and Cole come back here every week or so to see if any more cars have showed up, but I wouldn't be here by myself."

Kyle took one last look at the ring of junked vehicles, then suggested they return to the trailer.

The inside of the Smith's home reeked of marijuana smoke. Empty pizza boxes were stacked in one corner. Dust and grime covered every surface. Kyle removed a stack of bills from a rickety wooden chair while the brothers cleaned off two others. Kyle wondered about the stability of the furniture. Everything—table, couch, even the dresser in the living room—looked like yard sale or thrift shop odds and ends. Scratched and nicked surfaces, torn fabric.

"Let me see that map," Kyle said.

Cole went to the dresser and removed the top drawer. He set it on the couch and then reached into the slot on the dresser up under the frame. He must have released a catch, because the top of the dresser—thicker than one might expect—popped up. He lifted a panel on hidden hinges to reveal an empty compartment. Empty, save for the map he withdrew.

"Nice hiding place," Kyle commented.

"We use it for all the important secrets," Cole said.

He cleared the table of dirty dishes and laid out the map. A little over a foot square, the hide had thinned in places, but the symbols and markings were still legible. Kyle traced the various lines with an index finger.

"Well, this obviously shows a body of water." He indicated wavy lines near the map's center, then pointed at upside down 'V' markings. "I'm thinking this must mean some hills or bluffs."

On the right side, the water symbols continued, but were accompanied by others in the form of circles either complete or half-formed.

"I don't know." Kyle rubbed the stubble on his face. He hadn't shaved that morning, preferring a day or two's growth. "You didn't think to search the rest of the old Indian's trailer? Maybe he had some other reference on how all of this is to be deciphered."

"Well," Bubba drawled. "We were kind of scared last night when we were chased by that creature."

"What creature?"

"Don't know. We tried to break into the trailer, but something flew out of the air and started pecking at us. My head still hurts."

Cole took up the story. "We were okay to go back in the daylight to get the map but didn't want to stay around too long, you know, in case *it* came back."

Probably a harmless bat, Kyle thought. "Well, we can't figure out this map by looking at it. If this is supposed to lead to a treasure, I don't know where to begin."

"That's what me and Cole were doing today," Bubba said. "Trying to see if we could find something. We started out by going to the Cordova tower."

"But bees attacked us," Cole said.

"I still have some stringer marks on me.'

"The word is stinger," Cole said. "Stringer is what you use for a whole bunch of fish. A string of fish."

"Well, there was a whole bunch of bees. That's makes it a stringer, so I got stringer marks."

"Never mind," Kyle barked. "What did you find at the lookout tower?"

"Well, like I said, bees attacked us and well, we forgot," Cole said. "We didn't get a chance to see anything."

"Instead, we drove around," Bubba said.

"Where?" Kyle asked.

"All over. The whole lake. We figured the map shows this area, right? Otherwise, why would the Indian have it?"

"That makes sense," Kyle said.

"Well, we drove all over, but didn't see nothing."

"What were you looking for?"

Bubba shrugged. Cole said, "We thought we'd recognize some of these markings, maybe carved into trees or something."

Kyle shook his head, exasperated again. These idiots wouldn't recognize shoes on their own feet, let alone old map symbols.

"Look, guys," he said. "Let's sleep on this and try again tomorrow. Maybe I'll have some idea where to start."

Cole and Bubba glanced at each other.

"What?" Kyle asked.

"Well, the thing is...," Bubba began.

"So, like, we got some money for saving a kid earlier," Cole said. "You know, from the bees."

Kyle didn't know but waited for the explanation.

"We used most of it to fix the steering in the truck and buy groceries and chemicals," Cole said.

"We're a little short on gas money because we used almost the whole tank driving around," Bubba said.

"We thought we'd come back here tonight and cook up some more meth to sell."

Once again, murderous thoughts crossed Kyle's mind. Just one bullet each would end this stupidity. The average IQ in the county would jump several points. Instead, he reached for his wallet and offered a twenty he'd skimmed from the Woo Hardware till.

"Here. This should be enough to buy some gas."

He hated using his own money—stolen yes, but still his in the end—to finance these jokers, but they were useful in their own way. Kyle still needed them. At least until this treasure could be found. Then... well, two bullets.

He stood. "All right, I'm outta here. You two do what you have to do to get some cash, and we'll talk in the morning. I think I'll head into town, get a couple drinks, maybe find myself a woman."

He'd have to keep an eye out for the man in black clothes but thought going to the bar would be worth the risk.

"A woman?" Cole said. "What for?"

"You ain't planning on bringing in someone else, are you?" Bubba whined. "We're partners."

Kyle stared at them in disbelief. "No, a woman. For the night."

The brothers showed blank expressions. Kyle waved in dismissal and left them to their ignorance.

Chapter 22

The storm hit not long after Kyle left. Already keyed up about the treasure hunt the next day, Bubba & Cole became agitated with the thunder and lightning. It reminded the brothers of the previous night's storm and the horrific experience with the flying monster that had attacked them at the Indian's trailer. Before mixing a batch of meth, they decided to ease their nerves with a joint each.

"Only one," Cole insisted. "We can't be careless."

"I know," Bubba said.

"You almost ruined it the last time," Cole said. "'Bout got us killed."

"*You* almost got us killed," Bubba countered. "You asked me to pass you the sody-pop."

"You gave me the bottle with the ingredients for our batch. I told you to take off the Mountain Dew label, so you knew which bottle was which. If I hadn't seen what was in the bottle you gave me, I would have unscrewed the cap before everything had settled."

Bubba pointed at him. "See? You admit *you* almost killed us."

"I'll kill you right now if you don't shut up."

They settled back onto the couch, each working on handmade joints. With every inhalation, they held a contest to see who could hold the smoke in longer.

Sometime later, Bubba leaned over, trying to focus on the numbers on the digital clock resting on the lamp table.

"What time is it?" Cole asked.

"I think it's oh-forty o'clock."

"That doesn't sound right," Cole said.

Bubba leaned over again. "You're right. It's oh-four four o'clock."

Cole heaved himself off the couch, almost tripped over his brother's feet, and bent over to look at the clock. "Wrong again. It's 8:45. Come on, let's go make another batch. Maybe we can go into town and sell a few hits."

Cole banged open the trailer door, stepped to the ground, and splattered mud and water walking across the sodden yard to the barn.

"Speaking of hits." Bubba rolled and fired up another joint. He then followed Cole, protecting the joint from the drizzling rain.

In the barn, he took one more quick hit from the joint, set it on the counter, then handed Cole the ingredients. Cole poured the combination into a two-liter plastic soda bottle, screwed on the cap, and gave the bottle a series of vicious shakes.

Long ago, the brothers had decided buying a bunch of tubing, beakers, and other apparatus was going to be expensive. By going on the Internet on one of the town library's computers, they discovered the much easier 'shake and bake' method of making meth. All of the ingredients could be bought at the grocery store and Woo Hardware. With trial and a lot of errors, they were able to knock out several batches in a couple hours, especially if they used multiple pop bottles. Bubba had commented on how the whole operation was streamlined. Cole tried to correct him by saying the term was assembly line, like how cars were produced.

"First, the frame moves down the line," Cole said. "Then the engine is put in, then the tires, the fenders and doors, and so on. Assembly line."

"But it looks like stuff floating down a stream. It's a streamline," Bubba said.

Waiting for the mixture in the bottles to settle, the brothers relaxed in a couple chairs, Cole with a box of chips, Bubba with a plastic tray of chocolate chip cookies. They often discussed the reason they became so hungry for salt and sugary treats after smoking pot but never came up with a satisfying answer.

Cole slouched in his chair and munched a chip. He wondered where they could go to sell the batches, especially on a rainy night. The Swamp Fox was out. Spike had permanently banned them, threatening if he ever saw them again, he'd 'shove his fist down their throats and rip out their livers.' Maybe they'd try that new place on the north side of town. Heck, they could even head to Oskaloosa... no, they didn't have enough gas... wait, Kyle had given them money.

Cole shook his head to clear his thoughts. A faint red glow on the counter caught his attention. He squinted but couldn't identify the source. "What is that red light on the counter?"

"What?" Bubba asked. "Where?"

"Right near the bottom of the end pop bottle."

Bubba leaned forward and also squinted. "I think it's my joint. I laid it down when you gave me the Sudafed."

When the plastic bottle tilted a few degrees toward the joint, Cole's eyes widened, and his heart lurched into fourth gear. He grabbed Bubba's arm. "You dumb turd. It's melting the plastic. We gotta get out of here!"

The jolt of impending danger overrode the high and spurred them out the door. They made ten yards when the barn's side wall exploded outward. The brothers stumbled and fell face-first into the muck. Seconds later, another explosion disintegrated more of the barn.

"Head for the truck," Cole yelled.

Flying debris fell all around them. One burning chunk of wood skewered the roof of the trailer. Bubba screamed and ran for the door.

"What are you doing?" Cole shouted.

Bubba disappeared inside. Cole watched flames engulf his bedroom. His brother appeared in the doorway, something clutched in his hand. He leapt off the steps and rolled into a series of flailing somersaults. Then he stood and ran for the truc. Cole hurried to jump into the driver's seat.

As the truck sped down the muddy lane, fire consuming the barn and the trailer, Cole gave his brother a bittersweet look. Bubba had destroyed their home but had saved the treasure map.

Chapter 23

Spike's band kept the customers entertained at the Swamp Fox, but the place was pretty quiet for a Friday night. About ten couples, and as many unattached folks, relaxed at tables, sat at the bar, or took turns on the dance floor. The music wasn't so loud that conversations couldn't be shared. Spike had mentioned once that he didn't like to turn up the volume too much, because it distorted the singers' voices. The band played a mixture of upbeat country with some of the more popular George Strait and Willie Nelson songs. Every now and then they'd soften up for some slow dances.

Kathryn thought she and Justin ought to be here enjoying the music and swirling around the dance floor. Ever since yesterday, after the city council meeting and the trip out to the place where her casino was to be built, Justin had been acting strange. Actually, as she thought more about their relationship, he'd been out of sorts for a couple months. He'd been pulling back from her. Their times together were still enjoyable, but she'd noticed a... distancing.

Then he ignored her calls all that day and the argument at the school pretty much had infuriated her. She'd stopped in at the Swamp Fox, hoping to see him, talk over things, make a reconciliation. When she'd earlier asked Spike if Justin had been in, he shrugged, said he'd heard Justin had been at the hospital most of the day consoling Wildcrow's granddaughter. Apparently, the old guy had been assaulted. Spike mentioned seeing Justin and the granddaughter driving out of town in the direction of Justin's house. That made Kathryn livid.

"That's why he isn't answering my calls, I'll bet a dollar," she'd said. "What else do you know about her, Spike?"

"Not a lot. She's some kind of animal doctor in Ames. Came here because Wildcrow was talking crazy, and Sheriff Lockridge called her in to settle him down."

Sounded to Kathryn like Justin had become more interested in the Indian's granddaughter than in her. "I should just show him a thing or two," Kathryn muttered now.

"Hi, doll. Looking for some entertainment?"

Kathryn eyed the man who stood next to the bar two seats away. Kyle. She knew he was a recent hire at the hardware store. Kathryn had talked to him a few times when she needed some home supplies. Even though she knew where all the items were located, she let him show her the light bulbs, electrical tape, and graciously an economy-sized bottle of cleaner from a top shelf. While he had been attentive and she had felt a little spark of attraction each time she'd been in the store, she still considered herself Justin's girl.

However, with Justin's recent attitude and newly formed interest in another woman, Kyle's invitation sounded... well, more inviting. She smiled and took in his lean physique. His biceps, muscular, but not bulging under the smooth blue polyester blend shirt. He filled out the snug blue jeans well. Black hair styled with a hint of gel. A bit of James Dean boyishness with a sexy curl to his smile.

What the hell, she thought. She could play the game. "Might be, handsome. What you got in mind?"

He stood straighter, sipped from his glass of amber liquid, his eyes never leaving hers. "How about a dance and a couple drinks. See where that takes us."

She took a sip from her wine glass, also keeping his stare. Then she stood and led him to the tiny space they called a dance floor. She put her arms on his shoulder and let her hips sway to the music. "Lead on." She noticed his eyes had moved down her body. A frisson of anticipation shivered through her.

An hour and a half later, after five drinks and several dances, they left the bar, her arm looped around his. The alcohol and the music had loosened her inhibitions enough that thoughts of Justin vanished when Kyle suggested a 'nightcap' at his apartment three blocks away.

Yeah, she could play the game just fine.

Chapter 24

Grace had gone to bed early. She expected her anxiety over Grandfather's condition would keep her awake for hours. Mental exhaustion over the last couple days, though, had drained her and she drifted off minutes after her head rested on the pillow.

The sound of thunder awakened her from a deep sleep. An array of lightning flashes lit up the sky. Marion County seemed to attract overnight thunderstorms, she thought, and wondered what about small towns and country weather that made everything so miserable. At least this time she was in a lovely room at the Holiday Inn Express at Bos Landen instead of in Grandfather's trailer.

She woke to the sound of her dog barking. Chow sat at the end of the bed looking out the window. Grace rubbed her eyes and noticed digital lights on the clock had gone dark. She clicked the buttons to set the time. Nothing happened. Apparently, the power was out. For the second night in a row. She sat up and looked at Chow. He barked a few times then stood up with his attention locked on something.

"Chow. Shh," she said. "We're in a hotel. Keep it down." Chow jumped from the bed and leaped up in the chair by the window. What was he doing? She pulled off the covers and walked over to the switch for the overhead light. Nothing. No power, just like the previous night in Grandfather's Airstream. She tried it again. Still nothing. She sighed and leaned against the wall.

Chow kept barking. "Chow, what are you barking at?" She joined him at the window and placed a reassuring hand on his head. Jagged stripes of lighting danced among the clouds. Rain created a white noise effect and pattered against the window. The wind moaned and whined around the hotel. A crash of thunder shook the room startling Grace. "That scared me." She closed her eyes.

Chow barked again. "Chow, stop it." She looked out the window again and realized he reacted every time the lightning flashed. "You silly dog, it's just lightning. Quiet down."

Grace dressed in jeans and a T-shirt, grabbed the key card to her room, unlocked the door, and stepped out into the hall. "I'll be back. Behave yourself."

Out of the room, she waited until the door secured shut behind her. The hall lights had gone out and only the emergency lights gave faint illumination. A few other guests had ventured out to talk over the situation. She smiled as she passed them and descended the stairs to see what was going on.

Shadows gave a surreal view. She thought she saw a large form in front of her. Before she could take another step, the lights blazed to life. Grace gripped the rail tighter, eyes shut against the sudden bright. "Oh crap."

Seconds later, she blinked her eyes open and saw a man standing in front of her wearing a black suit. She gasped and dropped her key card.

"Sorry didn't mean to scare you, ma'am." He picked up the keycard and handed it to her. Water dripped from his sandy hair and streamed down his cheeks. His black shirt was matted to his chest and stomach.

"That's all right," Grace said. "I was coming down to see if the clerk knew anything about the storm and the power outage. However, for the moment, I see we're okay."

"Yes," the man replied. He didn't attempt to move around her but remained a few steps below her.

"My dog doesn't like the storm," Grace said. "Maybe the clerk knows how long this will last."

"I estimate another twenty minutes." The man cocked his head. "I believe I hear your dog now. Three barks, a silence, three more barks, a silence. Nice pattern."

"We're both a bit unnerved by the weather. Sorry if his barking is annoying you."

"It's no problem," he said. "Reminds me of my dogs at home, but you should try to calm him."

Counting his steps, the man hurried past her, but as she looked over her shoulder, he glanced over his to stare at her. An internal alarm sounded. She couldn't identify the feeling, but there was something off about him. Why would he be wearing a black suit so late at night?

The lobby was deserted and the check-in desk unoccupied. However, the clerk stepped from a back doorway as she approached the counter. This time both were startled.

"I'm sorry, I'm sorry. I didn't mean to scare you," Grace said with both hands up in front of her.

"It's okay. Can I help you with something?" the clerk asked. The lights flickered again.

Grace looked back at the woman and smiled. "Just wondering about the storm.

"Pretty bad tonight. I've checked the breakers, and everything looks alright. Don't know why the power's out."

"Thanks," Grace said.

Halfway up the stairs to her room, she stopped, hearing Chow's bark in his pattern of three barks, then a silence. She'd never noticed that before.

She turned the corner and got to her room. She swiped the card key through the slot seeing a green light. She opened the door and saw Chow take a few steps back. "Stop barking." She closed the door behind her. "You're going to bother the other guests."

She flipped the switch on and off and felt relieved the lights were working again. She undressed and readjusted the blankets. Chow jumped up beside her and curled up next to her.

For the briefest of moments, she imagined Justin... Digger, here with her.

"Oh, for heaven's sake," she chided herself. Chow glanced up at her. "Never mind, Chow, I'm having silly girl notions."

Still, Digger had been a gentleman all day. Driving her to the hospital, offering to care for Chow, taking her to dinner. No immature suggestion about kisses in the moonlight. Not even an attempt to hold her hand or drape an arm over her shoulders.

Even when she returned to Grandfather's room after dinner, she'd felt calmer, more at peace. The talk with Digger during dinner helped ease her fears.

However, she didn't want to feel she needed him here to comfort her through a thunderstorm. She was her own woman, not some Victorian damsel in distress.

Still... He flickered through her thoughts as she nestled in next to Chow.

Now, maybe she could get some sleep.

Chapter 25
Saturday

Saturday morning, Digger had driven to Grace's hotel, but she had already left. Disappointed she hadn't called, he drove to the hospital and parked next to her Escape. Not wanting to enter the hospital right away, he stood in the parking lot with the morning's first cigar. He took a long puff and twirled it between his fingers. On most days, he didn't enjoy his first cigar until the afternoon, but that day, it seemed right. He had made a good start in his relationship with Grace and felt confident with more time, he might get that kiss he had longed for back on campus. He couldn't push too fast, but a little nudge might make for pleasurable results.

A few lingering clouds after the previous night's rain skittered overhead in the brisk morning breeze. The forecast on KNIA had promised temps in the fifties with intermittent clouds. Digger had opted for blue jeans and a heavy sweatshirt, no jacket.

He also had chosen a Macanudo Court for his first morning cigar. Under five inches long, it had a mild-bodied flavor and, best of all, he could finish it in under half an hour. He wasn't sure what he'd be doing for the rest of the day, so he'd opted for a selection of shorter cigars for his pocket tin including one of his favorites, the Romeo y Julieta Petite Bully. When he'd first seen the cigar in the smoke shop, he'd been amused at its name. It sounded like a combination of Shakespeare and Teddy Roosevelt. He liked that and though it was a bit more expensive than some of the other cigars, he found it a worthwhile and enjoyable purchase.

After he disposed of the Mac's stub in the Gremlin's ashtray, he entered the hospital and followed the path to Wildcrow's room. Before he rounded the last corner, he heard a loud commotion, chanting, and cursing. He sprinted down the hall and into the hospital room to find Grace and a nurse trying to hold Wildcrow down on the bed. The old chief thrashed and bucked like a rodeo bronc, wailing away in his native language.

"What's going on?" Digger yelled. "It sounds like an entire Indian tribe preparing for war."

As if Digger's words had flipped a switch, Wildcrow relaxed and went silent.

"Mr. Wildcrow," the nurse admonished. "You must stay calm."

"Bah!" Wildcrow uttered and waved her away.

"Grandfather, stop this nonsense. Speak English," Grace demanded.

Instead of answering, Wildcrow met Digger's eyes, smiled, bleated another "Bah!" before he hoisted himself to sit against the headboard. He looked at Digger. "Ah, Digger, glad to see you this morning."

Grace shook her head. "Grandfather, can't you just—"

"You must excuse my granddaughter," Wildcrow said. "She isn't interested in her heritage, but that must change. I wanted to get her attention."

"You mean this whole episode was faked?" Grace asked.

The nurse huffed. "Mr. Wildcrow—"

"Oh, go away," Wildcrow told the nurse. "I'm perfectly fine. Leave me alone so I can talk to my friend and my obstinate granddaughter."

"You cannot cause a ruckus," the nurse said.

Wildcrow waved her off again. "I told you. I'm fine. Go away."

"It'll be all right," Digger assured her.

The nurse pursed her lips, glared at Grace and Digger. "Don't let him start up again."

"I promise," Digger said.

The nurse, with a last exasperated look at Wildcrow, left.

Wildcrow chuckled and looked at Digger. "I imagine the scornful look and folded arms you are receiving means my granddaughter can't take a joke either."

A blush reddened Grace's tan cheeks. "You shouldn't cause a scene like that."

"Forget that," Wildcrow said. "Now that Digger is here, I can tell you all that I've seen in the last few days and how you two need to be a part of it."

"Grandfather—"

"Sit and listen," Wildcrow commanded.

Digger laid a gentle hand on Grace's arm and said in a low voice, "Come on, Grace. It won't hurt to hear him out. Like I mentioned, I've been concerned about him for a couple months. Let's hear his story. You said to me yesterday that you promised to listen to him."

Grace narrowed her eyes in suspicion but pulled over a chair. Digger set another one beside hers.

"I have been having visions for a couple months," Wildcrow began. "Many vague images but some as if a scene were being played out in front of me. I knew they were important."

"Visions of what?" Digger asked.

"I've seen my people from long ago, how they lived and prospered. How they warred with other tribes and how they passed their heritage down through the generations."

"Grandfather—

"Be silent," Wildcrow interrupted. "I didn't know the meaning of these visions at first."

"Dreams," Grace said. "Nothing but dreams."

"No!"

Again, Digger touched Grace's arm. "Hear him out."

"No dreams," Wildcrow continued. "These were visions sent by the Great Spirit who watches over us. They were meant for me... and you, Gray Swan." He looked at Digger. "Maybe for you, too. Let me explain."

Wildcrow described his visions, detailed the scene through the hawk's eyes, the gathering at the Peace Tree, the prediction of Chief Saunuk of the white man's domination, and how they needed to preserve their heritage through the journey to hide a sacred bundle. Said bundle was to be found after other journeys of self-discovery by one who understood and also by one who had forgotten the old ways. They were to use the map that, unfortunately, had been stolen the previous morning.

He pointed to Grace and Digger. "We have been chosen to use this map and find the bundle. You, Gray Swan, are the one who has forgotten and continues to reject the old ways."

"Grandfather—"

Wildcrow reached for Digger's wrist. "I need your assistance. I also must take this journey."

"No, Grandfather," Grace said. "You've been injured. What you need is rest. I want you to stop this silly talk about visions and maps and relax."

"But—"

"No, you listen to me, now. I've made arrangements for you to come to Ames. I've found a nice room at a residential center where you can stay. I'll be nearby and can visit you whenever I can."

"Bah!"

"Listen to me, Grandfather. You're not a kid anymore. I can see you are—"

"No more talk about that." Grace opened her mouth to say something more, but Wildcrow asked, "Could you get me some water, please?"

When Grace left to request a pitcher of water, Digger caught Wildcrow's stare. The old man gripped his wrist tighter and whispered, "You know what I say is true."

"I believe you believe it's true," Digger said.

"You believe, too."

Maybe it was the intensity of the old man's words, the fierce grip on his wrist, a mystical solemnity in the air, or a combination of all three, but Digger felt a vibrant energy flow through him at that moment. Yes, he did believe. He knew Wildcrow had seen everything he'd related. Somehow, he had traveled into the past and witnessed an actual scene with Chief Saunuk and the revered bundle.

"Yes," Digger whispered.

"Talk to her," Wildcrow said. "Make her believe. Make them all believe. You must do this son, or all may be lost."

Digger didn't quite understand what the 'all' was Wildcrow thought would be lost but nodded. At that moment, Grace returned with the water. Wildcrow released Digger's wrist and sank down into the pillows. Grace poured water into a cup, inserted a straw and offered it to Wildcrow.

"Thank you," Wildcrow said after he drank.

While Grace returned the cup to the counter, Digger saw Wildcrow wink at him and knew the Indian feigned exhaustion. Digger stood. "Grace, why don't we let him rest, like you said? We can talk to him later."

"All right," Grace agreed. "But no more yelling those old Fox and Sac words."

"I promise," Wildcrow mumbled.

"Did you have breakfast?" Digger asked.

"Yes," Grace said.

"Well, I haven't. Why don't we grab some coffee and pastries in the cafeteria?"

After they'd purchased pastries and coffee and sat at the table, Digger decided not to waste time.

"Grace." Digger's thoughts formulated a plan. "I know what we're going to do. You do, too."

"What, Justin?" Grace's face drew into a tired frown.

"We're going to go looking for that treasure or bundle your grandfather talked about. He can't, but we can."

"What? I can't leave him. You're getting as nuts as he is. I'm sorry. I didn't mean that the way it sounded."

"Well, maybe he is nuts. I don't know. If he is, I just might be, too. I think we ought to do this. We *should* do this, if only for his peace of mind."

"Go then," Grace said. "Leave me out of it. I'll take him back to Ames and everything will work out just fine."

"Come on, don't be like that. We should do this together."

"Why? Give me one good reason."

"I'll give you three," Digger said. "First, because he's your grandfather. He loves you and doesn't want you to reject the heritage of his people. Whether you want to admit it, it's your heritage, too. Besides, what else are you going to do today? Sit around in a boring old hospital?"

He sipped coffee and continued, "Wildcrow got a lot of people excited the day before yesterday about a treasure. I think those people are reading too much into his words, but what if something really is out there like he saw in his visions? I don't know what type of treasure it might be, but we have a better shot at finding it. Come on, Grace, let's go have an adventure. It could even be fun."

Grace sighed. "What's the second reason?"

Digger shrugged and reached across the table and took Grace's hand. "Well, I get to hang out with a good-looking woman. Third, you get to see a decent looking amateur archaeologist in action."

Grace smirked. "Smooth one, Romeo."

"Romeo was thirteen," Digger said. "We're a lot older." He paused, then continued. "We're even a little older than we were at the university."

"You're still an incorrigible flirt," she said.

"You bring out the hopeless romantic in me."

"Don't push it, buddy." She took back her hand, but Digger caught the smile in her words. She sighed again. "Let's get back to the point. Even if I do agree, how would we know where to look? The map is gone, remember?"

"True, but I thought about it last night after I dropped you and Chow off to get your car. If it's the same one he's been talking about, I remember seeing an image of that map some years ago in a history book that I brought to class—I checked through some yesterday but didn't find anything—or from a book in the library. Actually, now that I think more about that map, I've seen it in one of the books in the historical museum in Pleasantville."

"You remember things like that? From years ago?" Grace said.

Digger smiled. "I may not look like much, Grace, but I can do many things besides drive a green Gremlin." He dug his cell phone out of his front pocket and showed it to her. "We'll take a picture of it just like you said the Smiths did at the Meat Market. We'll use that and the things Wildcrow told us from his visions. He talked about the Peace Tree. That's probably the starting point. We'll just follow the clues."

Grace frowned. "I don't know what to think. Sometimes Grandfather seems to know what is real and sometimes he...."

"It's the right thing to do, Grace."

She shook her head. "No, let's forget about it."

"Why?"

"It's a crazy idea." she said. "You're partly to blame for the foolishness my grandfather is involved in now. Don't think I didn't know you two were talking while I was getting his water."

"What are you talking about?" Digger replied. "Your grandfather has a strong mind. Stop looking for reasons not to go."

"You encourage him."

Digger sipped coffee. "He doesn't need my encouragement, Grace. He's convinced that he has some mission to fulfill. True, he's talked to me a bit about the historic precedents, broken treaties, white man's lies, but he is right, Grace. Your people were taken advantage of. Looking at the records in my history studies, I see that Wildcrow may be right in who ought to own the land."

"Really, Justin?"

"I'm not saying the government should give the land back to him or any of the Indians still in the area. We're talking about whole communities and farms. What I am saying is that if we find something buried out there, maybe we can convince enough people to change their attitude toward the Native Americans. At least enough to put a stop to this ridiculous casino."

Digger's cell phone trilled the ring tone he'd designated for Kathryn. He looked at the name on the screen just to confirm and placed the device back in his pocket without answering the call.

Grace arched her eyebrows. "That your girlfriend?"

The phone rang again. Digger rushed his hand into his pocket to stop the song from playing. This time he shut off the ringer. His face flushed with a boyish smile. He leaned across the table to whisper, "I'm sorry—"

Grace interrupted him, "Call her back if you want. This can wait."

"No, Grace. We need to make some plans."

He noticed the few people scattered around the cafeteria had gone quiet. Most kept glancing his way, trying to eavesdrop. Apparently, Grace also had noticed the attention.

"All right," she said in a lower voice. "We can go look for this map in a book if you want, but I won't play this silly game for too long."

"Give me the day," Digger said.

They stood, and Grace said, "Are you sure you don't want to answer her calls?"

"I will, later." He didn't think he would.

Digger deposited their coffee cups on the counter with the other dirty dishes. As they approached Wildcrow's room, Sheriff Lockridge exited.

"Morning," the sheriff said. "I was hoping to get some more details about what happened with your grandfather yesterday."

"What have you found out?" Digger asked.

"Well, now, I don't like to go passing information about an ongoing case, but if you asked him, he'd probably tell you anyway. He identified the Smith brothers."

"Just who are they?" Grace asked.

"Couple of local characters," Lockridge said.

"Couple of local losers," Digger muttered. "Nothing but trouble. Are you heading out to arrest them?"

Lockridge scratched the back of his neck. "Well, that's been a problem."

"Why?"

"We're taking this seriously, but…well, Wildcrow admitted they didn't attack him. He tripped and fell, which is how he became injured. Yes, the Smiths broke into his place and left him lying there, but we'd have a hard time getting them for anything more than that." His expression turned contrite. "We sent an officer out to their home a few times, but they weren't there. However, they must have come back later in the evening."

"Why is that?" Digger asked.

"The fire department was called out there last night. Early report is that it appears the barn exploded."

"What?" Grace said.

"Evidence points to a, uh, some type of chemical explosion."

"Chemical explosion?" Digger shook his head. "Sheriff, you know as well as I do, they were cooking up meth. Why you or the local police haven't arrested those two louses before is beyond me."

"All right, don't jump on my back. I've had plenty of calls this morning about it, including the guy out at Nearwood Winery."

"Winery?" Grace asked.

"Yeah, man and his wife have the property east of the Smiths' land. He called this morning saying a piece of debris from the explosion—which woke up neighbors for miles around, by the way—landed near a collection of vats he uses to ferment the wine. Said it melted two and ruined four more before he could put out the fire."

"Too bad." Digger turned to Grace. "They make some good wine. I've bought a few bottles."

"Anyway, the fire also destroyed the Smiths' double-wide," Lockridge said. "They must have hightailed it out of there once the barn went up. We haven't seen any sign of them."

"Our tax dollars at work," Digger said.

Lockridge smiled. "Don't be a smart aleck, son. I'll be hearing about it at the next city council and county board meetings. You need to worry about your grandfather. I hope you're planning on staying with him today."

"Actually, Sheriff," Digger said. "We were thinking about doing a little, um, exploring."

Lockridge narrowed his eyes. "Don't tell me you've gone off the deep end and gonna be out looking for treasure."

Digger shrugged. "We might even find the Smiths while we're at it."

Lockridge held up a hand. "Hold it. This is no job for amateurs. Leave sleuthing to the professionals. I had enough trouble with people digging up the countryside yesterday. I'll have more problems today, and I don't need you two out there adding to them."

He turned to go, then stopped and turned back. He glanced at Grace and Digger saw the glint of mischief in his eyes. "By the way, Digger, how is my sweet little cousin, Kathryn, doing these days? You two have been together for what... four years now? Ain't it about time you two got married?"

Digger gave him a blank stare. Sheriff Lockridge shrugged, nodded at Grace, and walked down the hall, saying good morning to everyone he passed. When he disappeared around the corner, Digger and Grace entered Wildcrow's room. The old chief was sitting up.

"Well?" Wildcrow asked.

Digger waited for Grace to answer. When she didn't, he said, "We'll drive over to the museum in Pleasantville. I remember a picture of the map in one of their books. We'll use my phone like the Smiths did on Thursday. Then, we'll... see what we can find."

"I knew you'd come through, son. Sit down and let me give you some help. I'll tell you what signs to look for."

They spent the next fifteen minutes discussing what Wildcrow had interpreted from the map. Near the end, he advised, "Keep a watch for the red-tailed hawk. He will be both guide and protector."

"A hawk?" Grace asked. "You're telling us to look for a wild bird? Do you know how many hawks live in Iowa?"

Wildcrow nodded. "Tell me, granddaughter, where do you usually see hawks?"

Grace shrugged. "I don't know."

"Signposts," Digger said. "Fence posts. Sometimes circling above the trees. I see them when I'm out hiking or walking."

"Correct," Wildcrow said. "I believe they show themselves for a reason."

"What reason," Grace said, and Digger heard the frustration growing in her voice. She looked tired of the lengthy conversation.

"They are waiting. Waiting for man to understand their wisdom, to answer their calling."

"But how can that be? I mean…" Grace said.

"Do not scoff, child. I have befriended many hawks throughout the years. Let me tell you a story. As a young lad of thirteen, I had a friend. Her name was White Dove. We used to explore the fields and woods together. She was only ten, but her father had taught her about being in harmony with nature and animals. How every animal, from the smallest ant to the largest moose, has their purpose, and if one has patience and time, one can befriend almost any of them. One has to be careful of Trickster Snake, though."

Digger smiled at Grace. "Serpents have been getting the bad rap since Adam and Eve."

Wildcrow continued, "White Dove had that gift. She could walk up to the biggest buck without fear and feed it berries from her hand. You don't know what an experience it was to watch her. Anyway, the incident I remember best was the day we were walking through a field of prairie grass and this red-tailed hawk came soaring out of the sky right at us. To me, it looked like a monster who was going to snatch White Dove up and carry her away. Instead, she told me to stop while she stepped forward, held out her arm, and the hawk landed as gentle as a butterfly."

"That's amazing," Digger said.

"Yes, well, I didn't know until later that she had befriended the hawk many months before. She did, however, teach me to connect to animals and, as I said, I have known many hawks. There is a red-tailed hawk that nests near my trailer at Elk Rock."

"What ever happened to White Dove?" Digger asked.

Wildcrow's face brightened in a huge smile, and he tapped a hand on Digger's knee. "I married her, my boy."

"Grandmother?"

"She never could charm those snakes, though." Wildcrow laughed.

"That reminds me of a story about Glady's Black," Digger said.

"Who?" Grace asked

"Ornithologist who lived in Pleasantville. For almost twenty years, she wrote a weekly newspaper column about birds. Did a lot of conservation work for Red Rock. She has a plaque at the Horn's Ferry bridge."

"Tell us the story, my boy," Wildcrow said. "I think I know which one you mean."

"Gladys died in 1998. A year later the community hosted an anniversary for the creation of Lake Red Rock. They invited some local members of the Sac, Fox, and Meskwaki tribes to join. One of the Indians was asked to bless the lake. The man talked about nature and how he wished humans could learn to be more connected to nature as the animals were. Just as he was wrapping up, a strange bird flew overhead squawking like crazy."

"What do you mean strange?" Grace asked.

"Some say it was a peregrine falcon, but they aren't known in this area," Digger said. "Anyway, the superstitious rumor was that it was the spirit of Gladys Black that came back to give her approval."

"No superstition, my boy. I was there. I know better." Wildcrow sighed and whipped away the bed covers. "You know, I think I'm feeling better. I'll go with you. Let me grab my clothes."

"Sorry, Grandfather," Grace said. "Dr. Browning has to release you from the hospital first."

"The day is growing long. We're running out of time! Tell that doctor to hop to it," Wildcrow said.

"I'll see if I can find him before we go," Digger said. "Have him stop by to check on you."

Wildcrow huffed but winked at Digger again when Grace wasn't looking. As Digger followed Grace out of the room, Wildcrow beckoned him back. At his bedside, the old man brought one hand out from under the blanket. He grasped Digger's wrist and presented the object he held. "When the time comes, give this to her."

Digger stared at what Wildcrow had placed in his hand. "I don't understand. When?"

"Don't worry; you'll know when the time comes. She will understand."

"All right."

"Don't let anything happen to my granddaughter. Promise me?"

"I promise," Digger said, but Wildcrow wasn't satisfied. He stared until Digger reaffirmed, "Yes, sir. I will take good care of her."

***

Wildcrow watched Digger and Grace from his window. He saw them drive out of the parking lot in Digger's Gremlin. He waited another five minutes until Doctor Browning visited, pretended to be suffering again from his head wound, and told him he felt like he could sleep some more. No pain, he said, just very tired. Browning checked off boxes on the chart, said he'd stop by again in a few hours, then left.

Wildcrow counted off two minutes, then he pulled out the IV lines, went to the closet, retrieved, and donned his clothes. He peeked into the hall and saw no one. Making no sound, he hurried toward the rear of the hospital. He managed to get out a door and start across the side lawn when a squawk above him caught his attention. He shaded his eyes, looked up, and saw the red-tailed hawk floating on a thermal drift. He froze as a wave of dizziness rippled through him. He reached for a nearby tree.

Wildcrow sank to the ground, his body motionless, but his spirit once again ventured out into the ether, on another trip into the past.

***

1790

After the adornment ceremony and Chief Saunuk's retinue had departed, Running Eagle, with heritage bundle in hand, prepared himself for the sacred task. He and his chief sat to discuss possible sites to leave markers for a descendant to follow. Many were rejected as unworthy or because of the length of travel time to the next.

With much debate, the decision was made to honor the land that had provided so much to the tribes. More specifically the rocks and the formations the Great Spirit chose to create of them. The stones that gave shelter against harsh winds, retained heat for the preparation of food and water for the newborn, and served as forever reminders of those who had departed.

Chief Saunuk pointed to the north bluff overlooking the river. "The hawk's beak, painted red, shall be the first. Prepare yourself this night. Begin just before dawn. Leave your first sign as the sun's first light strikes your face."

Together they called upon the Great Spirit for blessing, courage, and endurance. Saunuk then left to seek his own rest. The following day, for him, would be arduous, as he and his people prepared to depart the area.

Running Eagle, alone by the Peace Tree, closed his eyes, raised his arms to the heavens, and began the ancient chants and prayers, beseeching the Great Spirit for guidance, strength, and blessing.

The hawk, his sole companion, listened to the low drone of his voice. Its ever-moving head scanned the valley as a guardian protected a ward.

When true night blanketed the sky, Running Eagle rose, uttered a last prayer to the Maker and took the first step on the journey to the painted rocks.

***

Wildcrow awoke, stood, and took a deep breath as the cool breeze refreshed his senses. No one had witnessed his temporary slumber and as far as he knew, his disappearance from the hospital hadn't been discovered.

His heart hammered in anticipation. He hustled across the lawn. Digger and Grace had accepted the quest, but he was determined to lend whatever guidance possible.

Chapter 26

The cup of hot tea—one tablespoon of milk, one tablespoon of sugar—rested in the center of the round wooden table. White 3×5 index cards surrounded the cup, each in perfect alignment with the other, the cup, and the edge of the table. From above, the pattern resembled a strange mandala.

Other patrons of the Coffee Connection on the Square in Knoxville might have thought the man in the black suit seated at the corner table to be engaged in some sort of game. In one sense, they were correct.

FBI Special Agent Brandyn Antonaccio had never considered his mild case of Obsessive Compulsive Disorder to be a liability. Others, including his supervisor and coworkers, found the habit of straightening and counting objects annoying at times and often compared him to the television detective Monk.

Antonaccio, however, used his OCD as a mental exercise... or game. While laying out the cards around the cup, he'd let his mind collate the facts, observations, and speculations written on them. By the time the pattern was finished, with only two cards relocated, he also had a sketchy mental picture of the events of late around the Knoxville area. The jigsaw puzzle was missing some pieces but enough of the image existed to give him a satisfactory sense of order.

Around him, staff busied themselves with preparing coffee and food orders. Customers drank and chatted about the myriad topics small town residents often talked about. He heard bits of a discussion about the local high school football and the Central College basketball teams. One man pontificated about local politics to another in bib overalls who was mostly concerned about his latest visit with a "Doctor Obama" and "my damn prostrate." Two elderly women in the table next to him discussed the recent incident of sinkholes fearing one would pop up in the middle of the town square. An espresso machine hissed. Silverware clinked against cups. Antonaccio relegated everything to the background as he perused the note cards again.

He didn't worry about his surroundings. Upon entering, he'd taken in everything in one scan. The wall of windows looking out on Main Street and the stately courthouse. The chalkboard menus and coffee-themed artwork on the walls. The tight spacing of the wooden tables and chairs. Ceiling fans and the smell of bacon and melted cheese mixing with the aroma of imported coffee beans. When he entered, he perused the funeral cards of recently deceased citizens—something he'd never witnessed anywhere before. He flipped though the fliers advertising local "KACT" plays, farm auctions, and upcoming events at both the Peace Tree Brewing Company and the local winery. A knick-knack shelf held—what else?—knick-knacks for sale.

The people didn't concern him, either. They were local folk with a few out-of-town guests. Flannel, sweaters, jeans. A couple businessmen in shirts, ties, and slacks. No one gave him more than a glance when he had walked through the door.

He leaned back in his chair and recalled the previous days' events.

Upon his arrival in Knoxville, Antonaccio saw no reason to announce his presence to the city cops or the county sheriff's office. Not that he didn't like local authority, but in many instances, he found that word invariably leaked to the streets and his quarry could disappear before day's end.

The trail of Peter White, infamous Chicago gangbanger and general scumbag, had led him to this typical Midwestern town of Knoxville. Unlike the eponymous city in Tennessee, he found Iowa's Knoxville, much smaller, had a more laid-back, easy-going atmosphere. The people were friendly and not difficult to talk to. Many were farmers or small business owners. The popular topic was looking forward to next year with Sammy Somebody or Craig Whoever winning the sprint car series.

Instead of booking a room at one of the local motels, Antonaccio chose the Holiday Inn Express in the upper-class community of Bos Landen, adjacent to Pella, a dozen miles from Knoxville's town square. Pella was a unique city and saturated with Dutch influence. Windmills, architecture, and tulips all harkening back to the Old Country. Antonaccio found it almost overwhelming to take in so much at one time.

So, he concentrated on the case at hand and the evidence he'd gathered from poking around the edges of Knoxville society, chatting up the townsfolk. Who better to get a feel for the town, its inhabitants both long term, and more important, recent arrivals?

The bartender at the Swamp Fox—and he couldn't help but think with a nickname like Spike, the man should wear a studded dog collar—provided a couple of leads with some people who had stayed around after the sprint car races were over. He had given names of some Knoxville characters in the form of Bubba and Cole Smith. Brothers deemed relatively harmless with a limitless supply of stupidity but a potential for violence if pushed. Potheads who tended to smoke more of their product than they sold.

Antonaccio thought the Smiths important, because they'd be prime targets for Peter, who would exploit, then kill them with no second thought or remorse.

Someone bumped Antonaccio's chair as he walked by. The man mumbled an "Excuse me" in a Chinese accent and moved on. Taken out of the moment, the agent sipped more tea, counted the man's footsteps on the hardwood floor until they faded—seven—returned the cup to the table's center, and thought about Beau, his Beagle/Basset Hound mix back in Virginia. The dog had a knack for helping Antonaccio focus. It accepted a belly rub and a dog biscuit, but the comfort and relaxed aura it exuded helped him to stay within the 'zone' where puzzle pieces organized themselves. That happened only when Beau wasn't trying to hump Bella, the much larger and more sophisticated Lurcher. He made a mental note to later call and check in with the caretaker he hired to exercise and feed the dogs.

Antonaccio straightened a card containing notes about Hank Oliver. Fireman, manager of a hardware store called, of all things, Woo Hardware. Spike had mentioned Oliver had hired a new employee a couple months back. Antonaccio hadn't yet visited the store to see if the hardware man had seen White. Antonaccio didn't do things most people expected. He could wait and watch, identify him on the street, and follow White to his residence, approach him there, instead of risking innocents by confronting him in public. But he couldn't be sure Peter White was the new employee at the store. He could be working for any number of businesses and staying out of the public eye. He'd get lost in the crowd at some of the larger companies. If he was intelligent and still wanted to remain anonymous, he could have changed his appearance. Grown a beard or colored his hair or shaved it completely.

Patience. That was the key. Antonaccio suspected White would stay in town with the rumors of a treasure blowing around like a spring tornado. He figured given enough time, Peter would make himself visible.

Which brought up Justin Clay, otherwise known as Digger. Antonaccio shook his head in disbelief. An archaeologist nicknamed Digger Clay? Not too original, are you Mr. Clay?

High school teacher. Well-liked. Involved with county economic development director Kathryn VanSteele. This Digger fellow would be interested in treasure although Antonaccio doubted the man believed gold, silver, or precious stones actually existed, buried somewhere near Lake Red Rock. From the way they talked, other than Clay, many Knoxville residents had visions of riches keeping them awake at night.

Antonaccio didn't care whether the treasure, if there was one, turned out to be rare coins or twigs mixed with buffalo scat all wrapped up in deer hide. His concern lay with the capture of Peter White.

One by one, he collected the index cards and placed them into an inside jacket pocket. He sighed, finished his tea, wiped the cup with a napkin, disposed of the napkin, and returned the cup to the barista. Outside, he counted the cars parked on the near side of the street. Ten. A good number.

He sighed and made a decision. Digger and his 'treasure' would draw Peter like revenuers to a Virginia moonshiner. If Antonaccio stayed close to Digger, Peter would show sooner or later. If Digger and Grace stayed together, that meant the dog would be with them. Antonaccio had lied when he'd told Digger the previous day he, too owned a husky. It was a good cover story for his hand being inside the Gremlin, attaching the tracker under the dog's collar.

Chapter 27

Kyle flushed the toilet and before exiting the bathroom, stopped to check his image in the mirror. While women tended to be attracted to his face, he'd never liked it. Hated it at times. For as long as he could remember, it was always hard-edged. As a child moving into his teens and twenties, it had never filled out or softened. The abrupt angles and sharp features had worked to his advantage on the mean bullet-ridden streets of Chicago. People never knew his true feelings because his expression always conveyed a mixture of disgust, annoyance, malice. A twitch of a lip caused low level street dealers to shy away. The narrowing of the eyes upped the tension level in any room because someone risked losing status, the use of a limb, or in more than one instance, his life. He displayed this combination of emotions, including satisfaction, with an achieved goal.

Even when Kyle deigned to smile—and those times were rarer than killing a slacker subordinate or a woman who thought she was owed more than she deserved—people were unsure of his intentions. A shark's smile, some said. He rather enjoyed that phrase. A shark. He was the Great White or maybe a Hammerhead. No, a Tiger shark fit his lithe, lean body.

Kyle stood naked in front of the mirror and if he shifted viewpoints, he could see most of his body. He flexed muscles in his arms, pecs, abs, and tightened his thighs. Not massive or steroid enhanced but nonetheless developed. Hidden strength. He recalled the time when he was second in command and a third-tier lieutenant challenged him. The guy was 260, beefy, with linebacker shoulders, and stood four inches taller than Kyle. By tradition, the challenged chose the contest and Kyle opted not for knives, but an old-fashioned arm-wrestling match... with a twist. Victory was earned when the loser's hand was pushed far enough to be impaled on a nine-gauge, one and a quarter inch steel masonry nail driven up through the table.

The brute thought he had an easy win but didn't know Kyle used to lift concrete blocks for fun. Fifty curls per arm, twice a day, for months.

Kyle's iron cold eyes should have given the other man pause, but cockiness clouded good sense. Half a minute into the contest, fear moved across the guy's face like storm clouds over the sun. The closer Kyle pushed his hand toward the nail, the more sweat beaded and tremors increased in the man's neck and arm. An inch from severe injury, the man forfeited. After shaking off the stress of the match, he offered Kyle his hand in acknowledgment of the better man. Without a change of expression, Kyle accepted the gesture, clamped a painful grip, pulled the man close, and withdrew a four-inch blade from his back pocket. In a movement so swift no one saw the action until blood flowed, Kyle flicked open the knife and sliced up under the man's armpit through tendon and muscle to the joint. From then on, the man was barely able to hold a beer can, and never again made a challenge for superiority.

His thoughts turned to the woman in the next room. Was she ready for another round? They'd had a lot of fun the previous night after entering his apartment. Waking, she reaffirmed her insatiability.

Kyle had seen her around town a lot since his arrival, strutting her stuff like she owned the street. Little did he know then, beneath her brusque exterior lay—and he smiled at the irony—a tigress. The Tiger shark and the tigress. He thought the history teacher she'd been seeing must have been exhausted during class after nights with her.

Well, he decided, time to give it to her again.

He stepped from the bathroom into the room where his bed and a cheap three-drawer dresser were. The space couldn't be considered a regular 'bedroom' as it was contiguous—sans door—to a larger area with a threadbare couch, lamp stand, and television, the latter inset into a particleboard piece of furniture that could be loosely described as an entertainment center. The carpet was at least twenty years old. Stains from unknown origins formed Rorschach test blobs. In a quarter-sized patch just off the bed, it felt like a tuft of fibers had had glued dripped onto it. The strands had stiffened to the point of poking the bottom of Kyle's feet if he forgot to step over them.

The egg-shell white wall paint had yellow and black streaks due to either a previous tenant's smoking or candle burning. He'd hung no pictures or decorations after he rented the place, because he hadn't planned on staying but a few weeks, a month at the most. The hardware job, and the fact he'd seemingly dropped from authorities' radar, kept him around town. No, there wasn't much action in Knoxville other than a few bars to enjoy music on a weekend, and the lake, but inaction meant no one breathing down his neck or threatening violence. Now, with a potential treasure…well, he'd stick around long enough to find out the score.

He saw Kathryn, naked under the blanket, grimacing at her cell phone. When she noticed him, she put the phone aside, gave a sultry smile, and curled an index finger in a 'come here' gesture. "I just wanted to tell my jerk of an ex-boyfriend what went on here last night, but he isn't answering."

"Never mind him. Let's get—"

His own cell phone burbled and broke the moment. He snatched it off the dresser and swore again when he recognized the number.

He fingered the receive button. "What the hell do you want? I'm busy here."

"We're gonna need some help." Bubba's voice sounded strained, as if he'd just run two miles.

"What? You were supposed to call so we could meet up and look over the map."

Kyle had an instant regret talking about the map these two stole in front of Kathryn. Then, he figured she was as narcissistic as he was and wouldn't care.

"I *am* calling, but Cole and I got trouble."

"What trouble?"

"Um, well, you see…."

"What happened?"

"Our trailer burned up last night."

"How?"

"Well, it was after the barn exploded."

Kyle was stunned for a moment when Bubba explained what happened, then smacked his own forehead with the palm of his hand. What morons these two turned out to be. Why did he ever think these guys were worth hooking up with to get a bit of extra cash? "Where have you been all night?"

"Uh, we hightailed it out of there, you know, and hid behind the livestock auction building. We ended up sleeping in the truck."

Kyle placed his hand on the wall, dreading his next question. "What about the map?"

"We got it. I ran back into the trailer after it started burning and saved the map. I'm telling you, I was really scared—"

"Never mind," Kyle interrupted. "Just shut for a minute. Let me think."

The cops would be looking for these bozos, so he couldn't meet them anywhere in town. He'd bet anything Hank had been at the fire the previous night, so that meant Kyle had to open up Woo Hardware. He growled annoyance.

"Uh, what are we supposed to do now?" Bubba asked.

"You guys get anything further from that map?"

"No."

"Hold on," Kyle said and looked at Kathryn, who lay under the sheets, lips twisted in disgust. "What's the name of your boyfriend?"

"Ex-boyfriend," she huffed. "Justin, but everyone calls him Digger."

"Like I care," Kyle said, then back into the phone, "Find this Justin Digger guy or find the Indian's granddaughter you told me about."

"They're probably together," Kathryn interjected.

"Good point," Kyle said. "Maybe they're together. If anyone is out looking for that treasure, they will be."

"Where would we look?" Bubba whined. "The cops know the truck."

These idiots wouldn't last three minutes in Chicago. His own grandmother would have seen their lack of brain cells right off and shot them with the .32 she always packed in her purse.

Focus. What now? This map was the key. He was sure of it. Kyle had heard the Indian the brothers had stolen the map from had been hospitalized, so getting more information out of him was not an option.

He caught Kathryn's icy stare and figured he'd lost his shot at any more playtime. "You know anything about this old Indian we've been talking about?"

"Jacob Wildcrow. What about him?"

"This treasure he was raving about a couple days ago. He has to know more about it."

She shrugged.

"Come on. There has to be more to this than some stupid map. Where might he keep information, old papers, or records?"

"He lives in a trailer."

"Maybe." Kyle doubted it. Besides, the cops might check out there in case the Smiths returned to the scene of their crime. Kyle shook his head again. How had they escaped the law the whole of yesterday? He must not have been thinking straight himself, or else he would have figured there would be a deputy sheriff hanging around the Smiths' property. All three of them had been damn lucky.

Kathryn rolled her eyes to the ceiling. A sigh escaped, which told him she had better things to do than discuss demented Native Americans, even with the possibility of treasure in the picture.

"Anything?" he asked.

"I don't know. I remember he and his wife used to own a store in Harvey."

Kyle knew where Harvey was—stupid name for a town—but had never visited.

"What kind of store?"

"Indian related stuff. Artifacts, crafts, jewelry."

"Is it still there?" he asked.

"I don't know. Been closed for a couple decades. Could be torn down."

Kyle nodded. "How big is Harvey? Would this store be hard to find?"

"No," she said. "The town's not more than a dot in the road. Two, three businesses at the most. Biggest company is the quarry."

Kyle lifted the phone back to his mouth. "All right. Do you two know how to get to Harvey?" Silence. "Hey, you still there?"

He heard muffled scrapes and thuds. Then Bubba said, "Yeah, sorry, I dropped the phone."

"Listen, get over to Harvey. The old guy ran a store there. Sold a bunch of Indian crap. Look around for anything that might be related to the map or this treasure."

Kyle ended the call and looked at the time. He needed to get to the hardware store, but Kathryn had slid the blanket down to reveal more of her body. She bit her bottom lip and looked at him with sultry eyes.

Well, he wasn't scheduled for work until later in the morning. There was time to enjoy a project right here.

Chapter 28

Hank drove his pickup along T-14, still thinking about the mysteries of the numerous fires that had been flaring up all around the county. Until the past few months, Hank's duties as chief of the volunteer firefighters consisted of putting out spontaneous brush fires, farmer's burning barrels that had gotten out of control, or backyard fires of residents burning trash within city limits. The number of fires around the county had increased since August. A cornfield partially decimated. An abandoned house out near the Whitebreast Park area. After the fire at the old hotel a few weeks back, talk around town ranged from a serial arsonist, a group of teenage vandals, to the short-lived tongue-in-cheek rumor of a Chinese invasion.

Investigations resulted in shrugged shoulders. No evidence of any accelerant was discovered. No storms to blame for lightning strikes. The popular theory was someone had dropped a lit match or some other smoldering object, and the fire spread from there, destroying its own origin.

Hank hadn't gotten much sleep the previous night because of yet another fire, this time at the Smith's trailer south of town. With this incident, there was no doubt as to the cause. Those two goofballs let their meth cooking get out of hand. Both the barn and the trailer were beyond saving by the time he and the trucks arrived. All he and the crew did was to keep the flames from spreading to the tree line. The Smiths, no surprise, had vanished. City and county patrols were on the look-out. Sheriff Lockridge didn't like the fact he had to find a couple of pot-smoking losers while keeping folks from digging up the county on some fool treasure hunt.

Hank's thoughts turned back to the previous fires. He was certain *someone* had set them on purpose or by accident. Either way, the culprit hadn't bothered to call it in. Sometimes arsonists enjoyed the attention and made an anonymous phone call into the department. Other people felt no responsibility to report an accidental fire and just ran. Hank didn't know which way to think in regard to these county wide fires. If deliberate, why? What statement did the perpetrator want to convey? If accidental... well, that'd be a pretty huge coincidence.

Who? Local kids out for mischief? Someone upset about local government? A stranger or someone he knew? He had plenty of suspicions about his recent hire Kyle. Come to think of it, Kyle and the rash of fires started about the same time. Did the fires act as a diversion to get Hank out of the store. He already suspected Kyle of skimming. Maybe the guy had a partner who ran around the county igniting the fires to keep Hank occupied.

Before Kyle, everyone was okay with a *Closed* sign on the door whenever Hank received a call. Customers understood the need to attend to a fire and returned later. After a time, however, his bosses thought the practice detrimental to the bottom line. How many sales was he missing during the hours he was gone? They encouraged him to hire someone to fill in. Hence, Kyle Brewer. He had no evidence but wouldn't be surprised if Kyle were involved in the spate of fires. Somehow.

Nearing the edge of Knoxville, Hank spotted a familiar figure walking along the side of the road. He slowed, pulled off onto the gravel, and powered down the passenger window.

"Jacob Wildcrow, what are you doing out? I heard you were in the hospital."

Wildcrow looked back toward town, looked askance at Hank. "Uh, I am fine. They released me."

"And you're walking home? Where's your granddaughter?"

"She and Digger are... attending to other matters."

"It'll be another hour or so before you get home. Can I give you a lift?"

Wildcrow nodded and opened the passenger door. "Going for my pony. Need him for the quest."

"Pony? Quest? What are you talking about?"

"My pony is in the shed at my trailer."

Hank hadn't heard of Wildcrow owning a horse. Maybe it was a recent purchase. As for keeping it in the shed, that didn't seem right. He'd need a barn with a stall or two. "Well, I'll take you there. No problem."

In less than ten minutes, he pulled up at Wildcrow's trailer, just south of the campground. Wildcrow leaped out of the truck and hurried to the utility shed. He unhooked a padlock on the door that apparently hadn't been locked but gave the appearance of being so. He swung open the door and disappeared inside.

Minutes later, Hank heard an engine sputter to life. His eyes popped as he saw Wildcrow riding his 'pony.' A red Kawasaki ATV, about fifteen years old, lurched out of the shed. Wildcrow had covered the seat with a palomino-colored type of hide or blanket. A fashioned horse's head poked up between the ATVs handlebars. It reminded Hank of the bear skin and tiger skin rugs he had seen in magazine ads, though he had never seen a horse skin rug before. Slung over the driver's fender was a bow and a quiver of arrows. Wildcrow got off the ATV, held up one finger, and went into his trailer. A minute later, he came out dressed in deerskin tunic and breeches. His headdress sported few feathers but still gave him the appearance of a traditional tribe leader. He tucked a plastic bag of what looked like sunflower seeds into a sort of saddle bag draped over the rear of the ATV.

"Pony ready for quest!" Wildcrow gave a western movie war whoop and waved a fist. He gunned the engine, then roared off in a cloud of dust.

Hank laughed to himself and wondered what adventure ole Wildcrow was getting into this day.

***

Hunkered down on his ATV, Wildcrow raced along trails and through the trees toward the first marker on the map. So many years he had studied the hide, he knew every crease and every symbol's meaning. He had even visited the locations, but only at a few of them did he find the clues to the next location. That day, he vowed to help Digger and his granddaughter by leaving his own signs that they would discover themselves, re-affirming their own quest.

Nearing the bluff where he'd been the previous day before the Smiths showed up, he slowed the four-wheeler, then stopped and turned off the engine when a jolt of dizziness rocked his head. He knew what came next, so he climbed off the ATV, settled himself cross-legged upon the earth, and closed his eyes.

***

1790

A soft gray blue tinged the eastern sky. The hue blended into rose, then orange, and finally an all-encompassing yellow spread across the morning sky. The sun had not yet risen above the horizon, but glorious radiance would reveal itself in only minutes.

Running Eagle sat in a clearing of trees at what nature and the Great Spirit had formed to be the neck of a hawk's head in the rock. Only the beak of red stone gave proof of the hunter who watched over the valley. The flesh and feathered bird rested on a nearby branch, asleep. Only when Running Eagle moved to stand did the bird's eyes open, all senses on full alert.

With the ground still in shadow, Running Eagle gathered no less than fifty large stones, each twice the size of his head. He carried them up to the highest point of the cliff. There, he sat, eyes closed again, and greeted the new day with fresh prayers. So in tune with nature, he felt the slight warmth on his skin at the same time he sensed a bright shaft of yellow from the merest arc of the sun as it crept over the edge of the world.

Before the first sip of water or the first strip of deer meat passed his lips, he worked with diligence and determination to arrange the fifty stones into proper order. Each nestled into the earth so that even the strongest thunderstorm could not dislodge it. They were spaced so that only a single hair could be placed between one and its neighbor. Two hours it took to complete the task because of the difficulty of moving the stones to their correct location.

Once again, Running Eagle stood upon the bluff and looked down on what he had accomplished. The words of Chief Saunuk came to him.

"Straight and true is the arrow fashioned by our hands. Aimed and shot with confidence, it will guide us to sustenance and victory."

Thus, it was so.

Running Eagle's arrow pointed to his next destination.

***

170

Wildcrow stood and walked several paces toward the bluff until he found what he was meant to find. He smiled and sent up prayers of thanks that he was chosen to be one of the descendants to follow Running Eagle's path and to fulfill Chief Saunuk's quest. Grace would soon follow.

Wildcrow reached into a leather pouch looped around his belt and withdrew a handful of what Grace and Digger would recognize. When the two discovered what he'd left, they'd know who'd left it. Minutes later, he reversed course on the ATV, excitement and anticipation building, strength and vitality renewed.

Chapter 29

Cole and Bubba Smith used part of the twenty dollars Kyle had given them the previous night to buy breakfast at the Casey's convenience store. They hoped they could get in and out before one of the clerks recognized them and called the cops.

Cole waited in the truck while Bubba went inside. He watched his brother stand in front of the doughnut case so long he almost honked the horn. "Just grab a couple and get out of there," he muttered.

Seconds later, the clerk disappeared down an aisle toward the back of the store. Bubba no longer looked at the pastries, but out at Cole, smiled, and gave a thumbs-up. He hurried to the coolers, grabbed two quarts of chocolate milk, plucked a couple packages of mini doughnuts from the end rack and rushed to the door.

Cole figured the clerk must have gone to the stockroom. Bubba had opted for snatching breakfast rather than paying for it. "Maybe he isn't such an idiot after—"

His words cut off as Bubba tripped pushing the door open. He crashed to the ground face first. Chocolate milk erupted from beneath his body. He hauled himself up, wiped at the mess on his shirt, and retrieved the smashed doughnut packages. Cole switched his attention from his brother stumbling to the store to see if the clerk had spotted the shoplifting.

When Bubba closed the passenger door, he said, "Lost the milk. Sorry. I did save the doughnuts."

Cole eyed the flattened packages. Bubba had taken one covered in powdered sugar and the other with coconut shavings. Six doughnuts per package, but his body had mashed them into unrecognizable pulp. One of the plastic ends had split. Crumbs and white sugar fell onto the seat.

Cole shifted the truck into reverse. "You, dear brother, are a moron."

"What?" Bubba whined. "And don't call me *dear brother* in that tone."

"Never mind," Cole said. "Let's get out of here. Clean off the seat. There are a whole bunch of napkins we got from the Dairy Queen in the glove compartment. Wipe your shirt."

Bubba brushed the crumbs into the floor well, already littered with empty beer cans and food wrappers. After sopping up what milk he could off his shirt, he examined the coconut doughnuts."

"We'll take T-15 out to 92," Cole said.

"I always wondered something," Bubba said.

"How to tie your shoes the correctly?"

"No, *dear brother*," Bubba said. "I've always wanted to know how they number the highways."

"What?"

"Why didn't they number them in order? You know, start with Highway 1 way up in northern Minnesota and end with 500 or whatever number is last down in Texas."

"What?"

'It would make map making a little easier. You'd always know what highway came next."

Cole glanced at his brother, then back to the road. They were leaving the outskirts of Knoxville past the Hormel Foods plant. "You are sitting there with a milk-soaked shirt and licking coconut doughnut pieces from plastic. Do you really think you're intelligent enough to discuss cartography?"

"Cart— What?"

"Oh, shut up," Cole said. "That's map making."

"Then it should be called mapography. Cartography sounds like they make shopping carts."

"Shut up!"

***

The small town of Harvey lay north of Highway 92. Cole wondered how the old Indian and his wife stayed in business selling artifacts. Not a tourist attraction, the town had fewer than 300 people and covered less than a square mile. Many of the residents worked at the nearby Martin Marietta-Durham quarry producing concrete related products. Harvey could boast a couple churches, a post office, a lot of older houses, and not much else.

He and Bubba had visited Harvey once trying to drum up more pot customers. All they received were disgusted looks and Cole having the seat of his jeans torn away when a snooty woman sicced her Shar Pei on them. He didn't want to drive up and down streets looking for the old store. That dog might be out looking for another round.

"Where do you think we should start looking for this store?" Cole asked as he drove along Main Street past the white lettered green sign indicating the Harvey city limits.

"About 200 feet back," Bubba said.

Cole stomped on the brakes. Bubba lurched forward and hit his head on the dashboard. "What? Where?"

"Ouch! Watch what you're doing?" Bubba rubbed his forehead. "That old wooden building back there."

Cole steered the truck onto the shoulder to make the U-turn. "Why didn't you say something?"

"I thought you would have seen the sign." Bubba laughed. "Who's the moron now?

At a short weather-faded wooden sign that read *Native American Artifacts*, Cole turned into a small weed-choked gravel parking lot in front of a wooden structure tucked back into the trees. He hadn't seen it because he'd been looking in the opposite direction.

The store wasn't very big, perhaps the size of one of those compact bait and tackle shops around Lake Red Rock. It resembled an old log cabin he'd seen in books about settlers moving across America. Part of the roof had fallen in, and someone had spray-painted graffiti on one side wall.

Cole parked and the two brothers climbed out of the truck. They stood about forty feet from the front door. Grass had grown long before it browned. Bare trees formed a barrier between the store and the property to the southeast.

"Why do you think Kyle sent us out here?" Bubba asked. "There ain't nothing to see."

"I don't know," Cole said. "Let's look around anyway."

They circled to the back of the store where they discovered a stone hearth. Cole had seen something similar at one of the local campgrounds. The hearth was seven feet high, made of mortared stones, and looked like a giant chair with the rusting grill being the 'seat.'

The back door was locked, but Cole kicked twice, and it burst inward. The interior of the store smelled stale of trapped cool air. Spider webs curtained every corner. Part of the wooden floor had been damaged by burrowing animals. Dirt and grime covered the reception counter and the remains of shelving and broken display cases.

The front counter had also been part desk with four drawers. Cole yanked each one to find an old green colored receipt book, an opened box of condoms, and a half empty 750 milliliter bottle of Jim Beam. He guessed some kids had been out here partying.

He thunked the bottle on the counter. "Even if we don't find anything to help us with the treasure hunt, we found our own treasure."

Bubba's eyes widened when he saw the whiskey, and he gave Cole a broad smile. "I like how you think, brother. Shall we partake in a sip or two?"

"Not yet. Let's search the rest of this place. You take the storage room, and I'll check this main room."

Another five minutes passed. Cole found only mouse droppings and dust. Bubba reported that only a roll of paper towels and a cleaning bucket had been left in the storage room.

"Nothing," Cole said. "I think Kyle sent us out here to get us out of town so he could look for the treasure."

"Yeah," Bubba agreed. "He sent us on a wild moose chase."

"You mean a wild goose chase."

Bubba stood straighter, shoulders back. "I'm sorry to have to correct you again, but it's moose."

"As I said before, you are an—"

"Wait a second," Bubba interrupted. "I'm right, and I can prove it."

"You're wrong but go ahead and try."

"It's so simple even you can understand," Bubba said. "You see a lot of geese in town, right? Crossing the streets and hanging out in the park by the pond."

"Right."

"Well, you ever see any moose around town doing those things?"

"No."

"And why not?" Bubba asked.

"Because...."

"Because geese can't be wild if they're around town. You don't see moose in town because they're wild. So, we got sent on a wild moose chase. Now, let's have a drink and a toke."

Cole stared at his brother who uncapped the bottle and took a long swig of the whiskey. "That was the worst logical argument I've ever heard."

"By the way." Bubba belched. "I think if the plural of goose is geese, then the plural of moose should be meese. How's that for logic?"

Cole shook his head and withdrew his phone from his pocket. He pressed the speed dial number for Kyle. "Hey, Kyle, we ain't found nothing at this old store. This was a waste of time."

He heard a growl coming through followed by a string of profanities.

"All right," Kyle said. "You two clowns get back here. Meet me at the hardware store. I had to open up. Hank ain't here, yet. Make sure no one sees you coming in. Well discuss our next move when you get here. Make sure you come to the *back* door."

"Okay, we'll be there in a while."

"Hurry up."

Kyle ended the call and Cole replaced the phone in his pocket. "We have to get back to Woo Hardware and talk to Kyle."

"Relax, bother." Bubba pulled a joint and a lighter from his pocket. "Have a drink and a couple hits. We got time. We deserve a break from the stress of last night and this morning."

Cole sighed. He really wanted to get back to Knoxville to continue the treasure hunt. How they were going to drive back to town without getting caught, he didn't know. Everyone knew their truck. Maybe they could steal a car. Then Cole remembered the last time he and his brother tried that. They had broken into a nice-looking Jeep at Walmart only to discover the vehicle had a manual transmission. They'd never driven it before but gave it a try. After several rounds of hot wiring the engine, all they could do was grind the gears, lurch the car forward and backward, and stall the engine. To make matters worse, the elderly woman who owned the car showed up. She hit Bubba on the head with a huge purse and jolted him with a stun gun. Cole barely had time to haul his brother's twitching body to their truck and drive away before the cops arrived.

He sighed again and sat next to Bubba, back against the counter. His brother offered the bottle and the joint.

"Not too much," Cole said. "We still have to drive back."

"No problem," Bubba said. "We've driven high before."

"But not drinking, too."

Bubba belched again. "It ain't that much."

Cole wasn't sure how much time had passed. His eyes closed and he dozed, tired from being unable to sleep in the truck the previous night. He felt something heavy leaning against him. He opened his eyes to see Bubba's head on his shoulder. A wave of emotion washed through him. Ah, Bubba. He wasn't so bad. They'd gotten through some tough scrapes since their ma ran off and dad died. Yeah, Cole harped on his brother, but only because he wanted him to better himself, make something of his life. They couldn't go on growing weed and making meth forever, could they? Well, at least not at their place anymore. They'd have to find another piece of land and start over.

He felt a tickle in his nose and sneezed. Then he heard a crackling sound, like dry leaves burning.

Fire!

He leaned forward and saw flames licking at the counter on the other side of Bubba. *Crap!* Bubba must have dropped another lit joint.

Cole stood, and Bubba toppled sideways to the floor. "Come on. We have to get out of here."

He pulled on Bubba's arm. Finally, his brother woke to semi-consciousness.

"Huh?"

"Fire. Let's go!"

Bubba rolled and staggered to his feet. Together, they tried the front door, found it locked, then bolted out the back door. When they rounded the building and jumped in the truck, Cole saw smoke wafting up through the old roof.

"Aw, man," Bubba whined. "We forgot the whiskey."

Cole started the engine and reversed out of the parking lot. "You are a complete imbecile."

"What did I do?"

"You are no longer in charge of handling the joints," Cole sped southwest toward Highway 92. "You keep setting them down and starting fires."

Bubba opened his mouth to speak, but Cole backhanded his shoulder. "Last night our meth lab and trailer. Before that, the hotel in town, and before *that* the cornfield and a couple other places."

"But—"

"No more weed unless I give it to you, and then *I'm* holding the joints." Cole huffed in exasperation. The rearview mirror showed flames licking through the rotting board. Cole shook his head in disgust and turned west toward Knoxville.

Idiot!

Chapter 30

Digger and Grace headed to his Gremlin to begin the search. Digger was thrilled at being able to spend the entire day with her. Despite her anxiety over Wildcrow and her reluctance to join him on this search for an ancient bundle, she looked like the hearty flower still blooming with vibrancy even in the November chill. Her skin was clear. Her dark lined eyes didn't need any makeup. And her scent, Digger didn't know what it was, but it reminded him of the creams women were always trying to get you to sample in those large department stores.

Digger tried to get his mind back to the task. "So, off to the Peace Tree?"

At the hospital, they'd loaded Chow into the back seat and driven to Pleasantville. The Historical Society was open from 9-2. In less than five minutes, the attendant found the book regarding the Indian tribes who once occupied the area and the specific page with an image of Wildcrow's map. Digger snapped a picture with his cell phone, made sure they could see every detail on the image, thanked the attendant, and their quest began.

"Yeah, that's what Grandfather said. Something about the tree would point to some rocks somewhere. I hope this isn't one big lark."

"I think we're supposed to keep an eye out for a hawk."

"What?" Grace smirked. "Funny guy."

Still the skeptic, Digger thought. Well, maybe she was right, but her presence made the journey more enjoyable. He drove to Lake Red Rock via the county road. One of the offshoots led to Ruckman cemetery. Once back to Highway 14, he headed for Elk Rock Park.

"Why are we going toward Grandfather's trailer?" Grace asked.

"It's the first symbol on the map. It's supposed to show the correct direction to start looking for the first marker."

Near the drive to Wildcrow's trailer, a narrow strip of asphalt wound through the elms, oaks, and maples. Digger had been out here on few occasions, but knew the road went for a couple miles before reaching an outlook point. With branches devoid of leaves and dormant brown grass below, the woods had a sleepy appearance, as if settling in for the winter to come. Approaching a small clearing, they saw another car parked with a man and a woman rummaging around in the open trunk. They withdrew a long-handled shovel and closed the lid. The couple gave Digger a narrowed-eyed stare, but both flinched and cowered as a hawk swooped down and flew inches above their heads. Digger braked thirty yards from the other car.

"Did you see that?" asked Grace. "It was a hawk."

"Maybe your grandfather's hawk he's always talking about. He told us to watch for it."

The hawk dive-bombed the couple again. They started to run for the shelter of the trees, but the bird landed on a branch, squawked, then flew down as if in attack mode. The couple screamed and raced back to the car. While the woman ran for the passenger side, the man opened the back door, threw the shovel inside, then scrambled to get behind the wheel. The engine roared to life and with tires squealing, the driver tore past the Gremlin to disappear back up the asphalt.

"Well, wasn't that interesting?" Grace asked.

"Serves them right," Digger said. "Just another couple nutjobs out looking for this treasure."

"I don't believe what I saw. That hawk drove them away."

"I don't know what to make of it, either. However, it could be something as simple as the bird protecting territory. Maybe it has a nest nearby and thought the couple was intruding."

They got out of the car and let Chow roam at will. The husky galloped to the nearest tree, sniffed the base all the way around, then lifted his leg to mark his own territory.

"I don't see the hawk anymore," Grace said.

"Job accomplished, it probably flew away," Digger said. "Let's forget the hawk. We have a lot of exploring to do."

They walked to the edge of the bluff and Digger pointed out the stump that had once been the stately sycamore designated the Peace Tree. He had seen pictures when it had been a twelve-foot half trunk rising out of the lake, still a token of the past, still exuding a sacred heritage. Weather and time had reduced it to a tilting chunk of wood that stuck up perhaps five feet out of the water about fifty yards from shore.

"How can we get a direction from a stump?" Grace asked. "Besides, I can barely see it from here."

"Well, your grandfather said something about an arm."

"He said to follow the line the pointing arm makes... to the rocks."

"Hold on." Digger rushed back to the car. He returned with a couple of books. He and Grace sat on the ground next to each other, and Digger opened one of the books. "I brought along a few of these from my classroom. Some have territorial maps. As I recall, there was a treaty line settled on between the United States government and the Native American tribes specifying which area of land would belong to each group. Each group was to stay in its respective area. I think it's that line we're looking for, Grace."

Digger unfolded a page inset into the book like a pamphlet and pointed out the lines to Grace. "Look, Grace, over there at the pink and cream rock formation. That looks like it might be it!"

Grace moved his arm a few degrees to the east. "Yeah, could be. But what about that cliff over there? That looks like it could be the one also."

"No, we're going to the first cliff. That's the one."

"And you know that, how?" Grace's mouth scrunched into a pretzel as she shook her head. "You know, there's a lark and then there's malarkey."

Digger just stared across the lake. A light breeze rippled the water but created no white-capped waves. A few dark dots of far-off fishing boats, maybe a sailboat in the distance. "I know," he whispered.

"How? You think you know everything?" Grace shook her head. "You get my grandfather all psyched up about this stuff...."

"Three reasons," Digger said.

"More lists?" Grace asked, but with a teasing smile.

"The first is I want you to imagine the Peace Tree standing straight. Wait."

He riffled through the pages of the other book until he came to the photo he'd remembered. This showed the sycamore from the southern shore, looking across the water. "See how the angle of the trunk and the last remains of the stubby branch point toward the north cliff. Only from this side of the tree, where the photographer stood and from where we're sitting can you see it. The line points directly at that first set of bluffs."

"I think it's a weak argument," Grace said. "What's the second reason?"

"Look." Digger pointed to the bluff. Even from across the water, he saw a flash of red as, high above the bluff, riding the thermals, a hawk glided. Its red tail glinted like a beacon with each turn into the sun. The bird flew in a lazy-eight formation. Every time it turned to retrace the path, he saw a downward motion to its wings, as if the mighty hawk beckoned them to the pale pink cliffs.

Beside him Grace had fallen silent, watching the hawk. She still needed some convincing, but two appearances of the red-tailed bird had to have had some effect.

He knew she had an effect on him. The shine in her dark hair, the fine lines of her cheeks, the delicate curve of her lips, the softness of her hands. His throat tightened and his heart sped up.

At that moment, he knew he could easily fall in love. In fact....

She turned her head, caught his stare, and he looked down.

"What?" she asked.

"Nothing," he murmured.

"What were you thinking?"

"What? Oh, just about...." He almost said, 'about kisses at midnight,' but that would have brought back the wrong memories. "Just that I'm glad you decided to go on this little venture with me and that we should get going."

They stood, and he felt the pulling of something between them. Something... special? Whatever the moment had been, his standing broke the spell.

"Wait, what about the third reason?" Grace asked.

"Look where you were sitting."

She looked and saw what he noticed earlier. "Sunflower seed shells."

"Who do we know who enjoys sunflower seeds?"

"You think he was here?"

"I'd bet on it. He's leaving us a clue that we began this journey in the correct way."

"But he's supposed to be in the hospital."

Digger shrugged. "He could have been out here yesterday, although I suspect the rain would have washed them away. Either way, I still think it's a sign."

Grace frowned and looked at the shells in the brown grass. "Come on, Chow."

The dog, who had been resting his head on his paws, bounded over to her.

Grace opened the car door. "You really think this is something we should pursue?"

"I think if we don't, it won't be only your grandfather who's disappointed."

She smiled at him over the roof of the car. Had she felt that *something*, too?

Maybe.

Digger drove across the Highway 14 bridge. Grace craned her neck to keep the Peace Tree in sight. Five minutes later, Digger turned onto the gravel road that led toward the cliff. It ended at the edge at a tall stand of trees. A path covered with wood chips disappeared into the thicket. Digger walked around the car to open the door for Grace.

She looked up to the hawk circling above. "He's still here."

"Yeah. I've got a good feeling about this, Grace."

"I hope so. I want to believe in all of this stuff about a treasure, a map, and clues, but I want to protect my grandfather too. He's, well, he's old, ancient among our people."

"Our people? They're your people now?"

She shrugged. "I guess they are. A little."

"Come on, let's head on up the path." Digger and Grace walked up the trail. Chow sniffed around the edge of the tree line. It snaked back and forth for two hundred yards then narrowed with overgrown brambles and sticker weeds creating obstacles. Digger went first and held aside the thorny vines so Grace could pass. Finally, they stood on the bluff. The expanse of water below them was breathtaking. The hawk still circled above. Digger pointed across to where they had been and at the Peace Tree, now just a large dark brown lump in the water.

"What do we look for?" Grace asked.

Digger pulled his phone from his pocket and brought up the picture of the map.

"This is where we are now. See this pyramid or grouping of dark round objects just below the edge of the bluff. I think that's the first marker. It is supposed to point us in the direction of the second marker."

"What is this first marker? Where?"

While Grace searched the bushes and grass, and Chow snuffled and sniffed the ground, Digger studied the map again. He looked from the picture to the rock and an idea came to him. He climbed to the highest point on the bluff and leaned over to look at the boulders below.

"Wow!"

"What?" Grace asked. "What do you see?"

"I see a line of rocks. Huge rocks. Boy, it must have taken something to move them."

"I'm coming up." Grace put her hands on some of the outcropping to pull herself up.

"No, it's too dangerous. And there's not enough room."

"I'm coming up and that's all there is to it."

Digger figured she was too determined to be dissuaded, so he stretched his arm down to give her a lift. With a pull she leaped up, into his arms. He held her, caught the scent of her hair and looked into her bright brown eyes. Her lips, so near his. The soft lips inviting his to join hers.

"What?" Grace asked.

"I—uh...."

"What were you looking at up here?" she asked.

Oh well, he thought, moment gone for now, but he was getting closer. Literally.

"We're in a small space up here, so just turn your head and look down," he said.

She did and saw what he had seen. A plateau formed of boulders and earth lay almost ten feet below them. In this lone spot, surrounded by rock, earth had settled, and grass had grown. Even more amazing, was the grouping of large stones half buried in the earth. These stones weren't natural formations. Someone had carried each of them down the ten feet to the flat outcropping. The location and the symbol created could be seen only from this location, this one precarious perch of rock.

This first marker was in the shape of an arrowhead, the tip pointing northeast.

"I can't believe it," Grace said. "What does it mean?"

"I think we're onto something here," Digger said.

Grace looked back up into Digger's eyes. "This is real, isn't it?"

Digger took her meaning to be in regard to Wildcrow, his map, and the journey one of his ancestors took over two hundred years before. He also chose to infer the reality of their situation, his attraction to her. Maybe her attraction to him?

Forget about kissing at midnight, this was a perfect spot. Their proximity made the moment perfect. Made it real.

Inhaling slightly, he bent his head to kiss her.

With the slight shift in weight, his foot slipped on a smooth angle of rock and off the bluff.

"Oh, crap!" he cried out.

"Digger!"

His other leg, in sympathy, folded and he slid away. Instinct wanted him to hold tight to Grace but he knew if he did, she'd come with him and they'd both end up bloody and broken at the water's edge. Instead, he dug his hands into the loose scree of rock. Pain erupted in his finger joints, but he slowed the momentum enough, so he didn't topple backward away from the bluff completely.

He felt hands clutching his. Looking up, he saw Grace had dropped to her stomach, reached over the precipice, and tried to get a firm grip. She wasn't strong enough to stop his slide.

"Let go," he said. "I'll only pull you over."

"Give me your hand," she insisted.

"No, wait. Let go. I'm only a few feet from the outcropping."

Using his feet to further slow the fall, he slid down to step on one of the rocks used to create the arrowhead. A quick glance over each shoulder and below him showed he was several feet away from empty space, plenty of room to maneuver. Still leaning against the bluff, he gained his balance and surveyed the situation.

"Are you all right?" Grace called from ten feet above him.

"Yes," he said. "A little roughed up, but nothing major. I won't venture too much farther out, though."

"How are you going to climb back up?"

"That could be a challenge."

Though he stayed away from the very edge of the outcropping, he did move to the 'bottom' of the arrowhead for a better view.

"Amazing," he said. "I wonder how much time Running Eagle took forming this?"

"Don't worry about a bunch of rocks," Grace said. "You have to find a way to get up here."

"One second." He crouched and ran a hand over two of the rocks, each the size of a couple bowling balls and weighing at least thirty pounds if not more. "It's fascinating he took so much effort and meticulousness to find the right sized rocks and place them here."

"Digger!"

He stood. "All right. Let me look over this situation."

"Do I need to call for help?"

He held up a hand to forestall her. "I know nature has done some erosion in two hundred years, but Running Eagle managed to get up and down by himself."

He studied the rocky bluff and noticed an irregular pattern of jutting rocks up to level ground. With assistance of toughened grass roots and a thumb's diameter tree root, he had a chance.

Stepping his right foot upon the first jutting rock, he reached up for the tree root and gave it an experimental tug. It loosened but didn't break. He secured a firm grip and raised his left foot to the next step. This time, the end of the rock broke away, and he almost fell back.

"Digger, be careful."

"No worries."

Before he put his full weight on the second step, he tapped the rock. It held and continued to support him when he heaved his body upward.

The third and fourth smooth rocks presented more chances to slide back down, but his soles retained a firm grip. Finally, he was able to throw his body forward, over the edge of the bluff onto the path. Grace helped him stand while Chow licked his ear. He brushed away the dirt and dust and gazed back to where he'd climbed.

"Whew! That was what they call a harrowing experience. Hope something like that doesn't happen again," he said.

Snap.

Digger's head jerked around, and he stared back into the trees. Something or someone had stepped on a branch. From overhead, the hawk circled lower, and, in a moment, Digger was able to discern a vague outline of someone in the distance peering from around a thick tree trunk. In an instant, the figure disappeared. He heard faint footfalls moving away.

Chow barked three times.

"What's wrong?" Grace asked.

Digger gripped her arm in reassurance. "Stay put. Keep Chow with you. I think I can catch him."

Chapter 31

Grace waited for Digger to return after chasing the strange figure. She heard the fading thuds of running footsteps. When they disappeared, she realized how alone and isolated she was, even with Chow by her side. He pulled against the tight leash, wanting to chase after Digger, but a few harsh commands kept him close.

Who had been watching them? Why? Another hiker? Her mind recalled two nights before and the two figures trying to break into the trailer. Had they followed Digger's car? Was the other still out there?

An involuntary yip escaped her when her phone trilled. She removed it from her waist holster and looked at the unfamiliar number. With a quick glance into the trees to see if Digger was returning, she swiped her thumb across the answer icon.

"Ms. Snow?" an Asian-accented voice asked.

"Yes?"

"This is Soo-lee, the nurse for your grandfather at Knoxville Hospital. Is he with you now?"

"No. Why?"

"He hasn't contacted you?"

"No. We left him there after our visit. What's going on?"

"Well...."

"Are you trying to tell me he's not in his room?" Grace asked.

"He may have wandered off. We're searching the hospital now. I'm sure he's okay."

"I don't believe this," Grace said. "I don't understand. How could he have 'wandered off?'"

"Ma'am, please stay calm. We'll find him."

"Call Sheriff Lockridge or the police." She saw Digger appear among the trees. "We'll be there as soon as possible."

Digger jogged up to her. "No luck," he said.

"Digger, they can't find Grandfather!" she said in a panic.

"What?"

"The hospital. They called me. They say he's not in his room, that he wandered off."

Digger paused then reached inside a jacket pocket and withdrew out a metal canister. From one of the five slots, he extracted a cigar.

"Macanudo Cafe Hyde Park," he said. "Medium-bodied. I usually enjoy this on my front porch on a Saturday afternoon, but after my failed attempt to capture our watcher, I need to relax."

Grace's jaw dropped. "How can you talk about a cigar? Did you not hear what I said about Grandfather?"

She watched as he went through the process of lighting the cigar, becoming more exasperated with each motion. After a few initial puffs, he smiled. "Yes, and you shouldn't be worried."

"Why not?"

"Because I think I know where he is, or rather where he was."

When he didn't continue, she stepped up to him. "Don't stand there grinning like an idiot. Tell me."

"You need to relax, too."

"Justin Clay, if you don't—"

He held up a palm. "Follow me. I'll show you."

He led her and Chow back through the woods to the beginning of the trail.

"I'm thinking I should quit smoking these things," he said. "I thought I was in pretty good shape, but whoever was watching us disappeared before I could catch him. Drove off just as I reached the clearing. I didn't get a good look, but I think the car was an old Crown Victoria."

"Digger, where's my grandfather?"

"So, I checked on the Gremlin to make sure it hadn't been tampered with and when I started back to get you, I saw something we both missed at the time."

"What?"

He pointed to the ground near the head of the trail. She crouched to get a better look. Scattered and almost camouflaged in the brown grass were cracked and emptied sunflower seed shells.

"Just like at the outlook point at Elk Rock," Grace said.

"Yep. How long has he been eating them?"

"As long as I can remember. Grandmother used to scold him for not sweeping the shells from the store." Chow came up to nuzzle her cheek. She wrapped an arm around the Husky and looked at Digger. "You think he's been here?"

"I'm no detective, but these look fresh. I'd say those at the first site were put there earlier, probably while we were in Pleasantville. He came out here ahead of us and is leading the way."

"How?"

"I guess I'm *not* a detective, because I missed this earlier, too. Follow me and tell me what you see."

He walked around the perimeter of the clearing, staying about ten feet from the brush. She followed. After ten yards, she saw a regular pattern in the soft ground.

"Tire tracks," she said.

"Looks like an ATV. I saw one at Wildcrow's place on one of my visits. He customized that thing with some sort of animal pelt and a horse's head." He puffed on the cigar again, then looked back toward the sunflower shells. "Here's what I think happened. Remember how he was anxious to come with us?"

"Sure, but he'd been injured," Grace said. "He should still be in the hospital."

Digger shrugged. "Maybe. He'd been resting an entire day and night, though. I'm telling you, Grace, the old guy is pretty spry for his age. Determined, too. I'll bet he couldn't stand to be cooped up in that bed one more minute. Not after sending us out to follow the clues on the map. He probably sneaked out of the hospital, hitched himself a ride to his trailer, saddled up his ATV, and started out. He's showing us the way to go."

"But—"

"Those shells weren't left there by chance. No reason for them to be in one spot. Anyone else would be walking, dropping, or spitting them along the trail. No, I think he left them there on purpose."

"Why?"

Digger walked toward the Gremlin. Grace and Chow followed.

"He's on the quest that he told us about. He's following this Running Eagle's path, just as we are."

"Why didn't he wait for us?"

"I don't know, but he has his reasons."

At the car, he opened the passenger door. Chow bounded into the back seat.

"What should we do?" Grace asked.

"I think we should keep going."

"What do you mean?"

"Wildcrow will have known this was to be our first stop. I think he'll go onto the next location."

"Which is where?"

"I think the next mark on the map is near Bos Landen. The arrowhead formed by those stones back there on the cliff pointed in that direction." He secured the cigar in his mouth, pulled his phone from his pocket, and brought up the map image. "I seem to remember a huge boulder there. If my memory serves me, I think it was on the golf course. At first, I thought it was placed there by the developers, but maybe not. See this symbol here on the map? I'll bet it's that boulder."

"Bos Landen? The Pella golf course. That's where my hotel is. How do you know so much about this area?"

Digger shrugged. "I took the history teacher's position after graduation and have lived here ever since. I've explored the area a lot throughout the years."

Grace tried to calm her jittery nerves. "You really think Grandfather could have made it this far?"

Digger smiled and blew a smoke ring in the air. "I'll bet he's thrilled to be out here finally fulfilling a dream he's had for years."

She clenched her fist and shook it like she wanted to hit something that wasn't there. "I don't know what to think anymore. I just want to find him and know he's okay."

She felt Digger's hand on her arm. Her whole body stiffened as his touch set a wave of butterflies loose in her stomach. His soft smile reached from his lips to his eyes.

"He'll be fine," he assured. "We'll find him."

He helped her into the car, and she thought about the past several minutes. The almost kiss still hung between them. She hadn't expected that. What was worse was she needed his help finding grandfather but being around him made her flustered.

Chow huffed again and licked her cheek. At least the dog was enjoying the adventure.

"Are you sure this isn't a waste of time?" she asked when Digger closed his door and started the engine.

"You saw the arrowhead."

"That could have been put there by some kids having fun."

He raised his eyebrows. "Do you really believe that?"

She pursed her lips and realized how silly her statement sounded. "No."

"Then after a slight detour back to town for something we might need, let's follow your grandfather's trail. He'll show us the way."

She heard a squawk from overhead.

"I think our avian friend will be with us, too," Digger said.

He stepped on the accelerator, and Grace's heart hammered again. She didn't want to admit it, but she felt a bit of excitement. What would they discover?

Chapter 32

Kyle had received a call from Hank a few minutes after the Smith brothers had called, further ruining fun time with Kathryn. Hank said he'd be busy for a couple hours, and that Kyle needed to open the store. Kyle didn't like it. He hadn't been scheduled to arrive until later in the morning. He grumbled and complained to Kathryn who put on a pouty-face and lowered the sheet to just above her waist. That temptation was enough to change his mind.

A customer had been standing outside the store when Kyle finally arrived. The man grumbled that the store should have been open. Kyle apologized but added twenty bucks to the price of a small grill when he had to look it up in the catalog. Why would the dumbhead be buying a grill in November?

A steady stream of customers kept Kyle busy during the morning, and he didn't get a chance to retrieve the extra twenty from the till. When he remembered, Hank almost caught him. He had the bill in his hand when the bell over the front entrance jingled and Hank rushed in. Kyle tucked his left hand out of sight below the counter and closed the drawer with his right.

"What's going on here, Kyle?" Hank asked.

The counter was high enough, so Kyle deftly stuck the twenty down his pants. He figured if he tried to put it in his pocket, Hank would notice.

"Nothing, Hank. What's kept you busy this morning? Another fire?"

Hank eyed him then walked around the counter. "I hate to ask this, Kyle, but I will. Could you please empty your pockets?"

Kyle shrugged and reached into his pockets, drawing out a Swiss army knife, a handful of change, a BIC lighter, a worn wallet with three five-dollar bills, his driver's license, and a crumpled bandanna kerchief. For good measure, he turned his pockets inside-out.

Hank surveyed the small pile of items Kyle had dragged from his pockets. The suspicious frown on his face eased. "Okay, Kyle. Sorry. I guess seeing all that destruction at the Smith place put me out of sorts. Their barn and trailer burned to the ground. I was just out there checking on things. Had to talk with the arson inspector for my reports."

Kyle nodded. "Too bad. Anyone hurt?"

"No, we figured they cleared out just after the place went up. The sheriff is still on the lookout for them. I think this time they're in real trouble. He uncovered their marijuana patch out there. They're just lucky the fire didn't burn up the entire area. Then the department received a call out near Harvey. That old store Wildcrow owned also went up in flames. I'm telling you, the rash of fires around the area has a lot of people wondering."

Kyle walked into the small area at the back of the store where they kept a coffee pot going. First, out of sight of Hank, he retrieved the twenty from his pants and put it in his pocket. Close call, he thought. I'll have to pay more attention.

He thought about Harvey, where he'd sent the Smiths. Where were they? The two should have been back by now. Maybe they'd found something and covered their tracks. He filled a cup of coffee he had started when he first arrived. Several hours old, the brew was bitter, but hot. While he drank, he looked at the supply of some of the more lethal tools they stored. Axes, picks, and hatchets. Some were displayed behind glass cases out front, but the majority were kept back here to keep them away from any children. He saw the pair of shovels that had come in the day before and remembered Hank had asked him to put them up front but for some reason he was procrastinating. Oh yeah, now he remembered. He didn't want anyone else finding the treasure before he did.

He walked back up to the register in time to see the brothers' rattletrap truck roll by on the street out front. He set down the cup and rushed to the door to see the truck turn at the corner. Where were they going? In an instant, he knew.

Hank had gone into his office. Kyle poked his head in. "I've been pretty busy all morning. Haven't had a chance to clean up. I'll grab some cleaning supplies from the back."

Hank gave a dismissive wave. "All right."

Kyle opened the back door just as the Smiths stepped from the truck. "Get in here," he said. Without a word, they followed him inside. "Keep your voices down. Hank's up front."

"Okay," Bubba said in his normal voice.

Cole backhanded him. "He said keep your voice down."

"Both of you shut up," Kyle ordered. "So, you didn't find anything at the old Indian's store."

"Nothing," Cole said. "Lamebrain here ended up burning down the building."

"It wasn't my fault," Bubba said.

"Of course, it was," Cole said. "You're the one who dropped the lit joint."

Kyle shoved Bubba back a couple steps. "Are you kidding me? You're supposed to be helping us find this treasure, not getting high. You're both a pair of bobble heads." He paused when he thought of something. "Wait a second. You caused the fire?"

"Yeah," Cole said. "Just like at our home."

"Again, not my fault," Bubba said.

"You put the lit joint next to the pop bottle with the meth mixture," Cole said. "Of course, it's your fault."

"I swear," Kyle said. "I don't know why I hooked up with you pair of numbskulls in the first place. Your whole focus should have been finding clues to this treasure, not smoking your own…

The bell rang at the front door.

"Gotta go, you bone heads. Get outta here now. I don't want Hank to see you. I'll make some excuse to get out early if I can and meet you at the north end of the mile-long bridge at noon. Be sure to bring the map. It's digging time. Treasure awaits. Now go."

Kyle walked to the front. A young woman with hair tied in back and dressed in tight Capri pants and a Martha Stewart T-shirt walked to the garden aisle and Kyle, sensing an opportunity, followed behind, admiring the scenery.

"Can I help you?" he said.

"Well, yes, I guess. I'm looking for tulip bulbs." She smiled brightly, faced him, all of which Kyle thought were good signs.

"Pink ones," she said, "if you have them, or else…"

Just then, there came a loud thump from the back of the store. Kyle thought those idiot Smith brothers must have slammed the door on their way out.

"What was that?" the girl said, obviously startled.

"What was that?" Hank said, suddenly appearing at the end of the aisle.

Kyle swallowed. "What? I didn't hear anything."

Hank started for the rear of the store. "Came from back there," he said.

"No," Kyle pointed toward the front. "It came from outside."

"No," Hank said over his shoulder as he rounded the corner. "Someone's back there."

Kyle turned to follow Hank, took one step and then turned back when the woman spoke.

"If you don't have pink, I could go with red."

"Red?" Kyle found himself disoriented.

"Yes, but only the deepest red." She gave Kyle that smile again, and he almost forgot about Hank. Almost. He hadn't heard anything further from the stockroom. Had the Smith's escaped?

"You know the color I mean?" She held out her hand to him. "Just like this color."

Her long perfect nails were colored the deepest red he'd ever seen. He held her hand, toying with her fingers. She let him. He couldn't believe his luck.

For the next few minutes, he played a cat and mouse game with the woman, weaving through a collection of rooted bulbs, shoulder to shoulder, crouching to access the lowest bin where they were displayed. He wondered briefly if Hank had discovered the Smiths in back but whatever happened there was between them. He had more important things to do just then.

There came another thump from the back. That, he told himself, was actually the sound of the back door slamming shut.

The bell over the door rang and Kyle looked up to see a tall guy with red hair walk in. He turned his attention back to the woman, but the man walked up and asked for shovels. "The rack in aisle five is empty.

"Maybe we have some in back," Kyle growled. "Give me a minute here, okay?"

"Ohhh," the woman drawled. "I might need one of those shovels." She put one deep red fingernail to her lip. "No, on second thought, I think I might have one already. Somewhere at home. How are you doing Mr. Clay?"

The man smiled. "Doing just fine, Miss Edwards."

Clay? Kyle wondered if this could be Justin Clay, the one Kathryn was harping about.

At the cash register, Theresa Edwards, as Kyle saw the name on the credit card she handed him, paid for a dozen bulbs that promised a deep red challis of bloom. While he completed the sale, he realized Clay had actually gone to the back and was just then emerging with a small red shovel in his hand. Kyle had another heart hammering moment of panic. Clay didn't seem out of sorts, as if he'd seen anything wrong.

Kyle returned to the matters at hand. He memorized her name from the card but couldn't come up with a good enough reason to ask for her phone number. Instead, he jotted his name and number down on the receipt. "I personally guarantee these will grow amazing tulips next year. If they don't, you can call me. I'm Kyle. My number's right there." He pointed at the receipt lying on the counter. "If you want, Theresa, I could show you the best way to plant them?"

"I think I can manage." she said. "But…" She picked up the receipt, turned and looked back over her shoulder with a teasing smile. "But if I need anything, Kyle? Potting soil, stakes, maybe some fertilizer? Can I give you a jingle?" She turned and walked out, ringing the bell above the door.

Kyle looked around the store and saw no customers except Clay who waited with the shovel. He rang him up and the man, fortunately, hurried out.

Kyle walked to the back, unsure what or who he might discover. As to the who, there was no one. As to what, a lawn mower now sat in the aisle where it hadn't been before. A plastic quart of oil lay upturned next to it, its contents spilled in a pool on the concrete. It confused him but just then the back door eased open, and Bubba Smith peeked in.

"What are you doing?" Kyle demanded. "Get in here."

Bubba entered, panting as if from sudden exertion.

"What the…" Kyle said.

Bubba stood up straight and smoothed out his shirt.

"Sorry, sorry," Bubba said. "Cole sent me back for the shovel."

"Well, it's about time you idiots started digging. We can't let anyone else get to it first, you know. Where'd Hank go?"

Bubba walked to the corner and picked up the spade that leaned there. "Hank? Ain't he out front?"

"No, Bubba. He came back when he heard some sound back here. Was that you two freaks of nature making that noise?"

"We never saw Hank. Honest," Bubba said. "We just wanted to confirm you said to meet at the bridge at noon?"

Kyle wasn't sure what was going on. Where had Hank gone? If he had exited by the back door, wouldn't he and the Smiths have seen each other? The little bell at the front door rang. Crap, another customer. He pointed "Be there or else, Bubba."

Kyle walked to the front, anxious to be quit of the store.

Chapter 33

1790

Swift and sure were the feet of Running Eagle. With one stop per hour for water, he made a steady course toward the site where he would place the second marker, the next step on the journey of the Peace Tree heritage bundle. He recalled the words of Chief Saunuk.

"From the painted bluff, follow the course of the river, then seek out the field of rolling hills. Nestled in the earth amongst our ancients' burial mounds is their sacred marker. The giant stone designates a burial ground for our ancestors. Upon that rock, you will inscribe the symbol of your guide."

At that moment, the shadow of the red-tailed hawk drifted ahead, as if the great bird understood.

On through the cool day, Running Eagle ran. The warm sun and the fall temperatures created the perfect balance to sustain his energy. When he reached the field of mounds, tall grass hid evidence of any former burial place. The ways of the natives were long remembered, and soon he gazed upon the gray edifice. Stretching just past the reach of his raised arms, nature had formed the boulder with a smooth flat side, as if the chunk of rock had been sliced from a larger block by a sharp blade.

Similar to the previous evening, he prepared for meditation and the rituals to consecrate the site. As decreed by his chief, he sat vigil throughout the night. With the first rays of the morning sun, he took up his fashioned tools, approached the stone, and began his labors.

***

Jacob Wildcrow came to, wincing against the bright sun. Once again, he'd witnessed the past. The visions showing Running Eagle's journey followed his own.

Time had eroded the etching of the hawk upon the gray rock, but if one looked for it, the outline would appear. White men had turned it into a landmark, something deemed special to be part of transforming the land into a golf course and housing development for the wealthy. They completely ignored the sacred honor placed upon the stone by the people who once occupied the land. If the hawk in the stone had been recognized, it might have been taken for a child's playtime doodling activity.

Wildcrow scanned the land around the edifice and munched a handful of sunflower seeds. Even in November, die-hard duffers hit the little white ball across the flat fairways, laughed and joked about their shots. Maybe a few even negotiated weekend business deals. Wildcrow never did understand conducting business affairs during a round of golf. Serious matters should have been discussed around a meeting room table or at the very least, while sharing a meal. His ancestors formalized matters within and without the tribe around campfires, offering harvest bounties to honor those with whom they resolved conflict. Only afterward did they engage in friendly competition such as hatchet throwing, archery, and horse-riding skills. Victories weren't sacrificed to earn favor or to gain an edge in later talks. They were celebrated by both sides. Even those who didn't win received advice on how to improve their talents for when they next competed.

Wildcrow sighed. Yes, the years brought change, but how beneficial were those changes? He hoped his effort, and that of Grace and Digger, might bring back a little acknowledgment of the old ways.

With renewed determination, he mounted his ATV and roared off for the next marker.

***

Digger drove Highway G28 which roughly followed the contour of Lake Red Rock.

"You'd think as an amateur archaeologist, you'd remember to bring a shovel before we started out," Grace said.

He glanced at her, smiled, and shrugged. "Well, being around you, it's a wonder the shovel wasn't the only thing I forgot."

She pointed out the window. "I hope you haven't forgotten how to drive."

He looked out the windshield and saw they were coming up on a bicyclist. He eased over to pass and concentrated on his driving.

Grace eased down in her seat, looking anxious. He didn't need to be a telepath to know jumbled thoughts vied for space in her head. Wildcrow might be passed out in a ditch, suffering the aftereffects of his injury but as he deduced from the sunflower seeds, Digger thought the old guy probably was having fun leading the charge, as it were, on the journey his ancestor made centuries ago. Wildcrow was a tough ole bird. They'd catch up to him later.

Grace also probably worried who had been watching them at Painted Rocks. Digger wondered, too. How long had he been there? Had he been following them? How?

Despite the kiss he and Grace almost shared, she remained hesitant about both him and the entire venture to follow in Wildcrow's footsteps. Digger knew he couldn't push her too hard to accept and embrace her heritage. She might slam the door in his face, forget him and her grandfather, and go home to Ames. If she did, he could forget about any romantic relationship with her.

No, he had to be patient, persistent, and optimistic to make everything work out. He glanced back at Chow whose moist breath warmed his cheek. The dog met his eye and huffed once as if somehow it knew his thoughts about Grace. He reached back to give the big dog a scratch behind the ear. Chow uttered a throaty rumble of pleasure and licked Digger's cheek.

They passed Cordova Tower. Digger curled his lips in disgust as he saw half a dozen people with shovels scattered around the area. Each had staked a claim like the California gold miners of the mid-19th century hoping to find treasure. All they'd accomplish would be to put holes in the ground, tear up the land, and leave a mess for the county conservation personnel.

They saw more treasure seekers further along the route. This time county patrol officers were on site putting a halt to any digging.

What a mess a little rumor had become.

Ten minutes later, they arrived at Bos Landen. This area southwest of the Pella airport consisted of upper-class houses, a couple hotels, and an eighteen-hole golf course. A five-minute drive to the marina or into Pella, the subdivision provided exclusivity while remaining part of the Pella community.

At the west entrance to Bos Landen, near the second green, a huge boulder welcomed guests and residents. It measured approximately ten feet high and fifteen feet long at the base.

"I think the developers decided it was too much trouble to remove this, so they left it," Digger said when they stood in front of the massive rock near a sapling growing along the entrance road. "It doesn't interfere with housing or golfing and makes a nice decorative piece here at the entrance."

"Where's the marker?" Grace asked.

"I think this *is* the marker," Digger said.

"Okay, but what does it tell us? Is this where the treasure is buried."

"I don't think so," Digger said. "We may be looking at this all wrong." He pulled up the image of the map on his phone and pointed to their location. "Look here. We don't need to know where to go next. The map shows us." He moved his finger to the next symbol. "This is below the dam, near the Howell Station campground." He slid his finger to a spot just west of Knoxville. "And this appears to be another marker. The only way we're going to know for sure is to check out the third marker, see if it points in the right direction like these two did. This fourth marker looks like it's around Flagler."

"So, if the arrow at Painted Rock pointed to this marker at Bos Landen, and on *this* rock there's something that points toward the third one, then we can assume that one will lead to the fourth."

"Right," Digger agreed.

"Then why don't we jump ahead to go to the fourth one?"

"Because it's not about the destination. It's about the journey," Digger said. "It's about retracing the path Running Eagle took in the late 1700s. We're not doing this exactly like him—on foot—but we're taking the journey because it was sacred to the Indians back then."

"What does it matter now if we skip ahead?" Grace threw out her arms. "Look around you, Digger. It's a golf course surrounded by dozens of houses. There's nothing Indian related here, let alone sacred."

"You're standing on it."

"What?"

Digger stepped to her, took one hand in both of his. "The Indians considered the land itself sacred. The trees, the wildflowers, the rabbits, and deer in the woods. The river that provided water. All of it was sacred, given to them by the Great Spirit. Why do you think they were upset when the white man came through and took it all away from them? The land was their livelihood. It provided shelter, food, and protection.

"Wildcrow told us the story of Chief Saunuk and Running Eagle. About Saunuk's prophecy and the brave's journey to find the right place to hide the bundle, whatever it contains. I don't think the bundle itself is the key. Who knows? It may be, but I think our taking the journey following in the path is what's important."

Digger gave a small laugh, reached down, scooped up a handful of empty sunflower seeds that were scattered on the fairway, and showed them to Grace. "Your grandfather's been here."

Grace started to respond, but at that instant, Chow, who had been sniffing around the number two green, barked and raced toward them. In the next second, Digger saw the entire oblong circle of the fine-mowed grass collapse into the small rise where it had been located.

"Sinkhole!" Digger yelled. "Grace, back to the car."

Instead, Grace started to run toward her dog. Digger hesitated a second too late. A low rumble that reminded him of tennis shoes in a washing machine emanated from below. Five feet in front of Digger, the ground pushed up and turned over. For some odd reason, his mind jumped to a scene in a movie he'd seen years ago. He knew that any second, a groundhog would pop his head up. Just as the goofy face of Bill Murray came to him, the ground below him collapsed. He went down with it—another sinkhole—grasping at grass and dirt and then bare roots. Fear rose and he knew then that this was it, how he'd die.

He was sucked into darkness. He reached for a dangling root with his right hand and his left arm caught something. He kept falling with the dirt, but a bolt of pain shot through his left shoulder. He yelped in pain, but his descent stopped. Below him, the earth continued to fall away into a shaft of darkness.

He heard Chow barking. Funny that the dog barked three times in a row, hesitated, then three more times. The earth continued to rumble, and the sides of the shaft shifted.

"Digger!" Grace yelled.

He raised his head and saw only a rough circle of daylight. Then both the dog and Grace's head and shoulders appeared.

The agonizing pain in his shoulder continued. Digger saw in shadowy light that his left arm had somehow gotten caught on a loop of a root sticking out. He dangled, suspended, by his left arm. He'd been saved from further injury, or worse, by happenstance, a tree's roots extending farther, seeking moisture.

"Digger, Digger!" Grace shouted. "Are you alright? Talk to me!"

"It's.... I'm okay, Grace. It's a sinkhole, I think. I'm okay. My arm...."

"Digger, can you climb out?"

Digger embedded his shoe into the side of the narrow shaft to lift his body, take weight off the injured arm. He reached for another nearby root with his right hand, but he was too far down with nothing to help him climb. He'd fallen perhaps fifteen feet.

"Digger," Grace said. "What can I do?"

He looked up, saw tears and worry on her face, saw the dog's muzzle in the circle of daylight a couple of feet above his head. "Listen. My left arm is caught on a root. I can't touch solid earth below my feet. The side of this hole... it's a very tight fit. I can't move around much. I can kick at the sides, maybe get a foothold, but I don't know if I can get my right arm up to try to climb out." He took a breath and inhaled earthy dust. Coughed. Sweat rose on his forehead. "Get back, Grace."

"No. What? What do you mean?"

"I mean get back. This whole area must be unstable. It might get a whole lot worse before it gets better, more collapses, more sinkholes. Understand? You and the dog, get away from here. Go get help. I'll keep trying to climb out but get away and go get help."

"Digger. No. I...."

"I mean it Grace. Go get help. Call 911."

Digger saw her face collapse and a tear fell from her nose, fell and landed on his forehead.

"Grace! Listen to me! Do it now!"

"Hold on," she called back. "I know what to do."

Both she and the dog disappeared from his line of sight. Above, only the blue sky and the edge of a white autumn cloud. He watched it drift out of sight. In the distance, he heard the Gremlin's engine start.

He dangled for one long minute and then pushed his soles into the dirt on each side and twisted, his left shoulder screaming in protest. He gritted his teeth and through the pain, managed to shimmy his right arm up to his chest but he couldn't bring it any higher. He paused, panting, listening. The rumbling had stopped. For now, at least.

Sweat and tears stung his eyes. He jarred his head left and wiped it against his outstretched arm, feeling bright pain in the shoulder, feeling also a knocking deep in the joint.

"Huh," he muttered. "Dislocated."

So much for being Errol Flynn, he thought.

Complete silence. Above him, the air had a hazy quality. It's just dust, he thought. He remained still, gathering his strength, his thoughts. It could all collapse. Then where would I be?

Slowly, he lifted his legs, bent at the knees, and jammed his toes into the sides of the hole like he'd seen telephone repair men do when climbing. Instead of twisting left, he corkscrewed his body right, pushed his right arm up past his chin, explored the side of the shaft, found another root sticking into the hole, and grasped it. He felt as if he'd just won the lottery but realized that the root was way too small to support his weight. Still, he pulled at it, tried to haul himself up, even trying to use his left arm, despite the searing pain. He felt the root snap in his right hand, and he flailed again, finding another root, but smaller still.

He remained motionless then, hot breath mixing with hot dusty air. A dizziness came over him, as if his head was filled with helium. Pain, instead of slacking off, grew stronger, sharper. He looked to his left and saw his arm trapped above his head, which had by a stroke of luck kept him from falling to who knew where. He saw most his armpit and trickling blood. This is not good, he thought. His shirt below his armpit was soaked with sweat and blood to his waist. He tilted his head more but saw no blood seeping down on his trousers. Thank God for small miracles. Maybe I won't bleed to death before I can get out.

He went woozy, lost track of how long he hung in space. Even the pain dulled to a heavy throbbing.

Something bumped against his head. Surely, not the hawk. It bumped again. Digger looked around, vaguely remembered something had happened to him. Then he remembered the fall into the hole, remembered Grace, and the dog.

"Grab it, Digger. Grab the strap."

He managed to look up. Against the sky, there appeared a woman with a halo of light. He couldn't make out her features but a part of him began to see he might be in heaven. Then, a shaggy animal. So…that would be Chow, he told himself. And the saintly woman…

"Grace Snow," he said but could say no more. The opening, the circle of light above his head spun and jiggled about.

"Grab the strap. The strap. Try to get it around your waist," Grace said. "Can you hear me? Can you do that?"

"I... strap... waist...," Digger whispered. He remembered the tie-down strap he kept in the back of the car.

"Listen, Digger," Grace said. "Open your eyes, Digger. You've got to do this. I can get you out, but you have to tie the strap around your waist. Okay? Then I'll get you out and we can continue our search for the bundle. Do you remember the bundle?"

Digger nodded. The bundle. *Red-tailed hawk.* Grace's voice was strong but cracking, unsteady. Digger did not want Grace to cry.

With an effort that sucked his energy away, he grasped the strap and fumbled with it. An image of his father showing him how to tie his shoes as a little boy came to him. *Loop this way, throw the string that way, cross over.* Digger felt no pain as he went through the motions. No pain. Odd, he thought.

Then, pain like he'd never felt before. He was being pulled up. He heard an engine noise from somewhere above. Slow but steady, up he came, inch by inch. He saw a fringe of green grass again and then the sunlit expanse of the golf course. Again, he felt that same overwhelming and unaccountable joy and the pain seemed to back off.

The door of his Gremlin flew open, and Grace ran back past the long tie-down attached to the bumper she'd used as a strap. As Digger brought himself to a kneeling position, she wrapped him up him a hug. He was once again on the solid earth.

"Oh," Grace said and looked closer. "Can you lift your arm?"

To his surprise, he could. It hurt but not like before. In the extraction, it must have gotten re-positioned.

"Looks like the bleeding's stopped," she said. "Are you having pain anywhere else? How do you feel?"

He moved his left arm around in small circles, testing. "Like I just got dragged up out of a hole to hell."

"I've got you, Digger," Grace said. He heard the words as if underwater. "We got you. You're going to be okay."

A county police car drove up and parked. The officer rushed to them. "Everyone all right?" he asked.

"I think he's hurt," Grace said.

"I'm fine," Digger said.

"Take it easy," the officer said. "Don't move around too much. I've got the ambulance coming. The EMTs will be here soon."

Digger blinked the world into focus. "No, I'm okay. Please call them back and cancel the ambulance. Really."

"Digger, you should be checked out," Grace said.

The pain in his arm had eased. A laugh burbled up. He further tested the arm's mobility and, though it ached, it didn't hang limp. More laughter.

"Digger?" Grace asked. "What's so funny?"

"I think my shoulder was dislocated, but you're pulling me up jammed me into the side of the shaft and jolted it back in place."

He started to untie the strap and stand.

"Just relax for a few minutes," Grace said. "The ambulance is almost here."

Indeed, faint sirens wailed in the distance.

Digger brushed off the dirt. He reached into his pocket and pulled out his cell, punched in three numbers, and told the dispatch to cancel the ambulance. "No, I'm fine. Really…This is Digger. Is this Melanie? Melanie Sanderfield? I recognize your voice…Digger…Justin Clay… Yes…high school American History. That's right. Yes, it's been a long time." He paused and looked at the sky. "No really, I'm fine, Melanie. Yes… Fine. Nope, it's a waste of their time." He looked at Grace. "Besides, I have my own private doctor right here with me so not to worry."

The arm ached, but the pain's intensity lessened with each passing minute.

"Digger," Grace said. "Maybe you should—"

"Nice talking to you again, Melanie. Take care." He clicked off.

The officer, whose name badge read D. Chan, said, "You should be checked over."

"Digger," Grace said. "Are you always this stubborn?"

He held up a finger and cocked his head. The siren continued to become louder but abruptly, it stopped.

"I'm balanced out now."

"What does that mean?"

"Earlier this spring, I was walking along the bank of the Skunk River north of Oskaloosa, got too close to the edge, and the bank slipped away. I managed to catch hold of another tree root, just like I did here. Unfortunately, the angle of the fall wrenched my right arm. I wasn't hooked around the root like I was down that sinkhole. I lost my grip and ended up going for a swim."

"Oh, no," Grace said.

"The water was high and fast from the spring runoff. I just had to let the current take me and try to maneuver to stay close to the bank, maybe catch hold of a fallen tree. Well, I did. Smashed right into one…leading with my right shoulder. Before the current dragged me under, I hooked around a branch and pulled myself up. Hitting that tree, though, put my right arm back to working order."

"You have an amazing ability to find ways of risking your life," Grace said. "Still, I think…"

Some inner voice told him he and Grace had to continue their journey. It had to be completed today, or at least the majority of it. To break off now even for a delay of a few hours, could ruin everything. He didn't know how he knew that, just that he understood. What dangers had Running Eagle faced in his day? Certainly not sinkholes, but who knew. What risks was Wildcrow taking, venturing out ahead of them on his own?

No, the pain had subsided to a dull throb. He knew he had some extra strength Tylenol in the Gremlin's glove compartment.

"Digger, look!" Grace pointed behind him.

He whirled to see the giant boulder tilt, then as if sitting in quicksand, slowly sink into another hole. Just before it disappeared, he saw the image of a bird, perhaps a hawk, chiseled into the rock. Seconds later, the ground beneath gave way, and the second marker vanished.

Chan helped them move back toward the pavement.

Digger stared in awe, frozen in place. Reports of sinkholes earlier this week had made headlines, but they were all in rural areas, away from residential neighborhoods. Would others form? Were homes in Bos Landen in danger?

The officer called for assistance and emergency personnel to secure the area. The ambulance arrived sans lights and sirens. Chan hurried over to warn them of the danger. EMTs exited and approached Digger who had unfastened the tie down strap.

"Sir—" one of them said.

"I already told Melanie I was fine," he said.

"Digger, please let them look at you," Graced insisted.

The pain in his arm had reduced to a dull throb. He turned to face the EMTs. He couldn't let them persuade him to be taken to the hospital. Again, that inner yearning pulled at him. They had to finish the quest.

"Guys, really, I'm fine," he said. "I don't need assistance."

The EMT tried again. "Sir—"

"I'm fine. I'm relieving any responsibility from you. I'm officially refusing treatment. As I mentioned to Grace, her pulling me out of the sinkhole put my shoulder back into the socket."

"If you aren't going to the hospital, why don't we just go home, take it easy, call it a day," Grace suggested.

He ignored her. Instead, he rolled up the tie-down strap and popped it through the back hatch. Then he stripped off his sweaty and bloody shirt, cleaned his torso, and exchanged the dirty shirt for an old T-shirt he'd thrown in the back. He thanked the officer who was busy calling in his report and thank the EMTs who only shrugged. Grace stood by the car with Chow.

He approached her, took her hand. "Seriously, Grace, I'm fine. A little Tylenol from the glove compartment and I'm back in business."

"But—"

"We can't do anything about this scene. Let the police handle it." He smiled. "We have an adventure to continue."

She looked into his eyes, shook her head in disbelief. "You're absolutely crazy. You know that, right?"

"I think crazy is just about right. Come on Grace, shall we continue?"

He opened the door. Chow jumped in as if he was quite down with this whole mess. A last look at the sinkhole and the policeman, Grace eased into the car. Digger slid behind the wheel and while Grace strapped on her seatbelt, he reversed away from the sinkhole.

Back on Highway T15, he said, "You did say that if I grabbed onto the strap and was rescued, we'd still look for the bundle."

"Digger—"

He took her hand. "I'm holding you to your word." He lifted her hand and kissed the back of it. "I promise. I'm all right. Nothing else will go wrong today."

Chapter 34

Not many boats floated in the water at the marina. Most of the pleasure craft had been dry docked in storage sheds. Only a handful of dedicated fishermen and die-hard sailboat owners chose to leave their boats ready for use. When Cole drove past the long office storage building, he saw no one on the grounds. He pulled into the main parking lot that contained only two other cars.

"We gotta get closer," he said. "Can't be dragging the body all the way down to the docks."

Bubba scratched his left armpit. "What are you gonna—"

Cole bumped the car up over the verge, onto the walking path, and headed for the water.

Bubba braced his arms against the dashboard. "Watch out—"

Just before the truck splashed into the water, Cole yanked the wheel left and stomped the brake. The back end of the truck skidded but stopped at the edge of the dock entrance.

"How's that for fancy driving?" he gloated.

"You let me drive next time," Bubba griped. "You're gonna get us killed doing stuff like that."

"You're just a baby. Shut up. Besides, I ain't the one doing the killing."

"What do you mean?" Bubba whined.

Cole hiked a thumb over his shoulder to indicate the truck bed. "Him. Why'd you have to kill him?"

"I—I didn't," Bubba stammered.

"He's dead, ain't he?"

"But it ain't my fault."

"You killed him," Cole said.

"It was an accident. While we was trying to escape, he grabbed me. When I spun, I didn't know the point of the spade was gonna go into the side of his head." Bubba winced. "Man, did you see his brains all over the place?"

"Listen, we're darned lucky *I* had the brains to think fast, to get him wrapped up in that tarp and hide what happened."

"Yeah, well, what now?"

"What do you mean?"

Bubba aimed a thumb to the truck bed. "If we're gonna dump him in the lake, we need a boat and we ain't got one."

"You moron," Cole held up a pair of pliers. "We borrow one. Do you still have that camera you bought a few months ago?"

Bubba hefted his body over the center console and rooted around behind the seat. He produced a Nikon digital camera.

"Don't know why you bought that thing in the first place," Cole said.

"To take pictures of pretty girls."

"And what happened the first time you tried that?"

Bubba pouted. "How was I to know her boyfriend was nearby?"

"You're lucky he didn't shove that camera down your throat."

"What was she doing wearing that bikini anyway?"

"They were going swimming at the local pool, you dork. Never mind. I think we can get some good use out of it today."

"How?" Bubba asked.

"Come on, I'll show you. We gotta take care of Hank first."

They climbed out and looked across the water to the boats tied up to the floating dock. The covered part, used to protect some of the large craft, was empty.

"What kind we need, Cole? I want a big one. A really fast one."

"And I want that brunette that works at Casey's. We get what we get. We don't have too many choices."

They scrambled along the water's edge to the gangplank of the marina. Wobbling like drunks they walked down the wooden platform until they found a boat to their liking.

Bubba jogged to the last boat in the line. "That's the one we want, Cole."

Cole came up behind him and patted him on the back. "Well, you ain't as stupid as the principal said you were."

Colored sparkling green, with lettering along the sides that read Z18 Nitro, the nineteen-foot bass boat sported a Mercury engine, bow and stern slots for fishing chairs, and plenty of storage compartments. He pushed Bubba aside, climbed in, and crouched at the steering wheel. Squatting down he pulled wires out and stripped a couple of them.

"Okay, now it's ready to rock and roll. We won't start this until we're away from the marina. Bubba, bring Hank down and load him up."

"By myself?"

"Get Hank and haul him down here while I find the paddles."

Cole watched Bubba stomp back to the truck. He jerked open the tailgate, dragged out the body wrapped in the blue tarp and secured with rope. The body fell but didn't quite hit the ground. Bubba hefted the blocks out of the truck, then grabbed a length of rope lying near the front of the truck bed. He tied a knot in one of the holes of the tarp and dragged the body and blocks along the dock. By the time he reached the boat, Cole heard him gasping for air.

"I'll... need... some help getting him into the boat," Bubba wheezed. "He's too heavy."

Cole shook his head in exasperation. "I take it back. You *are* just as stupid as the principal said."

"Hey!"

"Why didn't you untie the blocks and make three trips?"

Bubba looked at the body, the blocks, then scratched his head. "Yeah, I guess that might have been easier." He kicked the wrapped body. Cole helped haul it and the blocks into the boat and set everything behind the cockpit.

"Now grab a paddle and let's push this thing away from the docks," Cole said. "Don't make no noise. Let's just ease this thing outta here."

They paddled away from the marina into open water. Cole touched the controls he'd wired, and the twin inboard motors purred to life. He pushed the control lever up, and the bow rose in the water. Cole kept a steady speed, until they reached deeper water, then nudged the throttle forward.

"How far are we going?" Bubba asked.

"Up near the Peace Tree," Cole stated.

"That's gotta be at least five or six miles. Why don't we just dump him here?"

"I got an idea."

The mileage indicator registered just over seven by the time Cole throttled back the engine. The stump of the Peace Tree lay about fifty yards away. Cole scanned the shore for witnesses, made sure no one was driving across the Highway 14 bridge, then said, "All right, let's do this."

They hoisted the body over the side of the boat, then each picked up a concrete block and threw them into the water. The blocks disappeared under the murky surface. Seconds later, the blue tarp was yanked down and it, too, vanished.

Bubba spat into the water. "Hope they never find you."

Cole took the seat behind the wheel and steered the boat near the stump of the Peace Tree. The stump rose above them for about six feet and measured about twice that around the base at water level. It resembled a black piling. Their boat nudged up to the rotten wood and Bubba reached out to grab hold of it.

"It's kind of loose, Cole. Think it'll fall over?"

"Naw, it's been there for hundreds of years. It ain't going no place. Find another rope and tie up to it. Use that notch near the bottom of the stump."

Bubba found the boat's anchor, leaned over the side of the boat, and wedged it into the notch. While Cole inched the boat around the stump, Bubba played out the rope, then tied it off just below where it connected to the anchor. He looked to Cole for approval.

"Yeah, yeah, that's okay." Cole shut down the engine. "Be sure to tie it to the boat."

"What're we doing here anyway? I thought we were looking for that Indian gold."

"We are." Cole pulled the map from a coat pocket and spread it out on the boat's deck. "See this symbol? I think is the Peace Tree, and this mark next to it looks to be a stack of rocks that'll show us where the gold is."

"Well, you ain't as smart as you think you are, brother. We don't have any scuba stuff and wouldn't know how to use it if we did. How are we going to see which way the rocks tell us to go?"

"Smarter than you, brother." Cole refolded the map and tucked it back into his pocket. "Grab one of those fishing poles from that compartment, and I'll show you."

Bubba discovered a rod and reel from the collection in one of the storage compartments and Cole pulled line off the reel. "Now hand me your camera and I'll show you how we're going to do this."

"Camera? Oh yeah, it's right here." Bubba reached into his pocket. "It's gone. It ain't here."

"What! You lost it! Now just how stupid is that, Bubba?" Cole's voice carried across to the high south bank of the lake and echoed back to them.

Bubba raised his fist at Cole. "Hey, who's stupid here? If you hadn't made me get Hank by myself, I wouldn't have forgotten it."

"Well, we can't go back for it," Cole said. "It'd take too long. We'll have to use my phone. It has a camera and video."

Cole dug his phone out of his pocket, picked up the fishing line, and wrapped it around the phone. He looked at the closeness of the stump and wanted more distance. "Now paddle us out more from the tree."

Cole activated the phone's video recording and dropped the unit over the side. The phone sank and he released more line. "The water isn't too deep because of the drought this fall. There…that should be enough. We'll let it work for a couple of minutes, bring it up and see what we have."

"Won't the water ruin it?"

"Naw," Cole said. "It ain't gonna be down there that long."

Their boat drifted back to the tree stump while they counted down the minutes for the video to capture what it could near the bottom. When the boat bumped against the stump, the impact lurched both brothers from their positions near the side.

"Hey, Bubba, you're supposed to watch for that. We don't want to lose the phone. Now get back there and push us off."

Bubba stumbled over the seats and using a paddle pushed on the stump. "Cole, we got a problem."

"Don't bother me. I'm trying to keep this line steady."

"I think the cops are coming."

"What?" Cole looked in the direction Bubba pointed. A large craft, way across the lake, sped toward them. The word *Patrol* was just discernible on the bow.

"Bubba, get this thing started. Now!" Bubba jumped into the captain's seat while Cole frantically reeled in the phone with its important video.

The Mercury engine roared to life. Bubba shoved the throttle to the highest speed. The boat's bow lifted into the air, and Cole grabbed a seat to prevent falling in the lake.

"Head west," Cole yelled.

They picked up speed as the twin propellers bit into the water and the boat slid across the lake. Cole looked over his shoulder hoping to see the cops getting further behind. The anchor rope tied to a rear cleat caught his attention.

"Stop! Stop!" he yelled.

The rope reached its end. The boat jerked sideways and almost capsized. Bubba fell out of the driver's seat, collided with his brother, and both toppled into the water.

Cole was dazed but not enough to keep him from paddling for survival. "Bubba? Bubba, you okay?" he yelled. He started to swim back to the boat, its motors still under full throttle, and the rope taut behind it. "Bubba, where are you?" He saw a hand wave above the surface. He swam to his brother, grabbed him by the arm, then pulled him to the side of the boat where they hung on for dear life.

Cole held onto the side while Bubba regained what senses he had. "What happened, Cole?"

"You forgot to untie the rope attached to the Peace Tree. Ask me another stupid question."

Bubba looked back toward the tree. "Why is the stump leaning, Cole?" At the other end of the anchor rope, the dead tree shook under the strain of the boat pulling at it. The boat kept jerking the stump until *Snap!* The anchor chewed through the notch. The top part of the stump tilted sideways and splashed into the lake. The boat jerked forward again, making it hard for them to hold on.

The weight and size of the stump still hooked to the anchor slowed down the speed of the boat as it made its way across the lake. The brothers clung to the side; hands wrapped around the cleats. The boat picked up a bit more speed. The stump forced the water up and over it like a huge fish skimming the water's surface.

"We need to unhook that anchor," Cole yelled.

"How?"

"If I can get to it, I can untie it."

Cole felt like a movie stunt man as he worked his way toward the side cleat. He wrapped both hands around the rope. Though he knew the wet rope would chafe his palms, he allowed himself to be dragged back to the stump. Three feet away from it, his legs were swept aside, and his head conked into the tree. He still had enough presence of mind to grasp the rope. He heard Bubba yelling something. When he could see clearly again, Bubba was trying the same maneuver.

"Crap!" Cole saw the collision coming. He looked for anything on the Peace Tree to grab, saw a small notch, and stuck his hand into it. He wrapped his other arm around the anchor and hauled his body out of the line of Bubba's just in time. His brother's head impacted against the trunk, but Cole grabbed his arm to hold onto when Bubba lost his grip. His brother thrashed for a second, then found a handhold on the trunk. Cole looked and found another depression and heaved a foot out of the water. The wood was slick, but he was able to pull himself out of the water and sit on top of the stump, legs on either side. Gripping the nub of a broken off branch, he reached down and helped Bubba up onto the stump. In seconds both were riding the tree like it was one of those floating rubber rafts pulled behind a boat. Both clung to the stump and gasped for air as the spray of lake water washed over them.

"Bubba, the boat's turning. We're heading to the bluffs."

Bubba closed his eyes and screamed. "Do something."

The stump hit an obstruction below the water. The bottom sheared off and created a sled from the part Cole and Bubba rode on. With a lighter tow the boat picked up speed sending the boys on their wooden wave rider toward the shore.

Cole yelled over the noise. "When I tell you, jump off."

"I ain't jumping anywhere. You jump."

Their wooden sled whipped across the boat's wake and when they came close to the shore, Cole shoved Bubba off their perch and jumped himself. He skimmed the water for a few feet then landed with knees sunk into the mucky bottom only five feet from shore. He looked to see his brother had landed in the same position, an arm out to keep from toppling over. He grasped Bubba's elbow and together, they helped each other to shore. Seated in the mud, Cole saw the bass boat had grounded itself forty yards up. The engine sputtered as the outboard's blades dug themselves into the bottom of the lake, then died.

Cole rolled and saw the remaining portion of the Peace Tree. Maybe the trip across the lake had loosened the rope or the knot around the anchor hadn't been secure. The heavy anchor, still lodged into the tree, was free of its tether. The Peace Tree floated with the momentum of being pulled for another five yards, then sank below the water's surface.

The patrol boat plowed across the waves toward them.

"Let's move it, brother!" Cole said.

They hauled themselves up, ascended the small bluff, and into the trees.

"Hey, that was some ride, Cole. Scary, but kinda fun."

"Shut up and run."

"Did you rescue your phone?"

"Shut up!"

Chapter 35

Sheriff Lockridge sat in his office; his feet propped up on a large oak desk. The desk was forty years short of being an antique. That designation was for a piece of furniture at least one hundred years old. He didn't think the desk would make it that long. Scratched and grooved from numerous Sheriff's boots resting on the top over the years, it had character but could never be refinished to its original state. The etchings ran too deep. Like himself, Lockridge thought. There were just some attitudes and ways of doing things that he could never change. Some of them had served him well through the years, although other people might call him judgmental or rigid for holding to them.

Take for example, that guy in the black suit he had seen driving the Crown Victoria. Lockridge knew deep in his bones that this man wasn't who he claimed to be. The man hadn't committed any crime but raised Lockridge's suspicions. A check of the license plates showed the Ford to be Hertz rental car out of Chicago O'Hare Airport, but the information on the renter was incomplete.

Whatever business the man-in-black had in Marion County had not been revealed. Generally, Lockridge felt, if someone kept secrets it was not for a good reason. The man didn't come across as genuine. His identity and background needed further checking.

Lockridge's thoughts were interrupted by the shrill ring of his office phone. The county dispatcher was on the other end.

"Sheriff, I've got Hank Oliver's wife, Ella, on the phone."

Lockridge grunted an acknowledgment of this and instructed the dispatcher to connect them.

"Hello, Sheriff." The voice of a woman wavered over the line.

"What can I do for you today, Ella?" said the sherrif.

The woman hesitated, then in a rush started speaking. "I don't know if there is a problem and I hate to bother you, but I am worried about Hank."

"What's going on?" Sheriff Lockridge shifted to a more formal position in his chair.

"Oh, it's probably silly for me to call, but I just don't know where he is. I know he went to the fire last night, came home, and managed to get a couple hours sleep before he went into the hardware store. I can't seem to get a hold of him. The guy at the store said Hank didn't come in all morning."

The sheriff paused. Ella was not the kind of person who was overly protective or who tended to raise false alarms. He'd seen Hank at the house fire last night himself.

"Have you tried his cell phone, Ella, or any of his friends?"

"Yes, but I haven't gotten any response. That's another thing. He usually keeps his phone on all the time. No one that I have been able to contact has seen him since last night."

"If you saw him this morning, then I'm not sure it's anything to get all worked up about. He might have turned off his phone."

"But where could he be?" Ella said.

Lockridge stifled an exasperated sigh. "I don't know. Maybe he had a special meeting to attend. Maybe a delivery out of town. Could he have had something important to do in Des Moines?"

"Nothing he told me about."

"Well, like I said, Ella, it's been not even a day. I'm sure he'll turn up, but I'll notify the Knoxville and Pella police to keep an eye out for him. Keep calling friends or family that he might be in contact with. I'll let you know as soon as we find anything definitive."

Sheriff Lockridge ended the call and contacted the local and Pella departments for a non-emergency Be On the Lookout For. He rubbed a beefy hand through his thinning brown hair. A good place to check would be the site of last night's trailer fire. Maybe Hank had returned to the scene. It was possible with all the confusion. Heck, he might be having car trouble or even got to talking with someone and lost track of time.

The sheriff rose, put on his leather jacket, and hurried to his car. The November morning was dreary. Sodden brown leaves lined the gutters of Knoxville and the trees looked skeletal against the leaden sky. The rain from the previous night had left shiny puddles of water that would be frozen in the next few weeks if the cold weather continued.

Minutes later, he turned onto the quarter mile muddy lane that would take him up to the burned-out shell of the Smith's residence. The area still smoldered with wisps of smoke rising into the cool morning air. The Sheriff drove around the site, then parked close to a cluster of maple trees that were singed but still standing. He hoisted himself out of the squad car and began to survey the area.

When he had been here last night, there had been three local township fire trucks and emergency personnel spread out over the acreage. Orders shouted, fire raging, thunder rolling overhead. He had assisted in the search for the two brothers but there had been so much commotion it was difficult to know exactly who had been on the scene. Bubba and Cole had not been found, and their bodies were not in the rubble. How much of the property had been searched?

Lockridge slogged through mud in the former backyard into the trees. The air was sharp with the smell of burning embers and dank grass. He stopped at the dormant patch of marijuana. A couple chunks of wood from the exploding barn had reached that far and, by a strange coincidence, only the pot plants were affected. No other trees or scraggly weeds had been touched. Nothing he read in the initial investigation report indicated deliberate arson, but this area being completely destroyed was... interesting. Karma, the sheriff thought, was a mean witch at times.

He heard a rustling sound farther in the woods, most likely a deer. They were always moving around here in the fall, trying to find a lady friend. There were no trails in the copse, but it looked like there were footprints mashed in the wet undergrowth. He followed the crushed grass back to the circle of junked out vehicles. Strange collection. Some of these had rolled out of the auto plant sixty, seventy years ago. They fulfilled their purpose in life, then someone had found a reason to bring them here, to form this circle of steel and rubber.

A snake-like feeling wriggled through him. No one about, but Lockridge felt watched. He spied the deer he thought he'd heard earlier. It looked back at him for a few seconds, before disappearing in a flash. He was all alone... except for this collection of rusting vehicles. Silent, sleeping vehicles, the stark-naked tree standing as eerie sentries.

He dismissed the horror movie relation, shivered once in the cool air to shake off the unwarranted ominous atmosphere, and returned to his car. He hoped there were no other missing people today. He supposed he'd better check in on the search for that old fool Wildcrow. Someone from the hospital had called in earlier saying he had left his room and possibly the building itself. Lockridge decided to visit the Indian's usual haunts. If Wildcrow had set up camp again where he didn't belong, Lockridge would lock him up, no questions asked.

In addition to the search for Wildcrow and Hank, he'd better help his deputies with the goofy treasure hunters digging up the county—all based on some rumor started by someone who'd overheard the Smith brothers talking. Lockridge had gone out earlier that morning to roust some people out at the Whitebreast Park. The idiots had brought in a backhoe on a flatbed trailer. If an observant neighbor along the road leading into the park hadn't been suspicious, who knows how much damage could have been done.

Lockridge loved the county, loved Knoxville, and for the most part, enjoyed his job. Some people though....

His cell phone rang.

"Lockridge."

"Sheriff, this is Deputy Chan."

"Yeah, Daniel."

"Sheriff, I've been trying to reach you for about twenty minutes or so. I don't know why I couldn't get through. Maybe it has to do with this sinkhole or something in the air jamming signals."

"Slow down, Dan. What are you talking about? Sinkhole?"

"Out here at Bos Landen. Actually, a couple sinkholes. Almost sucked in that high school teacher. What's his name? Justin?"

"Digger?"

"Right. Anyway, we rescued him, and I've called in some assistance to evacuate the neighborhood until someone can get in here and tell us the area is safe."

Lockridge didn't fully comprehend the situation, but it sounded as if his deputy was on top of it."

"Where are you?"

"Well, I had to drive about a mile out," Chan said. "Like I said, I didn't get any signal. Although, Digger managed to call out for some reason. Not sure what's going on. Anyway, we're at the west end of Bos Landen."

"Okay, I'll be there soon as I can."

"Thank you, Sheriff."

Lockridge ended the call and took a last look in the direction of the junkyard. One of the rumors he'd heard the Smiths had spread was that the place was haunted. Lockridge had dismissed the talk. Look at the source. Haunted? Nah!

Still, an involuntary shiver rippled through him before he yanked the wheel and sped back down the lane.

Chapter 36

Jacob Wildcrow barely had time to settle himself in a grassy patch amongst the rocks below the Horn's Ferry bridge before the next vision overtook him.

"The third marker shall be your most difficult and arduous task," Chief Saunuk had told Running Eagle.

The brave stood on the bank of the river. That year, the Great Spirit had chosen to decrease the amount of rain given to the land. The number of deer and rabbits hunted for food had fallen as they sought more water-rich earth.

Running Eagle had reached the riverbank as the sun set halfway between its zenith and dusk. He had plenty of time to start fulfilling his assignment but knew he needed the rest of the day and the night to replenish his own spirit and body. After pemmican and water, he made himself comfortable in a depression near a fallen tree, closed his eyes, and opened himself to receive the Great Spirit's guidance and renewal of energy.

When again the first rays of the morning sun pierced the tree line, Running Eagle stood, stretched, asked for one more blessing, then began his search for the materials needed to create the third sign.

Wildcrow opened his eyes. Three fat mallard ducks waddled along the shoreline below him, pecking at the tufts of the resilient plants. Overhead, the red-tailed hawk created lazy circles. The river burbled over rocks and a discarded industrial pipe half buried in the sand. After a handful of sunflower seeds, he rose, clambered up the rocks to level ground and up the steps to the partial bridge that used to cross the spot where Elias Horn once ran his ferry business. He walked out onto the bridge and gazed downriver. From nearly sixty yards away, his old eyes caught a vague pattern of rocks below the surface of the water. He couldn't discern the shape, but he knew what it was, nonetheless.

He smiled, spit out more sunflower shells, then hurried back to the ATV. With re-energized vigor, he roared off, continuing the sacred journey.

***

As they drove along toward Horn's Ferry, still shaken from the sinkhole scare at Bos Landen, Grace didn't speak much. All thoughts centered on Grandfather. Where could he be? What was wrong at the hospital that they didn't even know he was gone until now? None of it made sense. If he left the hospital on his own, what could he have been thinking? How could he be getting around the county?

"When you threw that strap down back there, I looked up and I swear I saw an angel." Digger said. "Turns out I did. It was you. I really like you, Grace Snow. Have I ever told you that?"

What was Digger doing? She gave him a half smile. "Thanks, Digger." She returned her attention out the window, not really interested in what he had to say.

"No, I mean it. You had a halo around your head." he said.

"Digger, keep your eyes on the road."

"Could we talk about us?"

"What do you want to know?" she asked.

"I realize now that I came on a bit strong back at ISU. However, after all these years, my feelings haven't diminished."

She gave him a pointed stare. "What about Kathryn?"

Digger shrugged. "What about her? The relationship was fine for a while. Recently, I haven't enjoyed it as much."

"How recently?"

He smiled. "Well, certainly in the last day or so."

"Digger—"

"More like two or three months. Probably around the time she started getting fired up about a casino. I think even then, I understood where each of us was headed, and it wasn't being together."

Grace saw the sign for the Howell Station Campground.

"I know we've just become reacquainted, but I was hoping you'd feel at least a little something toward me," Digger said.

"You're still pretty forward, aren't you?"

He shrugged again and gave her a wry smile. "This adventure is going to end in a day or two. Then you'll go back to Ames. After

230

that, who knows? I figured I might as well give it a shot now, rather than having to chase you down like the ending to a chick flick."

"Chick flick?"

"Sorry, like the ending to a *romantic movie.*"

She shook her head in mild exasperation. "Can we do this later? We need to find Grandfather."

Grace knew Digger was attracted to her, but right now was no time to fall in love. Her full attention had to be to find Grandfather.

"We're on his trail." He sighed. "We might catch up to him. Don't worry about it."

He rolled the window down so Chow could stick out his muzzle. A nice gentle breeze flew by his nose with his tongue flapping in the wind.

Digger drove on over the rolling landscape, passing fields now denuded of corn and beans. "Grace, could you do me a favor?"

"Of course," she said. "If I can."

"This one isn't hard. Could you reach into the glove compartment? I have one cigar left. Now's as good a time as any. It's in there somewhere. See if you can find it for me."

After a minute of picking between a small notebook, a collection of pens and a pair of sunglasses, she found the metal tube that looked like it might hold a cigar. "This it?"

"That's the one," Digger said. "Grab that butane lighter there, too, if you would."

She watched him run through the ritual of lighting and smoking he'd only talked about before, the clipper he kept in his pocket to trim the end, the licking part, the puffing part, the smooth and deep inhale. And while there was something intriguing in all that, she couldn't imagine herself smoking a cigar. She knew women who did, though.

Digger opened the window some to let the smoke out. Grace let her elbow rest on the center console and was surprised and mildly amused when Digger reached for her hand and held it like a schoolboy. Unasked for, a feeling of warmth flooded up from somewhere in her chest, and despite the chill of the late afternoon coming in through the window, the feeling flooded into her cheeks.

"I like that, Digger." She gave his hand a gentle squeeze and he did the same. "But please try to concentrate on driving."

Digger's face was lit with a pleasant smile. He turned to her. "We're almost there."

Besides the spaces for camper trailers and tents, Howell Station Campground offered a separate area for fisherman and hikers. Ample parking, restrooms, and a fish cleaning station. On the eastern end stood the Horn's Ferry bridge.

Digger parked the Gremlin, and they climbed up a short flight of stairs along the walking trail to the bridge. Chow happily ran back and forth, stopping to sniff trees and various patches of ground.

"I'm sure I visited here as a girl, but I don't remember," Grace said when they stood before a portion of fencing decorated with copper-colored silhouettes of some of the area's avian wildlife.

"Built in the early 1880s." Digger puffed on the cigar. "This was the first bridge in Marion County to cross the Des Moines River. Stayed open to cars and trucks until 1982."

"What happened?" Grace asked. "Did part of it collapse?"

"Yes, but not until about nine years later. One of the support pillars just gave way. Now, the bridge is just an observation point."

They moved to an information sign that told them of Elias Horn and his ferry business before the bridge had been built. The sign listed prices for people and livestock, including five cents per head of cattle and a quarter for a wagon and two horses.

The bridge itself extended about a third of the way across the river with fencing running along both sides and the end. Wooden planks made up the flooring. Another sign gave information regarding eagle watching, and a telescope, the same rust color as the railing, allowed visitors long distance views.

"Where do you think this third marker is?" Grace asked.

Digger puffed again on the cigar and leaned against the railing. "I don't know." He looked up and down the river and across to the opposite bank. "You have to remember ole Running Eagle made his journey about a hundred years before Elias Horn showed up in Iowa and long before this bridge was built."

"Sure," Grace agreed. "What are you getting at?"

"Our map shows the third marker on or very close to the river." Digger pointed west where the dam and the south overlook were located just over a half mile away. "No dam or campground." He pointed downriver. "Nice long stretch of water with plenty of woodland."

"Right."

"The challenge would be to create something that would last, that wouldn't erode or be washed away. Which means no pile of rocks or branches of trees. Who knows how often the river has flooded over decades?"

Currently the water level was below normal, despite the previous two nights of rain, with extended sandbars and a good portion of river bottom visible.

"I'm not seeing anything I'd consider a deliberate pattern," Digger said. "Maybe we're looking at it from the wrong angle."

"What do you mean?"

"Again, no bridge in Running Eagle's day. Let's walk where he would have been."

Back out on the walking path, they found a steep rocky trail that led down under the bridge.

"Let me go first," Digger said. He stepped down about five feet and steadied himself. Chow almost knocked him over as he slid past on his own descent.

"Careful," Grace admonished.

"No worries," Digger said. He braced himself and brushed dust from his hands. "Even managed to save the cigar. Come on, take my hand and go slow."

Foot by foot with shoes sliding on loose gravel, they made progress down the bluff until they reached a spot directly under the bridge.

"I could have guessed as much," Digger said and indicated a scattering of sunflower shells.

"Grandfather was here, too," Grace said. "How did he climb down that rocky bank?"

"He's still pretty robust and nimble for an old guy," Digger said.

Ten more feet and they stood at the edge of the water. With the water level so low, she had a sense she could walk to the other side without getting her knees wet. It was all an illusion. The channel was much deeper than suspected. Grace didn't mind Digger holding her hand as they walked perhaps fifty yards downriver along the edge of the current. At one point, she heard a soft sound like paper rustling. A dusty gray egret lifted off from the water's edge and flew to the opposite embankment. When the bird disappeared into the camouflage of the woods, she looked at Digger. He'd been looking at her.

"This is one of my favorite areas in and around Red Rock." He held her stare. "Who knows how many beautiful creatures you might see?"

Flirting again, she thought, but didn't release his hand.

When the river cut off further progress unless they skirted the steep bank, Digger stopped and did a complete circular survey. Grace also scanned everything. The flowing river, the trees on both sides, along the edge of the embankments, back to the bridge. She saw nothing unusual other than a couple of cement blocks upended in the water and a large drainage pipe half buried in the river bottom.

"Hey, there's our friend." Digger pointed to a circling red-tailed hawk above them. "I think we're in the right place."

"I don't see anything, though."

"I know, but I can't help but feel we're close."

She made another cursory scan but stopped when she saw Chow had ventured farther into the river than expected. "Chow! Come back here."

The big husky barked once, lapped some water, then continued walking.

"Chow!"

"Wait," Digger said. "Do you see what I see?"

"Yes, my dog going too far. He'll get caught in the current."

"I don't think so but look at him. He's not standing on the river bottom. Don't you see? He's walking along a line of rocks."

Grace harrumphed. "Digger, this is *all* rock we're standing on."

"Yes..., but something's different. I wonder."

"Different how?"

Digger continued to look at Chow for another few seconds, then turned his head to look back at the bridge.

"What are you thinking?" Grace asked.

"I have an idea." He clapped his hand once. "Come on, Chow. Let's go!"

The dog splashed and bounded back to them. Digger ruffled the dog's wet mane and vigorously scratched its head. Chow lavished the attention, bouncing and licking Digger.

"Why is he obeying you and not me?" Grace asked.

"Ah, probably just testing the limits. Children and dogs do that. Don't worry. He's just happy to get some exercise. Huskies need a lot of exercise."

"I'm a vet," Grace countered. "I know dogs."

"Well, this one may have provided the answer to our problem."

"How's that?"

"Follow me."

They returned to the rocks under the bridge, climbed up to the trail, made a quick stop at the Gremlin so Digger could dispose of his cigar stub, then he led them onto the bridge, really just a wooden walkway where the telescope was mounted near the plaque for Gladys Black.

"Think about the common denominator in regard to the two markers we've seen so far." He crouched to look through the viewfinder. He adjusted the angle of the telescope in the direction they'd been standing near the river.

"Well, obviously they're Indian related," Grace said. "An arrowhead and a hawk symbol."

"Sure, but where did we find the first, the arrowhead?"

"At Painted Bluffs."

"Right." Digger manipulated the focus wheel, then paused, motionless for several seconds. When he stood, he had a huge smile planted on his face. "Arrowheads were made of chipped stone. The first marker was an arrowhead created by stones, found on a precipice of a rocky bluff."

"Okay," Grace said, still unsure of Digger's point.

"The second marker was etched into a boulder."

"So?"

"Rocks. Stones. Don't you see?"

"No, although I think you may have rocks in your head," Grace said.

"You're cute when you get upset."

"Digger!"

"Okay, okay." He held up his palms in an I-give-up gesture. "What's more permanent than stone? Water can erode it away, but only after thousands of years. Weather may take its toll, but, again, over time. The arrowhead was relatively safe. The water never would have been that high. How many other people might have dared lean out so far on that bluff to discover what lay below?"

"And you told me Bos Landen developers might have thought destroying the boulder too costly."

"Sure. They may have thought the hawk symbol a cool piece of art."

"So, now we're at the river," Grace said.

"And what did you say we were standing on down there?"

"Rocks."

"Right," Digger said. "Chow was walking along a line of stones. I can imagine two, maybe three in a row, being something natural, but not a whole lot of rocks. Unless...."

"Someone put them there."

Digger gestured to the telescope. "See for yourself."

Grace placed her left eye to the glass, blinked a few times to focus, and saw... nothing.

"It's the river, Digger."

"That's the spot Chow was playing in. Look below the surface. Think about those pictures with hidden images underneath the complex pattern."

She blinked again and didn't focus on any particular point. She saw one of the stones Chow had stepped on. It looked securely embedded in the river bottom. Then she saw another... and another....

When a cloud partially covered the sun and the shadows moved, she saw a shape emerge. Okay, maybe not the entire shape, but enough she could fill in the rest.

"It's the hawk," she exclaimed. "I see it."

She stared and grinned at him with her whole face. "I see it." She gazed at the river over the bridge railing, then through the telescope again. The stone hawk wasn't visible to the naked eye, but with careful, concentrated observation, she made out the head, beak, extended wings, and tail.

"Why do you think no one else has seen this before?" she asked.

"Who knows?" Digger joined her at the railing. "In the last 250 years or so the river has been low enough people might have seen the stones, but not recognized *what* they represented. Even at ground level during a severe drought, they may have looked just like a bunch of rocks. How often do you think that happened? Most of the time, they'd be under water."

"If Running Eagle put these in place back then, knowing the water would cover them most of the time, how did he expect anyone to find the shape he created?"

Digger looked at the red-tailed hawk that continued to circle above its stone cousin. "I don't know. It may be one of those mysteries never to be solved, but don't you feel it, Grace? This time, this place. These circumstances. They all come together right here. A confluence Running Eagle was trying to leave something behind for others to follow and understand. Maybe everything has been destined for right here and now. Maybe he was leaving something behind for *you*."

She turned to him. Still caught up in the excitement of discovery, she yielded to the impulse. When Digger leaned down to kiss her, she didn't resist.

CRACK!

Digger lurched away from her... fell away.

"What the—" he yelled.

Digger clutched at her even as he fell. Grace saw that two of the planks they'd been standing on had broken. Digger was hanging in open air, only his arms, neck and head above the bridge. His right hand reached for a railing post while he tried to get a purchase with his left. The rocks loomed thirty feet below.

She grasped his arms but couldn't tighten her grip.

"Wait, don't pull. My arm."

"Digger, I'm sorry," Grace said." I'm sorry."

He reached for the fencing, managed to wrap three fingers around the links....

His hand slipped off and he fell farther. He hung, suspended by only his fingers gripping the wooden planks.

"Digger!"

"Hold on." He grunted with exertion. Chow barked three times and pranced in agitation around the hole.

"Digger!" she yelled again when one of his hands slipped off to be followed a second later by the other. "Oh, no!"

She couldn't look, waited in horror for the thud of his body hitting the rocks. The fear overwhelmed her, choking off any scream.

Seconds passed. She cringed; eyes squeezed shut.

More seconds and she heard... more grunting. Fearing the worst, she peered into the hole.

No body sprawled bloody and broken below.

"Digger?" she said, her voice a squeak.

"Hold on," came the reply, but it sounded as if it came from right under the bridge.

"Where are you?"

"One second."

Fencing covered the end of the bridge. Grace heard it bang and rattle against the end supports. A second later, a hand popped into view and clawed for a hold. Then another hand grabbed another section of fence links.

She ran and leaned over the railing. Digger was pulling himself up the end of the bridge, one foot on a steel support, the other finding the bottom railing. When he was within reach, she grabbed his forearms. She didn't know how much she aided his climb, but seconds later, he arched over the railing and collapsed to the wood planks.

"Digger, are you all right?" She wrapped her arms around him, tears streaming. "I thought—I—"

"Yeah," he said and drew a long breath. "Me too, until I saw the under supports. Figured the end of the bridge was closer than going all the way back to the bluff. I didn't know if my arm would hold out."

He stood with her still clinging to him.

"I'm all right," he reassured. "I've had to do some climbing in my time. Granted, not without safety ropes and a harness, but I did all right."

"So much for nothing more happening today," Grace said. "Oh, Digger, let's get off this bridge."

"In a second," he said.

She looked up at him. "What?"

"I want to finish what I started."

The kiss started tender, but she wanted more. She gave more. A rush of emotion washed through her. The previous stomach-churning fear morphed into pleasure, a thrill at the touch of his hands, his arms.

Too soon, he released her.

"We'd better tell someone about that hole," he said.

"Do you realize this is the third time you've fallen today?" she asked. "Each time nearly avoiding dying?"

He pursed his lips and looked off into the distance. What was he contemplating? When he looked back, he shrugged and smiled. "Well, this journey has been about your heritage, to bring you back into the fold, as it were. So, I'd say, in more ways than one, I've 'fallen for you.'"

"That is about the corniest line you've said today."

His smile broadened, and she kissed him again.

***

They hurried off the bridge. Chow was the first one to the car, acting like he wanted out of there. He jumped up on the side of the car clawing at the window.

"Chow!" Grace raised her voice. "Don't scratch the car." She opened the door and he hopped in and laid on the floorboard with his head down.

Grace looked in the back and saw Chow still hiding his head.

"Is he okay?" Digger asked.

"I never seen him like this before. Maybe he's relieved the danger is over and that you're safe."

Digger drove to the registration station of the campground to report the hole in the bridge. The attendant said he'd call in the proper people.

Back out on the road, Digger said, "The hawk in the water pointed toward the next marker. Somewhere around Flagler. Should be about a ten-minute drive."

"I'm hoping we don't run into any more dangers," Grace said. "Let's find this marker and finish this."

"Agreed."

They didn't see the Crown Victoria following at a distance.

240

Chapter 37

Earlier

Cole and Bubba Smith crouched at the corner of an outbuilding at the Red Rock Marina. A Marion County Sheriff's deputy stood outside his patrol car fifty yards away. Most of the time, the officer kept his attention on his cell phone, but Cole knew he'd see the brothers if they tried to run to their truck still parked at the boat dock.

"Keep an eye on him, Bubba," Cole said. "I'm going to sit back and think." He landed hard on his rear, back against the side of the building.

"We gotta get out of here," Bubba said. "I'm hungry, and we didn't wait to meet Kyle at the bridge."

"We couldn't very well wait out in the open, could we? He couldn't call us because I lost my phone. Just shut up and let me think of a plan to get us back the truck."

"Why don't we throw a rock and distract him?"

"That only works in movies," Cole said. "Besides, I see two problems to your dumb idea."

"What?"

Cole held up an index finger. "One, you can't throw a rock far enough that cop will want to investigate. Even if you could, he might not hear it." He held up a second finger. "Two, where are you going to throw it so he'll be out of sight when we run?"

"Those are three problems," Bubba said.

"What?"

"You said two problems, but you listed three."

"What?"

"First, you said—"

"Shut up. Your dumb idea won't work no matter how many problems I gave you. Your dumb ideas have almost gotten us killed."

"When?"

"Two others I can think of right away." Cole stuck the index finger back in the air. "One, tying the anchor to the tree and forgetting to untie it when we had to escape the patrol boat." The second finger. "Two, suggesting we jump on the back of that hay trailer."

Bubba shifted around to face Cole. "You keep calling me stupid, but you keep miscounting. Again, you just listed three dumb ideas instead of two."

"At least you admit they were dumb."

"The last idea got us here, didn't it?" Bubba countered.

"Keep your voice down or that cop will hear us." Cole scratched his left armpit. He hated to admit Bubba's idea *had* gotten them back to the marina sooner than they thought. Most of the time luck did not favor the Smiths. Cole didn't know how they had escaped arrest, serious injury, or death. It all had to be a miracle.

Somehow, they'd managed to get on a good roll in the last few hours. After dumping Hank's body but failing to get any images of the treasure under water near the Peace Tree, they escaped the patrol boat. Okay, almost dying in the process and destroying another boat, but they reached shore and eluded a bunch of county cops who showed up to conduct a search. Afterward, they walked all the way across the Highway 14 bridge without seeing a single vehicle.

Cole figured they would spend at least a couple hours to reach the marina, but their luck continued. At the Highway G28 intersection they met a pickup towing a trailer with hay bales stacked four high. Before Cole had time to consider the potential dangers of the decision, his dumbhead brother pulled him onto the asphalt. Together, they caught up to the trailer when the truck slowed for the turn. They timed the jump, but almost missed. Another miracle graced them as fingers found the tie-down straps of the end stack.

The truck increased speed while their legs hung over the trailer's rear bumper. Only when the vehicle again slowed, this time for a sharp curve, did Cole have time to haul himself up. He grabbed the top of Bubba's pants and pulled him aboard. Seconds later, he almost tossed his brother off when he looked at Cole and grinned. "I knew it would work."

When the truck slowed a third time to turn onto a gravel road, the brothers leaped off. They were at the edge of a housing subdivision near the marina entrance. A ten-minute walk brought them to the road that ended at the docks.

Cole thought there would be an entire troop of cops waiting but was surprised when he discovered a single officer guarding their pickup. However, too much open ground lay between the Smiths and their vehicle. They'd been hunkered behind the same building for almost twenty minutes. Cole didn't want to admit it, but his stomach churned with hunger. What they needed was a distraction other than the useless idea of rock throwing.

"Hey, Cole," Bubba whispered. His urgent tone captured Cole's attention.

"What?"

"He's moving."

Cole eased up beside his brother. The officer, who had been leaning against the driver's door of his car, still looked at his phone, but walked toward the main marina office and store.

Bubba started forward, but Cole gripped his arm. "Hold on until he disappears."

He held onto Bubba's arm even when the officer rounded the corner of the building. "Wait for it."

When Cole heard the entrance door shut, he said, "All right, let's go. Quick and quiet."

They thumped across the pavement and loose gravel to their truck. Even after the body-surfing and subsequent dunking in the lake, Cole still had the truck keys. He waited until Bubba climbed in to start the engine. "Hold on, brother, we're gonna go!"

Cole jerked the shift into drive and smashed the accelerator to the floor. Tires squealed and loose gravel ricocheted off the docks. He steered the truck around the patrol car, the office, and up the road. A check in the rearview mirror showed their escape hadn't been noticed. He figured the cop had gone to the restroom and was too occupied to respond if he heard.

"Where we going, Cole?" Bubba asked when they reached G28.

"We lost our cell phones, so we can't contact Kyle."

"We still have the map," Bubba said.

Cole touched his pocket where he'd put the map, also not lost during their fast ride across the lake. "Right, but no way to read it.

Let's go back to Knoxville and see if Kyle is still at the hardware store. We can discuss matters with him."

Cole turned onto T-15 which would take them over the dam. At Idaho Drive, he saw a green Gremlin turn south toward the dam. He thought he recognized both the driver and the passenger. "Hey, I think that's Digger and that Indian girl who was with Wildcrow."

What do you think they're doing?" Bubba asked.

"Let me see that map."

He took it from his pocket and gave it to his brother. Bubba held up the map so Cole could look at it and still keep an eye on the road. Cole jabbed an index finger at one of the symbols. "See this? It's near the river, and I think it's south of the dam."

"So?"

"There's the next symbol. This map ain't to scale, but I'll bet it's between us and Highway 92."

"Could be," Bubba said.

"I'll make another bet with you. Those two are out looking for the treasure. They must have gotten a hold of a copy of the map and are following the trail."

Bubba's grin widened. "Then we follow them and steal the treasure when they find it."

Cole nodded and concentrated on keeping the Gremlin in sight. "We'll be rich in no time, Bubba. I guarantee it."

Chapter 38

"Across the river, you will seek the cave of our ancestors, revered yet today by our medicine men for meditation. Upon its wall, fashion the final marker. Using the black stone we gather for our fires, draw the symbol so it will be recognized by all. By this sign, those who follow your journey will understand they must return to the beginning. Include the companion of the air, for it, too, shall serve as a beacon of knowledge."

This part of the discussion, even in acceptance of his chosen role, Running Eagle found difficult to comprehend. The journey would form a rough circle... and end where it began? He had asked Chief Saunuk for an explanation regarding the instructions. Saunuk's hard gaze held his for many heartbeats. The furrowed visage could have been set in stone. It was the first question Running Eagle had asked, and he wondered if the elder looked for a wavering of heart, a weakness in spirit, or loss of faith in the task.

Running Eagle never broke the other's stare but felt compelled to offer a reason for his inquiry. "I do not question the importance of what lies before me. I wish only to have a complete understanding of this particular segment and why I will be returning here. You have said that our people will have already departed before I am finished."

Saunuk's stare lasted another full ten breaths. The hawk perched on the branch above them remained silent, as if it, too, waited for the answer. The never-ending sigh of the nearby river soothed any rising anxiety within the young brave. A lone fish broke the surface, perhaps hoping to capture a hovering dragonfly. A sharp wood pop in the fire shifted an all but consumed branch. Short-lived sparks blossomed.

Saunuk spoke. "All things return to their origins, though certainly not in the same form. The acorn grows from the earth into the tall oak only to one day die to replenish and nourish the earth for another generation. Animals and men born from their mothers and inhale their first breaths of air will one day seek out those mothers after death as spirits of the air. Even the mighty mountains formed by nature shall someday return, possibly as dust and craters." He indicated the Sycamore behind him. "This Peace Tree will serve to return knowledge to those who will seek our ways. This is why our heritage bundle must return to the place from whence it was created."

After completing the hawk marker on the river bottom, Running Eagle spent the remainder of the day traveling to the next destination. Another night's prayers. As the sun broke the horizon, Running Eagle entered the cavern. Bits of bone and beads and feathers left by previous shamans lay scattered on the rocky floor. Deeper within the confines he discovered a circle of stones used for fires. Realizing he might be the last to do so, he set about gathering kindling to set one more fire.

Soon the flames danced as did Running Eagle with hands blackened by the walls. His movements executed a ceremony for one of his final duties as bundle carrier.

***

Jacob Wildcrow opened his eyes. The western sun, well on its way to the horizon, still left enough light to guide Digger and Grace to follow. While this would be the final marker, potentially, it might be the most dangerous... but maybe the most rewarding.

Wildcrow stood, sprinkled the evidence of his presence on the rocky ground so his granddaughter would be assured he was all right, then spurred his pony toward the cloud-paled yellow sun.

***

Digger turned left onto a gravel road.

"Welcome to Flagler," Digger said. "A mining town at one time."

Grace said, "I don't remember visiting too often. There wasn't anything here when I was a girl."

"Still not much to it," Digger admitted. "People built and rebuilt houses after the coal mines opened and closed." He pointed to his left. "That was once a post office and then a bait shop."

Digger drove up the hill to the right and took the next right up another hill. "This little house and the main house belonged to the

246

Clarke's. Well, I guess the little one is still in the family. Ole Tom Wood Clarke worked the mines and after a long day, he spent time building the little house using only lanterns for illumination."

They passed a two-story house with gray siding.

"That old pear tree back there in front of the porch? It's one of the oldest ones around. Lightning hit it and Tom Clarke's father, Irl Hicks Jr., filled the trunk with cement to prevent the plant from dying. I've always thought it was the weirdest thing ever. Bruce Clarke, one of my boyhood friends, lived in the house."

"Are you trying to sell me a house around here, Mr. Tour Guide." Grace shot him a quick wink.

"Why Doctor Snow, are you flirting with your tour guide," he asked.

Grace turned away, and Digger saw the rising blush in her cheeks.

He drove up a dead-end road to a gate fronting a cornfield. On the gate a sign proclaimed the land to be part of a reclamation area.

"Where do you think this marker is?" Grace asked.

Digger executed a three-point turn and returned down the hill. A road to the right dead ended at a boat mechanics cum storage operation and a couple of outlying residences. He rubbed the afternoon stubble on his chin and smiled. "You know, meeting you again and having a resurgence of those long-ago emotions for you have been a little distracting."

"What are you talking about?"

"Maybe you moved away before you were told about this place, or you may have forgotten it. There's a cavern back this way that the Indians used to frequent. Medicine men went there for meditation, but other members of the tribes were, basically, the first miners. They used coal as fuel for their fires. The particular cavern, a natural opening by the way, hasn't been as preserved as it probably should be, but it's enough off the beaten track it hasn't been completely ruined by kids partying or vandals. When one of the mining companies set up operation decades ago, they found a hole at the rear most part of the cavern. Maybe something similar to one of those sinkholes we experienced at Bos Landen, but on a smaller scale. Anyway, they found the marker. It's been known for decades."

"I don't believe it," Grace said. "People have known where this is all this time?"

"Yep. However, no one has figured out the meaning behind it in connection to the other markers."

"Grandfather knew," Grace said in a low voice.

"Yep."

"Do you think he's been there?"

"I have no doubts."

Digger eased around a soft curve as Grace looked out the window.

"Did you see that?" She pointed toward the sky to the left of him.

He leaned forward to peer out the windshield. "No. What was it?"

"Two crazy crows chasing a hawk."

"Interesting." Digger chuckled. "Do you think we're the crazy crows chasing after your grandfather?"

They looked at each other and then Grace said, "You're just trying to be funny, aren't you?"

"Whatever you think of Native American mysticism, you can't deny that hawk has been showing us the correct path all day."

He returned his attention to the road... and slammed the brake. Chow thudded with a yelp against the back of his seat.

In the middle of the road, three feet from the bumper of Digger's Gremlin was a frail looking man with white coarse hair and a beard which hung from his chin to his knees. Dirty and faded blue denim overalls sagged on his body. The shirt underneath looked as if it hadn't been washed... well, ever. He stood bent over as if studying something on the gravel. His gnarled fist clenched a thick and solid looking carved walking stick with a short rubber sleeve on the bottom.

"Where did he come from?" Grace asked.

"I don't know. He wasn't there a second ago."

Chow huffed a bark.

"It's all right, Chow," Grace said.

The old man rose to eye them but didn't stand fully erect. "What the Sam Hell do you mean by trying to run me over fur," he yelled.

Digger saw stained teeth and beard. The old man turned his head and spit. A glob of what Digger guessed was tobacco spattered the ground. Some of the juice dribbled into his beard. Digger put the car into Park and he and Grace got out of the vehicle.

"I'm sorry," Digger said. "I didn't see you. Do you need some help?"

In a high-pitched gravel coarsened voice, the man said, "No, I don't need no help, buddy. But you are in my way." He spit another wad of what looked like coffee grounds from his mouth, barely missing Grace's brown suede boots. She cringed and stepped back.

The old man looked at Grace with a smile and tobacco clinging to his gums and the only bottom tooth in his mouth. "Heh-heh! Little lady, don't worry. I missed your foot by a fat caterpillar length."

"Are you sure you're all right?" Digger asked. "I mean, you're walking in the middle of the road."

"Buddy, I told you. I don't need your help. That's what this here thing called a walking stick is for." He nudged Grace. "You, on the other hand, sweetie can hang on to my arm if you want. We can leave this here fellow you're with and find us a quiet little place." He winked, smiled, closed his mouth tight, and swished the black chewing tobacco around in his mouth. Seconds later, he expelled the stream of black gob and juice, sending it flying downward splattering on the side of Digger's pants.

"Aw, buddy I'm sorry, boy. Suppose I'm going to have to pay for your cleaning now?"

"No. No, that's OK." Digger brushed the stuff off his pants, then wiped his hand in the grass. He looked up at Chow in the car, bouncing back and forth along the back seat and then from the back to the front seats over and over. His barks were muffled until Digger opened the door. "Knock it off, Chow."

The old man tapped Grace's arm. "Oh, look, I went and made him mad. What can I do to make up for my orneriness?"

"I'm looking for my grandfather and also looking for a coal mine with a Native American marking."

Another huge smile revealed a few more stained teeth and a few places where teeth once were. "You sure I'm not your grandfather?"

Grace smiled. "I'm sure. My grandfather is Jacob Wildcrow." This was the first time she had ever said Grandfather's name like she was proud to call him by his Indian name.

"Why didn't you say so, honey? I know Wildcrow. He's a mighty brave Indian. I've heard stories about him." He adjusted his grip on the walking stick and rose as high as his arthritic back allowed. "I suppose a proper introduction is in order. I'm Rudy Spencer. Tell you what I'll do. You get lover boy...."

"Oh, he's not...."

The old man grinned. "Whatever, missy. I know where you need to go and whatchur' lookin' fur. Just be shor' to tell ole Wildcrow that Rudy treated you right. Okay?"

"Certainly," Grace said.

"All right. You two follow me to the barn. Keep that dog in the car, 'cause I don't want it to get hurt walkin' 'round my property and disturbing my snake. You're not afraid of snakes, are you? Oh, what am I saying? All girls are afraid. Come on. I'll get whatchu need and take you to the mine."

He didn't wait for a reply but shuffled away toward a decrepit barn. Both it and the accompanying house looked on the verge of collapse. The red paint on the wood siding had faded to brown. Both barn and house roofs sagged. Dust covered all the windows and doors hung at angles where a decent wind might rip them away.

The entire parcel of land was nothing but a junkyard. Rusted seventies vehicles. A gutted pickup with the front axle propped on crumbling cement blocks. Blackened car engines. Disfigured bicycle frames. Tarnished tools. Broken sawhorses and ripped vinyl card tables. Weeds partially hid bald, white-walled tires and a short stack of railroad ties. More weeds sprouted from the drain of a scratched and chipped porcelain sink. An aluminum wash tub half-filled with murky, algae clotted water had settled into the dirt. An electric washer, grayed by time and weather, tilted on a patch of uneven ground, door hanging on one hinge. Broken, rotting tree branches, limbs, and dead leaves made a patchy carpet over everything.

Rudy guided them between chunks of debris to the barn where Digger found more grime-covered car parts, broken tools, sheets of moldy drywall, slats of plywood that looked as if giant rats had gnawed the corners.

"Don't go explorin' too far or you might find that bull snake living in here." Rudy uttered a throaty laugh. "It do help keep the mice under control."

He spit another glob of thick tobacco juice into a pile of sawdust that had been stained and spotted by years of other globs. In a corner, he rummaged through a pile of miscellaneous items and brought out a coarse, thick, but intact length of rope, a couple of dark gray railroad spikes, and a sledgehammer. The latter he hefted over to Digger. "Here, buddy, you handle this, and I'll load the rest into your car."

They took the equipment to the Gremlin, where Chow sniffed everything as Digger placed it in the rear compartment. When he closed the hinged rear window, Rudy said, "Think there's room for me, missy, if we snuggle close."

Grace grimaced and looked to Digger for help.

"It's not a very long trip," Digger said. "Just slide as far to the left in the seat as possible."

Once they all crammed into the Gremlin, Rudy said, "Head on down that road there over the tracks." He waved a hand behind his head. "And keep that fool beast from licking the back of my head."

After they jounced over the single set of railroad tracks, Grace said, "Isn't this someone's driveway? I saw the mailbox back there."

"Yep, but it's the only way to the mine," Rudy said. "Take that there trail through the grass on your left. Hope your car's got some good shocks, buddy."

Digger turned left and followed the twin rows of the overgrown tracks through the grass. Nature hadn't quite reclaimed the foliage flattened by numerous vehicles throughout the decades. He kept his foot resting on the brake and tempered the forward momentum down the hill. At the bottom, the trail evened out with patchy weeds growing through loose gravel and rock. The path led around a short bend of the hill and ended at what looked like the opening to the old mine. Fallen support beams and rock chunks partially blocked the entrance. A hand- painted sign warned of danger in faded letters.

"We won't worry 'bout going in there," Rudy said. "Whatchu want is to the left here."

They exited the car and while Digger and Grace stood at the entrance to the cavern, Rudy took a crinkled pouch from one pocket of his overalls, reached into the pouch with three fingers, pulled out a hunk of what looked like loose tea—but Digger smelled the acidic tang of tobacco—and crammed it into the gap between his bottom lip and gums. Almost immediately, juice seeped out onto his beard. That's why his beard is so rusty-looking, Digger thought.

"Better keep Chow in the car," Grace suggested. "We don't want him running around that mine."

"That's it... all there is to the old place," Rudy said. "Any spare equipment left in there is nothing but rusted old parts. Kinda like me. Old, cricked, and rusty. Buddy, it's not fun getting old. People tend to give up on us old cusses. Say we lived a long life as though we have no more life in us. Like being kicked to the curb or thrown out like a worn-out rag. Well, let me tell you, this goat may be old, but only you know who knows when my time is up. Same with your grandfather, missy. Don't you go doing what his fool of a son has done. Why, I have a mind to find him and beat some sense in his noggin with this here ugly stick. One day he'll be sorry he turned his back on Wildcrow. Okay, you two gonna stand there listening to me or you gonna check out this here cave?"

Digger stepped up a little rise of loose gravel into the cavern and helped Grace up. When he turned to lend a hand to Rudy, the other waved him off. "I don't need no help. I been in and out of this cave and the mines dozens of times."

Digger stayed ready. The walking stick slid, and Rudy fell forward. Digger caught his arm and gently pulled him up to solid ground. Rudy huffed once but nodded when he became stable again.

The mouth of the cave rose perhaps ten feet and tapered to what looked like a solid back wall. The entire cavern stretched for about fifteen yards. The rock walls were colored a dusty black. Evidence of long-ago campfires lay scattered about the floor as well as bits of arrowheads and nubs of animal bones.

"Wildcrow was here," Digger said and pointed to a small pile of sunflower seeds.

"Did someone dig out this cave?" Grace asked.

Rudy settled himself with a firm grip on the supporting walking stick. "I 'spect this was a natural cave. When the Indians found it, they may have dug around a bit. Collected some of the coal to use for fires and such. When the miners discovered the cave, they had enough sense not to bother this cavern. Maybe someone figured it was sacred enough and left it alone. That's why they dug out the mine entrance nearby."

"That's what I understand from what I've read," Digger said. "I'm not faulting or criticizing the white man for settling and developing the land. The population grew and dominance was going to happen. However, every now and then, someone remembered."

"You're right, buddy," Rudy said. "The cavern and mine aren't well known. Oh, I come back here ever' so often, find that some kids have discovered the place and done a little partying. Usually, the people who live in the house call in the county sheriff. However, them kids are just out here for a little drinking—" Rudy nudged Grace's arm. "—maybe a little smoochin' but not much else. They don't vandalize or spray paint the rocks or nothing. I pick up a few beer cans is all."

"I don't see the marker," Grace said.

"'Course not," Rudy said. "That's why I brought the equipment. Buddy, check out the back of the cave. Careful. Don't want you slipping."

Digger crouched and duck-walked to where the rock roof met the floor. He stopped when he came upon a depression in the floor that angled down into darkness.

"Might have been weak earth," Rudy suggested. "Anyway, that's where the miners discovered some Indian marker. Down there. Come on, help me with the rope and hammer."

They retrieved the spikes, rope, and hammer.

"Listen, you two," Rudy said. "Ain't room enough for three of us back there, and while I can still do most whatever I want, I don't think I can help you with hammering in those spikes. But you pound them into the floor, they'll hold you when you tie the rope. Sorry, I don't have no professional mountain climbing gear, but this'll do fine."

With Rudy's guidance, Digger pounded the spikes into the rocky floor and tied the middle of the rope around them. The two ends dangled into the hole.

"That'll be long enough for you to slide down. There's a small chamber at the bottom. You'll see a smaller tunnel running off that, but I don't recommend crawling through it. It looks a mite cramped. The miners dug a back door, so to speak, sort of an emergency exit if need be. It connects to the main tunnel of the mine."

Digger retrieved the flashlight from the Gremlin. "I'll go first."

"Are you sure this is safe?" Grace asked.

"'Course it is," Rudy said. "Done it myself scores of times when I was younger."

"I think it'll be all right," Digger said. "What could go wrong?"

Grace put her hands on her hips. "Well, Mister Archaeologist, how about you're almost slipping off the Painted Rocks? Or the sinkhole? Or almost falling through the bridge? You're three for three on almost dying."

"The key word there is 'almost,'" Digger said. "Don't worry, I've done this many times myself. Granted, with better equipment, but...."

Rudy tittered laughter. "That's the spirit, buddy."

Digger lay face down, grasped the rope, and let his body slide. The angle wasn't too steep. Digger used the rope to ease himself down. After twenty feet, when the floor leveled out, he released the rope and squirmed backward until he could rise to hands and knees. The smaller chamber was egg shaped with a couple feet above his head if he was in a sitting position. On the far side, the hole Rudy mentioned disappeared into darkness. Digger played the flashlight around the ceiling and walls until he found what he had come there for.

"Found it," he called up.

"Great," Grace responded. "Now get back up here."

"No way. This is your journey, too. Come on down and look for yourself."

"Uh, no way."

Digger heard Rudy's high-pitched laugh. "Ain't no snakes or spiders down there. All you gonna get is a little dirty."

"Digger—" Grace started.

"I'm not moving until you join me."

Digger waited. Silence from above. He imagined the scene. Grace contemplating sliding down the rope. Rudy smiling with his stained teeth, tobacco juice dripping into his beard. After almost half a minute, he heard Grace mutter something he thought was, "This is crazy." Seconds later, he heard the sounds of loose rock and yips from Grace as she descended. She appeared faster than Digger thought. Maybe she didn't have a firm grip on the rope. He slowed her momentum and helped her into the chamber to sit beside him.

"I've ruined my clothes, you know," she complained.

"You look kind of pretty all smudged in black."

"Don't start," she said. "I scraped my knee and tore my shirt."

"Hey," Digger said.

"What?"

"Shush." He played the beam of the flashlight on the wall nearest Grace. Even after two hundred years the etching in the wall looked almost as fresh as the day Running Eagle created it. It resembled something made by a young child or possibly what people had discovered drawn on cave walls by early humans. A bit amateurish, but Digger had to consider the space in which Running Eagle had to work and the primitive tools he had to use.

The etching was of a hawk hovering above a figure with long hair, wearing a breechcloth, and holding an oblong bundle. He stood as if offering the bundle to a tall tree nearby. The scale wasn't exact, but each part of the image was easy to identify.

"What's it mean?" Grace asked.

"We go back to the beginning," Digger said.

"What?"

"Your grandfather didn't tell us the entire story of Running Eagle's journey. I think he did that on purpose. He wanted us to discover things as we went along. If I read this last marker and our copy of the map correctly, Running Eagle returned to the Peace Tree, maybe buried the bundle in among the roots. See this dark spot near the base of the tree? It could represent a small hole."

"You mean we've gone in a circle?" Grace asked. "Why?"

Digger shrugged and slipped an arm around Grace's waist. He felt her tighten, but in a moment, relax. "I could get really philosophical about birth and death but think of it this way. You were born in Knoxville and spent some early years here. Spent some wonderful times with your grandparents. Then you moved away. Yes, your father took you away, I understand, but you came back to Iowa to attend the university. Now, you're back here. Back home with your grandfather."

When Grace didn't respond, Digger moved the beam of light around the chamber. "Look at this place. Think about everything Running Eagle must have endured on his journey. From that precarious ledge at Painted Rocks, to finding the monumental boulder at Bos Landen. How long do you think he spent gathering and placing those huge stones into the riverbed? Finally, to come down into this cave—with no rope or spikes—to create this marker."

He pulled Grace closer, leaned his head against hers. "Compare his journey to yours. Think about all the ordeals and challenges you've had to overcome throughout the years to be the success you've become. Moving away to a strange city, the ridicule at school, getting the money to pay for college. Oh, and don't forget a pesky student who only wanted a kiss beneath the Campanile."

Grace lightly elbowed his ribs. "Yeah, he was the worst."

"I don't like it when newspaper articles or television news broadcasts feel they have to mention someone's achievement by starting it with what the person is. You know, 'the first black man to do such-and-such,' or 'the first Mexican woman.' Why can't we celebrate the achievement and the person who accomplished it?"

Grace nodded.

"In your case, however, I think being from Indian ancestry helped shape who you are. Your attitude, your perseverance. Heck, you're a vet. In your own way, just like the Indians, you admire and respect animals." He sighed. "This journey we've taken today is following in Running Eagle's and Wildcrow's footsteps. It was their way of keeping the Native American heritage alive. Through you."

"How about you?" Grace said.

"My ancestors came from Great Britain, and I don't care what journey I take, I'm not going to be into tea and crumpets."

Grace laughed. "You know what I mean."

"Running Eagle didn't have a guide other than his chief. However, sometimes, those on a journey need a partner." He paused, but emotions compelled him to add, "I'd like to continue seeing you even after we're through here."

Grace shifted to face him. She tilted up her head for a kiss. Digger inched closer.

"You two ain't gettin' nekkid down there, are you?" Rudy's laughter filled the chamber. "I could always come back later."

Digger smirked and released his hold on Grace. "What a mood killer."

"I think it's time to go," Grace said.

Digger pushed the bottoms of Grace's shoes to help her climb the rope. When she reached the top, he started up. Halfway up, the earth beneath him trembled. Digger held his breath, worried another sinkhole might be in his future. The vibration wasn't strong, as if the origin point lay off in the distance. It felt like the impact after the driver of a heavy piece of construction equipment slammed the ground with one of its appendages. However, the force loosened stones and dust from the roof of the shaft. When he moved another half foot, he felt another vibration and more stones loosened.

He scrambled upward, pulling himself as fast as possible. In his effort, he scraped his back on the roof of the shaft, and a section of the roof collapsed onto his legs. He cried out and writhed in pain.

"Digger!" Grace called from above.

"Dang'nabit!" Rudy ejaculated. "Sounds like a cave-in. Buddy, you okay?"

Digger's legs weren't crushed, but he'd bet he'd have a couple good-sized bruises in a day or two. He shifted out of the rubble. Forced to use his arms—his left shoulder throbbing again—one handhold at a time, he pulled himself up the rope. Near the top, he felt Grace's grip. With a last exhausting effort, he heaved himself to the upper floor of the cavern. Legs throbbed, but he didn't think any bones had broken.

"Use this," Rudy said, and offered his walking stick. "See if you can stand."

"Give me a few minutes," Digger said. He needed more pain killers.

He rested until he felt he could move without falling. Grace helped brace him on one side and clamping hands around the stick, Digger rose to his knees. Feeling as old as Rudy, he planted one foot and pushed up to a standing position. By then, the pain had diminished to a dull ache."

"Digger, what happened?" Grace asked.

"I don't know. I felt the earth move, then part of the shaft gave way."

Rudy tittered more laughter. "Felt the earth move? Heh-heh, maybe you was thinkin' 'bout what you wanted to do with missy down there."

Digger shook his head. The old coot was nothing but a randy rascal. "I think I can move all right now. Let's take it slow, but I think we should get going. It's getting late."

Still using the walking stick and enjoying Grace's hands on his arms, Digger exited the cavern. Back at the car, he rested against the driver's door.

"Are you okay to drive?" Grace asked.

"I think so," Digger said. "I think the shock of the rocks falling was worse than the actual pain. I'm all right now."

Rudy shuffled around to the passenger door.

"What about your rope and spikes?" Digger asked.

"Don't worry 'bout them," Rudy said, and opened the door. "I'll come back for them later."

Once again, they crammed into the Gremlin. Digger made a U-turn and drove them back to Rudy's house. His legs might ache for the next couple days, but he didn't think the falling rocks had caused any serious damage.

They thanked Rudy for his assistance and watched him claw his way out of the car, walk around the front, and tap on the driver's window with his stick. When Digger rolled down the window, Rudy said, "You know, I don't get many visitors these days. I shor' was glad to help you, though. I'm sorry you got hurt, Buddy. I had no idea that shaft was unstable."

"That's okay," Digger said."

"I feel bad about it, though. Anyway, I wanted to tell you...."

His words trailed off, and his face twitched. Digger wondered if he was trying to find the right words.

"Well, I just wanted to say to you... Grace. You take care of your grandpa. You listen to him and everything he says."

Grace nodded.

"I don't know all the particulars of what you two have been doing today, but, well, I hope you both find whatever it is you're looking fur."

"Thank you, sir," Digger said.

Rudy tapped Digger's shoulder with his stick. "You buddy, you take care of this here girl. Don't let me hear you mistreatin' her."

"No, sir."

"Doesn't mean you can't have a little fun along the way." He hiked his eyebrows a couple times. "If you know what I mean."

He exploded with mischievous laughter, turned, and shuffled toward the ramshackle house.

Chapter 39

"I knew it," Cole Smith had boasted when he saw Digger, Grace, and some old geezer drive off in the Gremlin. "Remember that mine and the second cave we found a year or so ago? Had a couple parties back there."

"Yeah," Bubba agreed. "Fun times."

"I'll bet that's where they're going. We'll wait for them, then find a chance to steal whatever they find."

Cole pulled into the boat mechanic's yard and circled to park facing the main road. The truck wouldn't be seen when that Indian woman and her pal drove past on their way out of town.

Cole had followed the Gremlin into Flagler. The small town had only three gravel streets and the other side lanes were dead ends. He and Bubba hadn't found any customers when they tried to sell their weed a few years ago, but while exploring, had discovered the mine and the smaller cave.

Not half an hour later, the Gremlin reappeared, stopped next to a house with a junk-filled yard. The old guy got out of the car but walked over to the driver's side window. Cole rolled down the truck's window.

"I don't know the particulars of what you two have been doing today, but, well, I hope you both find whatever it is you're lookin' fur," the old guy told Digger. A brief exchange, then the car drove off. The old man, using a gnarled wood walking stick hobbled up two steps and into the house.

"They didn't find the treasure," Cole said. "They're still looking for it."

"Let's go, brother," Bubba urged.

"Wait a minute."

"Why? They're getting away."

"Show me that map."

Bubba unfolded the parchment.

"Look here, Bubba. There ain't no markers left. Them two came from the direction of the third marker. They must have been to the others."

"So, what are you thinking?" Bubba asked.

"I'm thinking you're not thinking."

"Don't call me stupid again or you and me are gonna have problems. I'll whoop your—"

"All right," Cole said. "Shut up and listen. Those guys went to this last place. I heard that old guy tell them he hoped they find what they were looking for. Which means they didn't find the treasure."

"Right. Which means we gotta keep following them."

"Wrong. They didn't find the treasure, but it has to be here because this is the last spot. Ain't no more symbols."

"Three people didn't find anything?" Bubba asked.

"Who knows how big that mine is?" Cole said. "They weren't back there very long. I'll bet that treasure is there, and we're going to find it."

Bubba gazed at the map. Cole let him contemplate a moment. After ten seconds, his brother nodded. "Let's do it."

Cole followed the path and parked in front of the small cavern. "Let's start with this one. Then we'll try the bigger mine."

"But we were here partying," Bubba said. "This ain't very big. We'd have seen something."

"Let's look anyway. Grab the flashlight from the glove box."

"Why do you think it's called a glove box?" Bubba asked. "We ain't never put gloves in there. Mostly trash and stuff. Maybe it should be called a trash box."

"Never mind your word games." Cole grabbed the flashlight Bubba had retrieved. "We have a treasure to find."

They stood at the mouth of the cave while Cole shined the light over the floor, walls, and rocky ceiling.

"Look there," Cole said when the beam showed the rope tied around the railroad spikes. "Remember that hole we found when we were here?"

"Right. We weren't going to go down there. Too dark."

"Now we can. Come on, brother, I can almost feel that treasure in my hands."

Cole flopped onto his belly. Using the rope, he slid down the shaft. Bubba, the heavier of the two, became stuck at one point. Cole had to pull on his feet to get him through the opening. In the smaller chamber, they didn't see any sign of digging, but found the etched hawk, tree, and the roughly shaped human figure.

"What's it mean?" Bubba asked.

"I don't know. More Indian stuff, I guess."

"Do you think the treasure is behind it?"

Cole touched the wall. "No, this seems solid enough."

Soon, they found the tunnel.

"Maybe it's through there," Cole said.

"Maybe, but I'm too big to crawl through."

"Too fat, you mean."

"You shut up. I still have my size 38 jeans."

"You outgrew those jeans when you were twelve years old. Add about twenty to that size."

"No way."

"Shut up and let me think a minute," Cole ordered. He shined the light on the hole, back at the shaft to the surface, then back at the hole. "That tunnel goes toward the old mine. I'll bet it connects to one of the tunnels over there. Let's go see. Maybe we won't have to dig much to find that treasure."

Bubba turned onto his stomach and grabbed the rope.

"Are you going to be able to climb out?" Cole asked.

"Sure." Bubba squirmed a couple of inches.

Cole thought he looked like a large, beached fish. "Maybe I should go first, then I can help pull you out."

"Wait. What was that?" Bubba spat and coughed.

"What's wrong?"

"The ground," Bubba said. "It moved."

"What?"

"I think some of the roof came down."

"Get moving," Cole urged.

"I'm trying."

Cole tried to push from behind, to no avail. Seconds later, the earth trembled.

"Pull me back," Bubba shouted. "It's coming down."

Cole grabbed his brother's ankles and gave a mighty yank. Bubba wailed as he slid back into the chamber. He was followed by a hail of stones and dust as a portion of the shaft collapsed.

The brothers scrambled to the far end of the chamber. Cole aimed the light toward the shaft. For a long minute everything was obscured by dust. Bubba hacked and coughed beside him. Cole tensed, ready to dive into the small hole if the chamber threatened to dump more rock. He didn't want to leave his brother, but he'd go for help as quickly as possible.

When the dust settled, Cole saw the shaft almost completely blocked by a pile of rubble.

"We're never going to get out that way," Bubba said.

"No kidding."

"What'll we do?"

"I'm gonna have to crawl through the tunnel. Maybe, as I told you, it'll lead me to the mine."

"What then?" Bubba whined. "I still can't get out."

"I'll figure out something."

"Leave me the flashlight."

"What good will that do me?" Cole asked. "What if the tunnel branches off? I don't want to get lost."

"I guess."

"You'll be all right," Cole reassured. "I'll keep yelling back my progress."

Cole maneuvered around until he could stick his head and shoulders into the hole. If he stayed low, he thought he could crawl on hands and knees. If the tunnel went straight, he might have about fifty yards to the mine. Flashlight in one hand, he took his time. Fortunately, he didn't have a fear of confined spaces. His brother, on the other hand, while not terrified of complete darkness, still slept with a night light near his bed.

Every minute or so, he shouted to Bubba that he was okay. The reply became fainter and fainter.

Cole dropped to his stomach for a rest. Aiming the light ahead of him, hoping to see another opening, the beam caught the corner of what looked like an offshoot to the tunnel. He pushed himself forward to discover not another tunnel, but a niche inset into the wall. About four feet deep, the space wasn't empty. Cole saw the corner of a wooden box. When he was able to get the full beam of the flashlight on the box, his eyes widened in both surprise and excitement.

Bubba hugged his knees to his chest, his entire body tense. He waited for the ground to rumble again, for him to be buried by tons of rock, crushed lifeless. He wondered who had the stupid idea to slide down the shaft. Oh right, he remembered, his stupid brother. There wasn't any treasure down here. It would have been found long ago. All they had managed to do was get trapped. Cole had gone off, probably to get lost or trapped himself. He hadn't heard any shouts for a while.

Bubba thought back. This all started with that old Indian in the meat market. He and Cole thought they might have stumbled onto something valuable with that map. A real live treasure. They could have expanded their marijuana field, bought better materials for the meth lab, even a few cool things like a better truck and maybe a big screen television. Sure, they had run into a few difficulties here and there, but they were determined to get rich. Certainly, that Kyle was no help. All he did was order Cole and Bubba around. Go here, do this. What had been the result? Nothing. Sitting in total darkness, Bubba figured Kyle was a bully. He figured Cole complained too much whenever something went wrong, and he figured that Wildcrow was just crazy.

Just as Bubba was about to call out again, he heard shuffling and rock grating. These were followed by Cole's grunts of exertion.

"What happened?" Bubba yelled into the tunnel. "Did you find a way out?"

"Hold on," Cole called back.

Soon, Bubba saw the shadowy form of his brother's feet in the flashlight's ambient light. Cole inched his way out, but he also pulled something along with him.

Cole sat up and dragged the box in front of him. "No, I didn't go to the end of the tunnel. Didn't have to because I found this." He aimed the flashlight at the lid of the box.

Bubba's breath caught when he saw the picture of what the box contained and the warning underneath. "Dynamite?"

"You know it, brother. We can use some of this to blast our way out of here."

Cole opened the box. Inside, twenty eight-inch-long red sticks of dynamite lay in stacks of five. A coil of fuse cord rested on top.

"I guess someone must have forgotten this down here," Cole said. "I may have been close to the main tunnel, but I decided this would be better."

Bubba remained speechless, still stunned.

"I'll tell you what, Bubba, I was scared to death moving that box."

"Why?"

"Don't you remember Daddy talking about dynamite and these coal mines? When this stuff gets old, some of the nitro leaks. Any jarring movement could set it off. I held my breath every time I pulled on the box."

"How much you figure has leaked?"

"Who knows?'

"I—I don't know about this." Bubba's jaw quivered. "I'd rather take another ride on that out-of-control boat than mess with this."

"This ain't no different than the meth chemicals we use. Which, by the way, *you* caused to explode."

"Yeah, but we escaped by running outside. We're trapped in here. We set this off, the whole cave is gonna come down, maybe the entire hillside."

"That's why I'm smarter than you," Cole said. "Just like how we use the meth ingredients in the right amounts and, except for you, take care that it comes out right. Using this dynamite just takes a bit of... finessing as they say."

"But—"

"Don't start arguing with me about words. Listen, here's what we need to do." Cole explained how they were going to place the dynamite so the blast would go up the shaft. They'd break down the box and use the flat sides as shields to keep the blowback into the chamber to a minimum. The only tricky part, he said, was the extra bit of protection needed. He and Bubba, before lighting the fuse, would have to....

"No way," Bubba protested. "You know I can't fit in that tunnel."

"You're gonna have to. It's the only way."

"Cole—"

"Don't argue. You either force your fat behind in there or take your chances here."

Bubba's whimpering made him sound like a five-year-old denied a chocolate treat, but he didn't care. Meanwhile, lifting one stick out of the box with meticulous care, Cole pushed the dynamite into the pile of rocks.

"How many are you going to use?" Bubba asked.

"I don't know how much nitro is still left. I think I'd better use all of them."

Bubba whimpered again. By the time Cole pushed in the last stick, the whole thing resembled a weird black birthday cake on its side. Cole fashioned the length of cord around each individual fuse, so that once lit, everything would go off together.

Bubba helped dismantle the box and secure the flat sides and lid as a makeshift wall against the rubble, wedging them in as best they could.

"All right, we're ready," Cole said. "You go first into the tunnel. I'll follow and light the fuse."

Bubba made a final whimper that evolved into a painful grunt when he jammed his body into the small opening. "I can't see," he whined.

"Just keep going. There ain't any turns and nothing to see."

"I'll be stuck in here forever."

"Move!"

He felt and heard Cole move behind him. His brother had brought the flashlight. By craning his head around, Bubba saw the flashlight in one hand and the end of the fuse in the other.

"A little farther," Cole said.

"I'm stuck."

"A couple more feet."

Bubba groaned and heaved his body forward.

"That's good," Cole said. "Get ready."

Again, Bubba torqued his head. He saw Cole dig out his lighter from a pocket, thumb the wheel, but nothing happened. He thumbed it again.

"Must still be wet from the lake." Cole blew on the end and thumbed the wheel a third time. This time, a short blue and orange flame appeared. He touched it to the fuse. As the hiss of the fuse receded back into the chamber, Bubba's keening cry filled the tunnel.

***

Rudy spent twenty minutes searching the house and barn for a crowbar to pry out the spikes from the cavern floor. He started back along the gravel road.

His driving days were long behind him. Besides, none of the vehicles on his property had a complete engine. On very rare days, he could maintain a wobbly balance on an old Schwinn bicycle, but most of the time, he didn't mind walking. Once a week he walked to the southern edge of Flagler to pick up a weekly supply of groceries Bill Carruthers brought him. He also shared a nip or two of real moonshine—not that stuff in the liquor store labeled moonshine, even if it was in Mason jars—direct from Bill's still back in the woods. Bill kept offering to bring the bags of groceries to Rudy's house, but Rudy insisted he needed the exercise.

A walk to the old mine wouldn't hurt him. He crossed the railroad tracks, turned down the lane, and had reached the top of the downhill slope when he stopped. A beat-up pickup was parked in front of the Indian cavern.

"Where the blazes did that come from?" He spat tobacco juice.

Probably more dang kids. He'd have to threaten them with his walking stick.

He thought about Wildcrow's granddaughter and her friend in the Gremlin. That pair had promise. The girl was a pretty little thing. Must have gotten her looks from her grandmother, because ole Wildcrow was an ugly cuss.

The boom and shock wave from the explosion threw Rudy off balance. He fell and landed on his backside. When he regained his senses, he saw the cavern and hillside had disintegrated. A cascade of rock and dust rained down. On the ground. On the truck. A chunk cracked the windshield. Another took out the passenger fender and headlight. A spatter of rocks made a metallic machine gun burst in the bed of the truck.

Seconds later, quiet settled. Even the late season birds had gone silent. Rudy, stunned, could only stare. Not only was the cavern gone, but the explosion had also brought down part of the roof of the opening to the old mine.

He heard and saw a shifting of rocks near where the cavern used to be. Two figures emerged from the rubble, their bodies blackened by coal dust, maybe charred in a few places. They reminded Rudy of that old comedy team Laurel and Hardy, but the thinner of the two was still pretty stocky.

The pair pulled themselves out of the debris and stumbled to the truck. Laurel threw off the rock that had cracked the windshield, then both clambered into the cab. The engine coughed and wheezed to life, and tires threw up more dust and gravel trying to get traction. The truck picked up speed and skidded through a hard right turn. Rudy rolled out of the way seconds before the truck barreled past and raced out of sight.

Rudy sat up and saw his walking stick had broken. The truck had rolled over it.

"Dagnabit," he groused. "Now, I gotta carve me a new stick."

Chapter 40

Sheriff Lockridge sat at his desk, a foam cup of cold coffee nearby. One elbow on the desk, hand cupped under his chin, he skimmed the reports his deputies had turned in regarding their activities throughout the day.

Sinkholes at Bos Landen.

Four speeding tickets.

A gravel truck that overturned on Highway 92 east of Knoxville when it swerved to avoid slamming into an out-of-control speeding pickup truck with a cracked windshield.

A search for two suspects who'd stolen a fishing boat from Red Rock marina. In the subsequent chase from a patrol boat, the fishing boat was destroyed, but the thieves escaped.

An explosion at the old mine near Flagler.

A domestic call in Lakeside Heights. A woman held her husband at bay with a cast iron skillet claiming he was one of those pod people like in one of the Body Snatcher movies. Deputies suspected she suffered from a bad batch of meth.

Probably bought from those Smith boys, Lockridge thought. By the way, where were those two bozos?

He also read the preliminary report on the search for Hank Oliver. Nothing. No one interviewed or called provided any information.

Not much effort had been expended on that front because the biggest issue of the day was the widespread mania of treasure hunters. Officers had rousted at least twenty parties—individuals, couples, and families—from various spots all around Red Rock Lake, including one arrest of two intoxicated men. Lockridge sneered, because both men had to be Tasered, and the replacement cartridges cut into his budget.

He expected this kind of crazy behavior around July Fourth, not a week or so out from Thanksgiving. Treasure hunters popped up based on a rumor, explosions, an old man causing problems, people on both sides of the casino issue... what was wrong with everyone in this county?

Lockridge breathed a disgusted sigh. He wanted to chuck all the papers into the trash. Instead, he tucked them into a manila folder. He'd file everything in the proper place tomorrow. For the moment, he was tired and exasperated. Time to go home. He hoped his wife, Cheryl, had cooked up something besides leftovers. Three days of meatloaf concoctions had him all but swearing off hamburger.

***

Kyle Brewer turned the *Closed* sign on the front door outward and engaged the deadbolt. He turned his back on the last-minute customer who banged on the glass.

He'd grown tired of the store, this town, and especially the two lame brains, Cole and Bubba. Because Hank wasn't around, he couldn't leave the store to meet the brothers at the bridge. Anytime he phoned, there was no answer. He waited all day for them to call. Nothing. Where were those two bozos?

He managed to stay professional and acted duly concerned when a county deputy, a city officer, and Hank's wife visited the hardware store, all of them wondering about Hank's sudden absence. Customers also made inquiries, preferring to discuss their stupid plumbing, electrical, and home repair needs with the boss rather than the employee. Kyle handled each with calm and kind words. He told the truth that he didn't know anything about Hank's whereabouts.

Not long after the Smiths left, Kyle decided he wasn't going to return the following day. The time had come for him to move on. Knoxville and the county had gone off the rails. Conversation he'd overheard mentioned the treasure hunters, the Smith's home and meth lab blowing up, and other craziness. He'd have one more wild night with Kathryn, conduct his own treasure hunt, and be gone by the end of Sunday.

Woo Hardware sold a couple varieties of suitcases and duffel bags. He loaded one of each with supplies off the shelves he thought he might need. In Hank's desk, he found the combination to the petty cash safe—what moron writes down a combination on a memo pad then sticks it in the middle drawer—and emptied it and the till of several hundred dollars.

At his apartment, he packed clothes and other necessities and tossed everything into the car trunk. He could leave town that night, but two things stopped him. The first was the anticipated wild, lust-filled night with Kathryn. The second was that he was determined to ferret out that treasure, one way or another.

***

"Where is Grandfather?" Grace asked.

On the trip back to Knoxville, she and Digger had decided to end the search for the Indian bundle. The sun had almost disappeared. Both were hungry and tired from a long day's driving and constant danger everywhere they stopped. Grace insisted they drive to Wildcrow's trailer at Elk Rock in case her grandfather had returned. They arrived and discovered he had not.

"I don't know," Digger replied in answer to her question. "I wouldn't be too worried, though."

She whirled on him. "How can you say that? Where is he? It's dark, and he's out there on his own. He could be lying in a ditch unconscious or...."

Digger enfolded her quivering body in his arms. "Calm down," he soothed. "Look at it this way. He's been one step ahead of us all day. We know this because of the sunflower seed shells we found at each marker site. He's been living out here on his own for years and getting around just fine."

"But he was attacked," Grace said. "A concussion."

"Again, he seemed to be all right today. We haven't seen him along our journey, so I think he's been fine."

"But—"

"Who knows? Maybe he stopped for supper or visited a friend."

"Maybe he got lost."

Digger eyed her with raised eyebrows. "First, he's a Sac. I've never heard of one getting lost."

She lightly pushed his chest. "Don't be a smart aleck."

273

"Second, he's lived in this area most of his life. He has as much chance of getting lost as Kathryn and I have of getting back together."

"You're spouting romance when Grandfather could be out there disoriented and injured?"

Digger stopped any further words with a kiss. A cool breeze made her shiver, but Digger's embrace and tender kiss warmed her.

"He's all right," Digger whispered.

She nodded and hugged him close, head against his chest.

"What I suggest is we go into town for a Chinese dinner, then I'll drop you off at the hospital so you can pick up your car. During dinner, I'll call the hotel and see if authorities evacuated the entire Bos Landon area. If the hotel is still open for guests, I'll meet you tomorrow morning at the golf course clubhouse to discuss the plan for the day."

"I don't know how I'll be able to sleep tonight."

"You could always stay at my place," Digger said, then held up his palms. "No ulterior motive. I'll sleep on the couch."

"Thank you, but all my clothes are at the hotel."

Digger sighed. "Poor excuse, but I'll accept it. Are you ready to eat?"

"Sure," Grace said. "Could I make a suggestion?"

"Sure."

"I'm not prejudiced. I love Chinese cuisine, but I think I'm in the mood for Italian tonight."

***

A quiet settled around the trailer after the Gremlin's departure faded. A breeze clattered tree limbs and rustled fallen leaves. A lone twelve-point buck that had avoided hunters softly crunched through the underbrush. In an old tree trunk partially scorched by lightning, a family of squirrels nestled in for the night.

An all but silent rush of air sounded as a red-tailed hawk glided down to perch on top of the Airstream. Claws *click-clicked* on the metal roof. The bird uttered a throaty huff. The teardrop head twitched in all directions, eyes scouting for the slightest movement, ears sensing the merest sound.

Minutes later, the thrumming rumble of an ATV filled the air. Wildcrow, in the driver's seat, emerged from the trees along a trail behind the Airstream.

Not long after leaving the Flagler mine, the 'pony' ran out of gas. Wildcrow had walked miles before he found a charitable farmer with a supply of gas in his barn.

He'd stopped at the Hometown Market for some venison steaks. The owner, a long-time friend, agreed to add the cost to Wildcrow's tab, though he did warn him about not causing a fuss in the future such as the one two days before.

After parking the ATV in the shed, Wildcrow built a fire in the ring of stones. Soon, a nice blaze lit up the property, hunks of venison revolving on the spit.

While the meat cooked, he reflected on the long but adventurous day. The visions, instead of debilitating, had given him hope. While he'd not been in contract with Digger and Grace, he knew they'd been following his trail from marker to marker. He wondered what they had experienced at every site. Had the spirit of Gray Swan reemerged in his granddaughter? With Justin for a guide, Wildcrow thought it a distinct possibility.

The new day would bring further revelations. The quest neared completion. Grace would embrace her Indian heritage or not. If she did, Wildcrow knew what came after would be wonderful and enlightening. Challenges could be faced with new perspective, renewed strength. If she didn't... well, best not to think that way.

Wildcrow closed his eyes and gave thanks to the Great Spirit for the day past and the one to come, for the food in front of him, and for life and health. He asked protection for Grace and Digger and, if destined, for their relationship to blossom.

He opened his eyes, tilted his head to glance up at his avian companion on the trailer's roof, and chuckled. "We shall see, won't we?"

The bird's eyes gleamed yellow in the firelight. It lifted its head and cawed once as if in affirmative reply.

****

Brandyn Antonaccio sat at the desk in his hotel room. Notes of the day lay before him arranged in a linear timeline of events. He reviewed all he'd seen throughout his day of following Justin Clay and Grace Snow, reflected on the events he'd witnessed.

In his years as an FBI agent, he'd seen his share of people who seemed to have the proverbial dark cloud of bad luck hovering nearby, but these two, Justin in particular, had misfortune on their heels at every turn. Almost falling off a cliff and a bridge, almost being buried in a sinkhole and a cave-in.

Some people might have wondered why he, Antonaccio, hadn't rushed in to lend assistance in saving the history teacher. He felt guilty that he hadn't but wanted to maintain his anonymity more than anything. As he watched each incident from afar, he could see that the pair was taking appropriate action and they didn't need additional assistance.

Another review of his notes reminded him that he still had unanswered questions.

Why were Justin and Grace driving all over the county? What was the significance of each stop they made? Did each relate to this 'treasure' that had been the talk of the town?

Jacob Wildcrow, apparently the originator of the treasure rumor, had been attacked but left the hospital on his own accord to wander the countryside. What further part did he play?

The biggest disappointment for Antonaccio had been that despite his efforts, he'd not identified his quarry, Peter White. Of course, Grace and Digger hadn't discovered anything valuable. No buried box, bag, or chest. Because they didn't uncover anything, maybe White also held back in showing himself. Had he been following the couple as Antonaccio had, also staying hidden?

Patterns. Most of his cases involved patterns. Logical movements and motives, if only understood by the subconscious. Antonaccio's job was to recognize and take advantage of those patterns, to be a step ahead in order to catch his target.

In this case, except for the trip around Red Rock Lake, no other pattern existed. No other clues to White's whereabouts could be found. Although the idea of the gang leader's sticking around for a treasure seemed tenuous, it was Antonaccio's best—for the moment, only—idea. He'd stick close to Justin and the girl and hope for the best.

That decision made, he prepared for bed. Setting an internal alarm clock for six the following morning, he sat cross-legged on the bed, positioned for his nightly meditation that would evolve into real sleep.

***

"Bubba, did you hear something?"

"Only the irritating sound of your voice."

"Shut up and listen."

"How can I shut up and listen *and* answer your question?"

"Hush! Listen."

The Smiths lay on opposite sides of a double bed in a Yellowstone brand camper trailer from the 1970s. The camper rested on flat tires on the western end of the outer oval in the junkyard behind the Smith property.

Not wanting to spend another uncomfortable night in the truck, Bubba suggested the camper. It wasn't heated, but he thought they'd find extra blankets in their trailer if it hadn't been completely burned up. They were surprised to find a couple that survived the fire. Singed and still smelling of smoke, they provided enough warmth.

Months before, the brothers felt brave enough to explore a couple of vehicles in the junkyard. At high noon, of course. They found the Yellowstone, save for the tires, to be in pretty decent shape. Scratches on the cabinets, dirty and scuffed floor, couch cushions gnawed by mice and other critters, but the trailer as a whole seemed sturdy enough.

After driving back into town—narrowly missing being smashed by a gravel truck—they shoplifted—this time without incident—another Casey's. Cole had driven the truck into the trees and parked on the edge of the outer circle. The trailer door faced the inner oval of cars and panel vans. A quick check with the flashlight—no police lurking about on stakeout—and they hurried inside. By flashlight, they ate their meal on the trailer's foldout table. Exhausted after a harrowing day, they went to bed. Hours later, Cole woke thinking he'd heard something outside. Something large. Rumbling. A deep-throated growl.

"We should go check," Cole said.

"You go check," Bubba replied. "I'm too tired."

"I don't believe you, Bubba. I thought you'd be scared out of your pants. In fact, I thought you would have been too scared to even come out here after dark."

Bubba rolled over and half sat up. "I'm gonna tell you one more time, brother. Ain't nothin' in my whole life scared me as much as being almost crushed or blown up in that stupid cave you drug me into. I ain't never been so thankful to escape. My heart ain't stopped thumping, but I'm too tired to worry about it. I also am too tired to care about some noise outside. It could be the cops or Kyle or the darned old ghost that's been haunting this place, but nothin' could be as bad as almost getting killed by dynamite. Now, you're gonna shut up and go to sleep or do I have to wallop you senseless?"

That said, Bubba flopped down onto the mattress and turned to face to the wall. In less than a minute, snores punctuated the dark.

Cole, still sitting up, listened. The noise from outside increased in volume. Definitely some kind of engine. Maybe a semi? Whatever made the racket came up right outside the trailer and stopped. Metallic creaks and squeals, a squinch of what sounded like hoses disengaging, then the engine growled once more and rumbled off in the direction from which it had come. What the…? A minute later, silence, except for Bubba's snoring. His brother had remained asleep the entire time.

Cole stepped from the bed and walked to the door. Flashlight in hand, he pulled on the plastic handle to unlatch the door and pushed out. The door opened to almost six inches before it hit something solid.

Cole aimed the light outside. He saw a long gray wall that rose to just above the roof of the camper. When he recognized what blocked the door, effectively trapping his brother and him, he tried to swallow on a suddenly tight throat.

Just visible in the beam was the number 53, denoting the length of the semi-trailer that had been parked six inches next to the Yellowstone.

Chapter 41
Sunday

Jacob Wildcrow awoke Sunday morning an hour before sunrise. After morning ablutions, he re-stoked the fire to cook his breakfast. In the quiet cool woodland air—sky cloudy, but ground dry—he felt another vision coming upon him. Setting aside his empty plate, he submitted to the message.

***

1790

Running Eagle returned to the Peace Tree. The area, including the site of the inhabitants' teepees, was deserted. Chief Saunuk and the tribe had moved on in the hope of discovering a new land in which to reside and flourish. Running Eagle would catch up to them in time but first, he had one final task to fulfill on his journey. The ground was dry and hard, but using arrowheads and sharpened stones from the riverbank, he dug out the final resting place for the sacred bundle. Chief Saunuk had foretold of an expansive lake covering the land, including the mighty Sycamore. He gave Running Eagle instructions on how to secure the bundle within the tree's roots so that even the fiercest undercurrent would not dislodge it.

Task complete, Running Eagle spent another hour in meditation, thanking the Great Spirit for the strength during his journey. He asked for further guidance for himself, his chief, and his people. When the sun neared its zenith, Running Eagle rose to rejoin his tribe. He anticipated reuniting with Chief Saunuk and— touching the necklace given him—the chief's granddaughter.

***

The scene dissolved, and the vision formed a stretched starlight pattern as if racing through hyperspace. Wildcrow, momentarily startled, soon realized he had traveled through time to the present... no...to an as yet unknown future. He saw images flickering on his mental screen.

Two people and a dog.

More people arriving.

Water.

Trees.

Shouted words.

Danger!

Wildcrow's heartbeats increased in speed, and a grim portentous veil descended over his countenance. He didn't comprehend what the vision foretold, but he understood the warning. His role in the adventure wasn't over.

As the sky lightened, he gathered what items he thought might be useful and set off to be ready for whatever events occurred that day.

*****

"You should get a shot for that," Cole Smith told his brother. "Remember that time Dad had to get one. I think they stuck the needle in his stomach."

That morning, the two had eaten breakfast from their stash of stolen food, agreed to visit Kyle for the next step in the treasure hunt, but argued about how they were going to escape the Yellowstone camper. The windows were too small and while the trailer was over fifty years old, the walls were still solid enough. After heated discussion, they deduced that since a tube and hose combination ran from the toilet out underneath the trailer when it was at a campsite, removing the toilet itself would create a big enough hole for them to squeeze through. Bubba balked for a few moments about the size of the hole, but Cole pointed out how he had fit into the tunnel before the dynamite exploded.

Unfortunately, as Bubba forced his flabby stomach through the hole, he disturbed a nesting raccoon that had burrowed up under the flooring. He heard a growling hiss, then felt teeth clamp onto his backside. He thrashed and howled until the raccoon lost interest and released him.

"Yeah, I remember," Bubba now said. "Daddy was howlin' mad for days. What do you think, brother? Do you 'spose I could get rapid?"

280

"The word is rabid."

"Well, I'd still get sick, right?"

"It's a possibility," Cole said.

"How soon you reckon I'd be showin' symptoms?"

"I don't know. A few days, maybe."

"There you go. I'd be sick in a few days. That's rapid."

Cole glanced in disdain at his brother. "I think you're showing symptoms right now."

"What?"

"You're getting dumber by the minute."

***

Kyle stepped from the bathroom after his shower, towel wrapped around his waist. When he entered the bedroom, he found Kathryn still lounging on the bed.

"Do you know what I want?" she purred. "Another round with you under the covers followed by a big breakfast at Manny's Diner."

She lowered the sheet to her waist, tempting him. He considered her offer, at least the first part, but decided he didn't have time for either, let alone both.

"Listen," he said. "We had some fun last night, but I have important business this morning."

She pouted; lower lip stuck out. "Oh, pooh. You said Hank gave you the day off. I thought we could spend more time in bed."

He didn't want to bring up the fake conversation with Hank he'd told her about. She might start asking about Hank's whereabouts. Of course, like he'd told everyone else the previous day, he didn't know.

She gave him a smarmy smile. "What are you going to do? Join the treasure hunters?"

"Nope," he stated. "I'm going right to the source."

Kathryn leaped from the bed and clutched his arm as he buttoned his jeans. "You don't really think there is a treasure, do you? That's just crazy talk."

"I've seen the map, and I plan to collect."

"How?"

"Talk I heard from customers at the store yesterday was how this Jacob Wildcrow and his granddaughter are involved. People also mentioned your ex, Justin."

"The rotten bast—"

"Yes, well, I figured if anything had been found, it'd be all over town and the news. Since I didn't hear anything last night before I met you, I'm guessing all three are still looking for it. Wildcrow had the map and must have shown it to his granddaughter and Justin or told them about it."

"So, how did you see the map?"

Kyle glared at her. "I have ways."

"Okay." Kathryn stepped back, eyes widening in what Kyle thought was wariness.

Kyle wasn't going to tell her that Justin had visited the hardware store the previous day, but the man's buying a shovel convinced him he was part of the hunt. "Anyway, I heard Wildcrow ran away from the hospital, and no one knows where he is. However, his granddaughter is out at the Holiday Inn at Bos Landen."

"What are you going to do?"

"I expect Justin to show up, and they'll continue their search. I'll follow. When they find something, well...."

"Wait," she said. Her mouth tightened and her eyes looked toward the ceiling. Kyle wondered what she contemplated. After almost a minute, she gave him an innocent look, teeth biting her lower lip. "Maybe I could join you?"

Oh, how easily she'd been sullied. His power and persuasion over women had captured another one. Kathryn, the upper class, high society woman in a small town, a woman eager to be the center of attention, a woman who had been displaced from her self-relegated throne by one who possessed actual dominance. He knew she knew it. Kyle was amazed only in the short amount of time it took to accomplish the feat. Sure, she'd been overwhelmed by his sexual prowess but also by his presence and magnetism. He was the 'bad guy' after whom some women lusted. He exhibited dominance, a hint of danger. She wasn't the first woman to fall under his spell and wouldn't be the last.

He pretended to think about her suggestion. "If I—we—find that treasure, who knows what we could do with it?" Her eyes sparkled, and he knew he'd set the hook. "Better hustle. I want to leave in ten minutes.

He smacked her backside and laughed when she rushed by him to the bathroom, yelping like a little girl. Yes, he'd conquered another one.

***

Kyle's anticipation for the hunt faltered when he saw the Smith brothers drive up at the same time he and Kathryn exited the apartment.

"What are you two morons doing?" he asked when they ambled up to the sidewalk.

"We're ready for the treasure hunt," Cole said.

"You two should be in jail," Kathryn scolded.

Kyle ignored her. "What happened to you yesterday?"

"After we dumped—"

Cole interrupted his brother with an elbow to his ribs. "We followed Digger and that girl to see if they found anything."

"Did they?" Kyle asked.

"I don't think so."

"We were almost blown—"

Another elbow cut off Bubba's words. "Kyle don't need no details," Cole said. "Shut up."

Kathryn clutched Kyle's left arm. "You're not going to let them come along, are you? They'll just be in the way."

"We can help." Cole said.

"Yeah," Bubba said. "If it weren't for a couple, uh, accidents—"

"Everyone shut up," Kyle commanded. "Let me think a second."

He had hoped not to run into these yahoos, but since they were here, he couldn't tell them to shove off. They'd get it in their heads to do something on their own and might foul up things later. He stepped up to the brothers and stuck a finger in their faces. "All

283

right, you two, listen up. You do what I say when I say it, or I'll finish both of you for good."

"But—" Kathryn started, but Kyle held up his other hand to silence her. He glared at the Smiths. "Am I clear?"

Bubba visibly swallowed, but Cole nodded. "You bet."

"Good. Now get in your truck and follow us."

When they were in their pickup, Kyle faced Kathryn. "Don't worry, babe. Ain't no way they're getting any piece of that treasure." He indicated the gun stuck into a holster at the back of his pants. "They will, however, get exactly what they deserve.

Kathryn's eyes widened in momentary fear, then her lips formed an exquisitely devilish smile.

Chapter 42

Brandyn Antonaccio sat at a table in the cafe at the Bos Landen clubhouse. The dining area was not hometown diner ambiance but more casual-classy restaurant. Tall oval windows allowed in plenty of light that was enhanced by white tablecloths and pale tan flooring.

Antonaccio had laid out his dinnerware, not in a mandala pattern, but everything had a specific place, moved only when needed, then returned to its spot. Order comforted him, helped him focus.

With only a few forkfuls left, he turned his aural sense to two tables behind him. Justin Clay had just joined Grace Snow.

"You're looking quite gorgeous this morning," Justin said.

"Don't start," Grace replied.

"Uh, Grace, we shared a few kisses yesterday. Okay, so a couple were interrupted, but all were very enjoyable."

"You should be worried about Grandfather."

"For me, kissing means we have established a relationship. I know it's been only a couple days old, but I'd like to pursue it to see where it leads."

"I called Sheriff Lockridge this morning," Grace said. "He told me he'd send someone out to Grandfather's trailer."

"I'm not sure how we'd manage a relationship with you over an hour away in Ames. How about we check into the possibility of your opening a vet practice here in Knoxville?"

Antonaccio heard a sharp bang on the couple's table. Silverware and plates tinkled and clinked. "Digger! You're not paying attention. You don't care that Grandfather is missing?"

"May I start you out with something to drink," a waitress asked. "Coffee? Orange juice?"

Nice timing, Antonaccio thought.

After drink and food orders—Justin knew what he wanted; Grace caught up seconds later, and when the waitress walked away—Justin returned to the discussion.

"I *do* care, Grace. I cared enough to stop out at Elk Rock this morning before driving here."

"Did you see him?"

"No, but I saw evidence of his recent presence," he said. "Some charred chunks of wood in the fire pit were still warm, and his ATV is gone."

"Where is he?"

"I'm sure we'll find out later today."

Antonaccio made a mental note to keep watch for Wildcrow. He hadn't met the elderly Indian, but the man seemed to play an important, as yet unknown, roll in this case.

"We've gone to all the markers," Grace said. "What's next?"

"A return to the Peace Tree," Justin answered.

"What good will that do? The tree is almost covered by water."

"I did a lot of thinking last night," Justin said. "By the way, you have a lovely hand. May I hold it?"

"Stop that! Be serious."

Antonaccio heard the mock scolding in her tone.

"This journey we've taken has been for you," Justin said. "Wildcrow told us yesterday we had to follow Running Eagle's path, find the markers, and seek the bundle."

"I remember."

"What he didn't stress, but I realized soon after, was that the journey really *was* for you. To rediscover your Native American heritage. To reawaken the memories you had as a young girl. To have you remember the wonderful times when your grandparents taught you the old ways." Grace remained silent and Justin continued. "I hope we accomplished part of that. That's why we didn't jump to the end yesterday and why I wanted you to join me in the cavern. I think there's one more thing to be done."

"What?"

"I'm not sure, but when the time comes, I think I'll know."

"What about the bundle?"

Bundle? Antonaccio wondered. That was the second mention of a 'bundle.' What was it and how did it fit into this situation?"

"I have an idea about that, too," Justin said. "I'd have to make some calls. Who knows what type of treasure we may uncover?"

Treasure. Yes, there it was. They *were* after a treasure, a bundle quest. Antonaccio thought it sounded vaguely like some action movie. He knew he'd chosen correctly to follow these two. Peter White wouldn't be too far away.

He heard Grace sigh. Contemplation? Resignation?

"I think we could wrap this up in the next hour or so," Justin said.

All the better, thought Antonaccio. He was anxious to return home to his dogs.

"All right," Grace conceded. "But we *must* find Grandfather."

"I think he'll find us," Justin said. "Ah, here comes our breakfast. Now, relax and enjoy."

While the couple settled into their meals, Antonaccio finished his, slipped out of the cafe unnoticed by Justin or Grace, and returned to his room to prepare. Soon, he waited in his car to follow the Gremlin. He watched patrons of the cafe come and go. He felt he had good timing to overhear Grace and Justin when he had. Any later, he might not have been able to hear much more than a general murmur of conversation. A dozen cars had pulled into the cafe lot in the fifteen minutes he'd been waiting.

When Justin and Grace did exit the building, climbed into the Gremlin, and drove off, Antonaccio started his car, but didn't immediately follow. Even when the Gremlin was almost out of sight, he waited. There were two reasons. The first was that he knew where the two were going. The previous evening he'd done research on the Peace Tree and studied the roads on Google Maps that led to a couple of inlets within view of the Sycamore. He could afford to wait. More important, though, was the second reason. Twelve vehicles had entered the lot, but only ten parties or individuals had entered the cafe. From his position, he saw a tan Mercury sedan with two occupants. The passenger he recognized as Kathryn VanSteele, one of the local bigwigs and the major proponent of the planned casino. Antonaccio couldn't see the driver except glimpses of a partial profile. Dark hair, lean face, but not much more visible. For a moment, he pondered the possibility the guy could be Peter White. The other vehicle, a rusty faded red and silver pickup with a cracked windshield had parked next to the Mercury. Two men dressed in what looked like overalls filled the cab. Antonaccio had seen the two and their truck the previous day.

Antonaccio didn't think the four waited for the rest of a group gathering to enjoy Sunday breakfast. This was confirmed when the Mercury headed in the same direction as the Gremlin, followed by the pickup. Four others following Grace and Justin. Antonaccio felt his perseverance and patience coming to fruition.

Weapon in his shoulder holster, he eased out to the road, staying well back from the pickup.

***

"You need to get closer," Bubba said.

"Why?" Cole asked.

"'Cause you'll lose them. See, they disappeared around the curve."

"Calm down," Cole said. "I ain't gonna lose them. Besides, all we have to do is keep Kyle's car in sight. He's keeping an eye on Digger and that Indian girl."

"Well, then get closer to Kyle."

"Shut up, will you?" Cole griped. "I did a darn good job following yesterday."

"But we was almost blown up. It might have damaged your facilities."

Cole looked at his brother and shook his head, frustrated. "I'm gonna tell you three things, and then that'll be the end of it."

"What?"

Cole held up a finger. "One, the word is faculties." He put up another finger. "Two, I still got all mine, unlike you." He raised a third finger. "Three, shut up before I kick you out the door."

***

"Where do you think they're going?" Kathryn asked.

Kyle shook his head. "I don't know."

"Not into Pella," Kathryn said when the Gremlin turned west on G28, the road that wound along the north edge of Lake Red Rock and ended at Highway 14.

She had mixed feelings about what she and Kyle were doing, about even being with Kyle. Yes, they'd had some exquisite hours the last couple nights. Kyle's passion and fierce lust were what she had needed for a long time. She'd spent most of the previous day anticipating the coming night. She even entertained naughty

288

thoughts of going over to Woo Hardware and dragging Kyle into the back room.

Residual emotions for Digger still existed, and they made for a weird, squirming ache in Kathryn's chest. Part of her thought her reaction to seeing him with Wildcrow's Granddaughter was overblown. Maybe the argument with him at the school could have been handled in a more mature way. She just could not understand why he hadn't been more excited about the casino. Knoxville needed the income.

The blow up with Justin and the quick rebound fun with Kyle had messed with her head. What was she doing on a county road on a Sunday morning? Following two people in the hope of finding a treasure? Based on rumors from a crazy Wildcrow?

If she were honest with herself, she'd admit Kyle scared her. Just a little. She hadn't seen anything overtly violent from him, but she sensed the potential under the surface. Look how he had spoken to the Smith brothers the last two mornings. What was the relation between Kyle, Cole, and Bubba? The Smiths had committed crime after crime, but somehow stayed out of jail.

Who was Kyle? Where did he come from?

Nothing to do now, she thought, nerves becoming edgy.

His having a gun and threatening murder, even with thoughts about the treasure, didn't settle right with her. A treasure, though, changed everything.

Nothing to do but ride it out and hope to get lucky in the end.

Chapter 43

Digger slowed when he came up behind a late season Massey Ferguson tractor pulling a trailer filled with corn. However, the farmer edged onto the shoulder and the road was clear up to the next curve. Digger eased around the tractor with a two-finger wave to the farmer. Just before Highway 14, he encountered another farmer, this one driving an eight-row combine. This time, he had to wait a minute for traffic to clear and a long enough stretch of empty road to be able to pass.

"This is the type of slow down I ran into coming down here on Thursday," Grace commented.

"Ah, country life," Digger commented. "You people up in the big city don't have the pleasure of being delayed behind farm machinery."

"Come up to Ames when the Cyclones have a home football game," Grace said. "See how fast you get through traffic around Jack Trice Stadium."

Digger pursed his lips. "Oh, is that an invitation?"

She smiled at him. "Well, it could be."

"I don't think our relationship is going to work out."

"What? Why would you say that?"

He shrugged. "I'm an Iowa Hawkeye fan."

Grace rolled her eyes. "Hmph! I'm more concerned with the fact you think we *have* a relationship other than your chauffeuring me all over the county."

A pang of ache hit Digger's heart. *Could she be serious?*

He gathered his thoughts, figured his next few sentences had to show a more somber attitude. "I will admit to pushing things the last couple days," he said.

"Just like you did when we first met."

"Thursday night, however, I spent a long time thinking about you. Realized even though we never hit if off at the university—"

"I didn't even go on one date with you."

"You called campus security."

"You deserved it," she fired back. "Stalking me like you did."

"I wasn't—" He cut off his own words. "All right. Like I said, I came on strong then and now. But only because my feelings for you were strong. Thursday night, I thought a lot about you and realized those strong feelings never went away."

"If you say you love me, Digger, I'll make you stop, and I'll walk back to town."

"We're on the mile long bridge. I can't stop."

"That's not the point.'

"Maybe not, but my being with you these last couple days, with all our adventures, well, I…I do feel something, Grace."

"Just don't say it," she said. "I'm still worrying about Grandfather."

"Why couldn't I say it?" he asked.

"Because—"

"Besides, you're not really upset with me."

She shifted in her seat to face him. "Why not?"

He smiled and reached for her hand. She started to pull away but yielded to his touch.

"Because if you were truly mad, you would have called me Justin, not my nickname."

"That's—that's ridiculous," she sputtered.

Slowing for the turn onto County Road G40, he kept one eye on the turn while reaching up to Grace's neck to draw her in for a quick kiss. She felt hesitant at first, then returned the kiss.

"You're going to go into the ditch," she mumbled, lips still touching his.

"Nah, I'm an excellent driver." He released her, negotiated another soft curve, and turned onto a gravel road.

"Are we going back to the cemetery?" Grace asked. "Do you think Grandfather's returned there?"

"No, but I remember once, Wildcrow said before Ruckman Cemetery became a place for the dead, it had been a place for the living. His tribe inhabited the land long ago. That area around the bluff had been a haven for arrowhead collectors."

"So where are we going?"

A quarter mile north, Digger turned left.

"This is someone's driveway," Grace said.

"The road continues past the outbuilding and the house." Digger tightened his jaw and the grip on the steering wheel. "It peters out into a narrow track that leads to a couple inlets popular with fishermen. With the recent rain, I'm afraid the ole Gremlin's shocks may take a beating."

His concerns proved true. A hundred yards past the house, the road designated as 120th Place wasn't anywhere near as opulent as the name might have sounded—just two tracks with dips and depressions, leaving barely enough room for the passage of two cars meeting.

"I should have traded the Gremlin years ago for a four-wheel drive truck." His words rattled as much as the shocks on the ruts.

"If we end up stranded out here, you *will* hear me call you Justin."

Digger laughed. "No worries. This isn't as bad as I expected. I've driven worse."

About a half mile farther, they rolled down a gradual decline to the first inlet. Shaped like a skewed 'W' there was plenty of shoreline for fishermen. Digger thought there was too much shoreline now with the current water level. The river bottom extended out almost to the end of the 'W.'

They saw a couple makeshift stone fire rings and a discarded beer can indicating recent human presence.

The road ascended back into the trees for another half mile. It ended at the second inlet which also contained a fire pit of rocks, but no litter.

... and no Peace Tree visible.

"It's gone," Digger exclaimed.

"What?"

"The Peace Tree." He pointed toward the lake. "It should be about 1000 feet out. Especially with this low water level, we should see it."

He stopped the car, then climbed out and walked to the water's edge. Grace followed after letting Chow out of the back seat to run free and explore.

Hands on hips, he stared out at the water. "I've been here many times. Even during flooding, the top of the Sycamore is visible. Now... nothing. I can't imagine what could have happened to it."

"Maybe the storms knocked it over," Grace suggested.

He shook his head. "The Peace Tree has survived hundreds of years, even through the creation of the lake back in '69. Sure, the years and mother nature has taken most of it, but a good portion of the trunk should have remained for decades more."

"Digger, why are you upset? It's just a tree."

He whirled on her, gripping her shoulders. "No, you're still not understanding. That Peace Tree is why I've been driving you all over the county. It's been the key to this entire journey. Wait.... I think I have a picture of it."

He pulled his cell phone from an inside jacket pocket and brought up the Gallery which displayed thumbnails of stored images. Finding the one he wanted, he tapped to enlarge it.

"Look at this, Grace.'

He showed her the image taken when the sun rested just above the horizon, illuminating part of a line of bluffs in the distance. In the foreground, the Peace Tree stood perhaps twelve or fifteen feet out of the lake, stark and majestic even in the low light. From that angle, there was a notch near the base, then a long thick section of trunk. At the top, it resembled a plateau and, if one used his imagination, a castle built into the mountain. All around the Peace Tree, mercury-colored water shimmered the shadow of the tree and a ragged strip of sunlight.

"Have you ever seen this picture?"

"No," Grace whispered.

"Take the phone. I want you to try something."

She accepted the phone and held it up so she had a view of the picture and the spot in the lake where the Peace Tree once stood.

"Fix the image into your mind," Digger said. "When you have, close your eyes."

She glanced at him. He nodded and indicated the picture. Her body shivered. Digger didn't know if the light, cool morning breeze caused it or if it was a bit of nervousness on her part. Nonetheless, she stared at the picture on the screen for a while and then closed her eyes.

***

Seconds before Grace shut her eyes, movement from out on the lake caught her attention. Rather, it came from above the lake. A hawk glided in from the north. The morning sun highlighted glints of red on the bird's tail.

"Do you still see the picture?" Digger asked when her eyes closed. His voice came to her soft, just above a whisper, riding the thermals as the hawk did.

"Yes."

"I want you to reduce the size of the water to a river's width. Can you do that?"

She nodded. Her mental photo editing shrunk the lake to a band no wider than what she'd seen below the dam the previous day.

"Leave the tree where it is but imagine it not on a rocky river bottom but in a valley of grassland," Digger said.

Rocks faded, and green shoots emerged. The land around the tree sprouted wildflowers. Bees and birds buzzed and chirped. Only near the river did sand and stones remain.

"Around the Sycamore sit a group of Indians, a campfire nearby." Digger's voice dropped to a whisper. "Can you see them, Grace?"

Ten figures dressed in leather pants and vests rose into view. A stately man sat at the head of the circle wearing a headdress of feathers, beads laced around his neck. The group chatted among themselves. One gave a hearty laugh at another's story. A few relaxed, one smoked a long thin pipe. The chief observed the entire scene, contented, at peace. Every so often, he glanced up at the hawk perched on a branch of the tree. The tree itself wasn't the stump portion from the cell phone, but a full-grown Sycamore, sturdy branches full of green covering a diameter at least thirty feet.

"Do you see it?" Digger asked.

"I do."

"Do you?"

"Yes."

She sank into the scene, becoming an observer near the fire. Although she couldn't make out the words exchanged, somehow, she knew the discussions. The day's hunt; the coming rain; trading with a neighboring tribe. One described his young son's first hunt and how well the lad had recovered after tripping on an exposed root and falling face first into a fire ant mound. Another boasted about the recent birth of his second daughter. There was talk about the deer size that season and an upcoming contest among the young braves.

Without Digger's saying a word, the scene expanded to include a nearby settlement with teepees and fire pits. Indian women cleaned hides and prepared meat. Children laughed and played, while older youths sat with their mothers learning to make clothing and methods of cooking. A father taught his young son how to properly wield a bow and arrow. A boy and girl, both maturing into adulthood sat together talking about nothing important but stealing glances at each other. She accepted beads from him that she strung onto a thin strip of deer hide. Every time he handed her a bead, their fingers touched. They smiled, excited at the brief contact. The girl's mother, in the middle of her own project of securing together folds of hide for a teepee, monitored the young couple from a respectful distance.

"Every time I look at the picture, I imagine a scene similar to what you're probably seeing." Digger's voice blended into the vision as a narrator in a documentary. "It's magical, isn't it?"

She nodded.

"I expect it's more vivid for you than it is for me, because you are connected in a more direct way through your grandfather and his ancestry."

Grace, lost in the scene, marveled at the colors of the garments, the blankets. She felt the day's warmth, imagined she smelled the odors of cooking, leather, and the grass. What fascinated her the most was how she felt in tune with the people, as if she could walk into the encampment, sit near the fire with the other women, and be comfortable, accepted.

"It's... magnificent," she whispered, awed by everything she envisioned.

She felt a nearby warmth... Digger close to her. Then something touched the back of her neck and draped down her chest. She blinked away the vision and opened her eyes. Digger, not two feet from her, had placed a beaded necklace around her neck. She brushed her fingers over the shiny stones.

The next second, she gasped in recognition. "It's my necklace. Grandfather gave this to me when I was a girl." She met Digger's eyes. "How did you come to have it?"

"He gave it to me yesterday at the hospital as you and I were leaving. He said I'd know the right time to show it to you."

A memory stung her heart. "The day my father argued with Grandfather, that last day before he moved us to Colorado, he was yelling about Grandfather's ignorance, stubbornness." She shivered again, this time in how she felt when the argument ended. "Father... ripped off my necklace and threw it at Grandfather. Then he grabbed my hand, and we left. In time, he drove all thoughts of Grandfather and the necklace out of my head."

Digger lifted her chin with one finger to look into her eyes. "Now you're back, and the necklace is yours again."

She nodded.

"I hope, too, that... well, your grandfather hopes you can understand all he's been trying to do over the last few days. This journey of remembering and re-acceptance of your heritage."

By coincidence, or maybe not, the sun emerged from behind a cloud to illuminate Digger and her.

He glanced up at the light, then back at her. "Does that mean what I think it means?"

She laughed and hugged him. "Yes!"

Memories and emotions flooded in, from her days as a child learning from her grandparents, experiencing the pride of who and what she was, the lessons they tried to instill in her.

"Oh, yes," she said again and kissed Digger long and hard. Chow came and nosed his head between them. When they released, she asked, "Oh my, Digger. What's next in this bundle quest?"

"You're going to dig it up," a voice said. "Then I'll take that treasure for myself."

They spun around to see a man walking toward them. Black hair, tall, and lean, he pointed a large gun at them. His other hand held a shovel.

"Who are you?" Grace drew farther into Digger's arms.

"Kissy time is over," the man said. "Time to go to work."

"Hey, Kyle, let that louse Digger do it," a new voice called out. Seconds later, Kathryn VanSteele joined the gunman, a malicious smile plastered on her face. "It'll serve him right for being such a jerk to me."

The man threw the shovel toward them. Grace looked at it, then at Justin.

"Sounds good to me," the man said. "Start digging, Digger."

Chapter 44

Everyone remained motionless. Chow growled, but Digger, one arm around Grace, kept one hand locked onto the dog's collar. If the dog was determined to attack, he didn't know if he could hold it back. Water lapped up the shoreline, and the wind whispered through bare branches. Digger thought he heard a soft throaty squawk from the hawk perched in a tree behind them. Grace pressed close in fear. The gun in Kyle's hand never wavered. Kathryn, hands on hips, sneered in evil delight. Digger dared not move. He thought one twitch would set off an explosion.

The Smith brothers broke the moment. They stumbled out of the trees, arguing with each other.

"Hurry up, Bubba. We're gonna miss gettin' our share of the treasure."

"I'm coming. It was your lousy drivin' made us late." Bubba's voice went from griping to a screech when he slipped on a muddy patch. The shovel he was carrying went flying and landed in the weeds. He lost his footing, landed hard on his backside, and slid into Kathryn. She, in turn, yelped and landed on top of Bubba.

"Get off me, you big oaf." She scrambled to untangle herself.

"You're on top of me, lady," Bubba wailed.

Cole reached to assist his brother, slipped on loose rock, and also hit the ground hard on his behind.

Kathryn, who'd managed to stand, brushed dirt and pebbles from her clothes. "What are you two idiots doing?"

"Following you, like Kyle said." Cole stood but didn't bother cleaning his overalls.

"We're here for the treasure," Bubba said. "Just like you."

"What treasure?" Digger asked.

"The one you two have been looking for along with half of Knoxville," Kyle said. "Hey, you hold onto that dog. I'll use the gun on it if I have to."

"For heaven's sake," Digger said. "Where did anyone ever get the idea there was a treasure buried somewhere?"

"From you," Kyle said. "Or rather, the girl here.'"

"Yeah," Bubba added. "You was talkin' to the crazy old Indian at the meat market."

"We saw the map." Cole withdrew a folded hide from his back pocket.

Grace tensed and stepped forward. "You stole that from Grandfather. Are you the ones who attacked him? Were you the two I saw outside his trailer Thursday night?"

"Never mind," Kyle commanded. "All of you shut up. The important thing is the map shows where a treasure is hidden." He pointed the gun at Digger. "You look smart enough to figure it out. Tell us what that map means, where the treasure is buried."

Digger dropped his head in disgust. "You have it all wrong. There is no treasure."

"Don't give me that. I know better. Now you grab that shovel and start digging."

"I'm telling you, there isn't any buried treasure. This whole thing has been blown out of proportion."

"I think you're trying to keep it for yourself," Kathryn accused. "Maybe hoping to stop the casino."

"No. One has nothing to do with the other."

"Oh, please." Kathryn snorted. "Ever since the cutie showed up, you've been obsessed with her. You never wanted the casino. You know the town needs it."

"Kathryn—"

"Enough!" Kyle interrupted.

"We thought it was buried under the Peace Tree," Bubba said. He'd regained his feet. Mud streaked his clothes. "After we dumped—"

Cole elbowed his ribs. "We looked but didn't see anything."

"Well, we tried," Bubba said. "Then that patrol—"

Cole elbowed him again.

"Then I'm thinking it has to be close," Kyle said. "Let's go, *Digger*. Get moving."

"Why won't you believe me?" Digger said. "There is no treasure. The map and the symbols mean something completely different. Yes, there is an Indian bundle, but—"

"I knew it," Kyle said. "All right, no more stalling. Get to it."

"But—"

Quick as a striking snake, Kyle's hand latched onto Grace's arm. Chow pulled against Digger's hold, growling and barking.

"I'm tired of wasting time," Kyle said. "You have three seconds to leash that dog, grab that shovel, and start digging. Otherwise, the girl dies."

Grace quivered in sheer terror. Kyle squeezed her arm, and she uttered a sharp cry.

"One." Kyle pressed the gun barrel against her temple. "Two."

Digger started to crouch to take the shovel when he heard a soft, whistling *fffft*. In the next second, an arrow embedded itself into Kyle's chest. Kyle uttered a tight grunt and dropped to the ground, the gun clattering away.

Kathryn screamed.

The Smiths wailed.

Chow barked three times, then quieted.

Kyle fell to his side and lay on the ground. His last labored breaths sounded as if he was trying to breathe through a straw. Blood ran from his wound. Seconds later, he went silent and still. In the next instant, Jacob Wildcrow stepped from the trees and approached the group. Digger almost expected the next time he saw the old chief, Wildcrow would be garbed in the traditional clothing as befit his rank. Instead, he wore a leather jerkin-like shirt and protective trousers one might see on an Indian hunting game.

"Oh, Grandfather!" Grace ran to him.

With an arm around Grace, Wildcrow said, "Digger, I'm disappointed. I thought you'd do a better job of protecting my granddaughter."

"Um...."

Wildcrow looked at the corpse. "Pretty good shot for an old man."

Digger avoiding looking at the dead man.

"I used to be able to take down a running deer in the woods at fifty yards. Looks like I still got it. Who is he, by the way?"

"I think he's been working at Woo Hardware," Digger said. "Never knew his name until Kathryn said it."

Kathryn had knelt by the prone body. She looked up at Wildcrow. "You—you shot him! With an arrow. You shot Kyle!"

"Actually, his name is Peter White." This came from a man who appeared, as the others had, from the curtain of the surrounding woods. He wore a black dress shirt, pleated pants, and black windbreaker. He, too, held a gun, but kept it pointed to the ground.

"Peter White?" Digger asked.

"Who are *you*?" Kathryn asked.

The man withdrew a folded identification wallet from his jacket pocket and showed it to them. "Special Agent Brandyn Antonaccio. FBI."

The Smiths howled again and backed away.

"Everyone stay calm." Antonaccio looked at the brothers. "For the time being, no one leaves."

The Smiths slumped and sat on the ground.

"FBI?" Digger said. "What's the FBI doing in Knoxville?"

Antonaccio replaced his credentials and indicated the body. "I've been trailing this man for months. His name is Peter White from Chicago. Used to head up a small but vicious gang."

Kathryn bolted upright. "A gang!"

"I tracked him to Knoxville but wasn't sure what he looked like. The last time I saw him, he had slightly different features."

"I don't believe it," Digger said. "A real-life gangster in town."

"I deduced with all the rumors of treasure in the last few days that Peter would stay in the area in an attempt to capitalize on it. I've been following you, Justin, since you seemed to be in the center of it."

"You were at Painted Bluffs."

Antonaccio nodded. "I watched you all day. You have an uncanny ability to find danger." He indicated the group. "I didn't think you'd be so popular."

Digger shrugged and smiled at Grace.

"I would have been here sooner but was last in line of all the cars trailing you. I was delayed by the farm implements."

"Welcome to Iowa," Digger said.

He heard tires crunch on gravel. A county sheriff's car rolled into view, stopped, and Sheriff Lockridge stepped out.

"What in tarnation is going on here?" He hefted his body toward the scene. "I get a report of too many cars heading down this way, church-going folks wanting to know what's happening. Ain't any fishing this time of year, and I figured it wasn't a bunch of hunters."

"Just one." Digger smiled at Wildcrow.

Lockridge noticed the body on the ground, an arrow shaft sticking out of the chest. "Holy crap!" He laid a meaty hand on his service weapon at his belt and looked from the body to Wildcrow. "Jacob, I could have bet my next paycheck you'd be involved in this, but a bow and arrow?"

"It was justified, Sheriff," Digger said. "Kyle had a gun on Grace."

"Peter White," Antonaccio corrected.

"And just who are you, mister?" Lockridge asked.

The agent showed his badge again. "May I suggest we head back to Knoxville where we can sort out everyone's story?"

"FBI?" Lockridge threw up his hands. "Why the heck not? What's one more bit of craziness after the last two days?" He uttered a throaty grumble, glared at Kathryn and the Smiths, and shook his head. "All right, let me call this in."

"Wait," Digger yelled. "I don't think we're done here."

Grace spoke up. "But you said that there is no buried treasure. Nothing to dig for here."

"Yes," Digger said. "True enough. But…"

Lockridge, Antonaccio, and the rest of the group waited.

"When I bought this shovel, I did so in the off-chance that I might need to dig—not for buried treasure but possibly to find the clues along the way. And…" Again, he waited to be sure he had everyone's attention. "And when I bought it, Hank Oliver was not in the store. Only Kyle was there, helping customers."

"So?" Kathryn said. "What's that got to do with the price of bread in China?"

"Kyle was busy helping a woman buy tulip seeds, so I went to the back room to get a shovel. There were two left. This one that I eventually bought. The other was…" Digger pointed to a spade lying in the weeds. On its blade was the same dark stain he'd seen at the hardware store. "That one, the one the Smith brothers went back and got after they disposed of Hank's body, which was after they killed him."

Cole stepped back. "He's making this all up. We didn't…"

Bubba blurted out, "He was trying to arrest us."

"Shut up, Bubba!"

Digger went on. "I am just surmising this, Sheriff, but I believe Hank is dead. It was either Kyle or the Smith brothers. And Kyle is…was, a smart guy as far as criminals go. Smart enough at least that he would never leave a murder weapon out in the open at the store. But the Smith's…" He turned to face the brothers. "What happened there, Cole? Bubba? Were you there at the shop, waiting on Kyle to join you in the hunt? Did Hank discover you two in the back?"

"No," Cole shouted before Bubba could speak. "We never saw him."

"I believe that is a lie," Digger said. "What happened? Did Hank, the fire investigator, gather enough evidence from when your meth lab blew up to try to apprehend the two of you?"

"Never happened," Cole said. Bubba vigorously nodded his head up and down.

"When I went back to get this shovel, no one was there. However, I remember seeing a lawnmower dragged into the main area of the room as if someone was working on it. Next to it was a pool of motor oil that when I thought about it later, didn't look exactly like motor oil. The color was off, you know. And there was small chunk of something, oil coated, in the puddle."

"Doesn't prove anything," Bubba said. "And see? You don't even know what you saw. Was it a puddle or a pool?"

"Shut up, Bubba," Cole said.

"But then, when I grabbed this shovel, I saw that shovel in the corner." He pointed to the spade the brothers had brought. "And see? Even now, it has a large dark stain on it and unless my eyes deceive me, there are chunks of something there. What is that, Cole? Pieces of skull bone? Brains? A little hair?"

Everyone turned toward the Smith brothers. Cole took one more look at the group, turned, and tore into the forest. Bubba followed a step behind, and they disappeared into the underbrush.

Antonaccio started after them, but Lockridge ordered. "Let them go." The FBI man stopped in his tracks. Lockridge keyed his radio strapped to his shoulder. "All units, two male suspects, Cole and Bubba Smith, are now wanted in a murder investigation.

Apprehend and detain. They are driving a red and silver older pickup last seen one minute ago near Highway 14 and Stringtown Road. Repeat. Apprehend and detain. Set up roadblocks if necessary. Unknown if suspects are armed."

The Sheriff keyed off. "They can't get far. We'll catch up to them eventually. Until then, I'll need statements from all of you. And this is now officially a crime scene. I'd appreciate it if we all moved back to the road until we can get the team up here for photos and the like."

As Lockridge walked back to his car ahead of the group, Digger heard him mutter, "It's high time I started thinking about retirement."

Chapter 45

Six weeks later

Special Agent Brandyn Antonaccio walked through the front door of the law enforcement center. Janice, the receptionist at the front desk, busy with her headphones, nodded to him and pointed to the back door. "Go on in," she mouthed, pointing behind her.

Antonaccio tapped on the door and smiled at the big sheriff.

"Brandyn." The sheriff stood and extended his meaty palm. "Good to see you. Back for the hearing I assume?"

"Seems they need me." Antonaccio offered a big smile while at the same time straightening one of the framed pictures of Lockridge's wife on his desk. He eased himself onto a metal chair. "How have you been? Ever find the arsonist?"

The sheriff rolled his eyes. "Not officially, but it's interesting that in the six weeks that the Smiths have been behind bars, *poof*, no fires at all." He sighed. "Of course, what with all the national attention Knoxville has received in the last six weeks, we haven't had any chance to investigate any further on the fires."

"I've been reading about it," Antonaccio said.

Lockridge huffed. "Yeah, a dead gangster shot by an arrow from an elderly Indian, rumors of treasure, and the scuttlebutt about the casino brought in the media hounds from all over."

"I saw the casino idea faded in popularity."

Lockridge nodded. "Yeah, after all the attention Wildcrow, his granddaughter, and Digger received, as well as a resurgence of Peace Tree lore, Kathryn VanSteele left town quicker than a jackrabbit on speed. Moved to New York, in her words, 'To be with a better class of people.'"

Antonaccio offered a consoling smile. "Unfortunately, I believe her statement reflects more about her personality than those she was trying to demean. I'm sorry. I realize she's your cousin."

Lockridge shrugged. "Her side of the family and my side never did see eye to eye on a lot of things." He sighed. "Anyway, if you saw the declining interest in the casino, you know about most everything else. I think you were gone by the time anything was arranged to look for Wildcrow's bundle under the Peace Tree. The diver was able to cut through the roots into the river bottom to extricate the 'treasure' everyone had been seeking. A lot of people were disappointed when the unwrapped hide revealed nothing but bits of bone, an arrowhead, and a few beads. Wildcrow described the meaning behind each item. They were mementos from his ancestors. The real purpose for all his antics over the previous months, of course, was to bring Gray Swan back into the fold."

"The real treasure was the map," Antonaccio said.

"Native American authorities were brought in to oversee the excavation of the bundle but deemed the map the real prize. Along with newly discovered and even more valuable artifacts in local mounds, city and state officials were able to secure a government grant for a museum for Native American studies and preservation. I don't think it'll ever outshine the annual sprint car races; it looks like the city can get out of the red, though."

"Other than Miss VanSteele, what is the latest on the other parties involved?

"Grace Snow is making arrangements to sell her veterinary practice in Ames and open up one here in Knoxville," Lockridge said. "She and Justin have been pretty much inseparable since November."

"Marriage?"

"Wouldn't doubt it."

"Jacob Wildcrow."

"He's been all excited being part of organizing the museum," Lockridge said.

"And the Smiths?"

"That's what the hearing will be about today."

"Any news on the DNA from the shovel?" Antonaccio asked.

Lockridge crossed his arms in front of them and leaned back in his metal swivel chair. "I keep calling up there, you know how these folks are at the state lab. Last I heard they were a year and a half year behind on DNA evidence. Maybe if we ever find Hank's body someday, we can get a rush job done."

"So, still no sign?"

"No. We're at a dead-end until we find him."

Antonaccio looked at his watch. "Are you required to go to the hearing?"

"Not really. Thought I might, though. Mainly for the intimidation factor. The Smiths aren't my favorite people. It's going to be a big waste of time though. One of their distant cousins ponied up the money for legal funds. Their defense attorney is pretty good but even if he weren't, it's a foregone conclusion that they'll get out on bail today. Again, no body. No identifiable fingerprints on the spade handle. Eyewitnesses saw the truck in town that morning, but no one saw them at the store. Their truck being at the marina is suspicious, but the patrol boat officer couldn't identify the occupants of the stolen boat."

"Everything is circumstantial. Not the first time I've heard a case like that." Antonaccio stood up and stretched. "Well, maybe when the formalities are done today, we can grab a cup of coffee or lunch? Make the trip worth it."

"Funny you should bring that up. I was about to ask you the same thing. My wife tells me I'm getting a little too old for this job. I don't believe a word she says, but there's something I'd like your opinion about. Might be an opportunity in it for you. Could I buy you a drink at the Swamp Fox and talk it over?"

Chapter 46

Five months later

Cole and Bubba Smith sat in the woods on a fallen tree trunk and snacked on fried chicken, coleslaw, biscuits, and fruit punch they'd snitched from the banquet tables in the enclosed tent. In the clearing, fifty yards away, where the catering tent was located, other people enjoyed the meal at folded tables under a splendid windless June afternoon.

"This chicken's shor' is tasty," Cole said.

"You bet, brother," Bubba said. "Definitely is good treating."

Cole stopped mid-chew. "What? Come on, Bubba, you know the phrase is good eating."

Bubba sniffed. "Wrong again, brother. How often do we get chicken this good?"

"Well, not often—"

"Then it's a special treat when we do. Hence, good treating."

"Hence?"

"Yeah, what about it?"

Cole shook his head. "I thought the warmer weather would have smarted you up, Bubba, but you're still an idiot at times."

"Me?" Bubba smacked Cole's shoulder with greasy fingers. "Who was it got us a still and learnt how to make the hooch? If it weren't for me, we'd be flat broke. "

"Bubba, it was me that got the still and you know that. You about fouled it up for us."

"Did not," Bubba countered.

"I'm gonna explain it to you one more time, because you don't seem to understand. Cousin Joe was gracious enough to give us a place to stay, right?"

"On the second floor of his old barn."

"Right," Cole said. "As long as we could pay our own way."

"Which is where the 'shine comes in."

"And the small marijuana patch out back in the woods Joe and his family don't know about, but I'm not talking about that. I'm talking about the still, which I found in the woods."

"I learnt how to make the hooch," Bubba insisted.

"No, you learnt how *not* to make it when you almost burnt up the woods."

"But I did it right the next time."

"Yeah."

"Well, then I learnt the right way, by doing it the wrong way."

"Just shut up. You're still a moron."

They finished their meal in a few more minutes. Cole tossed away a bare chicken bone, flicked a gnat out the plastic drink cup, and slurped the red fruit punch. "Well, you have to admit, this was a mighty fine wedding."

They'd read about the upcoming wedding between Justin Clay and Grace Snow. The event was to be held at Elk Rock Park, not too far from where they'd invaded Wildcrow's trailer. Of course, the Smiths had received no invitation, but Bubba had pointed out, "A wedding means a reception, right?"

"Right," Cole agreed.

"Reception means food. Since this is going to be outside, we might be able to sneak in and get us a free meal."

The day wasn't humid, but the fake beards they wore itched. Bubba had persuaded Cole that even though they'd been released from jail, their faces had been all over the news. If they were going to sneak into the wedding, they should wear disguises. In an old footlocker tucked behind a workbench in the barn, nestled among a variety of costumes that might have been used for skits of stage shows, Bubba found a couple pairs of sunglasses and a pair of stick-on beards.

While Cole reluctantly agreed, they soon had three problems. The first was the beards were long enough the ends touched the middle of their stomachs. They had to be careful not to snag them on the undergrowth in the woods. Second, they couldn't find any spirit gum, but Bubba found a small tube of glue. Cole noticed what type of glue only after their beards were firmly settled on their faces. He came the closest he'd ever had to punching out his brother.

"Super glue? You have qualified for idiot of the year."

The third issue was that not only did the glue irritate their faces, but it and the beards itched. Bubba had scratched his neck and lower jaw red in the couple hours since they'd worn them. Cole would bet his own neck looked the same.

They'd arrived in time to find a spot in the woods in which to view the ceremony. A small crowd had gathered including Sheriff Lockridge and the old coot they'd seen out at the mine talking with Digger and Grace. Cole figured the couple had invited a few friends and what family lived in the area. A husky, a dachshund, and a German Shepherd sat at the edge of the chairs, content to watch the proceedings, accepting any pats and scratches behind the ears. And some table scraps.

Justin stood near the edge of the bluff overlooking Red Rock Lake. He wore brown trousers, a white shirt and tie under a brown vest. Two groomsmen in similar garb flanked him. To his right, Wildcrow stood dressed in his chief's finest. Beaded vestments, feathers sprouting from a headdress that gave Cole the impression of a peacock about to flare its colors. Several necklaces hung around his neck. Bubba made a whispered comment about how the jewelry might bring a few bucks at the pawn shop.

To Cole's surprise, when Grace Snow walked down the center aisle, flanked by rows of folding chairs, the traditional wedding march didn't play. Instead, a single flute trilled a serene melody. Cole saw the musician in the distance, near the tree line, but the peaceful tune filling the air was full and rich, as if it had been amplified by speakers.

The bride wore white with decorative browns and soft greens woven into triangular patterns. Cole remembered seeing something similar on Indian blankets. Instead of a bouquet of roses, she carried a bird's feather, brown and black, with a touch of red highlights. The feather matched the one Justin held. Two bridesmaids accompanied Grace and took their places.

When the ceremony began, Wildcrow looked at Justin and Grace in turn, smiled, raised his arms to the sky, tilted back his head, and proclaimed a string of Indian words.

"What's he saying?" Bubba asked.

"I don't know. Probably giving thanks or something. Just shut up and watch."

Cole couldn't hear all the words said by Wildcrow, Justin, and Grace during the next few minutes. Maybe reciting vows or whatever usually was said at weddings, all that 'I do' and love, honor, and cherish stuff.

At one point, Grace and Justin handed Wildcrow their feathers and Grace turned to accept a small jug from an attendant. Facing Justin again, she poured what looked like water into his cupped hands he held in front of him. After returning the jug to the attendant, she dipped her hands into the water. Then, she and Justin made motions as if washing their hands. Another attendant handed them small towels.

"The old life has been washed away," Wildcrow said. "A new life, one together, begins."

The scene fell quiet. What breeze there was held its breath, and the insects ceased buzzing. Cole thought the only sound he heard was the soft lapping of water far out on the lake. He felt himself pulled into the moment. Though he crouched hidden in the woods, he could have been right there, yards away in one of the chairs, sharing the scene. His own breathing slowed, eyes barely blinked as he watched, entranced. Overhead, a red-tailed hawk made lazy figure eights.

Wildcrow lifted one hand and held up the feathers. The merest of breezes riffled the tips and the vanes.

"Listen to the wind. It talks."

The old chief's voice resonated strong, clear, and firm. He returned the feathers to the couple. They accepted them but kept their eyes on Wildcrow. He laid his index fingers over their lips.

"Listen to the silence, it speaks."

He moved his hands over their upper chests.

"Listen to your heart, it knows."

Finished, he took a half step back, smiled, and nodded. Grace and Justin exchanged feathers, clasped hands, and shared their wedding kiss. Overhead, the hawk swooped low, cawed, then flew off.

Cole's heart pounded so hard he felt the rhythm in his ears. "Wow," he whispered.

Bubba sniffed. Cole looked to see his brother wiping one eye with the back of his hand. "Are you crying?"

"No." Bubba sniffed again. "I think a bug got in my eye."

"Right. Look, the wedding is almost over. They got the food set out. I think I see a basket of chicken. Before anyone notices, let's go grab a couple pieces."

He moved forward through the brush, but paused when he heard Bubba utter, "That was so awesome."

The reception commenced. A band set up instruments and speakers. People lined up for the food.

Bubba and Cole, finished with the stolen meal, stood to leave. They wiped greasy hands on their pants and stuffed the paper plates under the tree trunk. Cole figured it wasn't really littering. The paper would wash away in the next rain.

Bubba pointed toward the lake. "What's that guy doing?"

A man, the one who had played the flute, stood near the tree line. He had shoulder length hair flaunting a white feather. His arms were raised to embrace the setting sun. The big husky sat next to him. A hawk circled overhead. After a few minutes, the man lowered his arms and bowed his head. The dog lay at his feet until someone up the hill called his name, and it ran back. A minute passed and then he looked about his surroundings and noticed Cole and Bubba. He headed towards them.

"We've been spotted, brother," Cole said.

"We're in trouble now. Let's get out of here."

"Hold on, he don't look angry. Good thing we're done eating," Cole said.

"Hello there," the man called when he was twenty yards away. "Beautiful wedding, wasn't it?"

"You're right," Bubba said. "A mighty fine wedding."

"Why aren't you both at the reception? There's some good food up there."

"Oh, we weren't..." Bubba started, and Cole poked him in the ribs.

"We've eaten and just enjoying the fantastic view," Cole said. "You?"

"I'm sorry, I should have introduced myself. I'm Michael. Michael Wildcrow. Grace's father." He extended his hand to both of them. "I'd best get back to the reception myself."

The man turned, started up the path, and turned back to Cole and Bubba. "Actually, father named me Mahkah. Means 'one with the earth.' You know? I tried to bury my and Grace's heritage. I was so upset with my father years ago. I let that anger come between me and my family. So much I couldn't even stand my own name." He sighed and shrugged. "Anyway, I think the Great Spirit intervened to bring us all together as one again. Sorry for rambling. Come on up to the reception. Time with family and friends is so precious. I know Grace and Justin wouldn't want you sitting here by yourselves!"

Mahkah extended his arm to guide them up the path.

"We'll be up in a few! To enjoy the party. You go on ahead," Cole said.

"Okay." Mahkah turned to rejoin the reception.

"Wow, that was close," Cole said.

Bubba said. "Come on, let's go before someone else sees us."

"Yeah," Cole agreed but hesitated before following his brother. "You know, I should look into maybe doing one of these for me someday."

"What do you mean?"

"A wedding, you moron. What did you think I meant?"

"You?" Bubba snorted laughter. "What girl would want anything with the likes of you?"

Cole stopped and turned to face his brother. "Shut up, stupid. We got a nice gig going with the 'shine and the weed. We got money. I'm just sayin' it'd be nice having some, you know, companionship other than you."

"Yeah, but, a full-time wife type companion?"

Cole shrugged. "Why not?"

"Because she'd want you to buy her nice things and, you know, clean up, and dress a certain way."

Cole put a hand on his brother's shoulder. "Bubba, we ain't getting any younger. I'm not saying we bring in women this afternoon, but maybe, you know, think about... the future."

Bubba nodded. "I see what you mean. But if we did find a couple, we'd have to tell them about all we done. I mean, not all, but people talk. They know or suspect some of the stuff we done."

"Ain't nothing we done can't be explained. We don't got the meth anymore. Sure, a little weed now and then, but that ain't no big deal."

"What about... Hank?" Bubba asked.

"What about him?"

"Well, you know, we—"

"We agreed that anything that happened was an accident, right?

"Right."

"And we was let go last year because no one saw nothing. Kyle or Peter or whatever his name is, won't be talking. He's dead."

"We was lucky they didn't find the body when they went diving under the Peace Tree."

"If they didn't find it then, they'll never find it."

"But—"

"No buts," Cole said. "Now, let's get back to the truck and talk more about women."

"All right."

"You worry too much." Cole stepped over another fallen tree. "We disposed of Hank's body right proper. Ain't no way it's ever turning up."

Chapter 47

One month later

"Digger, hon, would you run back in and grab my umbrella in case it rains?"

The June sky had dawned clear that day but now clouds marched across the southern horizon. The meeting was scheduled for 2 PM, and Grace figured the weather would turn on them. She hoped it wasn't a bad omen. Before moving into Digger's house, she was not the kind of person who normally put much faith in hunches or much weight on serendipity. In the last few months however, it seemed that good fortune did indeed smile on them.

Notwithstanding that, the sun, at least, wasn't smiling. "Better get one for yourself," she said.

The trip to the Marion County Courthouse took twenty minutes. It started sprinkling when they walked up the courthouse steps. The meeting had already started when Grace and Digger stepped into the meeting room. The three members of the Board of Supervisors sat at the head table. The man in the middle chair, Mark Coffee, was reading through some final directions for the previous petitioners, a man and woman interested in getting the Board to force their neighbors to remove a large collection of rusting vehicles on the basis of it being an eyesore. From what Grace could tell, it seems their petition had been approved. They were all smiles.

Wildcrow, who had begun calling himself Chief Wildcrow, and Grace's father, Michael, sat side by side in the second row. Grace and Digger took seats next to them.

Coffee called for a short break and the three supervisors stepped out. The happy man and woman gathered their documents and their umbrellas and left the four of them alone.

Grace's father leaned toward her and whispered, "I sure hope this goes well."

Grace turned to her father and said, "After all you've done, I can't see how they could say no. I mean, you have all the financing put together, the grants from the State and the Feds, all the rest. I guess I always knew you were a banker, but I never would have guessed you did so much in project financing."

"Well, part of that is my fault," Michael said. "You were busy getting your degrees and I was busy on my side playing with numbers. Still, that's no excuse."

"We should have kept in touch better," Grace said. "Still, where would we be without you?"

"No, where would *I* be without *you?* Since you called last fall, having to research all the details for this project has, well, educated me. I've learned so much about the ways of our native culture that I've been blind to it all my life. Turns out it doesn't matter so much that Native Americans never used the written word, didn't appreciate the value of numbers. I began to appreciate the real a power our culture and traditions have—connections to the land, to the spirit world, a reverence for everything. Thank God you reached out. It helped, of course, that you needed my special area of expertise, help I was more than glad to offer. It's a good project. But I've learned so much along the way. I feel whole, Grace—or at least more whole—maybe for the first time in my life. I love you, honey."

"I love you, too, dad."

Michael sat back and looked at Wildcrow. "Thank you for forgiving me, father."

"Humpf," Wildcrow crossed his arms. "That's Chief Wildcrow to you, son." The old man couldn't hide a smile of satisfaction.

Michael nodded at Digger. "I guess you're okay, too."

The trio of city officials walked back in and sat at the table in front. True to his name, Mark Coffee had scored a cup of java from the Coffee Connection across the street.

After everyone settled, he picked up a sheet of paper and read from it. "The next order of business is the petition to cede 12.3 acres of Marion County land on the south shore of Lake Red Rock—platte 72, Division four, Lots 1 through 19—to the Sac Nation for the purposes of land preservation, and the provision for a building intended to house the proposed Peace Tree Heritage Museum. Do I have that correct, Phil?"

Phillip Vander Bandyvonvander nodded, looking bored. The other member, Alonzo Jones, said, "I can't remember seeing the EPA filing, Mark. Did I just miss it?"

"It's in there," Phillip said. "Everything's fine."

"As you know, we talked about this at the last meeting and since then, all the paperwork is in order," Coffee continued. "I will say on behalf of supervisors, we are very pleased to see a project like this taking off. This likely will do wonders for our economy and tourism in the county." He looked to the other supervisors. "Are there any questions gentlemen?"

"I'm good," Phillip said.

"Me too," Alonzo said.

"Okay then," Coffee said. "All in favor of this project as stipulated, raise your hand."

All three hands shot up.

Chapter 48

The late summer clouds overhead were puffy white, tinted pink along their western edge by the setting sun and carried along on a southern breeze high above the sustaining water. He is called to the memory of huntsmen, warriors, mothers, and daughters traveling to better hunting grounds. He saws himself as if from above, sitting on an earth-toned blanket, chanting words from before, surrounded by a dozen others, mouthing their own words to the Great Spirit. In his right hand he held a walking stick, adorned with beads, hollowed out singing gourds, and a single feather, black, tipped with red. A heavy familiar and ever-present weariness pressed over his old body, but his mind was infused with joy. The spirit of the earth had shown what will be.

A great coming together has started, of minds and bodies and everlasting souls. A strength now where there once was only feebleness. A commitment where once was only a great dissipation. The man who will lead his people who gather here and elsewhere across this sacred land is growing in strength, as is his granddaughter, blood of your blood. Here this day for the sacred rite.

***

Chief Wildcrow opened his eyes and smiled. He waited while the others completed their own inner journeys and one by one, their eyes, too, opened.

"Thank you all for being here," he began. He proffered a faint smile at the young men and women gathered around the fire, part of the hopeful future of the Sac nation.

"This is now the third meeting of the Council of the Talking Stick," he said, his tone solemn and respectful. I welcome you all. Let me introduce our newcomers. On my left is Michael, my only son, whom you've met before. Next to him is his daughter, Grace Snow-Clay, and her husband, who I call by his given Native name, Digger. Grace, will you be called out again tonight?"

"I hope not, Grandfather. I apologize about the last two weeks. Horses have their own timetable for birthing foals."

"Those of you who farm may know Grace as one of our local veterinarians. And Digger is our high school's history teacher." There were nods around the circle.

Wildcrow spread his arms wide. "Were it not for these two people, all this may not have come to be. So let me be the first to hold the Talking Stick."

He stood and with the Stick in hand, walked close to the small fire burning in the center surrounded by red rocks from the shore. He gazed down and after a minute looked toward the sky.

He lifted his free arm and pointed. "See, the hawk remains our friend."

Above, making small circles in the growing dusk, a red-tailed hawk swooped high on a warm updraft and spun down to land in a tree in the distance.

"People, we sit tonight on the sacred ground of our ancestors which has now been consecrated." He pointed to the south. "In the distance the machinery soon to begin construction of our museum and new home."

Then he pointed to the west, toward a machine shed near the cemetery which held a large, wooden crate. "The last section of the fabled Peace Tree awaits us. While it may not have always represented the best in us—both Native Americans and European settlers—it does remind us of our heritage. My sentiments for all of this to the Great Spirit who showed me the path and to the people who would be moved to make it happen. It is nothing short of miraculous. My thanks are especially for grace—I don't mean my granddaughter Grace—but for grace in the sense of that force that leads us, sometimes against our own desires, toward destiny, toward a future that might not have been, but is now bright and clear."

The chief bowed his head for a minute and then again lifted it. "Who would like to be passed the Talking Stick now?"

"I would." All eyes turned toward Digger Clay. Wildcrow handed him the wooden staff which Digger held with one hand while rooting in his shirt pocket and coming back with a cigar. "Would anyone mind? I'm at my best when I'm smoking."

"Digger…" Grace said.

"Light up, my boy," Wildcrow said. "Reminds me of peace pipes if you want to know the truth."

Digger uncrossed his legs and stood, took two steps to the fire, knelt and lifted an ember, and used it to get his cigar going. He turned to the group. "Havana Black," he said. Among the best in the world." He went back to his place and sat again cross-legged, cigar in one hand, Talking Stick in the other.

"I want to say I, too, am grateful. I'm grateful for Wildcrow who followed his calling and found the map that led to all this. And led Grace to join him, with me tagging along, which is how she got to know me, the way I am now, and fall in love, no matter how stupid I showed myself to be. Call me selfish but I'm very grateful."

With that, he leaned to nuzzle Grace's neck.

"Not now, Digger!"

Even in the fading light, he flushed up, looked around the circle and laughed a nervous laugh. "Ah, sorry, my timing has never been the greatest."

"My turn, Digger," she said.

He passed the Stick to her, and she held it with both hands in front of her. "All kidding aside," she said. "When I was practicing in Ames, and teaching students, I thought I had everything, all I'd ever need. Now, I see how wrong I was. Please, don't get me wrong. Digger's taken some getting used to, as has living out in the country, but life *has* gotten better with each new day. My life has expanded, and I'm happier than I've ever been.

"I always heard people talk about how important family was to them. I thought, well, okay. I guess. But I had no idea. I don't blame anyone for that, but I guess I'm confessing." She lifted the Talking Stick. "I see now that I was naïve, ignorant of how beautiful family can be. And I denied that possibility, made my choices. Lived by my choices. My eyes have been opened now. So, I guess I'm grateful, too." She passed the Stick back to her grandfather.

"Thank you, granddaughter. Before we get to the business of the Heritage Museum, does anyone else want to speak up tonight?"

As if on cue, the hawk in the distance cawed twice, attracting everyone's attention, took flight and after swooping low over the fire, landed on the shed that housed the Peace Tree, then cawed again.

"A good sign," Grace Snow said.

Chapter 49

Three weeks later

Midnight on Red Rock Lake. Joe Dorman cast his line, reeled in a couple times to tighten it, and placed the pole in the holder attached to the side of his bass boat. The LED sensor clipped to the end of the pole glowed a solid soft amber. If a fish took the bait, the light would flicker.

He sipped from a can of Peace Tree beer, leaned back in his seat, and sighed, contented. The late August temps had stayed mild. Clear sky with a canvas of stars. No wind meant the water lapped against the boat with soft pats only occasionally because of the natural undercurrent. The live well already contained three small mouth bass and a two-pound catfish.

Beer in hand, fish ready for cleaning, and girlfriend gone for the weekend at her mother's. What could be better? Joe had come out to the lake in the late evening, planned to stay until the sky faded into the new day. He'd sleep until the afternoon, restock bait, beer, and provisions, and come evening, motor out onto the lake for another quiet night's fishing.

The sensor light blinked once. He set down the beer and reached for the pole. Easy, easy. Something just curious.

He felt the pole dip. The light went wild. One swift yank to set the hook. A turn or two on the reel to tighten the line. Another jerk pulled him forward. Whew, baby, what did he hook?

He let the fish have its lead until it tired, then pulled back, reeled in. Repeat.

Not sure what he had—maybe a bass, but some catfish offered a good struggle—he went with the give and take. Close now, the fish dove under the boat. Wait, a bit more line. Wait. Reel.

Joe enjoyed the challenge; confident he'd be the victor in the end.

Reel in. Not too much tension. Didn't want the line to break.

Ten minutes later, he kept one hand on the pole while the other reached for the nearby net. He waited until the fish neared the surface. Yes, there it was. Ease the net underneath... yes, a good-sized catfish.

With a last second effort, the fish flipped out of the water and must have spit out the hook. It landed just outside the net and disappeared.

"Crap!" Joe muttered. "At least five or six pounds easy."

He reeled in the line. The bait still secure, he cast out again.

"Come on back and try one more time."

Peace and silence settled in again. He'd just finished the last of the beer when he felt and heard something bump the bottom of the boat. Not a fish or a floating limb. He sensed this object larger, longer. He unclipped the Mag Lite from his belt and pressed the power switch.

Whatever had hit the boat slid along underneath until, with a soft splash, surfaced.

"What the—"

What would a blue tarp, wrapped and tied, be doing in the lake?

Joe reached for the tarp, curious as to the treasure within.

Chapter 50

From the *Marion County Express*
August 28

KNOXVILLE—Two fugitives wanted for murder are being returned to Iowa for trial. Cole and Roderick 'Bubba' Smith were arrested in the city of Lynchburg, Tennessee, after an alert officer spotted them exiting a convenience store. Each was concealing several packages of food under their shirts.

The Smiths, longtime residents of Knoxville, had been arrested the previous November on suspicion of the murder of Hank Oliver, former manager of Woo Hardware, but were subsequently released due to lack of evidence, including the fact that Mr. Oliver was still missing. With the recent discovery of Mr. Oliver's body by a man fishing on Lake Red Rock, arrest warrants against the Smiths were issued.

Former Marion County sheriff, Brett Lockridge, tracked the brothers to Tennessee.

"My wife and I had been enjoying our retirement out at South Shore Estates, but when I saw the report of an unexplained fire near the Jack Daniels distillery, I suspected the Smiths," Lockridge said. "Turned out there were three other fires in the area, causes unknown. I felt obliged to go down and provide the local authorities with any information I had."

The brothers haven't been seen in the Knoxville area since early June. Lockridge reported that Roderick Smith had been cited in Tennessee for driving without a license plate, but the violation had occurred before the discovery of Mr. Oliver's body.

"It was only a matter of time," commented Acting Marion County Sheriff Brandyn Antonaccio.

Antonaccio, former special agent for the Federal Bureau of Investigations, had come to Knoxville the previous fall in search of Peter White, a known gangster from Chicago. In November of last year, a day after Oliver was reported missing, White died after being shot with an arrow from Chief Jacob Wildcrow, local resident and member of the Sac tribe. Wildcrow wasn't charged for the incident as it was proven he acted in defense of his granddaughter, Grace Snow-Clay, who was being threatened by Mr. White.

Antonaccio was appointed Acting Sheriff by the Marion County Board of Supervisors after Lockridge resigned the position earlier this year. He continued the search for Oliver.

"It was an open case that needed solving," Antonaccio said.

Currently, Antonaccio is assisting city police with security arrangements for the upcoming National Sprint Car races.

When asked about the chances the Smiths would be convicted, he said, "Even with the discovery of Mr. Oliver's corpse, the evidence is still circumstantial. However, they have been suspected of numerous crimes here in Knoxville and Marion County as well as in Tennessee. At some point, their pattern of crimes will catch up to them, and they will be held accountable."

Sheriff Antonaccio wrapped up the short interview by making one last comment regarding the Smiths. "Some people never change.

History of the Peace Tree
By Larry Brown

An iconic symbol in the history of Iowa is the Peace Tree. It was the second largest sycamore tree in the nation at that time and grew on the south side of the Des Moines River, in what is now Marion County. The Native American tribes of Sac and Fox would have seen it start from a seedling in the early 1500's.

The tree was rumored by early pioneers as a place where native tribes would meet in peace, a place to hash out problems, regroup and refresh. From a seedling 500 years ago, the tall sycamore grew to stand as a symbolic boundary marker.

Across the Des Moines River, traders established Red Rock in 1842. It became a lawless, rough neck town and had the highest murder rate in Iowa at the time. Even Jesse James may have stayed in a Red Rock hotel after robbing a bank in Corydon, Iowa, in 1871. Wyatt Earp who lived in nearby Pella, could have ridden along the river banks under the Peace Tree.

In 1843 the Peace Tree was in line as a boundary marker between the settlers and the natives. The Red Rock Line ran from Hardin County, through Marion County to the Missouri State Line.

In Marion County, a marker designating the original The Red Rock Line is on County Road G40, east of state highway 14.

The formation of Red Rock Lake in 1969 spelled the end of the tree. Over the next 23 years it stood as a proud symbol of our heritage. In 1992, the elevation of lake waters to compensate for silt, covered its roots. The tree died, until only a stump stood. Finally, a brutal winter uprooted the Peace Tree, and its roots towed away. They are on display at the Red Rock Marina.

The Marion County Writers Workshop

The Marion County Writers Workshop is what came out of a clarion call (posters placed in local businesses) to organize into a loose conclave of wordsmiths dedicated to the writing life, inspiring the best pen on the page writing, self-educating on skills and tools, work-shopping individual manuscripts, and publishing.

Founded in 2003 by Michael Van Natta, the group has no membership fees and no requirements, other than participants bring their best work, their best mind and their best self to the group. Each writer has learned, grown, and become better writers. Many have gone on to become published authors. Some have dropped out, others have joined over the years. The group has met in coffee shops, churches, parks and now, as it always has, meets weekly Thursdays at 6:30pm until 9, hosted by Nearwood Winery in Knoxville. Lately, with the pandemic, the group utilized Zoom, which has added some far-flung members.

The workshop continues to have an interest in writers who wish to pursue their craft in an informal friendly group. It holds an annual "Camp Write" retreat in the late autumn and annually gives an award to the best scary short story (the recipient automatically becomes the next year's group facilitator.

Writers of all levels are urged to contact us on Facebook: The Marion County Writers Workshop.

www.ingramcontent.com/pod-product-compliance
Lightning Source LLC
Chambersburg PA
CBHW071233300726
48975CB00002B/404